Tides Must Turn

Gaynor Hensman

Cover picture Sancta Lilias by Dante Gabriel Rossetti used by kind permission of the Tate Gallery, London.

© Copyright 2004 Gaynor Hensman. All rights reserved.

No part of this publication may be reproduced, stored in a retrieval system, or transmitted, in any form or by any means, electronic, mechanical, photocopying, recording, or otherwise, without the written prior permission of the author.

All characters in this publication are fictitious and any resemblance to real persons, living or dead, is purely coincidental.

Co-published by Grantham Press and Trafford Publishing. Sales enquiries should be directed to Trafford Publishing.

Book Design by Moyhill Publishing

Note for Librarians: a cataloguing record for this book that includes Dewey Classification and US Library of Congress numbers is available from the National Library of Canada. The complete cataloguing record can be obtained from the National Library's online database at:
www.nlc-bnc.ca/amicus/index-e.html
ISBN 1-4120-3369-1

TRAFFORD

This book was published on-demand in cooperation with Trafford Publishing. On-demand publishing is a unique process and service of making a book available for retail sale to the public taking advantage of on-demand manufacturing and Internet marketing. On-demand publishing includes promotions, retail sales, manufacturing, order fulfilment, accounting and collecting royalties on behalf of the author.

Suite 6E, 2333 Government St., Victoria, B.C. V8T 4P4, CANADA
Phone 250-383-6864   Toll-free 1-888-232-4444 (Canada & US)
Fax 250-383-6804   E-mail sales@trafford.com   Web site www.trafford.com
TRAFFORD PUBLISHING IS A DIVISION OF TRAFFORD HOLDINGS LTD
Trafford Catalogue #04-1196   www.trafford.com/robots/04-1196.html

13   12   11   10   9   8   7   6   5   4   3

FOR JASMINE AND IN MEMORY OF CHRIS

ABOUT THE AUTHOR

GAYNOR HENSMAN worked in many capacities including artist's model, sales representative, retail manager and estate agent before returning to study as a single parent. Having attained a BA Hons (Drama, English, Art) and a PGCE, she subsequently worked as a Lecturer in Drama and Theatre Studies and latterly, Programme Leader for Performing Arts. She directed both student and community productions in West Yorkshire and Cambridge. In 1999 she successfully adapted the screenplay *Brazen Hussies* by Martyn Edward Hesford which was originally screened by BBC2 and starred Julie Walters and Robert Lyndsay. This world premiere stage adaptation was performed by students at the ADC Theatre in Cambridge receiving approval and praise from the writer, Martyn, who attended the production.

Gaynor is justifiably proud of her three children, Gibran, Tamasin and Sarah – Jane who have now flown the nest and found their own paths to skip along.

Tides Must Turn is Gaynor's first novel.

ACKNOWLEDGEMENTS

I wish to thank my dearest mother, Doris, for her unfailing belief in me and for her advice, guidance and fastidious editing of this novel. As always my children, Gibran, Tamasin and Sarah – Jane have been my inspiration. My father, Desmond was quietly yet steadfastly supportive and for that I extend my gratitude.

Suzanne by Leonard Cohen. Copyright 1969, Leonard Cohen. Used by permission of the author.

Cover picture, *Sancta Lilias* by Dante Gabriel Rossetti, used by kind permission of the Tate Gallery, London.

For research I used the following publications: The *Pre-Raphaelites* by Timothy Hilton, 1970 – Thames and Hudson; *The Tate Gallery* by The Tate Gallery Publications Department, 1979; *Spain, The Rough Guide* by Mark Ellingham and John Fisher 1999 – Rough Guides Ltd; *Barcelona* by Sue Bryant, 1997 – New Holland Publishers Ltd; *The Director and the Stage* by Edward Braun, 1982 – Methuen London Ltd.

For further information about Isadora Duncan I consulted the *Encyclopaedia Britannica* on-line. For historical information about Liverpool in the 1960's I accessed the *Lonely Planet.com* website.

Hope is the thing with feathers
That perches in the soul,
And sings the tune without the words
And never stops at all.

Emily Dickinson

There is a tide in the affairs of men which
Taken at the flood leads on to fortune;
Omitted, all the voyage of their life is bound in shallows
And in miseries.
On such a full sea are we now afloat
And we must take the current when it serves,
Or lose our ventures.

William Shakespeare

Prologue

She could hear voices; they had an intense surreal quality punctuated with echoes like those often experienced underwater. There were moments of intense dancing light teasing her senses and facilitating her escape to this other place. Then suddenly it revealed itself, like the ever present demon around the corner in a nightmare, but worse because it clearly existed. Now, with a fierce and determined precision it was permeating the very core of her tolerance— pain so excruciating she had no ability to control or bear it. A grunt, slowly metamorphosising into a scream, so overwhelming and piercing it shook her into wakefulness and brought knowing and understanding glances from the women in the room, prompting further activity that she wanted no part of.

Melissa was aware now that the sequence was complete, the transient embrace of denial was unable to contain her, and she was being propelled back to the present. It was relentless and somehow beyond her control as certainly as the use of the gas and air machine had seemed to be within it some time ago. The women had turned away momentarily dealing with the routine business associated with the immediate minutes after childbirth. The infant, calm and unusually subdued as if she was aware of what was to come, endured the customary checks and invasions without protest.

The midwife looked at the young mother, just a girl really. It was hard the first time especially when you were so young and not a soul there to support you. She had seen it so many times, especially over the last few years since women had supposedly been given more control over their own destinies. Joyce Harding did not hold with all this natural childbirth business either – women screaming their heads off and men in the delivery room getting in the way, neither use nor ornament or so it seemed to her. Give me tradition, she thought, and a loving husband who knows when to let women get on with what they know best, allowing him access only when all the detritus had been cleared away and newborn and mother alike had been made presentable.

Old fashioned it might be but Joyce knew she was right; hadn't she given birth to, and brought up, four of her own and husband Jim none the wiser about what went on in the labour ward. After all this was Lancashire not London where anything seemed to go these days. Well it might be 1971 and times had changed, but childbirth was still a joyous occasion; even after all her years of experience it still brought a lump to her throat when a child entered the world despite the unpredictability of its future. As she turned back to the mother and their eyes locked, Joyce knew in an instant that the next few hours, if not days, were going to be crucial. Who knew what the outcome might be for the little girl as yet untouched and, to all intents and purposes, rejected by her young mother. As for Melissa herself, Joyce could only sigh and thank God that she had never been in such a predicament.

"No I don't want to hold her. Take her away and give me some pain killers before I go out of my mind." Melissa knew what they would all be thinking but she could not make herself feel what she assumed should be a maternal reaction; she was experiencing the pain and indignity of this whole process without any of the associated joys. How could she feel elated or maternal when she did not want, and never had wanted, this baby? She must maintain this distance or she knew she would be lost. The memories and grief were waiting in the wings to take centre stage and glory in her fall. What a fall that would be! If these nurses thought they had heard even an iota of the pain she really felt just let the curtain go up on the real drama and they would be running to the emergency exits in an attempt to escape the ferocity of her anger, self loathing and abhorrence for the man who had given her the responsibility of making this choice.

Joyce spoke softly now her professionalism and experience breaking the tension, "Come on Melissa, the baby needs you. Just try to hold her and I am sure you will feel better, love."

"I have already told you I don't want to hold her and I bloody well don't

Tides Must Turn

need you to take that condescending tone with me. All I want is for her to be gone and for you to give me some painkillers." She was resolute, despite the tears welling and a tightening in her chest that threatened to squeeze the life from her if she had to be here a moment longer. As she spoke a cloud momentarily obscured what little late afternoon sunlight had pervaded the room, and she almost lost her resolve as the gloom reflected both her present state of mind and her destiny. She was eighteen and felt a great chasm of uncertainty open up before her; the sense of being totally and irrevocably alone. A choice she had made some months ago, but the full impact of what it meant was now surfacing and cloaking her with uncharacteristic apprehension.

Despite all their attempts to get her to hold or even look at her daughter, Melissa held out and found herself some time later being offered something inedible to eat accompanied by unwanted and overpoweringly cheerful banter. As visiting time was nearing an end and she watched the selection of doting fathers and grandparents leave she retreated further into the comfort of the sterile sheets. Before the onset of much welcome and obliterating sleep she reached for the crumpled piece of paper in the drawer by her bedside and, as she read, the tears won their long battle and ran endlessly down her flushed cheeks.

FOR MEL

Often I feel at one
    with the universe.
Sometimes it seems that time
    is only a hand's breath away,
That I can almost reach out
    and touch it.
And if I caress your cheek
    or put my arms around you
I could carry you away
    into a different future,
With no pain, darkness
    or bitter choices.

Jonathan

Melissa read and re-read the poem and wondered if he really had any idea when they last met six months ago, just how bitter and unendurable her pain and choices had been. He had written many poems for her, but for some reason she had clung to this penultimate one, perhaps hoping that in some way it held the answers she had failed to find within herself. Yes she felt an irrefutable resentment but it was so intermingled and embodied in the overwhelming love she knew she still felt that she completely mistrusted herself to even think of the events which began almost three years ago when she was fifteen. It was as if she would lose all her determination and resolve if she went back. She could not make herself so vulnerable again; she must cling to this strength she had found and let it carry her to a future of unbroken promises and sweet possibilities.

Melissa was not aware, as she crept from the ward much later that evening and made her way to the nursery where her daughter lay, that she had taken the most momentous step of all. She was barely conscious but driven by a powerful urge that would not be denied, would not be repressed and which was propelling her beyond her own ability to reason, compartmentalise and discard. This involuntary action, brought about by some deep and undeniable maternal instinct which was beyond intellect and dwelt in the realms of intuition, was to seal their futures irrevocably.

It was Joyce who found her as she was going off duty. A practical, well built and unpretentious woman, she was wrapped and protected from the bitter cold outside the hospital with her woollen hat and matching gloves, knitted by her neighbour Marion a hardy Glaswegian who had given up on such winter armour when she had come further south to the 'warmer climes' of Lancashire! The colour seemed incongruous somehow; this deep claret intermingled with flecks of a lighter red was not in keeping with Joyce's usual navy or brown attire. Her coat almost reached the ground forming a protective carapace around her which she would shed gratefully when she reached the warmth of her cosy little semi, the door shut firmly behind her, and the flickering of the fire beckoning from the living room. Beneath the coat a sensible pair of fur lined brown suede boots could be discerned, ready to guide her safely through the intimidating winter terrain which lay in wait once she had left the familiar cocoon of the labour ward.

Something stopped her from opening the main doors and starting her arduous journey home to the eventual welcome and warmth of her beloved Jim; something she almost didn't register. Joyce thought it was a heap of bedding or some other discarded linen from Ward 2, even though her reason told her that no member of staff wishing to retain their position would create such a potential health hazard. As she moved swiftly down the corridor she began to hear soft yet agonised sobbing. Sweet Jesus, she thought, it's that young girl, Melissa Johnson, who gave birth this afternoon and wanted nothing to do with her baby. "Melissa," she spoke gently but there was no response from the crumpled girl. Louder now, her voice insistent and containing an edge of authority, "Melissa can you hear me? Come on love you must get up. Whatever is it pet? Come on now hold on to me and we'll get you back to bed." She was attempting to lift the girl but she was leaden, her very weight protesting a need to be left to suffer.

The activity and increased noise brought help and although she never spoke a word or lifted her head, Melissa was brought into a small room containing two beds presently unoccupied. She allowed Joyce to wipe her face and change her nightdress which was by now smeared with blood and wet with a mixture of her tears and perspiration. Before long she was in one of the beds and slowly responded to the soothing and welcome words of this woman who could have been her mother. Except Melissa's mother no longer had any words, soothing or otherwise, for her.

"What happened love? Do you feel a little better now? I think you will be allowed to stay in this room tonight and they will keep an eye on you. So if you need to have a cry you can do it in privacy and you won't be disturbing any of the other mothers." Joyce tried to be professional and remain reasonably detached but it was not her way, especially in these sorts of circumstances. How could she go home to the nice stew that she had prepared this morning and which Jim would have put in the oven, when this girl needed a shoulder, an ear perhaps if she was patient? She knew that Melissa had been alone since the birth and had remained so throughout visiting time; no phone calls had been received either from a relative or from the baby's father, whoever that might be. Joyce felt the questions, which she could not and would not voice, amassing. The very name Melissa was unusual around here. But this was not one of the disquieting thoughts that were preying on her mind in this bubble of female isolation she found herself in. No. Joyce felt with an uncanny certainty that this young woman had experienced a level of pain and suffering that she, despite her age and experience, could only begin to imagine.

She had called Jim who, although he was not so pleased about her coming home even later on such a 'bloody awful night', was as understanding as he could be without knowing the details. He would go to bed if she was home too late and leave her some bread and cheese and a nice apple. He knew that when she couldn't sleep and came downstairs for a 'bit of a read' she enjoyed a piece of tasty Lancashire cheese and a little of the bread she still found time to make at weekends. When their youngest son Paul had left home he had tried to encourage Joyce to take it easy, pamper herself a little and cut back on some of the time consuming household tasks she insisted on taking charge of, despite working such long hours at the hospital. She wouldn't hear of buying shop bread or ready made pies and, although she had the hint of a smile when she spoke, she threatened him with divorce when he had told her about his Aunt Mildred's new cleaning lady! So, Jim undertook as much of the household work as he was allowed to and, having reached a level of compromise, they continued to live in the easy and harmonious way that many of their friends and neighbours marvelled at.

They were sitting now side by side. The girl slender almost waiflike with her long auburn hair brushed back, her face devoid of colour and her deep green eyes a tempestuous sea spewing forth her memories without mercy. The rest of her body did not betray her, each part was so calm and still, the perfect antithesis of the turmoil that reigned within. Her hands lay limply in her lap and if Joyce looked closely she could see the small broken pieces of skin and miniscule areas of scar tissue, which were the remnants of Melissa's habit of biting at her fingers around the nails when she was anxious, nervous or excited. Her legs swayed very slightly in the space between the high hospital bed and the floor below. Then very slowly, her voice almost inaudible like a whisper from the past, she began to speak and as she did so Joyce took her hand and stroked it affirming an unspoken trust that now seemed to exist between them.

Chapter one

"If you think you are going to school in that state Melissa, you can think again. When I bought that skirt I know it was at least five inches longer!" It was late April 1969 and the morning was surprisingly warm; the usual languid demeanour of Melissa at eight in the morning had been replaced by a very discernible level of excited anticipation. The weather may have had some bearing on this, but her state of mind and body was related more closely to the fact that Melissa had a double period of Art at nine o'clock.

Her mother was later than usual going to work this morning or Melissa may have managed to leave the house in the aforementioned skirt undetected! They stood there in the hall of the orderly, visibly respectable small terraced house ready for the ensuing argument and the impasse that more often than not concluded the swift and predictable proceedings. Each had taken up battle stance and if observed closely it was difficult to determine who the parent was. Melissa and her mother Carol were almost like sisters; Carol, although severely dressed and with her thick red hair forced against its natural inclination into an unflattering short bob, looking much younger than thirty five and Melissa displaying a maturity of physical development that belied her fifteen years.

"For God's sake Mum do you have to go on at me every bloody morning about the length of my skirts. You are so out of touch. Everyone else has skirts this length and their parents don't give them a hard time! You should be satisfied that I get good grades for my work instead of being so petty and small minded and, if you don't mind, I have an important assessment in Art this morning so I don't have time to stand here arguing with you again!" Melissa folded her arms rigidly and simultaneously her face became a shield, her features defiantly locked in fortification, posing a definitive and belligerent challenge to Carol.

Carol was losing patience with this familiar line of reasoning and would miss her bus if she didn't get out of the house very soon, "You really have developed a foul mouth since you got friendly with Susan Posthlethwaite, it's just not acceptable Melissa and God knows what the neighbours will think when they hear you screaming at me constantly every time you disagree with what I ask you to do! You can start treating me with a bit more respect. I have every right to tell you how to wear your uniform and whist you are living under my roof you will do as I tell you." As she finished she saw Melissa's right hand move involuntarily to her mouth in preparation for the relentless onslaught of her teeth which sometimes caused the area around the nail of her choice, to bleed. Carol could not be certain when her daughter began to gnaw at her fingers causing them to look so ugly, but she felt it may have been immediately after she married Stuart and he came to live with them. As an afterthought, and with a sudden escalation of speed and a marked increase of volume, she almost shouted, *"And stop biting your fingers it's a disgusting habit!"* She was reaching for her coat and bag and at the same time managed to block the doorway. Melissa frozen with obstinacy maintained her stance of rigid defiance. "Go upstairs now and find a longer skirt and put your tie on correctly and hurry up or I will be late for work!"

As she watched her daughter walking, listlessly now, up the stairs she felt a wave of debilitating tiredness which threatened to engulf her, obliterating her conviction and tossing her to the ground with a force she was powerless to resist. If anything she welcomed it, embraced the essence of this power which was making her gasp for breath and sink as she knew she would on to the small telephone seat which Stuart had fixed to the wall near the front door. She became inanimate, functionless as if the puppet master who gave her life had discarded her carelessly and with some haste as he moved on to the next scene. Carol sank into this sea of flotsam and in doing so she abandoned all the former resolve and energy she had displayed to Mel. In a moment of intense clarity she saw her guilt; it rose like heat will from tarmac on a hot summer day, almost a mirage.

It was her need for this man, her undeniable selfishness in bringing him into their previously balanced and ordered lives, which had brought about this gulf between daughter and mother. Of this she was certain.

For the few moments it took for Melissa to change and return to the hall she attempted to regain her composure and re-establish a tone of authority albeit one suffused with tenderness. " I am so tired of this atmosphere Melissa. Most of the time when you have eaten your tea you go to your room without a word and have that awful Leonard Cohen wailing from the record player and your joss sticks making the house smell like India! You never show me your sketch books or paintings like you used to and I can't remember the last time you confided in me about anything; to be honest Melissa I feel barely visible as far as you are concerned." Her daughter rolled her eyes heavenward and shook her head in disbelief at this knowing it would inflame the situation. Carol remained calm however, as the gesture had lost some of its former impact. She continued, "It seems that you would rather be on your own for hours than spend even a little time with me. Then when we do speak you seem to show me nothing but contempt. We used to get along so well and now I feel that the house is becoming unbearable - and not just for me."

The final words Mel knew were a reference to Stuart, her mother's husband of just over a year, a man she could not bear; yet her mother had gone ahead and married him despite her obvious antipathy to him. This was clearly established at the outset, when she was introduced to him at the local fish and chip restaurant, where she had been taken to meet him on the pretext of a 'treat'. When they had arrived at the restaurant and Carol had revealed the true nature of the 'outing' Melissa noticed a middle aged greying man wearing what she could only describe to her best friend Susan as being tramp's clothes. She conceded that they looked ironed, yet she experienced a caustic foreboding in the very predominance of the pervading greyness that emanated not only from these clothes but from the essence of the man. Even his eyes were grey! He had a new growth of stubble clearly visible on his chin and although he smelled clean, the cleanliness was of such an overbearing and obvious nature it reminded Melissa of the carbolic soap she associated with her grandmother's house, vaguely threatening in its inimitable virtue.

Her mother might need updating, she thought, she was surely a fashion victim – dressing like a librarian, and had been going to the same hairdresser for years maintaining an unflattering and ageing hairstyle, but at least she seemed alive, youthful in her features and figure. Carol had been blessed genetically, for she used only Nivea crème once a day, with beautiful clear skin that Melissa envied, hers being problematic lately. All her initial feelings were confirmed like a death sentence when Stuart rose from his seat, kissed her mother on the cheek and proffered a hand to Melissa; she looked up to see an uncertain smile which revealed teeth that seemed……. grey! He also held her mother's hand, overcoming considerable logistic difficulties to do so, whilst devouring his food like a locust; Melissa felt like she was witnessing a grotesque spectacle of adult absurdity. She wanted it to be a dream, a mistake, be taken by the hand, led immediately out of this foul place and have her mother explain that everything would return to how it was, just the two of them. But her developing awareness of womanhood told her otherwise.

She had felt betrayed by her mother. What had been wrong with their life together? It was secure, devoid of the turmoil that had affected them both deeply when her father had left and, above all, Melissa enjoyed the exclusivity she had over her mother's time. Now with the presence of this man in their home it seemed to her that nothing would ever be the same between her mother and herself. She was, she felt, powerless in her youth and inexperience to affect change and was determined therefore to be as difficult as possible and reject all Stuart's efforts to establish a friendship with her. Melissa, with the self absorption of teenagers, interested only in the way the altered circumstances adversely affected her world, remained ignorant of the seeds of doubt that had begun to sprout sporadically in her mother's mind. Carol was a woman of extremely low self esteem who sought injudiciously and indifferently to develop a sense of her own identity through the eyes of the two men she had married. Those two men could not have been more widely divergent.

Melissa's father, an American journalist whom Carol had married in haste and under some duress from her parents, had returned to Virginia nine years ago and had divorced her. If she was honest with herself Carol had always known that the relationship was a non starter as the passionate and unexpected love she had felt was never reciprocated. Jay Johnson was only a few years older than her but he was well travelled and worldly in a way that attracted and also thrilled her with an addictive sense of danger. He was also, she later realised, engaged in affairs with numerous women in as many countries. She knew he was attracted to her looks and inexperience and in his shadow she felt unempowered, stunted, an outsider looking in on her own life with no ability to affect it. She was an observer of his fleeting and always transient world, clinging to his moments of undeniable physical passion to gain a sustenance that simply did not exist. He had married her because she was pregnant and because at the time it was the path of least resistance. It suited him to have this pretty and undemanding young wife to come home to after an assignment had given him a few days respite from small town British suburbia which he found unendurable.

Jay had always felt claustrophobic in this little town with its parochial mentality and its rows and rows of regimented brick houses. He had never understood the thrill that his wife had felt when they spent a day shopping at nearby Lancaster. He conceded that it was a quaint town with its castle and the River Lune running through it. It gave the place, to some extent, a life and vibrancy that still did little to relieve his incredulity at the geographical limitations that these people, he now lived amongst, seemed to impose on themselves so willingly.

Jay had wanted a son and was visibly disappointed when Carol delivered him a girl. He had however, insisted that she be named after his mother despite Carol's protests that the name was not traditional and would create even more tension between her and her already somewhat estranged parents. He maintained his stance and, as he knew he would, won the minor skirmish with the small concession to his wife of the addition of Ann as the second name. Carol and Jay barely had sex after the child was born. He lacked the sensitivity and finesse of spirit to submit his greater ego to that of the bond that was developing between mother and daughter. He knew Carol would re-establish their 'married life', albeit in a less impassioned manner if he was patient and empathetic, but he was as shallow as the formulaic writing with which he managed to provide an income for them.

Gradually he spent more time away from his new family and felt more than sustained and satisfied with the undemanding and uncommitted sexual encounters he sought out with an escalating urgency. At each taste of this available and intoxicating fruit his addiction grew until he passed on a particularly virulent dose of gonorrhoea to his wife during one of their rare couplings. This was the word which now described what had once for Carol been a haven for her senses and flesh, but was now reduced to a loveless act which served only to satisfy a perverse need for Jay. After this final indignity Carol had asked him to leave and although she had no idea how she would manage or maintain a vestige of the dignity she valued so much, she was resolute.

The divorce settlement she finally accepted had transferred the house Jay had bought outright for them into her name, on the condition that she accepted a clean break without regular maintenance payments for Melissa. It was her overbearing father, prosaic but shrewd when it came to matters of finance, who persuaded Carol that this would give her the most security. He was a little unusual amongst his work colleagues at the printing firm in Lancaster, for few of them thought it worthwhile struggling financially in order to own their own properties. Brian Rawlins however, believed otherwise. He tried to instil this ethic in his only daughter whom he felt had been duped by the charm of this American who had made her pregnant then continued to live the life of a bachelor humiliating his daughter throughout their marriage with his numerous affairs.

A taciturn man, he found it hard to open up to his daughter, even avoiding the front parlour when he heard her crying and discussing her marital problems with his wife. Janice was altogether different and was able to deal with emotional turmoil and offer some comfort to their daughter who had so far proved disappointing to them. The opportunities that she had missed by getting herself into trouble *and with an American to boot*! She had been a pedestrian child and had never shone at school but both Janice and Brian thought she possessed all the qualities necessary to make a good secretary; she was efficient, well organised, able to follow instructions and, albeit very occasionally, act on her own initiative. She had not listened to their advice however and at the time she started this disastrous relationship with Jay she was working at a nearby petrol station, a job with little or no prospects. Once married to Jay, Carol was more than happy, if not relieved, to hand in her notice and enjoyed the months of homemaking and preparation for the birth of her baby.

Blissfully unaware at this stage of her new husband's infidelities and feeling incredibly lucky to have married such a handsome and somewhat 'exotic' man, she developed a sex drive that almost equalled that of her husband. Being pregnant only added to the pleasure for she was now relieved of anxiety and was more than willing to experiment with some of the more outlandish positions that Jay had suggested to her before they were married. In her innocence and ingrained propensity for conventionalism when they had first become lovers, she had refused outright to submit to his, at times very persistent, requests for what she had been reliably informed was 'kinky' sex. Now though, it was through the physical act of love that she tried to possess him hoping she would secure his loyalty with her mortise lock of passion, yet this was in essence the only form of communication they had between them and her endeavour was destined to fail. When she had given birth and was experiencing a joy and contentment she had only dreamed about, it was the sexual contact that had previously given her so much pleasure, and that Jay wanted to resume rather too hastily, that revolted her.

Her feelings were polarised; she desperately wanted to keep him, yet she could only view sex now as a form of submission, equating it with a level of subservience which she no longer needed to sustain her identity. Her daughter had more than filled this gap – through her she felt she became closer to the essential core of her femininity. For Carol, sex had been a fruitless search for this ultimate pleasure that she now found as a mother. Jay, as was his wont, constantly rebuked her, "It's a month since you gave birth Carol, any normal woman would be desperate for some attention from their husband by now. Do you imagine I enjoy being sidelined by my own daughter? What do you think I feel when you sit there feeding her, taunting me with your breasts when you refuse to let me near you in the bedroom when she is finally asleep? It's about time you put her on the bottle and we resumed some of those games you used to enjoy before she came along." His eyes bore no love, no warmth; all they conveyed to Carol was a selfish lust which made her retreat back to the now welcome confines of her conservative roots. She would turn away from his piercing gaze that made her blush uncharacteristically and feel ashamed about some of the things he had persuaded her to do when she was pregnant. The worst aspect of this recognition for her was the unspoken acknowledgement that she had enjoyed it. Now it was anathema to her.

"Jay how can you be so selfish, thinking all the time about sex and about your own needs, Melissa is a baby and she must come first, you are just going to have to learn to be patient." As she spoke she hastily replaced her left breast into the nursing bra, clearly agitated at his closeness and the scent of his intent which unnerved her. "In any case they told me at the clinic that it was dangerous to have sex before the six week check, and even then it could be some time before I feel ready." I will never be ready, she thought. But how will I hold on to him when I know he is so attractive, sexually insatiable and probably committing adultery already for all I know. How could she keep this perfect, respectable family unit without re-establishing their sex life; it was a dilemma to which she as yet had no answers. On this occasion he said he was going out to interview someone for a story he was working on. She knew he would be late coming home and as usual she would have to deal with all the domestic chores alone.

About two months later, in her growing sense of desperation, she attempted to give Jay some sexual comfort, as he had begun to call it lately in his effort to shame her into submitting to his needs. It was a disaster. Carol felt that she had lost all sensitivity and this was compounded by Jay's selfishness, devoid of any attempts at arousing her through tenderness or the sensuous and protracted foreplay she had so enjoyed before giving birth. The lack of finesse and the seemingly ferocious way he penetrated her, thinking, she realised, only of himself, left her sore and in tears. She stayed awake for hours crying gently and silently as she sat in the enchanted, gratifying milieu created by the narrow shaft of moonlight that fell on her daughter's cot. A poignant contrast; her beautiful and innocent daughter sleeping peacefully, her breathing methodical and her plump cheeks flushed as only a baby's cheeks can be. Carol conversely with a tear stained face, her cheeks also flushed, but with a weary sadness that would not abate despite the joy she always felt when she watched her daughter sleeping.

Life went on for the next six years in much the same vein, with sporadic sexual encounters between them, always at Jay's instigation and always to satisfy what could only be described as a perverse pleasure for he was fully aware that his wife was only capitulating, not participating. Essentially their lives were totally separate and Jay was often away for days and occasionally weeks working on various assignments and also working his charm on numerous and varied women. Carol was convinced of that now, as Jay did not attempt to conceal the fact that he had sex with other women. She was resolute in her refusal to engage in any position other than the missionary one, despite him goading her about his exploits with other women in an iniquitous attempt to stimulate an animated interest in him. How shallow he is she often thought when he talked this way. After all she was giving him what he wanted even though it left her cold and often precipitated extended nights of lonely protracted weeping to which he was utterly oblivious as he lay temporarily sated and in a deep sleep. It was, Carol thought, a waiting game; she was too diffident to take the initiative and ask him for a divorce, or even to leave.

Her interests and limited leisure activities revolved solely around the domestic, a self imposed limitation which gradually and relentlessly began to not only define her world, but define her. It imprisoned her spirit as certainly as Jay had imprisoned her soul. She sought solace in her daughter and the few girl friends she saw weekly at the coffee mornings these mothers organised. Mentally, if not physically, she was prematurely middle aged; her life predictable and without great depths or heights of emotional frisson. Of course they all thought Carol was lucky to be married to such a fascinating, charismatic and wildly handsome man and to her constant amazement and horror; she found she still loved him. What sort of callous game was he playing with her? If only she had asked this question in relation to herself. What merciless game was *she* playing with the future happiness of both herself and her young daughter? Perhaps then she would have shaken off the cloak of inertia and found the key to unlock her ability to control her own destiny.

Unusually Jay was present and actually participated in the preparation for, and the organisation of, Melissa's sixth birthday party. Carol continued to convince herself that this family unit was sustainable. She clutched at and ate eagerly the crumbs of involvement her husband scattered that day. He was charming to the parents who brought their children to the party and was disproportionately gregarious when they all shared a few bottles of champagne on the terrace whilst the children were being entertained, at great expense to him, in the lounge. For a fleeting moment Carol thought she detected an aura of sexual tension manifested in an exchange between her husband and the conspicuously attractive wife of a corpulent, somewhat offensively rich used car dealer. She chose to ignore it. She was actually enjoying herself and feeling a little of the old sexual attraction to Jay stirring; it surprised her, shocked her and almost thrilled her.

Later, and after a few glasses of the champagne Jay had been so generous with, she found herself divest of her usual cosy pyjamas, entwined with Jay on their predominantly chaste bed. She did not stop to question the fact that she actually wanted him for the first time since their daughter was born. She followed her instinct, her pleasure at rediscovering her libido knew no bounds. Initially he was gentle, slowly arousing her as he had when they first met: coaxing her now, encouraging her to stimulate and tease him. He whispered what he wanted and for a few moments she was lost, lost in a passion she never expected to experience again. He pulled her across the room and sat on a chair, flinging on to the floor their discarded clothes and as she sat on top of him, she began to move slowly and rhythmically up and down pleasuring not only him, but herself. Her whole body plunged down on him as she eventually reached orgasm for the first time in years and as she cried out in sheer ecstasy, there elicited from Jay's enraptured lips a long animal groan which as he climaxed, evolved into a guttural and all encompassing scream.

As Carol eventually came out of her reverie she realised the name he had called out was not hers but that of Maureen, the woman he had been speaking to earlier. She extricated herself from him, her momentary bliss shattered yet again, *and* for the last time she vowed, as she instantly regained her abstemiousness. Jay tried to pull her back on to him, too insensitive to realise what he had said, too shallow to realise that this was what she needed to propel her in to action; the catalyst she had thought, just a few moments ago, was extraneous. His fate was sealed when some time later she discovered he had passed on to her a vile and particularly virulent dose of gonorrhoea.

After the divorce was made final her father enrolled Carol in a secretarial course without thinking to check with his daughter if that was what she really wanted. They knew her well enough to realise that she would acquiesce if they did the ground work and presented her with confirmed and watertight arrangements. When at last Carol was offered a position with a firm of local solicitors they felt they had been vindicated and said so on numerous occasions to her whenever she came for Sunday lunch with Melissa. The solicitors were relatively flexible with her hours and it seemed to Brian and Janice that their family had regained some of its standing – Carol had a respectable job, was earning reasonable money and perhaps in time they would learn to live with the fact that their daughter was a single parent. It also helped that she lived some distance from them so they were not constantly reminded of her status and were able to deflect the questions and false concerns of even the most persistent neighbours. Some semblance of equilibrium was restored.

Chapter two

Melissa watched as her mother's bus disappeared out of sight around the corner and made an immediate and rapid about turn, fumbling in her rucksack for the house key whilst simultaneously checking the time on her wrist watch. Amazingly neither of these activities precipitated a need to either stop walking, or place her Art folder anywhere but over her right shoulder! Where the bloody hell is the key she thought, as she reached the front door still absorbed in the earnestness of her task! When she located it her face became transformed by a smile which totally encompassed her feeling of utter satisfaction at her ability to placate her mother so easily. Melissa had come back downstairs contrite, telling her mother that she was sorry for swearing and that she would try much harder with Stuart. Her mother had vaguely believed the first but knew with certainty that her daughter was blatantly lying about the latter. She was not a malicious or devious girl, and she maintained a deep love for her mother despite the escalating frequency of these stormy altercations which threatened to engulf their relationship. But Melissa did want to wear her skirts the same length as everyone else to avoid the label of *frump* which really was embarrassing!

In most matters Melissa relished being different, embracing her sense of individuality like a possessive lover: often eliciting whispers and disdainful looks from the girls who had group mentalities and always seemed to be on the prowl for someone to isolate and demean. Melissa had a predilection for arousing the animosity of such girls and yet it was not a premeditated or confrontational act, merely the calling of her senses as they demanded to be inspired and taken on a journey of exhilarating exploration. Delighted with each new experience her senses danced with her until she was exhausted finally - needing only isolation and the voice of Leonard Cohen or the poems of W B Yeats to send her into a sleep that was often more turbulent and fitful than the events of the previous day. Even the seemingly innocuous act of asking occasionally for homework in English, or openly admitting that she often stayed behind in the Art studio to complete the GCE course work that had been set, or being unfazed when questioned about the uncanny amount of Shakespeare soliloquies she learnt by heart – *for pleasure*, was enough to compound the animosity of many of her school peers.

Worse still was the fact that Melissa was an incredibly and naturally beautiful girl who had the innate and unrefined ability to charm members of the opposite sex. Melissa relished school and had a voracious appetite for the acquisition of knowledge; this fact alone gave her all the space she needed to pursue her interests and allowed her the luxury of isolation. This was a much welcome commodity in a crowded and often noisy school, especially now that her interest in Art and Art History had become so intermingled with her developing womanhood and the arrival of Mr Pritchard.

Melissa opened the door with some haste and ran upstairs to change into the forbidden skirt! She arrived at the school gates with ten minutes to spare before the bell went. She scoured the playground for her friend Susan and discovered her lurking in the school entrance and made straight for her. Her growing sense of anticipation and nervous excitement at the thought of double Art made her seem breathless, although the walk to school had barely exerted her. She noticed and disregarded the admiring glances and inane comments she received from two Lower Sixth form boys as she brushed past them taking in the odious musty smell of male pheromones so prevalent on teenage boys!

Susan Posthlethwaite was Melissa's only real friend at school although there were some boys and one or two 'non-group' girls whom she spoke to occasionally. Essentially the two girls had very little in common but had developed a rapport and close friendship since they had met, both loners for fundamentally different reasons, in the first year at secondary school.

Susan, a vacuous girl, hated school and could not wait to leave and work in Woolworths at the record counter. This had become her aspiration since she had begun to spend Saturday afternoons promenading with Melissa around 'Woolies' and had discovered the incredible number of boys engaged in the same pastime – one eye on the record in question and one eye on a girl or girls in question!

Susan often became frustrated with Mel who genuinely wanted to look at records and make-up, *even books*, ignoring the veritable feast of young men seemingly gathered there solely for their pleasure. She seemed far too serious, unnatural for a girl of fifteen. Even when they had giggled together after two delicious boys had asked them out on a date a few weeks ago, Susan sensed that Mel was indulging her. Even if she turned up once an arrangement had been made, she knew from previous experiences that her friend would frighten her date with animated talk of bloody Shakespeare or God knows what other writer or artist had taken her fancy that week. Very strange behaviour in a young woman who should be enjoying all the attention they seemed to elicit from the opposite sex.

Susan also had much more freedom than Melissa's mother and new stepfather seemed to allow her. She could stay out quite late and not too many questions were asked about her whereabouts either. In any case when she got home her mother and father were usually out down the pub anyway. It was so embarrassing when that man Stuart turned up at the disco at ten o' bloody clock to collect Mel, and consequently her, in that decrepit old banger of a car. Once they had persuaded him to wait round the corner in a side street it wasn't too bad – but still *ten o' bloody clock*, even on Saturday night! What chance did they have to flirt with boys and get dates if they had to leave visibly before the end of the disco?

Susan had already tried sex and although she would never admit that it did not seem all it had been cracked up to be, being a very quick and messy experience with Norman Bishop after the school Christmas disco a few months ago, she now felt that she belonged somehow. She was not sure to what, but she did belong and it made her feel special and exclusive even though she had turned down Norman's requests to see her again. He professed to love her which was nice but despite his ardent and persistent entreaties to be with her and, she presumed, repeat the dubiously gratifying experience, she was not convinced and repeatedly turned him down. Even after those few seconds of utterly forgettable intimacy, which was the culmination of several weeks of after school fumbling behind the bike sheds before she finally allowed access to her knickers and what lay underneath, she didn't want to continue any form of relationship with him.

He was OK but a bit spotty and smelly really and she had decided that she wanted one of the gorgeous boys from Woolies; she wanted a boyfriend that every other girl would envy, perhaps even Mel, although that was doubtful. Mel was a virgin and Susan was only too aware that her friend was developing an unhealthy interest in Mr Pritchard, the Art teacher, but she assumed it was just a crush and would pass. But what was worse in Susan's eyes, was that her friend seemed to really enjoy being alone in the evenings and had recently admitted to writing poetry. *Poetry*! She even preferred Leonard Cohen and bloody Bob Dylan to the Beatles – but perhaps that too would pass.

Susan had been wondering where Melissa was, she was usually on time for school, when she spotted her flying across the playground, an unwitting siren; Art folder over her shoulder, skirt fulfilling its task of covering her buttocks and her feral hair almost obscuring her field of vision. "Hi Mel, bad news, well bad news for you anyway! There has been a timetable change; that snotty cow Miss Jones has been out to tell us that we have her for double Maths first today instead of Art." Susan grinned knowing how disappointed her friend would be to miss her Art lesson and the attention of Mr Pritchard. She found it unbelievable that Mel could be so besotted by a teacher, although she had to admit he was fun and his class was more enjoyable than bloody Maths. God though he must be at least thirty, positively ancient, foreign looking and not really what she thought could be classed as handsome.

She dropped her bag on the floor and spat out her chewing gum her aim, as always, perfect. It landed in the far corner of the waste bin congealing with the remnants remaining from previous days to form a vulgar, but ingenious, veneer to what was in effect a very ordinary and dull bin! She took out her mirror and found the small tin of Vaseline which she carefully applied to her full lips making them shine and immediately handed it to her friend who performed the same ritual. They both combed their long hair; Susan's was as black as coal and straight whilst Melissa had even longer silky deep auburn locks which just touched the base of her spine. She had a substantial maroon hair band to contain it as its outrageous tendency to fly about her face, like serpentine tendrils blissfully released from captivity, affected her concentration. Lately it also impeded her view of Jonathan Pritchard!

The procedure continued with both girls engaged for some minutes in the desperate attempt to make their skirts look longer. They knew they would be in serious trouble if they did not touch the knee because the aforementioned Miss Jones was notorious for her inspections. She was a woman who, for some obscure reason, seemed to be in a permanent state of disapproval. They undid the zips and expertly balanced the skirts delicately on their hips thus giving the appearance of respectability. It was during these manoeuvrings that Melissa looked up momentarily and almost caught the zip in her knickers as she let out an audible gasp for she had seen Jonathan going in to the staff entrance and her heart sang.

After morning break Melissa and Susan reapplied the Vaseline to their waiting lips and restored their skirts to the fashionable shorter length as Mr Pritchard did not seem in any haste to enforce school regulations. As they walked in to the Art room, Susan whispered to her friend, "Mel could you cover for me and say that I left my Art homework on the bus when I came to your house at the weekend?" Melissa looked dubious; she had heard this one before, many times in fact over the last two years and was losing patience with Susan's obvious lack of interest in any subject. It particularly grated when she pulled these stunts with Mr Pritchard who seemed to be taken in, believing Susan who was actually an accomplished and somewhat imaginative liar in such matters. As he was relatively new he had not been subject to the full gamut of Susan's stock of insouciant excuses and those she had utilised so far, with Melissa's unwilling assistance, had seemed plausible.

Mel scrutinised Susan's taut, expectant face and despite her genuine love for her friend, she found herself saying, "Not this time Mel, the exams are in two months and I can't afford to get on the wrong side of Mr Pritchard. He will start to question you soon if you never hand in any work or prepare for assessments. I don't know why you don't just own up and ask him for more time, it would be better in the long run." She knew she was sounding more like an admonishing parent than a school friend and a part of her hated herself for it, but the stronger pull was from her sense of what was right, her steadfast resolution to achieve excellent grades to take her place in the Sixth Form and her undeniable need to please Jonathan.

"You bloody cow Mel! It's not the exams at all is it? You just don't want to get in his bad books 'cause you fancy the pants off him that's why. Just bloody admit it and stop trying to kid yourself. Some friend you are Mel Johnson!" Susan's raised voice brought a concerned look from Jonathan Pritchard, who had just arrived in the room to a perceptible appreciation from the female class members. There were also audible giggles from some of the 'group girls' who dearly hoped that stuck up Melissa Johnson and her stupid, pasty faced side-kick Susan Posthlethwaite would be in trouble. Susan had to admit to Mr Pritchard that she had not completed her work and was sent to an annexe to make a start on completing the required sketches. She threw a dagger glance at Melissa's self righteous face on the way out!

When it came to Melissa's turn to show her work and receive Jonathan's considered opinion and grading prediction, she felt her mouth become dry and an unfamiliar and delicious feeling overtake firstly her stomach, making her feel almost sick yet expectant, and then move like a determined and relentless avalanche of sensation to her groin. Her head spun and she clung to familiar, formulaic and welcome words to stop herself becoming a stupefied wreck. She rightly assumed the feelings she was experiencing – painful, pleasurable waves of attraction, were the first stirrings of lust. Melissa had never had such feelings until Jonathan Pritchard's arrival at the school, but embraced them greedily - welcoming their relentless onslaught as one might welcome the momentary pain of the dentist's drill prior to an extraction, knowing it would bring eventual release from pain. She could see no relief in sight here however; she was going to be spending the next two years studying for her Art A Level and would be in even closer proximity to the fascinating Mr Pritchard.

"Melissa were you listening to what I have just told you?" Jonathan's voice laced with faint whispers of the sun penetrated her thoughts and she realised she had drifted, losing concentration momentarily. She looked up, his face only inches from hers and was lost again in the dark nights of his eyes, pools of intensity reflecting her own. His skin, enticingly and exotically Latin and with an intensified golden sheen from his half term visit to see his mother in Spain seemed to be a magnet which she was powerless to resist. Having no adroitness to control the dictates of her body, she brushed her bare arm against his as she turned the page in her sketch book to show him the still life she was particularly proud of. She had no words for the electricity of that moment; no adjectives could be plucked from her wide vocabulary to adequately describe that beat of time. Words, her friends, failed her.

But Jonathan was twenty eight and he had the words. He found them where they had been discarded, lying dormant for years, deep within a restricted place, locked away where they could not reveal themselves and cause pain and confusion. The key he had thought was out of reach, cast away in some distant corner, manifested itself miraculously and unlocked his words. If he could have spoken them at that moment to Melissa, the sheer indisputable intensity of them would have been totally overwhelming casting them both into a tempest of forbidden, reciprocal yet impossible passion.

The moment was suppressed by his instant return to professionalism as he shocked himself into the realms of reality by saying, "Melissa, what I was trying to tell you when you stopped paying attention to me was that if you continue to produce work of this standard and range, I can't see any reason why you should not achieve an A grade," his voice was faltering as the tidal wave of the unspoken appeared on the horizon threatening to engulf him and crush his resolve. Jonathan was certain that she affirmed what had not been spoken when she drew his eyes into her own intent depths and held them there for what seemed like an eternity, before she answered him.

"Are you sure that I have the ability to get an A Mr Pritchard? I'm really pleased if that *is* the case because as you know I want to continue with Art as one of my subjects at A Level in September. It's really important to me especially as the course will also cover Art History which I enjoy.

Tides Must Turn

Actually I bought a lovely book last weekend." Melissa was amazed she could retain some composure when she could still feel the heat of his breath on her right cheek as he moved away from the antler lock of their eyes and looked over her shoulder at her sketch book. It made no difference that she could not see him; he had invaded every cell in her body like a benevolent despot. Her mind was straining like an overfilled balloon ready to explode and cover the room with her fragmented expectation.

Genuinely interested and pleased with any enthusiasm pupils showed for his subject he said "What is the subject matter of the book Melissa? I didn't think that the reading lists for the A Level course had been distributed yet. They are usually given out immediately prior to study leave next month."

"It's a book on design. I thought it looked really interesting, especially as it covers some of the work of Gaudi; I love Gaudi - I find him so incredibly inspiring." She rummaged in her bag as she handed it to Jonathan, "Here it is, Pioneers of Modern Design by Nikolaus Pevsner. My stepfather gave me the money to buy it because I was taking too long looking at it and he got a bit embarrassed in the book shop actually, thinking that they would make me buy it if I mauled it! Probably he was bored as well; I don't think he has a great deal of time for Art really. I think he takes me to book shops and galleries to please my mother and keep me happy but he never enthuses. He is a man of few words and I don't like being chaperoned by him it's archaic, but my bloody mother insists. I have virtually no freedom compared to other girls of my age. Even when I meet Susan on Saturday mornings to go to the shops I have to be picked up from the bus stop." *God where did that come from?* She realised suddenly that she had spoken to him in a much too familiar manner barely stopping for breath, even saying *'bloody'*. Now she would be in trouble she was sure! After all he was her teacher and the school did have rules!

Jonathan fought the burgeoning smile that was hovering like an expectant understudy in the muscles around his mouth ready to undermine his equanimity. Ignoring the relative intimacy of her reply, he said stiffly, "An excellent book Melissa, can I recommend in particular the chapter on the Arts and Crafts movement." With some reluctance, because he would have preferred to stay and talk about Gaudi whom he also found inspirational, he had to move on to his other pupils. He took the opportunity when Sandra, a girl devoid of talent but with an indefatigable and fervent enthusiasm for the subject, called him over.

He had a monster of a headache and needed to get home quickly after school. He could not possibly go to the pub with his two friends and colleagues tonight, a Friday ritual he usually looked forward to from about Thursday lunchtime! He needed to be alone to think, to try to decipher what had occurred today. He knew it was momentous; he needed though to acknowledge and deal with it. For it must be dealt with. He was a professional of seven years standing and he valued his career, his position and the trust placed in him as teacher. He had been at this school less than a year and wanted to make a success of the move. It had cost him dearly.

Chapter three

When Jonathan Pritchard was offered the post of Head of Art at his old grammar school in Lancashire he accepted what was, in fact, a good career move with some reluctance and many misgivings. He knew that his wife Lydia was rooted in London, where she was born, and where they had set up home together when he was undertaking his probationary year teaching at a particularly rough east London secondary school. He also knew that they were making each other miserable; had lost track and direction and were now looking at the future with very divergent aspirations and expectations. Once they had seemed inseparable, united in their goals and seeing their future with a shared vision.

He wasn't sure now when they had started to seek different paths and develop separate and mutually exclusive circles of friends. He was certain it was not related to the birth of their son Jack five years ago. It was Jack who bound them together irrevocably, no matter what course their lives would take. He was the product of what was at the time a deep and satisfying relationship – he had been created through their love and born into a home filled with expectancy and calm. It had seemed perfect and Jonathan was happy to map out his life with this secure and unsinkable raft as its epicentre. When had it become vulnerable, taking on water like the Titanic, with the definitive prospect that there would be no survivors if they continued to drift aimlessly in what were rapidly becoming hostile waters?

Jack was his joy. They had a nanny who lived with them and sometimes

Jonathan envied her; envied the special moments of Jack's development which she shared exclusively. There was no replay button for parents who worked full time: milestones missed were often recounted second hand, but new achievements were already hovering on the horizon like birds at dawn waiting to sing Jack's new song. Jonathan and Lydia were fully involved in all aspects of their son's life and tried to spend as much time during the evenings and at weekends reminding him that they were indeed his parents! They tried to compensate for a lack of presence during the day and sometimes it exhausted them, but they need not have tried so hard. They were dearly loved by Jack who adored them both and, even though their own relationship with each other was floundering, they had a surfeit of love for their child who was lucky enough never to hear them arguing. They were so careful it was painstaking, a military manoeuvre, even going to the extremes once of getting a babysitter whilst they went to the local pub to continue a particularly vicious argument that had been simmering for days.

Lydia had an affair when Jack was one year old; it lasted for almost a year before Jonathan found out. He knew that he had been extremely busy that year as the school was undergoing an inspection and simultaneously a structural change was being implemented by the new Headmaster; this was rather daunting for a relatively new teacher to deal with without becoming preoccupied to the extent of obsession. Well that was how Lydia recounted it when they were in the midst of a violent argument one weekend when Jack was with her parents. He recalled that most of their crystal goblets, a wedding present from Maggie and Jock their closest friends, were smashed onto the concrete kitchen floor by Lydia as she took them one by one and hurled them with utter satisfaction and a look of deranged glee as they reached their random targets!

Jonathan took the stance that most problems could be resolved through discussion and ultimately compromise. It was not that he lacked passion; he had a surfeit of passion – for music, art, literature, for beauty in all its myriad and multifarious manifestations, for Jack and indeed for Lydia. He always knew she could be volatile; they were opposites temperamentally but they had complemented each other, creating a delicate balance which worked until someone stepped on one end of the seesaw. Correction, he was invited as a willing yet ultimately debilitating passenger. He was called

Matthew and worked with Lydia at Selfridges in central London. They worked in the food hall and she was his boss although he was several years older than her. Even now looking back he did not think that the affair was the catalyst for the break-up, it ran deeper than that. He thought now that the affair was a symptom and not a cause; their relationship was sick and neither of them had the time to work out how to heal it. Perhaps it had always been doomed – two people so polarised emotionally were bound to create pain for each other eventually.

Now here he was putting as much distance as possible between himself and Lydia and consequently his beautiful son. He had access to Jack one weekend a month formally but in reality he was able to see him whenever he wanted. He missed him; it was as if his heart had been lacerated so many times that as one wound healed another opened up again - constant pain to remind him of his loss. He could only bear it by immersing himself in his work, both at school where he was well respected and liked, and with the paintings he was commissioned to produce. He was a very popular local artist now; having gained an excellent reputation during the year he had been living on the outskirts of Lancaster. He lived in a small cottage he rented from a local spinster who charged a reasonable rent in return for his occasional gardening services in her own rambling and overgrown garden.

Recently Jonathan had begun to feel that he was settling into a relatively happy routine despite the ever present pain when he thought about his son. He had made two very good friends at the school and was well known at the local village pub where he took his Sunday lunch and had a couple of beers during the week. He had been commissioned to do a series of paintings for the landlord depicting the quaint thatched roof pub over the last two hundred years; it had been time consuming and the landlord, Bob, had supplied him with some old faded pictures and archive material. Jonathan had found it incredibly therapeutic, he could utterly lose himself in the project and like a drug or exhaustion it almost obliterated haunting and painful memories.

The more he immersed himself in his art and the more time he took at weekends marking school work or preparing for the forthcoming week's classes, the less he cried as he fell asleep. He was a man who had always experienced the full range of emotions; unusual in a man who was half

Spanish and who had been exposed to the influence of 'machismo' not through his mother, but from contact with his male cousins and uncles who lived in Madrid. He had been an only child and his father who was English and a Lancastrian had died when he was two so the major influence in his very happy childhood had been his mother, Maria Luisa, who embraced emotion as she embraced her love for her country and its traditions. She was devoted to her boy and it was with a great reluctance that she returned to Madrid just after Jonathan married Lydia. She did not like Lydia.

"My son why you marry this cold fish?" she said when he told her they intended to marry, "She never make you happy with her stiff heart and her face of stone. Believe me I know about these things. Your father, I did love him too much, God rest his poor soul, but he had the voice of an angel and the eyes that sparkle and laugh right in your face. You love this girl, this Lydia, but her eyes are dead, grey as these old British gravestones."

He chuckled at the last comment for it was true that when Lydia was in a temper or even when he had unwittingly said something to irritate her, her face was set with a concrete rigidity that only his gentle touch or his persistent and ubiquitous smile could penetrate. "But mamma you will not give her a chance, you are so extreme. You make your mind up without really getting to know her and I know it makes Lydia unhappy. She wants you to be pleased for us, she wants you to feel you can come down to Leytonstone and stay with us whenever you want."

"Cariño mio why you not listen to your mamma? I worry for you. You need a girl who will look after you and cook you good food and be good to you in the bed. This one, this Lydia she bring home the stale food from that shop she work in and she look so tired she be no good in the bedroom. Listen to me cariño. Come for holiday with mamma and find a nice girl in Madrid." Then she started to cry in to her apron, spasmodically blowing her nose into its depths with vigorous fervour, but it subsided almost as quickly as it had begun when he cuddled her. That usually did the trick with his mamma; sometimes he lifted her clear off the ground, she was only five feet two inches in height. When he did so she would end up giggling breathlessly amidst fake protests, repeatedly telling him to put her down!

He adored her but she did not seem to realise that times were different now and that women had careers and needed much more from life than being enslaved in the home. She had been in a time warp living in the same house she had lived in with his father, nothing had changed except that now he was not here and she was living on a widow's pension and some money that came from an obscure source in Spain. She would not divulge any details about this money even to her beloved cariño! Her only response to his now less frequent inquiries was to create an embryo of a smile which faltered and aborted never growing to its full potential, disappearing almost as quickly as it had begun to emerge. That unformed smile seemed complicit, aiding her with its artifice, in suppressing information that his mother almost relished keeping from him.

Now though, Maria Luisa was living in what she described to her boy as 'la casa de mis sueños'. This house of her dreams was in a little village just outside Toledo a place Jonathan had great affinity with since he had discovered the amazing art of El Greco when he was a student. He went to visit his mother as much as he could and always found peace there; she spoiled him as she always had when he was a small boy – in fact he still felt like that small boy when he was with mamma in Spain! Just being there nurtured him, absolved him of some of the guilt he felt and ultimately it cleansed his soul so he could return refreshed and able to deal with whatever work or life threw at him.

She loved it when he brought Jack who doted on his abuela and had developed a wide vocabulary in Spanish with a touching and adorable accent, according to his grandmother! He could empathise with his mother's description of her house; it was picturesque, serene, a cornucopia of tranquillity containing Maria Luisa and two lazy, contented and very fat cats. The house was utterly Spanish and what made Jonathan happy was the fact that she had good neighbours and an active social life in the village. She was content. Jonathan even suspected his dearest mamma was having a little activity 'in the bed' of her own with the local carpenter, but he couldn't swear to it!

Thoughts of his dear mamma were far from Jonathan's head on this Friday evening as he lay on his sofa with a large glass of Merlot and the mellow, comforting voice of Sarah Vaughan wrapping him in a silken cocoon of delusion. For he was not comforted, he was not relaxed and soporific despite the wine, music and the soft glow of the tiffany lights which usually combined to create a delicious need for his bed where he slept more contentedly now. He was even devoid of thoughts of Jack this evening, despite his self inflicted melancholia. There was only one thought, one name, and one unnerving, pervasive and inescapable fact – he loved a fifteen year old girl. He loved her utterly and as surely as he breathed. He loved Melissa. He had recognised it today when it revealed itself like a previously dormant and camouflaged snake, slowly unfurling, teasing the eyes as it emerges as a definitive and potentially lethal wholly separate entity. It was a fact. He could not deny it, even when he presented himself with logical arguments and reasons against it. Yet it was insane, the reckless action of a madman to submit to this potentially wretched and irresolvable state; it was agonizing but utterly, utterly beyond his control.

He knew now what he had denied for the last few months since she entered the art room like a typhoon of Pre-Raphaelite beauty with an intoxicating zest for life. The moment had been unforgettable and had literally taken his breath away. She was so absolutely and visibly alive, so vibrant and with an amazing talent and passion for art that was so contagious it threatened always to consume him. She was so young yet could not be categorised by age, generation, gender or type. She was unique: an enigma. Melissa was unusual amongst her peers in that she embraced wholeheartedly and delighted in school and any other means by which she could acquire knowledge. She was multifaceted, inordinately beautiful and absolutely incomparable, just thinking about her now that he had acknowledged his feelings brought a tender smile to his lips, but he could not have a relationship with her.

How did he let this happen? Why could he not have fallen for a woman his own age; a much more preferable scenario even though he had certainly not been seeking love. Far from it; his priorities were firstly his son, Jack, and secondly his art both as a teacher and practitioner. This overwhelming torrent of emotion currently engulfing his senses was so different to the manner in which he had fallen in love with Lydia when he was twenty. That had been a relatively slow and progressive journey from friendship to the realisation of love and from that realisation they had followed the traditional, albeit predictable, route from engagement to marriage and from marriage to parenthood. But this love he felt for

Melissa had been an electric shock of immediate yet painful recognition; an instantaneous blood transfusion of all encompassing love. Not only was he almost twice her age, he would be twenty nine next month, but he was also a professional with all that was entailed in such a position of trust. There was real danger here, if he did not take remedial action and avoid close contact with her. It would certainly help that study leave was imminent and then of course the long summer break before she returned to undertake her A Level courses including Art.

The logistics would be difficult especially if he was her personal tutor in the Sixth Form. How would he cope? He could not deny these feelings especially now that he had acknowledged them. The long summer break would be famine enough without her vivacity and beauty to feed from. From where would he find sustenance? He must lose himself in the joy of fatherhood, the pursuance of his art and the ample embrace of his mamma in Spain. After admin week and his duties as examiner for the GCE board were completed he had planned to spend a month with Jack in Spain. He would take sketch books, charcoal, gouache and watercolours and hope to find solace in the sundrenched landscape of Spain and the infectious Latin cadence and singing intonation of the language of its inhabitants.

Lydia welcomed this arrangement as it would give her time to devote to the new man in her life, a Surveyor, who seemed an improvement on the guy from Selfridges. From conversations he had had with Lydia, Jonathan knew that this was the first serious relationship she had embarked on since the divorce and he genuinely hoped it would make her happy where he had failed. He imagined it must be difficult to enjoy any real privacy with a five year old as chaperone. Jack had confided to his dad that he liked David, Mummy's friend, and that they had all been to have an ice-cream together last weekend. As Jack's welfare was his prime concern this pleased him and eased his worries somewhat about the potentially devastating changes that they had both inflicted on their young son's life His thoughts about Jack filled his whole being with joy and gave him momentary respite from the turmoil that was Melissa.

Jonathan sought respite from the torment of his thoughts by writing a poem for the unattainable and forbidden object of his love. Over the course of their fateful relationship he was to write many poems to Melissa and would often be delighted and in awe of the sophistication and passion of those she wrote for him. When he lingered, even for a moment, on the shiver of excitement that was elicited by her arm brushing against his this afternoon, he knew he was lost and his resolve vanquished by the power of his yearning. He eventually went to bed much later than usual even for a Friday night and sleep when it eventually came was spasmodic. During the few hours he did manage to achieve the semblance of deep sleep he had a disturbing and particularly vivid dream.

He was walking on a beach somewhere, he was not sure where because there were no recognisable landmarks or visual signifiers, the only certainty was that it was not summer as he felt unbearably cold and distraught; the latter was not usually associated with the accepted perception about beaches - being the stuff that dreams, romantic dreams, are made of purportedly. This beach offered no such illusion. It was comfortless and alien with a looming and threatening sky overhead and terrain so coarse it made his feet bleed. He could see his mother in the distance with another figure which he could not make out for certain except that it appeared to be male. His mother was being assisted somehow by the figure as if she had difficulties remaining upright and would fall without the supporting arm of the stranger. He tried to catch up with the couple and despite the agony he was experiencing as his feet bled profusely and the flesh tore at each movement, he never shortened the distance despite the seemingly slow pace his mother and her companion maintained.

He cried out but his voice was weak and he elicited no response from his darling mamma despite frequent calls making him hoarse and frustrated. As they neared a bend where the beach became a rocky inlet, seemingly impassable, he seemed to be gaining ground and was heartened when his mother turned round and looked pointedly in his direction. He relaxed his pace momentarily and simultaneously began to cry, the tears forcing their way through the barrier of spurious composure he had managed to maintain. His mamma's friend steered her away up the grassy track that led to the cove and even though Jonathan was sure she had recognised him and made the first tentative movements towards him, she went willingly and without glancing back even for a second.

Suddenly he was screaming amidst the tears, calling for her unashamedly as if he would never see her again, as if this was his last chance to talk to her to communicate something. Again he could not pinpoint what the something was but it seemed imperative that he made contact. It was at this point that Jonathan sensed he had left something behind, something vital, and as he turned round he saw Lydia and Jack some distance away, being engulfed by the tide as it threatened to cut them off from land. They waved frantically and beckoned him to help them but as he ran towards them he felt himself weaken, his knees buckled beneath him and he sank to the ground, despair emitted from his pores as inertia. He would never reach them, they were lost.

Jonathan watched from the ground as a scene unfolded before him; a man who he recognised from a photographic record rather than from life as his father, frozen in time at the age of thirty years old, raced from nowhere and gathered Lydia and Jack into his arms. With the sure knowledge that they would now be safe Jonathan let himself collapse completely face down, giving way to the torpor as rivulets of sweat ran down his back and in-between his buttocks despite the freezing temperature. At that moment he woke up in his bed breathless the same rivulets of sweat invading his buttocks and with an overwhelming feeling of insecurity and an inability to decipher what had to be the most horrific unresolved dream he had ever experienced.

He did not trust sleep. He would not submit himself again tonight to its torturous embrace. He made his way downstairs to the kitchen and made a cup of coffee gulping it down gratefully and in anticipation of its stimulant effects ensuring he maintained a wakeful vigilance for the rest of the darkness hours. He finished the first and made another cup before making his way to the second bedroom in the cottage, where he had created a makeshift studio with his landlady's permission. He had painted the walls a stark white and removed the old musty carpet which had hidden a beautiful and well preserved wooden floor, which he had painstakingly sanded and stained. At once the room had seemed to double in size and the large window, unusual in cottages of this type, had afforded enough natural light to facilitate his art.

His landlady, a Miss Glossop, had been thrilled when she discovered that her house was in fact being let to a serious artist *and* one who sold his work. You would never have known to look at him she thought: he looked so respectable! All the same she was thrilled and had gained a distinct elevation in status within the local community, for not everyone could boast that they let their cottage to a successful and famous artist! Well at any rate she was sure he would be famous some day and word had it that he sold his work so he was clearly successful. She wondered if he lived a somewhat bohemian lifestyle and if in fact that encompassed life drawing? How notorious her cottage would become if that was the case! She had read about such antics, she was a voracious reader of novels, her own life having been so dull for the last twenty years or so, since her Cyril had died.

They had not been married and indeed no-one knew he was 'her Cyril'; to everyone else he was the local baker, a respectable and distinguished widower who, to his additional credit, had brought up his two sons unaided yet ultimately successfully. A great feat for a man according to the locals! Once they had left home however, Cyril had become her beau, and what a romantic and unforgettable few years they had shared in illicit and contented companionship and sexual joy. She had no idea why they had to keep their relationship a secret; it was Cyril who insisted, saying it would spoil everything for them if it became known that they were involved and thus sanctioned by the local busybodies. He thought the relationship would lose its thrill and immediacy if they 'went public' and became official. The community would expect them to marry, which of course was the respectable and expected outcome of their new found love.

Looking back Mary Glossop had to agree in retrospect with her Cyril; the time spent with him, in and out of his bed, had been the most wonderful years of her life. Every night she would rush home from the library, where she was a respected member of staff and at times a sombre and intimidating fixture, and prepare herself like a new bride for a romantic dinner and the activities of Cyril's bedroom which always delighted and thrilled her. Ah well those days were long gone and she had sought solace in her novels when Cyril had passed away, but now there was a real artist living in her cottage and heaven knew what went on there! She undertook a fictitious journey of discovery in her fertile and under stimulated imagination! If only she could climb into Jonathan's head and experience the turmoil and sheer trauma he was experiencing having acknowledged his love for Melissa, she would have no further need for fiction for a while!

So her tenant sought his solace in art and from memory, and in this case a vivid and photographic memory, he began to draw Melissa with the red and black charcoal he so favoured over pencil. He worked for two hours or so with free and at times abandoned strokes and as her image became recognisable he was momentarily assuaged and sated and found a renewed resolve to avoid close contact with her until study leave began. He would put off dealing with the perturbing and potentially untenable situation that would arrive as surely as the September term would start, until his mind was clearer and the vibrant colour of this anarchic internal turmoil had faded somewhat. He surrendered to sleep's compelling embrace at dawn; the birds chorus which usually welcomed the new day became a lullaby, gently and soundly inducing the respite of slumber. Jonathan had placed Leonard Cohen on the turntable before laying down in a stupor of tormented emotion and as he listened, and slowly succumbed to sleep, he murmured the words of his favourite song: *For she's touched your perfect body with her mind.*

Chapter four

"Ok I really am sorry Susan but I didn't have a choice you must realise that. Susan for God's sake please wait for me and bloody listen. *Susan wait can't you*! Stop being so childish and slow down." Melissa was quickening her pace with some difficulty, as she was heavily laden with work for the weekend, to catch up with her friend who was doing all she possibly could to snub her and create as much distance between them as possible! Melissa was genuinely concerned for Susan and had not wanted her to get into trouble with Mr Pritchard, *Jonathan*; she had not imagined for one moment that she would be so angry with her, even threatening not to go to the disco tonight which had been arranged for weeks.

Melissa was not very concerned about missing tonight's disco which would have too much Beatles, Cliff, Beach Boys and other chart music for her liking. She knew the DJ who would be selecting the music and he was really mainstream! Some Friday nights were completely given over to Motown which she loved but rarely featured the artists she truly favoured, like Neil Young, Moody Blues, Donovan, Dylan or her incomparable Leonard Cohen. Melissa knew her taste in music was not on Susan's favourite list, she considered it too 'hippy' and 'bloody impossible to dance to'. In an effort to make her happy she had agreed some weeks ago to go tonight, even though she knew she would become an appendage to Susan's rampaging trawl of the potential boyfriend material. It was strange how Susan had hankered after Norman Bishop for so long and now wanted nothing to do with him. She must question her about that. Why had her ardour lessened after the Christmas disco? Melissa was determined to discover the reasons behind the dampening of Susan's lustful attentions towards him. Perhaps she could ask her tonight when her friend would be in a much improved state of mind, particularly if she was receiving the level of male attention she usually attracted.

She finally caught up with Susan and yanked her arm more to elicit an immediate response than to get her to turn round and have it out. There must inevitably be a row followed by numerous accusations and recriminations before the two would return to a precarious and potentially transient, status quo. "Ow you bloody cow, that hurt and now I'll have a sodding great bruise and I was going to wear my sleeveless pink top with my bell bottoms tonight," It was clear to Melissa from the retort that there was still a distinct possibility that tonight's outing was on. In any case she knew her mother would be angry with her if she caused Stuart to change his plans. As if he had anything better to do than give her a lift. It seemed to Melissa that her mum and Stuart should go out more themselves instead of sitting together every night watching television or listening to some boring radio station until bed time. It might make them a little more interesting to be with, as it was there were no points of contact, no common ground between the three of them and conversations at the rare mealtimes they did spend at the same table, were stilted and protracted in their futility. Her mother seemed watchful and unusually sombre compared with the way she had often behaved with Melissa prior to this marriage.

Although her mother had always been reserved and fairly strict, she had been less rigid and guarded before she had met Stuart. In fact they had often had fun together, relishing in each other's company, her mother displaying an unobtrusive flexibility and at times an unstinted and absolute joy in her daughter's company. Those times were a rare if non-existent occurrence now. Her mother complained all the time that she shut herself away in her room, but surely she could not expect any alternative behaviour from her daughter since the arrival, well invasion actually, of the greyness that was Stuart. Melissa thought she was under scrutiny for some reason and if the conversation ever veered towards a rare moment of tangible communication, even a semblance of a conversation between herself and Stuart, her mother seemed to summon clouds of disapproval to engulf and obliterate the momentary brightness that had entered the room. It was as if she deliberately imposed this anomalous and dank atmosphere. It was dichotomous therefore that Carol often berated her daughter for not making enough effort with Stuart. Actually, Melissa had decided she could not win and so opted out, preferring her room and the welcoming and unconstrained embrace of her senses.

Susan rubbed at her arm vigorously because she had read somewhere that this lessened the potential bruising caused by such an attack. Without looking her friend in the eye and resuming her marathon pace, she added, "If you just admit you wanted to keep in soppy Mr Pritchard's good books 'cause you fancy him rotten, I'll forgive you. Then I might reconsider about going to the disco tonight." She was certain her friend would give in and agree with what she had said because, despite Melissa's strange taste in music and the bloody nightmare of being met by Stuart, Susan naively thought that going to this disco would take Mel's mind off the Art teacher and the homework she insisted on doing every weekend. She knew that Mel would be going reluctantly but perhaps she could be convinced to have a good time and Susan had something hidden in her wardrobe that might help – a bottle of QC sherry which she had saved her pocket money to buy. Well actually she had begged a friend of Norman Bishop's to go into the off licence to get it as he looked older and gave a certain impression of sophistication.

He was rather good looking actually, but completely off bounds as he was seriously involved with an older girl in the Upper Sixth and everyone said they were bonking for England! Apparently they were doing it everywhere and anywhere, even, according to school gossip, on the floor of the science lab after school! God knows how they managed that undetected! She wondered if what they were doing was more fun than the forgettable minutes she had spent with smelly Norman; logic told her that it must be pleasant or they wouldn't want to be doing it all the time. Mmm perhaps one of the gorgeous boys from Woolies would be there tonight, and soon she might discover if there was sex after Norman Bishop and more importantly if there was enjoyable sex after Norman Bishop! After all she was sixteen and almost three months older than Mel, so there was no reason why she should not be doing it all the time as well; it sounded a lot more exciting than completing boring homework for Mr Pritchard and the rest of those stuffy teachers!

She was brought out of her reverie of profligate thoughts by Melissa's soft laughter and the realisation that she had caught up and they were now walking at a snails pace, arms linked and her friend's Art folder making inroads into her left hip. Even more bruising she thought, but never mind at least the now close proximity of Mel meant there was a strong possibility they may still be going out tonight. Hopefully her little ploy had worked and Mel felt guilty as hell for getting her into trouble this morning! "I am not admitting to anything Susan Posthlethwaite but I accept whatever criticism you want to make, even the label swot which you can't deny you have called me more than once. I had a bad row with my mum this morning and don't want to fight with you tonight. OK we will go to the disco even though I hate the bloody DJ, will probably be bored to tears and will have to spend the whole evening making sure I avoid the vipers at all costs!"

"You twist everything round Mel so that it seems like *you* are doing *me* a favour; it was me who said I might not go out tonight if you remember. I didn't think you were so bothered. And what do you mean, vipers?"

Mel was now in fits of laughter as she knew her rather asinine friend didn't see it as she did. "Susan don't you know by now it's those lads you ogle who I refer to as vipers; they are only after one thing and once they have had it they move on to the next girl."

Susan's face was set with defiant obstinacy as she was certain that Mel was wrong; she knew of many boys who were seeing girls for ages, weeks, even after they had supposedly bonked them so they couldn't all be that shallow could they? She was adamant that you got a better class of boy at Woolworths and as it happened many of them also went to the disco in Market Street. Everyone knew they denied entry to riff raff and the boys who went to the under eighteen nights were renowned for being the best looking in town. It was a fact, how could Mel be so dense. She said abruptly, "Stop being so stuck up Mel you'll never attract boys by being so bloody snotty. It's not true what you say and anyway maybe some of us don't want to be prissy virgins until we are old and withered." With that she retracted her arm from Melissa's and started to move away but was stopped by her realisation that Mel may not go with her if she flounced off and anyway she reluctantly acknowledged that her friend was entitled to her own opinion even if it was behind the times and more in keeping with her boring mother, Carol's views.

She immediately retraced her steps, gave her friend an unexpected and vigorous hug and said, somewhat meekly, "Truce ok? Sorry about what I just said Mel. The annoying thing is that even though you are so aloof with boys they seem to flock to you anyway, although it's me that makes all the bloody effort. I think they see you as mysterious; you know like someone who is a bit glamorous and out of their reach!" She said this with total sincerity, because although Mel did annoy her quite a bit really, she was unusual and it was clearly attractive to boys. "So what time will you and 'Mr Grey' (Susan had dubbed Stuart Mr Grey, having listened with glee to Mel's initial, graphic and hilarious description after her first encounter with him in the fish and chip restaurant) be picking me up?"

God she can be fickle Melissa thought, but weary of games and acerbic remarks she replied, "See you about seven o'clock then and remember to bring that little pink angora dress with you so I can change in the toilets when we get there." She had bought the dress with money she had saved, it was absolutely gorgeous, but it barely covered her thighs and her mum had taken one look at it and refused to allow Melissa to wear it. She had been instructed to take it back to the shop and exchange it for something longer. Something longer! God her mum was old fashioned! Had she ever been young? Melissa had therefore deposited the garment at Susan's who was sworn to secrecy. Tonight would be the first time she had worn it and she was thrilled to think of it wrapped around her, its softness caressing her and accentuating the intense glow of delectable anticipation which had been awakened when she brushed her arm against Jonathan's. The memory of that sensation alone should sustain her for the ordeal of the evening ahead.

The evening was bearable, sporadically fun, and passed without too many surprises except that when they went into the toilets for the somewhat subversive and positively surreptitious change of clothes, Susan proudly produced a bottle of sherry from the depths of her voluminous purple bag. Susan loved purple: purple nail polish, purple stockings, purple fruit: even her bedroom walls were painted purple and if she ever spotted purple underwear she simply had to buy it even if she had to beg, borrow or almost steal to afford it! Melissa was once prompted to look up the word fetish in the dictionary after reading about similar activities in a magazine article which had been described utilising this word. She was loath to reveal her new found knowledge to Susan who might be offended by the label and so Melissa did not openly rebuke or criticize her friend for this obsessive behaviour. After all she had a similar predilection for poetry books, which could not however be described as a fetish, being simply the product of a ravenous and voracious appetite for the beauty of the written word. Melissa was sceptical about the sherry which she associated with stinking drunks loitering in doorways; an image most probably fashioned in her mind by her mother some time ago and having not been disproved by Melissa's, as yet limited, life experience, there it remained. She did, however, partake of some and openly admitted to Susan, who seemed to love the stuff, that it made her feel queasy. She had tried Vodka and Lime previously stolen from Susan's parent's drinks cabinet, which she found quite pleasant, but this QC sherry it was positively disgusting. Melissa had been too distracted by purple, sherry, giggling, changing clothes and her friend's voracious appetite for flirting with boys, to remember to ask her about Norman. Oh well she supposed she could wait until tomorrow and Woolworths to find out!

They had been duly picked up by 'Mr Grey' who loitered around the corner so they did not have to suffer embarrassing taunts, and whispered together about nothing in particular all the way to Susan's house. Once she had been deposited, the remaining ten minutes with Stuart were punctuated with his disingenuous and unsolicited attempts at conversation; on arriving home Melissa escaped from the stuffy confines of his car like a prisoner recently released from death row! Melissa welcomed the solace of her room and gratefully made for its tranquil sanctuary. She got undressed for bed, scrutinising her body in the mirror before putting on the tee shirt she liked to sleep in. She found her woman's body absolutely fascinating. The onslaught of puberty, like the invasion of a relentless and determined parasite which had taken up permanent residence, had taken her completely by surprise despite being conversant with the biological facts regarding the changes that would occur.

One major disquieting factor was that her body had taken on a life apart from her since the age of about eleven and now she realised there were aspects of this woman's body that were very difficult, if not almost impossible, to contain. She must bring this reprobate under some semblance of control especially as the incident at school today had unnerved her, breathtaking though it was. She had brushed against Jonathan's arm involuntarily, but must acquire some adeptness in order to recognise those moments and avoid the circumstances that may precipitate them. She knew she adored him, had absolutely no ability to quieten or dissolve these delightfully heightened feelings and did not want to rid herself of the bliss of longing, of anticipation and mostly of the sheer joy being in his presence brought her.

Melissa had endeavoured on numerous occasions to engender within herself an interest in young men even at a modest level, for to rival Susan's appetite would not only be impossible, but distinctly undesirable! Whilst she was affable and relaxed with one or two Lower Sixth Form boys, when it came to their inclinations to establish romance it was almost as if there was an invisible, impregnable barrier created by diametrically opposed expectations. (They found her fascinating and under the auspices of charm they were relentlessly following the path dictated by their raging hormones! Melissa, on the other hand, had no such inclination!) It was an insurmountable blockade which she had unwittingly created and now fiercely protected. The more the boys tried to break it down, inundating her defences with their incessant attacks - futile attempts to attain her attention - the greater its strength became. She didn't dislike them or despise them she simply found them for the most part dull and somewhat vacuous. For Melissa the inspiring and the beautiful, both mentally and physically, went hand in hand with her ideas of romantic and sexual love. The inevitable consequence of her anomalous state was that she spent more time alone; she was not lonely, but sought stimulus in her interests and studies. Melissa was not in any hurry to experiment with sex although she often felt sexual and at night her body often whispered promises of rapturous sensations as she luxuriated in its nascent potential.

She finished scrutinising her body, deciding she was satisfied with its image but wished her breasts were a little more voluptuous like Susan's but admitting to herself that as she was slim they may in fact look incongruous, attracting even more attention from adolescent boys. She certainly had no intention of escalating the already problematic, and at times totally distracting, situation which conversely elicited much pleasure for Susan Posthlethwaite! They really were draining these escapades of Susan's and she had to get into bed and sleep quite soon to gather strength for the Woolworths debacle tomorrow morning! She put Leonard Cohen on to the turntable and with only the faint hint of moonlight and her soaring thoughts for company she listened to *Suzanne*; euphoric, gratified and totally unaware that in a few hours, in a house just a few miles away, the object of her awakening desire would also fall asleep listening to this song. *For he's touched your perfect body, with his mind.*

Chapter five

The last few weeks of school before the fifth form went on study leave passed like a tornado of instruction, revision, confusion, anticipation and an undeniable and significant level of stress. For Jonathan Pritchard and Melissa Johnson it would seem like the longest few weeks of their lives and certainly the most difficult strategically. How they managed to avoid close contact and discourse of any kind was a commendable feat and seemed to have been as carefully planned as a military manoeuvre. But it had not. This artificial and excruciatingly torturous dance of avoidance, they both unwittingly succumbed to, strained at their combined tolerance. Jonathan sought refuge in the departmental meetings he had organised and immersed himself in the development of improved teaching and learning strategies; Melissa's innocence and lack of guile ensured that she gave her wholehearted attention to exam preparation.

She was confident about her Art, English Language and English Literature; her teachers led her to expect good results in French, History and Geography. She was less confident about Maths and Biology and had given up totally on Chemistry. She needed excellent grades in order to further her studies at A Level in Art, English Literature and History - her favourite subjects. She had begun to worry somewhat about the History syllabus and knew that if she did take it at A Level it would be far more demanding and draining of her mental energy and time than the other two put together. For this reason she declined to take four A Levels like some of the more assiduously intellectual students, despite her teachers' persistent attempts to gain her assent.

Melissa was being extricated by circumstance from the whirl of social engagements which were Susan's mainstay now she had been interviewed and had the prospect of her dream job at Woolworths within her grasp. This suited Melissa as her friend was an unwelcome and potentially destructive distraction from the now very tangible possibility of achieving her goal of Sixth Form study in September. Susan had recently befriended two other girls who were as uninterested as she was in furthering their studies; it took a great deal of parental persuasion and threats of gloomy futures without prospects being levelled at them by their teachers, to get them to sit their GCE's at all. All three girls were determined to do as little work as possible and seemed intent on distracting and ridiculing those who were in their eyes *swots,* and that included Melissa. She had been hurt by and disappointed in Susan until she realised that her friend meant no malice and was only finding her own path to skip along, albeit with dubious company. She did not envy her the job, the boys, the present, or the self imposed limitations of her future which for Melissa would be a barren prospect without her art, her studies, her music and....... and possibly Jonathan.

Now and again she caught glimpses of Jonathan, now and again their eyes met briefly and now and again she remembered, with a shiver of yearning, the thrill of his arm against hers but was able to contain the ominous waves that rose spasmodically from the sea of calm she had so precariously bathed in. She was apprehensive however, as the last school day heralded the torment of time she would be apart from him. The onset of despair was curtailed by the contrived, almost manic, hilarity of her classmates and friends as the last few hours of their confinement drew to an end. Many made tenuous promises to keep in touch, but who could predict what contact if any they would retain with each other? Even less substantial were the proclamations of Susan and her cohorts to involve her in all their adventures and boy hunts. It was a token and completely false gesture especially as Melissa's perspective about the nature of the ultimate aim of these nights out had changed radically.

She had been told the awful truth about Susan, Norman Bishop and the Christmas disco 'encounter'! Whilst Melissa wasn't shocked, well apart from the seediness of the chosen location of the copulation, she was not planning to go down the same route. So she knew with absolute certainty that she would not be invited on their jaunts; why would they want to be lumbered with her - she would serve only to dampen their collective ardour. Susan denied it of course, for after all they had been close friends for so long hadn't they and she cared more about Melissa than anyone, apart from her mum and dad obviously.

She had said with an uncharacteristic reflective tenderness, "Come on Mel, you know we will always be really special friends, I don't know how I would have coped with bloody school without you, I really don't. Sandra and Anne are just mates to go out and have a laugh with, you are my friend. Even though we won't see so much of each other now that I will be working and having a lot of fun looking for Mr Right, we can still do other stuff together. I'll even come to see Donovan or bloody Leonard Cohen with you if you get tickets to go to any concerts. Now that *is* love because you know how much I like Leonard Cohen!! Susan gave her friend a bear hug thinking to herself that she really was sad that they would be seeing less of each other from now on and wrongly assuming that Melissa would miss their intimacy.

Melissa would miss the close proximity of Susan, her infectious laughter, her ruses to avoid detection when she had failed to complete homework, her genuinely kind yet fickle nature. What she relished however was the thought of the new term without Susan's assiduously prying eyes reproachfully watching her every move with Jonathan and the chance to enjoy her studies with abandon. She felt a little sad for Susan, after all she had passed the eleven plus, was certainly bright, but had thrown it all away to follow, and then be confined by the limitations of her dream. Come to a Leonard Cohen concert with me, ha! That will be the day! Even if he did plan to tour Britain, the chances of getting to see him would be slim, if non existent.

As the day drew to a close and they were dispatched by the education system to embark on their respective futures, she was unavoidably placed within touching distance of Jonathan as he gave an impromptu pep talk to some of his prospective Sixth Form students. They had already been given the reading lists, advice on which galleries to visit and encouraged to undertake as much sketching and painting as the freedom and excitement of the summer would allow. (Melissa remembered thinking when the advice was given that it was somewhat patronising. It was also such an inaccurate description of her own impending, interminable summer that she could very easily have given way to an outburst of uncontrolled, nervous laughter in front of the whole Fifth Form Instead she starting biting around the cuticle of her left thumb and was contained by the soothing distraction of teeth against flesh.)

One of the boys asked, "Where are you going this summer Sir? Will you be having a holiday somewhere nice?" It was an inconsequential, innocuous inquiry but Melissa was thankful to glean any information about Jonathan's whereabouts so she could visualise him as the days became weeks and the weeks slowly stretched to months; her mental horizon a blur of sea and sky, separate yet indistinguishable.

"Actually Malcolm I will be spending some time in Spain this summer and like you I hope, I will be taking my sketch book with me." His voice was resolute and factual, giving no insight into his private life, but hinting at the human dimension beyond the confines of the school. His face fluid now, answering final questions about the A level course and fending off further attempts to elicit personal information from an excited, amiable yet potentially uproarious group. "So that's it for now, have a good summer once the exams are over. Good luck and see you all I hope in September." The group dispersed but they remained, Jonathan and Melissa, rigid as bronze before the sculptor gives it depth, contours of light and shadow and, ultimately, the semblance of movement and simulated life. They were alone in the room; time hovered like a bird of prey waiting with a stealthy stillness to steal this unexpected tremor of intimacy.

He spoke first his voice tentative and barely audible, "Melissa, I hope you have a really good summer whatever you choose to do after the exams. It's been a joy to have you in my GCE group this year; you've been an exceptional student and a pleasure to teach. I think you will be an asset to the Sixth Form and the Art department in particular. I know you appreciate the work of Gaudi so I have prepared this fact sheet and bibliography for you which the secretary was going to post to your home address, but you can take it now if you wish." As he finished, although neither of them had moved, he nervously ran his hand through his thick black hair whilst his eyes unwittingly revealed his soul and his body keeled involuntarily to the left causing him to hold on to his desk. She saw everything in a second, the camera flashed recognition, blinding her momentarily with

its brightness.......flash......... unequivocal love.........flash............
she embraced his vulnerability....... flash........the silence of absolute
certainty..........flash...*he's touched your perfect body with his mind.*

Melissa knew she must leave the classroom immediately and allow the composure and dignity that had characterised the last few weeks to remain. He loved her. *He loved her!* The murmur of possibility waited in the silence that seemed prolonged but was in fact only a moment. It waited to be acknowledged, whispered and then proclaimed, shaking them both from denial.

"Goodbye Mr Pritchard. Thank you for having faith in me and for your advice and encouragement over the last year." She sounded in control, almost blasé and was about to proffer her hand to shake his but was saved by an intuitive interdiction, a certain knowledge that neither of them could cope with touch, no matter how innocent. The shiver of unease she now felt was the memory of his arm on hers and she was afraid to touch his hand.

As the door closed behind her, Jonathan realised he was shaking. He sat in his chair as he listened to her walking towards summer and he recovered his composure sufficiently to realise the full import of this second 'encounter'. He must renew his determination, seek inner tenacity and develop watertight strategies to deal with September. Right now he wished he could confide in someone, a friend who would advise, comfort and help him discover the answers he was sure were waiting to jolt him back to professionalism and the stability of his world before Melissa. How could he confide in the two colleagues he had befriended – that was impossible given the circumstances. His best friend had always been Lydia, God knew what she would make of all this. No, he had no-one with whom he could confide.

This was not an intellectual dilemma; not a situation created by choice, but an organic and self determined entity with a life of its own, apparently determined to survive the first attempts at repressing it. One fact above all the turmoil remained impervious, he would not betray the trust placed in him by his profession or indeed by Melissa's parents He knew that the feelings had not abated for Melissa over the last few weeks, they had grown like a multifarious and determined collection of exotic plants, needing only a glance of water to soar heavenward; now threatening to besiege him and strangle the shoots of his precarious steadfastness. He picked up his agenda and walked distractedly to his staff meeting.

Jonathan Pritchard was a good teacher and was well respected by his colleagues and the members of his department. He was an excellent head of department and was able to lead and motivate his team of three experienced teachers with vision; his leadership skills encompassed the ability to reflect the views and valid expertise of his colleagues, always listening, evaluating and acting with principle. His humour was infectious and was often brought to bear to lighten the sombre mood that often resulted from those meetings which were solely concerned with such aspects as retention, results, forward planning, timetabling and factual administrative detail. So much paperwork they all said, were they teachers or administrators? Those meetings where they debated and discussed aspects of curriculum content were without exception, the most enjoyable. Their combined acumen and enthusiasm blended with a genuine vocation for teaching seemed to make even the most protracted meetings pleasurable, thus ensuring that their current and prospective pupils would have a varied and stimulating experience.

A great deal of time was spent by all the team organising extra curricular visits to exhibitions and galleries, and this year they were all very excited by the prospect of a two week residency at the school by Julian Long, an acclaimed landscape and wildlife artist. The team had been pushing for something along these lines for years before Jonathan had joined them as head of department, his predecessor had always believed that contact with working artists on a daily or even weekly basis would enrich the curriculum and benefit those students intent on a career in the art world. Fortuitously the residency, one of several Julian would be undertaking throughout the year, was sponsored by a large educational charity and thus the school's tight budget would not be affected. Whether the students would appreciate the amount of time and effort being invested in their futures by these highly motivated teachers was another matter! It was an indisputable fact that teaching could at times be a thankless task. It was sufficient for most dedicated teachers to think that they were remembered, and hopefully appreciated, by a small percentage of those young people who passed through their classes displaying varying levels of interest, ability and commitment.

Jonathan's term, unlike Melissa's, was far from over as he had many teaching groups throughout the school. His work for the examination board would coincide this year with one of the momentous events of the twentieth century, for on July 20th Neil Armstrong would be the first man to walk on the moon. As he watched the events miraculously take place he would be disconcerted that even such an incredible feat for mankind could not completely take his thoughts away from Melissa. It was as if she had burrowed into his skin and erupted, leaving fragments of her being in his bloodstream creating a paroxysm of images appearing and distorting without reference to time or situation and without respect for circumstance or location. It drained him of his usual fervour and energy and the art he produced became the therapeutic carnage of the tormented, meant only for his own eyes. As soon as it was completed, he discarded it for it had served its finite purpose.

The business of organising his trip to Spain gave him renewed pleasure and when he spoke to his mamma on the phone her enthusiasm for the visit of her beloved son and grandson was infectious, creating a domino effect he was helpless to resist. The plans were completed and Lydia would actually bring Jack to his home at the beginning of August so at least his son's travelling wardrobe, which was extensive, would be arranged by Lydia. It was too long he thought since he had held his son and he knew that in a small child's life change and growth were daily occurrences and the first couple of weeks they were together would be a renewal and affirmation of their relationship and a reestablishment of parameters and routines. Of course it went without saying that both he and his mother would spoil him. How could they resist; he was such an affable, beautiful child who needed very little discipline really. In fact he had coped well with the potentially devastating changes his parents had brought into his young life and seemed remarkably well adjusted.

July was almost at an end and with great effort and concentration and many sleepless nights, Jonathan finished the work for Bob at the pub and went for lunch to celebrate. "On the house of course," said Bob who was amazed at the fantastic job the newest village incumbent had done for his little establishment. Whilst he was there Jonathan had a couple of pints to wash down his sausage and mash with a topping of brown sauce, not his favourite meal by any means but one provided in generous proportions by Bob who proudly carried a girth some equated to an eight months pregnant woman! Bob loved his traditional pub grub cooked by his wife Marian, and indeed it was sought after locally being truly home cooked and sustaining. Jonathan was however partial to Marian's Sunday roasts and he particularly enjoyed the succulent pork and apple sauce she placed on the menu twice a month. So dissimilar physically to her husband, Marian was a spindly woman, sporting a very tight short perm which gave her a startled expression, and was somewhat surly except where Jonathan was concerned.

As soon as he walked into the pub her face was transformed and years were lost as she instantly became a girl, vaguely flirtatious and always with the same opening greeting, "Ello love, how are ye chuck? Looks like you'll be needing a good meal inside ye to cope with them kids at yon school." With that she would pile the plate with whatever he had ordered and much to the dismay of all the other customers she would always serve Jonathan first. If he had been the type to frequent this establishment on more than one day a week he was sure he would follow in Bob's footsteps despite the fact that he kept fit by riding his bike and swimming at the local baths. He also loved to cook and was partial to the Mediterranean cooking that had been his mainstay as he grew up. For although his mother had been born in Madrid, her own parents were from Valencia and brought with them the influences and the flavours of the coast. But the food he enjoyed was unfashionable, particularly where he was living and indeed some of the locals he had befriended thought of salad, strangely cooked fish that did not originate at Nora's 'chippy' and even pasta as potentially lethal substances for the body!! Foreign muck they said but not in front of Jonathan who they would never want to offend, such a pleasant young man, by all accounts a good teacher and now with the proof on the walls of their own pub, an acclaimed artist, living amongst them. They were right proud.

Lydia and Jack arrived in her weary, battle-worn Hillman Minx which she managed to keep on the road at great expense and with a stubborn pride that would not see the logic of trading it in for something less fraught with mechanical idiosyncrasies. They got out of the car mother and son, and as they walked up the path to the cottage Jonathan caught a glimpse of Jack skipping, full of the carefree energy which had been restricted by the confines of the car, with his favourite teddy bear on his shoulders and he caught his breath at the wonderful sight of his son who had visibly grown in just a couple of months. Jack was a joy, encompassing the hopes and aspirations that had once characterised the lives of the parents who conceived him. Behind him laden with bags and looking tense and weary after the long journey was Lydia, still his wife in name, still very beautiful and still with the ability to stir a fleeting flutter of desire in him. She had her hair coiled on top of her head creating an elegance he had not remembered her possessing; she looked slimmer, assured and despite being tired she seemed energised when she greeted him, possibly precipitated by the prospect of temporarily relinquishing the burden of responsibility she had gracefully carried since he left.

Jack allowed himself to be swept off his feet and swung around vigorously by his father whom he missed terribly. In his young mind he thought this separation of his parents a temporary one and he hoped that despite what Mummy and Daddy told him that they would all live together again soon. He liked Mummy's friend David because he took him and Mummy to the pictures, bought him ice creams - chocolate ones - and made his mummy laugh and that was good because she used to cry too much. But David was not Daddy and what was worse he didn't even speak Spanish and had confided in him that he had never been to Spain. *Never been to Spain*! How could any one not go to Spain it was so nice and the grandmothers there were all lovely like his very own abuela! He got cuddled tightly by all his grandmother's friends and he was allowed to stay up very late and eat with grown ups; when he was grown up himself he would live in Spain with his mummy and Daddy and his lovely abuela and be a shop keeper selling ice cream and cakes. Spanish ice cream was, he believed, all made by abuelas and tasted like nothing he had ever tried here in England.

He looked at his mummy and daddy as they sat talking in the garden with their tea. Yuk what did grown ups see in tea, it was nasty. He had tried it once at home, when Mummy went to answer the phone, and it tasted like soil and crumpled old leaves off the trees mixed with nasty hot water! It made him feel sick and yet most of the adults he met loved it! It was nice to see Mummy and Daddy talking and being friends; they were he knew good friends and that made him hope even more that they would all live in the same house together soon. It would have to be in London though because his friends were there and his new school was there, Mummy and David were there and well - it was home wasn't it? Perhaps David would learn Spanish and he could still visit and everything like now. Mmmm he wondered if there was any more chocolate cake in Daddy's tin.

Jonathan had settled his son down for the night, having read two of his favourite stories and was cooking pasta with chicken breast and a tomato, basil and white wine sauce for Lydia who was steadily imbibing the best part of a bottle of Rioja. She was talking of her plans with David and it seemed that the weeks in which she was relinquished of her parental responsibilities would be a whirl of social engagements for the pair, sandwiching a two week trip to Madeira an island Jonathan knew Lydia had always wanted to visit. He had never been keen to go thinking it would be too confining for a two week trip; he liked to explore, often randomly, and if necessary book into somewhere overnight then take a road to the next place that looked intriguing on the map. He liked the uncertainty of it, the semblance of pioneering even though logic told him this was fatuous! Madeira he felt would limit this spontaneity and he knew he had disappointed his wife when she had suggested going some years ago, just before Jack was conceived.

Thinking about it now he realised for the first time how selfish he had been thinking mostly of himself, his sketchbook and his need to be open to possibility, kismet, chance. As it turned out though, his choice of a tour around Tuscany and Umbria had fulfilled both their holiday aspirations. Lydia's initial truculence when he had presented the trip as a fait accompli, had faded when she saw the beautiful countryside and they explored the towns and villages which would remain rooted in their hearts forever, for their wonderful son was conceived after a delicious meal eaten at a small family run trattoria just outside Siena on the final night of their holiday. They had taken a long stroll on the still balmy July evening and made love on the loggia of their villa, tasting the distinctive pervading perfume that characterised the area as deeply and as hungrily as they tasted each other.

After their supper and a couple of glasses of Hine cognac, Lydia's favourite, (actually Lydia's bottle that Jonathan had packed by mistake or so he said) they made their way to their respective sleeping places. Jonathan had given Lydia his bedroom with a fold down bed for Jack alongside his bed and he had made up the chaise-longue in his studio needing only a crisp white sheet and a pillow as the night was warm and induced a pleasant, welcome somnolence. Tomorrow they would leave early and after she dropped them both at the airport, Lydia would continue the drive back to London returning to work the following day. Jonathan knew that Jack would miss Lydia but he also knew the great affection and bond that existed between his own mother and his son which within a few days would take precedence in Jack's daily routine filling his days with exclusive attention and unconditional affection. As always their lives in Spain, for whatever length of time, prioritised Jack. Jonathan knew that he was over compensating as absent fathers are wont to do, but he could see no adverse affects on his son who was he felt well adjusted and balanced. Of course he was not aware of Jack's naïve young hopes of reconciliation between his parents and his fantasy of a reunited home in London with David as house guest!

He had the window fully open and was lying naked on the chaise-longue, which he preferred during the summer despite the rather endearing vagaries of the British weather. The thin white cotton voile curtains were billowing comfortingly in the light breeze and Jonathan sought sleep and visions of Melissa to complete the perfect mood. He was almost asleep, gently tapping on the doorway to dreams when he felt a presence which should have unnerved him but his semi-conscious brain found it familiar, comforting, allowable. Now he felt warm breath, sweet slightly intoxicated breath next to his cheek and he became fully and startlingly awake. It was Lydia kneeling beside the chaise-longue and gently stroking his cheek, her face glazed with a look Jonathan recalled from their early years together. She was whispering now, incoherently at first, and he was paralysed unable to glean the reason for her actions but as her words became audible, insistent, he began slowly to comprehend what was happening.

"I still love you Jon. Every time I see you I want to touch you, to feel what we used to feel, even for a moment. I suppose I engineered staying overnight to see how it was between us now. After all we have been such good friends since you left and it may be that that was what we needed, some breathing space in order to understand each other better, to communicate instead of arguing." Jonathan was genuinely shocked, he had assumed, thought it was a fact actually, that Lydia and David were serious from all the indications and from everything she had told him. Was she playing a game with him, a drunken game? She had drunk quite a lot over the course of the evening.

His voice was husky from the onset of sleep and he said tenderly, "Lydia, what are you saying to me? Are you saying you don't feel anything for David, that it's all a sham? Because if you are then I don't understand what the last six months have been about. You couldn't tell me enough about him; what a great bloke he was – so accommodating and understanding, how much you had in common and how good he was with Jack."

"All that is true," she spoke with a voice that he recognised was on the verge of tears. "But Jon he is not you, not the father of my son and he is not, despite being a considerate and generous lover, he is not my beautiful, familiar Jon who always made me happy in bed." As she spoke she moved the sheet away from the top half of his body and lay her head on his chest uttering a slight murmur of contentment as she did so, the sound of someone at peace rather than an expression of desire. Despite his logic, his intellect, his common sense, Jonathan found to his shame that he had an erection. His body with its fickle male hormones was betraying his newly acknowledged love for Melissa: his as yet illicit fantasy lover he had seen undressed only in his dreams. He told himself it was a spontaneous reaction beyond his control, after all they had desired each other for many years and it was only to be expected that the close proximity of his semi naked wife should elicit such a response from his body. His head told him he did not feel anything but friendship, but the signs of desire were visibly there.

She had slipped into the cramped space now, lying beside him in the humidity that epitomised his dilemma. As she turned to hold him he saw the wetness of her eyes, the sadness that was hope and at once he felt trapped, cornered, manipulated. He felt she had stage-managed and contrived this whole scene and by doing so had betrayed David, her own dignity and their friendship. He had been happy to be friends with her, to work with her to create a harmonious workable relationship which would support and offer stability to their son. It had been a difficult journey, at times fraught with his guilt and a complexity of polarised emotions he had been forced to confront and deal with. It had taken over a year so far and here she was in his bed creating turmoil. He moved as far away as the narrow chaise-longue allowed which was only inches and hoped she did not feel his erection lying like a traitor between them.

It was too late. Lydia lifted off her thin nightshirt, which had in essence concealed very little, and began to caress him, the darkness a blanket covering her deceit and the silence an ally affirming her actions. She manoeuvred herself underneath him, kissing his neck gently and whispering she loved him as she did so. For a while Jonathan gave way to the pleasure of her familiar touch, his frustrated libido relishing another's flesh. He kissed her tenderly and began to touch her breasts in the light fleeting way she enjoyed but as she urged him to enter her, instigating a dance of uncertainty, confusion and ultimately chaos, Jonathan was jolted into sensibility by a sense of right and of the realisation that he wanted this to be Melissa. More than anything in the world he wanted Melissa in his arms right now, even though she was forbidden to him now and possibly for ever. He was responding automatically to his estranged wife without thought for the potential consequences, the destabilising affect on the reciprocally established equilibrium, the fragile status quo. Did he still love her? Yes he loved her as a friend and as the mother of his child but he was *in* love with Melissa. What had he been thinking? God! "No," he almost shrieked. "*No Lydia, I can't do this.*"

He moved off her and grabbed a robe from the floor and went to stand by the window. Suddenly he felt cold; he was shaking and had no words now. No words to say sorry. No words or indeed inclination to even begin to explain to her; in an instant she had managed to invade his space ruthlessly and undermine the calm embrace of potential that had lingered on the edge of sleep, waiting to take him on his journey of dreams. Perhaps he had made her believe he still wanted her. Had he? He had not thought so. Clearly signals had been crossed here somewhere and now he was feeling both sorry for seeming to reject her and angry at the way he thought she had attempted to induce an erroneous state of intimacy between them.

Lydia was undoubtedly a very attractive woman and his body had responded automatically and without question physically to her touch, her presence. No, it was the shock of manipulation, of betrayal really, that made him momentarily vulnerable, lost. He didn't like this one bit and now there would be this knowledge, this guilt, hovering like an assassin in the shadows ready to attack him with unwarranted doubt every time they met. As for David, how could he ever face the man? He seemed like a decent person and clearly he was hopeful that his relationship with Lydia would develop on a permanent basis. From the events of tonight, Jonathan had to deduce that this would probably not be the case. He turned round and realised that she had left the room as silently as she had entered it without another word being uttered. No explanations, apologies, pleadings, or recriminations, just a silent void where a moment ago a love scene of her own invention had almost been played out.

The next day she drove them to the airport after an early and relatively silent breakfast which was made bearable by the routine of starting Jack's little engine – a slow process as he was not it would seem a morning person. Once filled with cereal or his favourite 'eggy bread' he seemed to begin to tick over and once he had partaken of at least one glass of orange juice, he was almost ready to start the day. Jonathan and Lydia sat beside each other on the journey and managed with some logistical difficulty to avoid eye contact. Although there was no discernable atmosphere as such, they were communicating only through the unwitting medium of their son. Both were respectively and silently peeling back a complexity of layers revealing a unified, tangled core of latent emotions. They were stinted by these unacknowledged and as yet suppressed deliberations about last night, which would not be communicated in words to each other until some two years later.

53

Chapter six

"We are going to Morecambe for a week Melissa. Stuart has booked us a lovely little caravan just on the outskirts so we can have the best of both worlds. There are two bedrooms so you can have your privacy and there's even an awning so we can eat outside if the weather is good. You remember the canal and the coast there don't you, it's so pretty and we can take walks when we feel like it or just laze on the beach. Of course we can also go to see the lights when it gets dark and even go to a restaurant on a couple of evenings. What do you think Melissa? Are you pleased?" Carol had only just walked through the front door and Melissa was making tea when she was assaulted with this totally unwelcome news. She threw the teaspoon noisily and dramatically into the sink, grabbed her mug of tea whilst indicating to her mother that the pot had just been made and stormed upstairs without a word.

As she had expected she heard Carol's footsteps on the stairs a few moments later and the inevitable knock on the door which was followed by a suspiciously calm entreaty, "Come on Melissa it will do you good, keep your mind off the results which won't be out for a few weeks yet." Then silence pierced at length with, "Oh and Stuart said you could bring your record player as the caravan has mains electricity laid on. That was good of him wasn't it especially as he does not like much of your music; well not as much as I do anyway." Melissa listened as the record began to turn and the stylus was about to bring Bob Dylan to life. The semi darkened room was currently lit by six candles placed strategically to create the mood she sought, despite the intrusion of the glorious sunshine of the early August evening creating a tentative, transient latticework on her carpet. Strange, she thought, a revelation in fact, that her mum liked some of the music she played for she had never communicated this to her. Was it Dylan, Moody Blues or one of the American groups she had recently discovered? She knew for a fact, because it was reiterated almost on a daily basis, that Carol hated Leonard Cohen with a vengeance and presumably Stuart was of the same opinion, so it clearly wasn't him. She hated bloody Morecambe and could think of nothing worse than being confined in an even smaller space with her mum and Mr Grey, especially if they were going to bring the records *they* both enjoyed in anticipation of utilising *her* record player.

She was sixteen now for God's sake so why couldn't her mum and Stuart go to tedious parochial Morecambe on their own? It might do them good; she had sensed an atmosphere over the last few months and she worried about Carol's state of mind, she seemed nervy, totally unpredictable, constantly on edge and overtly critical of Stuart when he was attempting to communicate with his step daughter. Melissa had no idea why her mother was like this, after all Stuart was her choice and she had been pushing her daughter to at least attempt to be civil to him for so long. Yet now that the demarcation zones had been eased and she had been getting on a little better with him her mother was behaving strangely. She recalled a prime example of Carol's erratic behaviour: it happened on her birthday, the 26th of June. They were having a small party in the garden and despite some showers in the morning the weather held out for the evening gathering. Melissa had come downstairs in her new beige suede hot pants and a lacy black blouse underneath; she felt good, because her mother had actually gone shopping with her for birthday treats and raised no objection to these items of clothing she had chosen. They had been bought without derogatory comment or protests!

No one else had arrived at that point and when she walked into the living room, Stuart jumped to his feet, almost spilling his brown ale and gave her a hug saying how great she looked. Well this was a decided improvement as far as Melissa was concerned because he usually declined to comment openly on her clothes just in case it provoked an outburst from his wife who without exception disapproved of her daughter's proclivity for current fashion. On this occasion he knew that Carol had approved the outfit so he felt he was on safe ground. Wrong, he was on very dangerous and potentially treacherous ground. Carol, without a second's hesitation, leapt up from the sofa, her face contorted with what Melissa realised later was irrational jealousy, and physically pulled Stuart away from her confused and visibly shaken young daughter.

"What do you think you are doing Stuart?" she yelled, spittle emitting relentlessly from her mouth spraying the room with her venom." Get your hands off her for God's sake its disgusting. As for you Melissa why are you being so provocative? If I had realised that you were going to look like a little tramp I would not have agreed to you having those dammed hot pants. I thought they would be longer. You've probably altered them; I wouldn't put it past you." She broke down in tears and shocked speechless, her daughter and husband could only watch as she collapsed into a chair with her instability lingering like a foul smell in the room. Melissa was hurt beyond endurance and found it impossible to understand what this was all about and even more impossible to forgive her mother for spoiling her birthday which had always been such a special occasion in the past. What the hell was going on? What had happened to her mother over the last couple of years?

It took Carol about three days to fully apologise to Melissa who listened to her mother's implausible explanation without betraying the full depth of her anger at the still raw incident. Carol said she had been confused, not fully realising that her daughter was a young woman now and she had felt a misguided need to protect her; it had been a shock to see her look so, well so exposed. Melissa was too angry to roll her eyes in disbelief, because that was what she felt; she had no inclination to argue either, she had grown tired of the repetitive and fruitless disagreements that erupted all too frequently between them. What baffled her more than anything was the fact that Carol had been trying to 'protect' her as she had put it, from her own husband. Now that took some understanding and Melissa was at a complete loss to grasp whatever underlying adult complexity precipitated her mother's actions.

Without fully realising it, Melissa was outgrowing the confines of her mother's limited and stifling insularity and this recent outburst just served to compound her feelings of being suffocated. She desperately needed to breathe the exciting, vigorous air of freedom and discovery, to shake off the confines of this predictable and dreary daily routine that was her mental and geographical prison. Of course she was completely aware that there were another two years to endure as she finished her studies, but she acknowledged that some drastic tactics must be deployed in order for her to cope with the ordeal! In fact Melissa was sowing the seeds of her own survival, for it would be through her self sufficiency, her love of discovery, an insatiable thirst for learning and her ability to express herself through her Art and the written word that she would truly discover the intrinsic strength that would become her sustenance.

Carol was an unhappy woman. She very rarely had sex with Stuart, indeed this state of affairs had existed since they first got together and despite his redoubtable patience and dogged understanding she had shown him very little physical affection. He had been happy to wait until they were married thinking that Carol, would learn to trust him. She had not revealed any details about her first marriage except that her husband had been unfaithful many times and that when he finally returned to America for good, she had been satisfied with the life she had created for herself and her daughter. In isolating herself from relationships with men and reserving all her love and nurturing for Melissa, Carol had created the perfect anaesthetic. Being a mother was her joy and being a good mother was an aspiration she now felt she had not achieved.

When she had agreed to marry him after their friendship had clearly progressed to what Stuart described as courtship, Carol's self esteem had been boosted. Not only had she given up on the possibility that anyone would actually want to marry her, she felt she was drab and dull, but she knew that Stuart was well respected and admired at work. He was pleasant, caring and above all courteous with his colleagues. She felt he was a catch and considered herself privileged to have caught him. A bonus of course was that from the outset he had told her he adored children and assured her that her having a daughter was not a barrier in any way to their being together. In her heart she felt a slight wave of guilt begin to overwhelm her decision to accept his offer, because she knew she would never agree to have any more children and he had once confessed to her that he would dearly love to have a child of his own one day before he was too old.

Stuart had befriended Carol whom he had admired for some considerable time, and now loved her in the safe and pedestrian way that characterised his limited emotional plateau. It was no less valid for lacking great heights because Stuart's logic told him that they would be saved from plunging eventually and inevitably to those awful depths of anguish and mutual torture that seemed to epitomise relationships based, he felt, solely on passion. He did like the physical side of love even though he was very inexperienced more through an innate shyness manifesting itself as diffidence, than a lack of inclination. He had only made love to two women prior to Carol and he had found the experience rather pleasant. He knew he was not very good looking and did not take an interest in his own appearance but felt gratitude that such an attractive and bright woman had shown him some interest and eventually even agreed to marry him.

On their wedding night, Melissa had been dispatched to her grandparents so they could have a little privacy, he remembered feeling excruciatingly nervous and almost physically sick with anticipation. They were staying at a small bed and breakfast establishment in Grange-over-Sands, a place they were both fond of. Carol had chosen the accommodation, which was in a prime location offering sea views for a supplement, and he had organised a meal at an exclusive restaurant with wine as a treat. When they had returned to their room and both were changed and in bed, he in his blue striped pyjamas, new for the occasion, and she in a long floral winceyette nightdress, he lost his nerve somewhat. He took her in his arms and attempted to kiss her deeply but she would only permit the superficial and rather unsatisfying kisses that had been his only allowance prior to the marriage. He was disappointed, but the close proximity of this lovely woman, despite her uninviting attire, gave him the confidence to attempt to undress her.

Carol for her part, with absolutely no feelings of desire whatsoever pushed his hands away and took off her own nightdress, thus encouraging her new husband to do the same. This way she could dispense with the indignity of foreplay which she had absolutely no intentions of indulging in. So she lay there like stone and he had sex with her inert body. But thankfully, being as inexperienced as he was, he did not know better and thought the sterile offerings most satisfactory as he deposited his seed into the waiting condom that she had miraculously proffered, and he had obligingly slipped on prior to the crucial moment.

Carol was glad it was all over, she wanted no part of these sordid proceedings and would have to engineer a way to avoid them totally if that would be at all possible. She wanted companionship with Stuart, an enduring friendship, not passion. What good had passion and sex ever done her? It had been her downfall with Jay. Despite giving him what he wanted and even on that last occasion experiencing such physical joy with him, he had betrayed, discarded and trampled on her leaving her limp, crumpled and lifeless like a fallen leaf after an autumn shower had relentlessly pounded it. Now she was apprehensive for her daughter as she was growing into a very beautiful young woman and she worried continually about what would befall her when she started to have relationships with boys. As yet there were no indications that this was occurring, but Carol did think it was unusual that her daughter was not showing a healthy interest in the opposite sex. She found it difficult to relate to her at all lately; either they argued needlessly about superficial things or she was ensconced in her room with her artwork, music and books.

She had wanted Stuart and Melissa to like each other and be able to live in the house together with some semblance of harmony, but until recently her daughter had been defiantly belligerent and the ensuing strain had caused her to argue with Stuart, especially when he reached for her in bed. In fact she couldn't bear it at all now; the last time they had made love was several months ago. What a dreadful dilemma she thought. I have created an awful home life for my beloved daughter, so much so she barely communicates with me now and this man who is so good to me is probably going to go down the same route as Jay and take a lover if I don't sort myself out. Carol subconsciously envied her daughter's blank page as yet pristine, waiting for the colours that would define her life's experiences; she perceived her own page to have been irrevocably scribbled on, firstly by Jay with calculated and manipulative deception and then compounded by her own perfidious hand. No matter how hard she searched for answers, solutions, she could not find a way to erase even a little of the deleterious mess that constituted her life.

This trip to Morecambe offered a lifeline of potential. Perhaps she could re-establish the friendship with Melissa and show a little kindness to the ever suffering Stuart. In any case she needed a break herself. "Can I come in Melissa; I need to talk to you?" She spoke calmly and with a determination to enter the darkened space that her daughter preferred to the lovely evening sunshine. She began to turn the knob on the door; certain that if she gave a little more detail about the trip, she might engender some interest from Melissa if not discernible enthusiasm! It was worth a try. Her eardrums were greeted by the, not unpleasant but rather loud, lyrics of *All Along The Watchtower* and she swiftly turned the volume down. She was offered no resistance as she sat on the white wicker chair next to Melissa's bed so she reiterated the points she had already made about the holiday and tried to make it appeal to her as much as she could. Melissa sat, unresponsively, staring into space and greedily gnawing at her left thumb.

"Mum, why couldn't you have thought to ask me my opinion before you let Stuart go ahead and book the bloody trip," she said listlessly, her thumb gaining momentary respite from the attack. Avoiding her mother's penetrating, pleading gaze, she continued, "Why is it so important that I come with you? I may have plans of my own you know. Had you asked me I would have told you that Susan and her parents have asked if I want to go to Liverpool with them for a couple of days. Well you know how I love Liverpool, lots of places to watch bands playing and cool shops, I was certain you would let me go especially as her parents are taking us. It would be like last time I went remember? You were quite satisfied with the arrangements." Melissa did not communicate to her mother the fact that Susan's parents had a far more relaxed attitude to parenting than Carol had and that she and Susan would be allowed to do virtually whatever they pleased during the evening, so long as they agreed a somewhat flexible time to get back to the bed and breakfast place which was fortuitously placed very near the bars and clubs they had discovered on their last visit in early June.

Melissa was she knew being somewhat hypocritical when she went on these sporadic trips with Susan and her parents, for the two girls had grown apart since the last days of school. But who could resist the offer of some freedom and fun, an escape from the engulfing dreariness that enveloped her at home, especially as she had saved some birthday money and could get some great clothes and art books in Liverpool.

Her mother's response was studied and offered a conditional olive branch that appealed to Melissa, "Look I have no objections to you going to Liverpool with Susan and her parents because as you know I can't stand the city myself, I'd rather go shopping in Lancaster it's cleaner and quieter. But on this occasion I really want you to come with us and I promise that when we get back you and I can talk about the house rules you always object to, particularly the time I expect you back in the evenings if you go out. It's true you have grown up this last year rather more than I had realised, and perhaps I have been too restrictive with you. I can't promise to let you do exactly what you want, but if we both try I think we could reach a compromise don't you?" She placed her arm loosely around her daughter's shoulders, an affectionate gesture somewhat lacking in their lives these days, and as she did so Melissa's stubborn stance of defiance dissolved as she saw the efficacy of the bargain about to be struck.

The Morecambe trip was actually rather pleasing as the caravan was some three miles from the town and Melissa was able to take long walks, thankfully alone, delighting in the beauty of the unspoilt coast, sketch book under her arm ready to record her inspiration. She also found the canal and the walk along the tow path a welcome distraction from the seemingly renewed and escalated courting rituals of her mother and Stuart who had diversified from grey slightly for this holiday. He sported a rather modern white cotton polo neck sweater which Melissa was sure was too hot for August and no doubt hid a plethora of unpleasant smells. Anyway she was mellowing where Stuart was concerned as he always seemed to support her when her mother was being unreasonable and after all there were worse things in life than grey. She was pleased to discover that it was only her own choice of records that were played on the record player which remained firmly rooted in her allocated small bedroom. She could listen to a carefully chosen selection and drift in to the delicious realms of fantasy and longing that she so assiduously protected from being detected by the other two.

She lay in the late evenings safely naked, as her mother and Stuart had developed a habit of late night walks when they told her it was cooler and the humidity more bearable, for it was humid. On their eventual return, they would go directly to their own bedroom and she knew she would not be disturbed. She would play music quietly and soar with anticipation, relishing her own innocence which she fully intended to maintain vigilantly until she could share her young body with Jonathan. How could she be so certain? She did not analyse or question, she just knew that one day she would experience this wonderful act of love that as yet she only fantasised about. She was so sure now that he loved her she almost became manic; should she cry with the frustration of circumstance that had engineered their meeting when it was so impossible to give way to the discovery of each other. Or should she laugh out loud at the sheer unadulterated happiness he had engendered within her. She moved like a metronome between the two polarised emotions, sometimes rhythmically for hours, helpless to stop the relentless beating of her dilemma.

One evening they went into Morecambe for a meal and as they ate their 'wholesome fare' she observed Stuart and her mother and was immediately reminded of the first time she had been presented to him at their local fish and chip restaurant, when they had announced their awful intention of marrying. The last few months at home had been a strain as Carol's erratic, unstable and verbally vehement behaviour was difficult to predict let alone avoid; now however the state of harmony had reasserted itself between them and unlike previously when it was anathema to Melissa, now it gratified her. Her life at home would be easier; she would be under less scrutiny if these two were getting along better. Whatever the underlying causes of her mother's transparent insecurity had been, she hoped they had resolved them.

Later on their return to the site bar, she was separated from them for a time as they talked to another couple they had befriended, presumably when she had been out on her own walking, and Melissa began to feel that she was being observed. She was. The son of the couple whom she had not had the opportunity of getting to know was indeed openly staring at her in such a way that she felt extremely uncomfortable. He was she suspected about her own age or a little older, probably here under some duress. Melissa noticed when she returned his gaze with a magnanimous yet steadfast challenge, that he was very good looking. He had clearly spent much of his time outdoors as he was tanned and glowed with health and a spectacularly high level of confident audaciousness. A Woolworth's boy to be sure, Susan would have remarked! How had she not noticed him before? She had after all been in Morecambe and on the site for four days now and had never to her knowledge seen him around. Perhaps she had been preoccupied, blinkered with fantasies of a deliciously uncertain and unpredictable future. He began to grin, displaying almost perfectly straight, gleaming white teeth and a warmth that permeated the stark surroundings and infectiously induced a responding gesture from Melissa.

"Hi. You must be Melissa," he said with a honeyed, uncontrived huskiness. "I am Luke, nice to meet you at last after hearing so much about you and your art." He placed an opened bottle of beer in her hand and opened himself another from a supply near his caravan which she had unwittingly wandered towards in her state of absorbed contemplation. My God he was bloody confident, she thought sipping the beer automatically even though she had never imbibed alcohol other than Vodka and Lime, by choice! She found in his young face an uncanny resemblance to Jonathan, precipitated she was sure by his tan and the grin which was almost a mirror image of those she had observed Jonathan indulging in when a student had amused him. The beer tasted good and she found he was proffering her a chair and as she sat down she realised to her horror, being fully aware of correctness and manners, that she had not spoken a word!

"Hi Luke, yes I *am* Melissa although I don't know how you could possibly know that as I am certain we have never met. I don't recall you from my school either so go on reveal all, how come you know *me* and yet until a moment ago, I had no idea who *you* were?"

He clearly enjoyed her bemusement and his voice had a hint of innocuous, genuinely good humoured laughter as he replied, "Well, for a start your mum has been raving on to my mum about your art work and how you will be taking it further in the Sixth Form at your school and secondly I know someone you know, a sort of mutual acquaintance if you like."

"Oh and who might that be?" She was a little indignant now, especially as she was beginning to be irritated by his evident advantage and the fact that he was relishing it.

"Susan Posthlethwaite," he replied in no hurry to enlighten her further. He took a long, noisy slurp of his beer and waited for her response which he had no ability whatsoever to predict. He had only met Susan once when she had been allocated to show him round the grammar school as he would be starting the Lower Sixth in September, having transferred from another school when his parents moved house. She was something else that Susan Posthlethwaite, God knew why they asked her to show him round because she clearly hated the place, couldn't wait to leave and was totally uninformed. She hadn't been able to answer any of his questions except the ones about what there was to do after school and at the weekend, that sort of thing. What he *had* felt though, was a suffocating sense of unease as she quizzed him about his current status in the girlfriend department, unashamedly proffering herself as suitable material and unabashedly determining the date of his move to the area. She had even asked him his new address!

Well he liked girls, that was without doubt, but he was not desperate and did not need it offered on a plate. Where was the mystery when that happened, the thrill he felt when he started to court a girl, find out about her, see if she had as much to interest him in her head as she had in her looks? Looks were undoubtedly important but it was also necessary to be at ease, share some common interests and be good friends with a girl. He liked this Melissa already. She was unbelievably beautiful – breathtakingly so, her boyish figure was so sexy, her hair was an incredible, seemingly separate entity with a life of its own and her eyes so subtly penetrating and unnerving. As he himself loved art and would be taking it at A Level, he knew that they already had at least one thing in common.

Although he should actually be starting the second year of his A Levels, he had no choice but to recommence the whole course of study because the examination boards and therefore the syllabuses were too different for it to be possible for him to progress directly to the Upper Sixth. So Luke found himself at seventeen with the prospect of being older than all the other students in the Lower Sixth and wondered if that would affect his ability to make friends; it would be difficult anyway as the others would all have a shared history of progressing through the same school together and he would in essence be an outsider. Another factor that he had to acknowledge was that he found boys of a similar age to himself, let alone those a year younger, rather immature and he had a tendency to prefer the company of girls as friends. He was sure that being the youngest in a family of five children, his siblings being all female and older, had facilitated his ability to be at ease around girls.

"So Luke, how do you know Susan?" Melissa was curious to elicit this potentially juicy piece of information, although she had a feeling, an intuitive feeling, that there had been nothing of an intimate nature between the two of them. "You know she has left school and is working now do you?"

"Sorry to tease you Melissa," he chuckled, "I only met her once and that was enough! She did mention you though and said that I would meet you if I was taking A Level Art in September. The description she gave of you was absolutely spot on I would have known you anywhere. She showed me around the school when my parents were talking to the Headmaster about the details of my transfer."

"Oh so you are coming to our school are you? I am very surprised that *she* was given the task of showing you the school. I'll bet she had nothing good to say about it! Personally I think it's a great school and I don't care if you think that's unfashionable and uncool, because I genuinely like school and actually I can't wait to start the Sixth Form. At least I have chosen the subjects I want to study and not had some forced on me like at GCE level." Melissa realised as she finished talking that she had almost drank the whole bottle of beer! She felt at ease now, anticipating his reply and with a feeling that he was actually tolerable for a boy; he seemed willing to sit and talk as if they had known each other ages. It was a relief to think that there was going to be at least one person she could have a decent conversation with at school over the next two years. It would perhaps ease the pain of seeing Jonathan every day and knowing that she would never be able to have a relationship with him outside of school.

He opened another bottle for her and as she reached for it automatically, her parents and Luke's came back from the bar together. Amazingly Carol said "I see you two have met then, that's good. Melissa you have your key don't you so let yourself in and don't be too long it's almost eleven thirty now." With that she walked in the direction of their own caravan saying goodnight to Luke's mum and dad and with Stuart diligently following in her wake like a bobbing tethered dinghy!

With a similar message for their son and having expressed their delight in meeting the first of Luke's new schoolmates, his parents also went to bed. Luke said "Actually I don't think it's uncool to like school. Personally I really enjoyed my last one and hope I'll have a good two years at yours. I am so glad we met Melissa; I hope we can get to know each other a little better before term starts." He noticed her half empty second bottle which, quite honestly, she had drunk because she was genuinely thirsty and it readily if superficially quenched her immediate thirst, rather than from any notion of becoming intoxicated. She had experienced that with Susan about a month ago and was in no hurry to repeat the experience. Thank God she had been staying round at Susan's or she was sure her mother would have utilised her very alert powers of detection and found her out! "You like beer do you?" He grinned and then rose to his feet asking her if she wanted him to make sure she got back to her caravan safely. She acquiesced and as they walked the short distance he told her about having to repeat his first year of sixth form studies and she realised as she got to the door of her caravan that she had not thought about her darling Jonathan for almost an hour and despite the fact that she was enjoying Luke's company and feeling so at ease, it disconcerted her considerably.

As the clouds, that had been hovering ominously, finally claimed the moon's autonomous reign that night, Melissa found sleep eluded her. The music she had placed on the turntable barely registered and even attempts at reading would not ease her into a somnolent state. When she finally found a level of superficial sleep begin to claim her, it was accompanied by the almost deafening intrusion of a violent and relentless storm which would last for most of the following day.

Chapter seven

Jonathan Pritchard parked his black Morris Minor in the staff car park and attempted to adopt the necessary mien and appropriate mindset for the arduous admin he would have to plough through before the school reopened its doors to the pupils after the summer break. He was ambiguous regarding his own personal dilemma that characterised the term ahead, for he had enjoyed himself so much in Spain, he had barely acknowledged the impending problem of dealing professionally with Melissa. He had however thought about her almost continually, her visage appearing as if by his command, a silent almost ethereal presence as he fell asleep to the cicada's chorus and the soft, comforting sounds of his son sleeping in the other single bed.

Her presence in his thoughts was, he felt, fragile and he was almost afraid at times to attempt to conjure up his private and covert image of her. Perhaps her colours would fade? Perhaps it was after all only his perverse imagination that was tricking him into believing the feelings, he now realised he had unintentionally revealed, were reciprocated by her. They had been marooned for a moment, locked in complicity and at the mercy of fate and circumstance which seemed to mock them. Yet it continued, entrenched now, despite his mamma introducing him to the obviously available daughters of at least three of her friends! He was coerced by his well meaning but utterly misguided mother to agree with her that their collective beauty was indeed a peculiarly Spanish phenomenon and their counterparts in England could never compete! He kissed, ate, talked, smiled and drank with mothers and fathers of marriageable young women until he was forced from sheer exhaustion and with his face set in an almost permanent, genial and now painful smile, to tell his doting mamma to ease up He really could not face another voluptuous, simpering, expectantly nubile and obviously, desperately interested young Latin woman! There was a dearth of eligible and prospective husbands in the still staunchly parochial village. Mamma would have to rectify the misconception she had engendered in these families: that he was looking for a wife to take back to England and give him plenty of 'the babies'!

He had come to be with her and Jack and have a holiday. He also needed some solitude for sketching and reading; at this rate he would go home utterly exhausted and if mamma had her way, with a betrothal in the bag! He smiled now as he walked into the Art block at the relentless campaign his mother had engaged in! Eventually she had conceded that he must be allowed to find his own way in these matters of the heart; she had only wanted to help him she had said a little sadly. Her son and grandson were the two most important people in her life and she would be overjoyed if Jonathan found a woman truly worthy of him; her fears (that she did not voice to her son) were that he would go back to that cold, unpleasant girl – that cold fish Lydia, and then she was sure she would see less of both him and her beautiful Jack.

Simultaneously, Melissa was sitting with Luke in his parent's house which was only a few streets away from her own, listening to music, Colloseum - a band they had discovered together a couple of weeks ago and had simultaneously enthused about. They were lying on his velvet floor cushions, multicoloured and dynamic, two joss sticks burning scenting the air with musk and faces gazing fixedly at his ceiling where he had painted a psychedelic, quite awesome mural. Carol would never have given me free reign to decorate my bedroom, Melissa thought resentfully. The intense silence was interspersed with easy conversation with this unusual young man whom she had grown to like and trust over the last month or so. This summer she had made two major discoveries. Firstly after watching the moon landing with her mother and Stuart she became fully aware perhaps for the first time, that anything was possible; this amazing achievement proved that no barriers were insurmountable, no goal unreachable, no limitations could be placed on the imagination and aspirations of mankind. Secondly, after endless discussions with Luke, arguments for and against and finally, at his insistence, a visit to an intensive pig farm which disgusted her, she discovered she was a Vegetarian.

Her mother was in disbelief! Stuart said, somewhat quietly as he was being scrutinised for displaying potentially disloyal tendencies, that he could see the merits of it. Susan, in her simplistic way, thought she was trying to please Luke because she fancied him. Well God who bloody wouldn't and the annoying thing was that she had seen him first and now Melissa Johnson had him wrapped around her little finger in only a few weeks without even trying! He was absolutely crazy about her, you could see it a mile off – so bloody unfair! How did she do it for God's sake? Vegetarianism, who would have thought when they were all in Liverpool devouring roast beef and Yorkshire puddings at a pub close to their B&B, that a month later Mel would be eating bloody pulses and nuts as if they were going out of fashion? God it made her feel sick to think of her friend's diet now; I hope that turncoat Luke Scott is worth it, she thought rather disingenuously.

"But what will I feed you Melissa? I mean what do Vegetarians eat apart from vegetables? I don't know any other Vegetarians so I really am at a loss. Will you still eat eggs because I could do you a nice omelette and chips when Stuart and I have fish? We like our Sunday roast dinner though and I really don't think you can have gravy on omelettes can you, it would be almost inedible." She sighed deeply, as if she didn't have enough to think about what with work and Stuart trying to replicate the somewhat relaxed and increasingly tactile week they had enjoyed at Morecambe. She had mistakenly thought that if she gave a little physical attention to him whilst they were away, it might keep him happy for a few months and he would stop pestering her. Even though they had been sexually active on holiday, she had been as frigid during each brief encounter as she had been previously, yet perversely it had encouraged rather than dissuaded Stuart. He seemed to think, well from what he said to her quietly in the darkness of their bedroom after each event, he certainly seemed to think it was all wonderful. She knew she had been like stone, for she had the early relationship with Jay to compare it with; how could he be satisfied, overjoyed it seemed, with her paltry offerings?

She had also begun to notice, disconcertingly, that Stuart frequently gave her daughter admiring glances when she showed them both her new outfits (she was less inclined to criticize Melissa now after that upsetting incident on her birthday), or when they had been swimming whilst on holiday. She berated herself for being stupid and paranoid to think that a grown man of forty two would be interested in a young girl. Perhaps she was being irrational and it was just innocent and the sort of behaviour a father would display. But he was not Melissa's father and had only known them all for two years. She had moments when she felt such overwhelming doubt and foreboding, often thinking she did not know this man at all. She questioned the fact that he had never married or sustained a long term relationship even though he was older than her and she assumed most healthy, normal men would have been married when they were younger and perhaps had some children of their own. She dare not talk to him of children as she knew he had hoped she would want to conceive very soon after their marriage, and he barely concealed his disappointment when the condoms were installed in the bedside cabinet.

Now she had to deal with Vegetarianism! That boy Luke who had seemed so nice was clearly behind all this. Perhaps she should have been alerted to the possibilities of an alternative lifestyle when she saw the embroidered shirt he was wearing and the beads he displayed proudly around his neck! (Melissa herself was no better though, often to be seen around the place with a garish, voluminous caftan and rows of what she told her mother were called love beads. Carol had to admit to herself that she preferred these unconventional clothes which covered more of her daughter's body, to the hot pants and mini skirts she still wore sporadically). Knowing her daughter's strength of mind she realised she would not have followed his lead blindly and that discussion and debate had probably taken place. So she concluded that if Melissa had now come to the decision that 'meat is murder', a phrase she had heard bandied about elsewhere, it was a considered and possibly permanent decision. So for the foreseeable future she would be preparing separate meals for Melissa when she was already feeling she couldn't cope with all this teenage antagonism and defiance.

Luke had been there at her house when the post arrived with Melissa's grades and shortly after she had opened them, Susan (despite her own appalling results) had generously telephoned to see how she had got on. She did achieve an A in Art and both English Language and Literature, with a disappointing B in History and French; surprisingly she achieved a C in Maths and Geography and the same for her Science subjects. If only I had revised the earthworm, Melissa thought, it may have pushed my Biology grade up to a B! Luke lifted her up and swung her around the kitchen much to the annoyance of Carol; Stuart gave her a platonic kiss on her cheek which was closely observed and also a cheque to place in her account for her University fund. Melissa in turn gave him a protracted hug which elicited an icy stare of disapproval from her mother. He still smelled of carbolic soap! Susan's squeals of genuine delight could almost be heard in Lancaster and were reciprocated by Melissa, deafening all those present in the cramped kitchen. It was a joyous occasion and only marred slightly by Carol's barely concealed apprehension. Carol gave her some money, a lot of money actually, to spend on whatever she liked. "This is not for your savings Melissa it's for you to treat yourself. I am so proud of you, I really am and I know you will do well in your A Levels, you are so much better at all this than I was, you will have a great future I just know it"

Now in Luke's bedroom the album had finished and he removed himself from the floor and the womb like comfort of the cushions to lift the stylus off and seek another album that was conducive to the relaxed mellow mood they had created in this haven from adults. He found Melissa's favourite Moody Blues album and after it was safely turning and the stylus made contact with the first track, he rejoined a sleepy Melissa, his burgeoning desire for her barely concealed by the tightness of his jeans. This physical manifestation of his attraction to her was matched by a fervent admiration of her mind, her intensity and passion about things she believed in and her determination to achieve her goals. He knew she was a virgin for they had spoken at length one evening about their respective levels of experience.

He was shocked to discover that she had never had a boyfriend and was not fazed by it at all. She revealed very little when he asked what type of boy she might go for and he was no wiser for having asked. He had had one serious girlfriend which had lasted from when he was almost sixteen to just over four months ago when he had found her rather enthusiastically kissing another boy at a party. He had ended it instantly. He had two short relationships, what he termed intense friendships really with girls when he was fifteen, but they had not involved sex.

Sex! He did not think he knew so much about it actually. He had lost his virginity in the most unusual and unbelievably pleasant way when he was on holiday in France at a camp site in Brittany with his parents – he was fifteen. His parents had befriended the wife of the owner who was away on business for the duration of their stay and had left her completely in charge. She explained to them in fluent English that she usually involved herself in the bookkeeping and other secretarial aspects and that she found the day to day running of the site, unbelievably exhausting, leaving her little time for her preferred leisure activities: sunbathing and swimming. She was a very glamorous woman of about thirty five, still inclined to prefer the clothes that were prevalent in the 50's with their tight waists and full skirts, presumably because they enhanced and indeed revealed her voluptuous figure. Her make up was very fastidious, her lips always painted deep red even when she was in the pool or at the seaside. To a young adolescent boy she was a fantasy pin up, unobtainable, and even when Luke thought about it now he could not believe that she had been the one to initiate him into the realms of sexuality.

It had happened one night when she had called in to the tent to say good night and ask if everything was OK. Luke was sitting reading and he explained that his parents had gone to the nearby village for a meal and would not be back until later. She had perched on the end of the bed and slipped her shoes off saying, in a comical, yet sexy, combination of French and English, that walking around the campsite in the evening after the interminable rain of the day had ruined them. She then said something very quickly in French and to Luke it sounded like a gasp, not a sentence. She was looking at him intently. He suddenly realised he had only his briefs to cover up his modesty and yet rather than hide or climb under the sheets, he felt a strange sense of pleasure that she had seen his body. He made no attempts to cover up and as she came closer to him, asking to see what he was reading, he had no doubts about her intent even though the only knowledge of such things he really had, had been gleaned from talking with other boys and from looking at and reading the odd forbidden magazine. Her breathing changed perceptively and without realising it Luke's began to echo hers and he felt the familiar stirring of an erection. He was thrilled beyond belief; she took the book from his hand and asked him in English if he would like her to kiss him, he assented with his eyes but without words and returned the kiss which she was shocked to discover was more satisfying than any of those she had received from the more experienced lovers she had taken.

When he thought about it now, he knew she did not realise he had not reached his sixteenth birthday, yet he also sensed that she would still have attempted to kiss him even if she had known. She retreated slightly after the initial kiss which he enjoyed thoroughly and made as if to leave, but he pulled her back and was surprised at his own confidence and lack of guile. He was absolutely certain she did not know he was a virgin until the actual act took place as he seemed natural, intuitively sensing what to do, how to touch, how to explore her. He was amazed at himself, really amazed; it was as if he was a grown man with years of experience behind him, not a kid of fifteen! She certainly had not taken advantage of him and he was as willing and complicit as she, for he was eager to learn. It had been most enlightening and gratifying as had the next three encounters they reciprocally arranged before he left with his parents for the arduous, and now unwelcome, drive back to England.

He was a sensitive, intelligent and mature young man who reflected on the loss of his virginity and concluded that it was simply that – there was no relationship, certainly no emotions, merely a mutual lust and a need to discover on his part. He knew without any doubts that it had been a quite wonderful way to explore the delights of his own sexuality, but he was also unequivocally aware that he wanted the next time to involve deep feelings, and preferably love. The girl he had been serious about for almost a year had told him she loved him. Yet Luke never quite felt he could reciprocate, unsure if the feelings he had which were strong and ultimately more steadfast than her own wavering devotion, could be uttered as or described as love.

As he attempted to lie down again, his erection safely subsided after great mental efforts, he realised that Melissa, Mel as she allowed him to call her, was someone he could love. She was so unlike any other girl he had met and he was absolutely thrilled that they would be studying together for two years. He could barely contain his enthusiasm and yet there was something reticent about her at times; she seemed to retreat to a place that he was totally excluded from. Her eyes would glaze and often he would detect tears when she did not realise he was observing her. He thought that perhaps she thought sometimes of her father and he felt great sympathy for her if that was the reason, for he could not imagine a life without his own fabulous and supportive dad.

She stretched her sylph like feline body and as she opened her eyes, he could see that she had again been to that place he was excluded from. My God she looked beautiful and before he realised what had happened he was kissing her and sleepily she actually kissed him back, tentatively and so sweetly it made him tremble. Then abruptly she drew back, fully awake and obviously shocked at what had occurred.

"Luke what do you think you are doing?" she said softly without discernible anger or reproach. "We are supposed to be friends aren't we? Why would you want to spoil it?" Melissa stretched, moved to a sitting position and looked at Luke fondly. She said gently as she saw the hurt in his eyes, "Don't worry Luke and please don't look so hurt, I am not really angry with you I just like us being friends, we have so much fun and I've already told you I am not looking for a boyfriend."

Luke lay there feeling that her gentleness was a far worse form of rebuke than if she had been angry with him. He had nearly blown it after just a short time and he couldn't bear the thought of losing her friendship and her amazing and stimulating company for a moment's thoughtlessness. "I am sorry Mel, I really don't know why I did it, but you did look so gorgeous and well it just happened and if you are not happy for us to be anything more than friends at the moment I can be content with that. God what I want more than anything is for us to be friends. I am so sorry." She placed a finger on his lips and as she did so she got up from the floor and grabbed her cardigan from his chair. "Where are you going Mel? Look it won't happen again I promise, you don't have to go." He almost pleaded but managed an edge of decorum! He got up and followed her to the door.

"Don't be silly Luke; I'm not going because you kissed me. Look at the time, I am supposed to be going into town with Susan remember it's her day off today and she said she would help me spend some of my treat money my mum gave me. I expect she'll try and get me to frivol it away on rubbish, but I already know what I am getting. See you tonight OK?" With a flourish she left his bedroom and almost ran down the stairs nearly crashing into Luke's mum as she soared off the bottom step. Once she had apologised and said goodbye she hurled herself like a fireball into the street and only when she was safely out of sight around the corner, did she stop and lean heavily on a wall; as she got her breath back her right hand went automatically to her mouth and she punished her smallest finger relentlessly until it stung with pain.

What had she done? She had kissed him back, kissed someone who was not Jonathan, but with whom she felt totally relaxed. Why? She half excused herself because as always when she dozed or relaxed totally, she thought of Jonathan and she had so, so missed him. Even now developing this truly great friendship with Luke, she missed Jonathan. It was not logical and she had analysed herself until she had developed a severe headache and could bear it no longer. Her own self criticism was always more brutal, more relentless and unswerving than any other form. There was no logic in loving someone you didn't really know when there was a definite possibility of developing a potentially wonderful relationship with Luke, who was her own age or thereabouts and who she was getting to know and admire and really like. She knew other girls would go crazy about Luke when he came to the school; he had those classic good looks that, linked with such a genuine and sexy persona, couldn't fail to attract girls and probably lots of them.

She couldn't tell him she had never kissed anyone before, how could she say that when it would take on a special significance to him and may encourage him to pursue a romantic route, which she really did not want. She had wanted it to be Jonathan when she had returned the kiss instinctively, and in her half sleepy state she had thought for a moment it was. She had to admit to herself though that it was a nice kiss and that was important for her first kiss. If it could not be with Jonathan she was glad it was Luke who had given her that memory to cherish. Yes it really was a very nice kiss.

Chapter eight

The first day back at school, even with the purported privileges and the supposed relaxation of rigid rules that epitomized being in the exalted position of a Sixth Form student was, according to all those prepared to voice their views, a nightmare. It seemed that the veneer of organised efficiency took only a slight scratch to come peeling away mercilessly leaving the teaching staff vulnerable to open criticism. The main problems, as far as Melissa and Luke could see related to the unusually high numbers of students and the fact that two of the classrooms were still closed to them as the refurbishment, due to be completed by the start of term, was obviously behind schedule. Well, thought Melissa, not quite the intimate small groups I thought would characterise my two years study; obviously the results had been good this year and all those who were offered places had therefore been able to take them up.

Once term got underway and the refurbished classrooms were made available, the day ran almost like clockwork. Melissa was surprised and thrilled to discover that Luke was in her tutor group and her Literature set, which would certainly make the sessions more stimulating and eventful. They had both joined the debating society and although Carol was disconcerted to discover as half term drew near that Melissa had not formed any close friendships with other girls, Melissa herself was adamant that there was no one whom she wished to get even remotely close to; no one at all.

She had two acquaintances at the debating society whom she admired for their depth of knowledge on a variety of subjects and their determination to research and present a solid and reasoned argument, but she had no inclination to become intimate friends with these girls. She was satisfied with Luke as her confidante; he was so easy to talk to, even about female issues like periods. Luke had never tried to kiss her again after that rather embarrassing faux pas in his room a couple of weeks ago and she truly respected him for that, for not invading her precious need for distance, for not encroaching on or enquiring about her reasons for wanting to remain simply good friends. He was certainly in touch with his emotions and unlike many young men he was happier in the company of girls, especially in the company of this particular girl. What Melissa was blissfully and genuinely ignorant of, was the very pertinent and single minded manner in which he still harboured hopes; hopes that she would become his girlfriend and that one day she may return his affections which were deepening the more he got to know her.

Melissa was developing an even broader interest in theatre and theatre design in particular, and for the first half term she had been reading avidly about the ideas of Bertolt Brecht. She became utterly captivated and intrigued though by the staging ideas of Edward Gordon Craig, which were revolutionary for his time; she also admired his lifestyle and the fascinating, yet doomed romance with Isadora Duncan. Carol had been bemused as her daughter almost fell into the house on one occasion, laden down with books from the library and as she took some of them from her she became somewhat confused about the actual subject matter and its relevance to her A Levels. She was in no doubt about Melissa's voracious appetite for knowledge and its acquisition which seemed to be a major source of joy in her young life. But books on Isadora Duncan? She had read once that she had lead a rather scandalous life and was disconcerted to find books about her life, her dancing and worst of all her amorous adventures, amongst the supposed reading matter for her courses.

Much to Stuart's consternation and embarrassment, Carol had voiced this concern at the inaugural parents evening when she had spoken to Melissa's Art teacher, a Mr Pritchard who had taught her daughter in the last year of GCE's. He had simply smiled and said he thought it admirable that Melissa was broadening her knowledge of related issues. He explained that it was probably Isadora Duncan's association with the theatre designer Edward Gordon Craig, whom Melissa found stimulating, that had prompted her to seek out material on the innovative dancer. They should not worry unduly, or feel that it was an unsuitable or irrelevant digression. She really was doing awfully well, he reassured them.

The next day, clutching at this genuine reason for a moment alone with her, he asked Melissa how she was enjoying the year so far and in particular how she was finding the syllabus for her Art A Level. Almost unable to meet his eyes which she feared would unnerve her, she continued to sketch as she replied with a composed, almost distracted tone which belied her unease "It's fantastic Mr Pritchard it really is especially Literature and Art. I am finding the History tough, but I was prepared for that and make sure that I try to prioritise the homework for it as I can only cope with it when I feel alert. There is absolutely no chance of me attempting an essay for History when I'm even remotely tired." Now she must look up because she felt she was being rather rude and even more importantly, as it was the first time they had been in such close proximity to each other all term, she was unable to cope with the searing heat emanating from his eyes as they almost bored a tunnel of molten entreaty straight to her core.

She had no choice in this – she was compelled to move her face until it was upturned to his, slowly removing the wisps of hair away from her eyes, and said softly, meeting the intensity with indisputable admiration, "Thank you so much by the way for preparing the fact sheet on Gaudi for me, it was very informative, fascinating actually, and I have read more about him during the holidays which has reinforced my interest in his work and life. A few weeks ago when I was reading in the reference library, I discovered the staging and scenic designs of Gordon Craig, God what an amazing man and so misunderstood. I know it's not on the syllabus strictly speaking but as both you and Mr Brown have reinforced, we should look at as many great practitioners as possible to stimulate our own ideas and broaden our techniques. I am beginning to prefer looking at the diversity of applied art, rather than merely studying fine art as such. Do you think that's OK?"

OK, he thought, it's more than OK. She seems to have a very deep appreciation and vocation for this subject and she reminds me a little of myself at her age with her enthusiasm and undisguised, unashamed hunger for a wider, unrestrained knowledge Then what he wanted to say, to let her know unequivocally was, 'I've missed your voice, your incredible beauty, just your whole presence so much Melissa; what the hell are we going to do? This is just so painful, having to speak in these stilted, laden sentences when what I really want to do is pick you up and carry you out of here, carry you to the future, to some remote place where we can be ourselves and really begin to get to know each other.' But he spoke different words, breaking the almost imperceptible but significant silence, the teacher at the fore, "Yes of course it's OK Melissa, you are finding your own way in the subject, creating your own niche if you want to describe it that way. I knew you would prove to be as individualistic now as you were in the fifth year. So tell me," he continued, unable to resist and with a humorous lilt to his voice knowing her response before the words were uttered, "what do you think of Isadora Duncan!"

"Sir ....Mr Pritchard, how do you know I've been reading about her?" Melissa was genuinely shocked. How exactly did he know? She hoped that Luke had not been discussing her interest in Isadora with him, but she knew deep down that he would not betray her confidence, her trust. OK it was not exactly a secret, but still, she'd like to know how he knew! Was nothing sacred? And the way he said it with such a look of impish glee! He was teasing her and he was bloody enjoying it! He seemed so young at that moment, she thought, in his almost adolescent exuberance. Oh how she would like to kiss away that triumphant, boyish grin and feel his arms about her! How long will I have to dream, to fantasise and remain a virgin, occasionally hopeful, yet for the most part barely managing to endure being so close to you and not being able to touch you. "Really Sir how *do* you know?"

"Let's just say, I have my sources!" He left her to go and speak with another student, bewildered and a little infuriated wishing she could enjoy a less formal relationship with him and therefore make him tell by utilising some terrible device like tickling or, or yes that's it she'd read about that - withholding her body or...... No she knew that once she had known him physically, she just knew she would never have the strength of mind to do that!

Luke was at her house that evening, Carol had cooked omelette for them both (God how unimaginative Melissa thought to herself, how many bloody eggs can a person consume in one week!) and when they had all finished, Melissa asked Luke if he wanted to go for a walk. She was feeling tense somehow, stifled and needed some fresh air.

"OK if you want to Mel. Are you sure you've finished all your homework though, 'because I don't want you blaming me if you haven't."

"Yes I have Luke Scott, stop tormenting me, you know very well I finished my History essay last night and as I told you at lunchtime, we haven't been given any specific Art homework today." She gave him one of her famous digs in his side which he responded to by tugging her hair playfully and grabbing her hand as they walked out. She didn't wriggle her hand free as she usually did and her very real need for the warmth and closeness of Jonathan was making her feel strangely disoriented, confused and in a way this manifested itself in a morose pessimism. Perhaps it would never be. He had not let his guard down, even unwittingly like that last time just before she went on study leave. There really were no tangible indications of his feelings. Melissa felt so alone, confused, lost in a void of uncertainty, even with Luke walking, talking animatedly about his Shakespeare essay and how much he was enjoying the lessons where they were encouraged to act out scenes in small groups.

She would never know what prompted the next action she took and she would regret it always. She stopped dead in her tracks and pulled Luke back to face her and said, "Luke do you think I'm attractive, you know desirable?" They were still holding hands. He had felt that she was attractive and utterly desirable since the day almost three months ago when he had first laid eyes on her.

"You, Mel? Attractive, desirable? Are you kidding, don't you bloody well know how gorgeous you are? Remember the other week when I kissed you and you got so annoyed with me. Why do you think I kissed you, you silly girl? But why are you asking me Mel?" She had her head hung down now and from the soft undulating movements of her chest and shoulders he knew she was crying gently." Mel? Mel, look at me. My God what's the matter? I hardly ever see you like this. Have I done something to upset you? Did I tease you too much over dinner? Speak to me please Mel?"

She didn't speak to him. She pulled him closer to her and with tears streaming down her beautiful face and her hair distorting her vision, but with a fierce determination she kissed him and he thought he was in a blissful, unexpected and undeserved heaven. They stood in the street and kissed again and as they did so Melissa felt a sense of relief but failed to understand it or dissemble it, she just really needed to be kissed. They were isolated from the bemused, occasionally shocked and mostly curious eyes of the world around them; isolated in their innocent reciprocal need of each others physical proximity and isolated from each other in their divergent perceptions of its significance.

Half term proved problematic for Melissa for despite the amount of homework she had to plough through and the very real difficulties she was having understanding, or mustering up enthusiasm for Chaucer, she could not bring herself to telephone Luke. She had promised she would and even though they had not spoken about 'that night' in the two weeks since it occurred, it remained like a cloak of complicity binding them in what could only describe as a perplexity of intent. If she rang they would have to talk about the kissing and the tentative caressing that followed and how could she respond without hurting him and betraying their incredible friendship. She felt so miserable.

How could she have behaved like that, in that awful and 'easy' way when she was in love with Jonathan? She was angry with herself and failed even after considerable and agonizing analysis of her actions, to understand her motives or what was worse her need to kiss, let alone touch, Luke. She was so surprised therefore when Luke called round just before they were due to begin the second half of term. She was alone in the house listening to Leonard Cohen and completing an unfinished pen and ink drawing, temporarily absenting herself from further self criticism and protracted inner debate.

The door bell was relentless, she knew it was him and really did not want to answer, but the noise and the potential disturbance to the neighbours, forced her to run downstairs and answer it. He looked forlorn, standing there in the rain, his hair dripping into his eyes, a veil effectively camouflaging his misery. "Hi." That was all he said and she indicated to him to come in out of the appalling downpour. She took his jacket and placed it on the radiator and at the same time went to the kitchen to get him a towel to dry his hair, grateful for the distraction of the activity. She gave him the towel and asked him if he wanted a drink or some food as it was almost lunchtime and she had been about to make a sandwich for herself anyway. He declined and she indicated that he should follow her to her room where the music now permeated the whole house seeming intrusive and sadly inappropriate for the sudden change in mood. In any case Luke hated Leonard Cohen, much to her consternation, stating that he was depressing and morbid, very similar observations to her mother! She took the stylus off the LP and they sat for a while silently looking at the way the rain was creating patterns of molten sadness on her window. Finally he broke the silence.

"Mel, I don't understand why you haven't called me. No, that's not what I wanted to say – I feel right now that I don't understand you at all actually. What is going on Mel? Was it so awful when we kissed, was it so dreadful and disgusting for you that you completely blanked me for a whole week? I've been so bloody miserable and it was only my mum telling me to 'get yourself out of the house and cheer up for God's sake' that sort of encouraged me to come here. I need to know what is going on."

"Luke, I'm so sorry about not calling you and you'll probably think its an excuse when I tell you that it has taken me until today to finish all my homework and then I got involved in this sketch and as you can see the time just went. It's as simple as that, there really isn't anything to read into it, honestly," she lied.

"I suppose you think I'm being paranoid or something, but do you realise Mel it's the longest time we have not seen or at least spoken to each other since we met. OK I know it was you who initiated the kiss the last time but I thought, after what you said a few weeks ago, about just wanting to be friends, that you really regretted it and realised it was just a gigantic mistake and perhaps that you didn't even want to remain friends with me. I've just been going over and over it until its all I can focus on; but Mel I am still so bloody confused." He was looking so plaintive, so utterly vulnerable and she felt so guilty and responsible she held out her arms for him to cuddle up beside her and for what seemed like an eternity of time and with only the soft murmurs of her apologies in his ears,

Tides Must Turn

Luke felt comforted, consoled, and unfortunately – aroused.

Melissa had to try and explain to him soon that she couldn't bear the thought of losing his friendship, but she did not want to become his girlfriend and for the physical attraction, which clearly was manifesting itself and sparking between them, to overwhelm the mental rapport they had developed. She could not find the words, she was lost in his misery and her own despair and frustration and so, when he gently lay her down on the bed and cradled her face in his hands whispering words she only half registered, she responded to the kiss, the touch and allowed her need for closeness to obliterate her reason. It was bliss to be wanted, to feel desired, she thought and the certitude that she was not emotionally free to reciprocate the depth of feeling he was expressing as he caressed her, did not dissuade her from her need to make her wonderful friend feel happy and cared for.

What did disconcert her was the presence against her right thigh of what she reasoned was an erection; it scared and amazed her at the same time and she was left in no doubt whatsoever that she had been the cause of this occurrence. She had never ever been in this position and she was gauche enough to wonder what the correct procedure was if, like her, you did not want to proceed along this sexual highway going through all the stop signs. She was enveloped in his adoration, aware of his desire, yet believed with absolute certainty that she would be able to put the brakes on at any given point. She would wait for Jonathan. What she was feeling now was comforting, safe and quite pleasant but it did not even begin to compare with the way a simple glance or an everyday pleasantry from Jonathan made her feel. And the electricity of the touch of his arm against hers a lifetime ago, well if that was a foretaste of the sensual pleasures she would perhaps enjoy with him one day then she really would be in the blissful heaven she often conjured up in her dreams.

She loved Jonathan Pritchard – it permeated her whole being, yet here she was again in the warmth and safety of Luke's arms, allowing him to kiss and touch her, even responding to him as though she had no ability to control her own body anymore. Again a wave of self disgust at her lack of willpower overcame her momentarily and then as he kissed her throat, it vanished with her resolve. Her body and mind were diametrically opposed, giving her conflicting and alternate messages which she could not ignore; she was being relentlessly propelled into pleasure by the roller coaster of her physical inclinations whilst her mind struggled ineffectively to locate and securely grasp the safety brake.

"Luke," she whispered almost inaudibly as he started to move her caftan away from her shoulders, "Luke, you must stop, Luke you must….." He kissed her and then she was quiet for a moment luxuriating in his touch as he stroked her shoulders, but as he moved his hand towards her breasts she managed to move away, gently removing his hand and kissing his closed enraptured eye lids. "Luke, no more, please Luke, I can't."

He stopped and held her so close it became unbearable. "Don't worry Mel, we are still friends you know, it's just that we kiss sometimes that's all! It's better this way, I love to kiss you and if that's all you want to do then it's OK really. I think you know though that I really do care for you Mel. I find it difficult to stop myself from touching you, so you must always stop *me* when you feel I've stepped over the line. Promise me you will. I can't bear for us to have an atmosphere between us and this last week when we didn't speak, God I was almost demented! No wonder my mum kicked me out into the street!" This was OK, Mel thought, when he put it like that they were just friends who kissed and it was lovely so why was she berating herself; it would have to stop - this self inflicted inner turmoil and constant analysis. Jonathan was unobtainable, but she adored him.

What she was beginning to feel for Luke was a deep and stimulating friendship; he was probably the best friend she had ever had. Certainly their friendship was on a completely different level to the somewhat superficial knowledge that Susan Posthlethwaite had of her. The two areas of her life were mutually exclusive and yet not diametrically opposed. She supposed that Jonathan who was a man of what, twenty three or something and probably even married for all she knew; she supposed he had sexual experiences. After all he was so perfect, so beautiful, he must have had many lovers - but she would not think about that now for it made her feel jealous and that really was absolutely ridiculous!

Melissa was in the timeless dilemma created by an awakening and importunate sexuality, which demanded to be acknowledged, to sing its unique song, but was thwarted and repressed by her self imposed determination to remain chaste until the man she had set her heart on became available to her. Had she not met Jonathan Pritchard there would be no predicament, no necessity for self recriminations and she would have followed the dictates of her body. He heart without restraint and having not been contained by clandestine expectations, would have followed her body's journey to reciprocate Luke's love. For he did love her. So, in other circumstances Luke Scott would have been the one she recalled many years later, as her first love, unencumbered, unrestrained and untainted by unnecessary complexity.

Chapter nine

To Carol's consternation, particularly as the costs were debilitating, Melissa signed up for every available theatre visit organised by the English department, whether it was relevant to her current studies or not. This expenditure had to be added to the less expensive but significant outlay she and Stuart were making for Art trips. Luke would have liked to go with her, but his parents had to put a limit on extra outgoings as they had recently taken on a new mortgage and were finding it somewhat difficult to meet all their commitments despite his dad's prestigious new position. Carol had discussed with Stuart the need for them to ask Melissa to curb her extra curricular involvement but he had completely disagreed, stating that they only had one child between them to spend their money on and what could be the harm when it was educational and not frivolous. He had been adamant that Melissa should be allowed to continue, without restraint.

The first trip organised by Mr Pritchard for her Art group was drawing close; they were to go to the Walker Art gallery in Liverpool, the mini-bus had been arranged for 9.00 am the following Tuesday and Melissa had the whole weekend to endure before she could be in really close proximity to her beloved Jonathan whom she had had very little close contact with so far this term.. It was fortuitous that the take up on this trip had been poor, probably because as it was now December there was very little money to be spared in most households for school trips and other unnecessary expenditure, and rather than a large coach they would be travelling in a much more intimate mode of transport, perhaps she could even manage to sit next to him. She felt bizarrely immature and enjoyed the pleasure these secretive plottings and intrigues made her feel! She was glad that Luke was not in her group and as she had obviously never revealed to him, especially not to him, her feelings for their teacher. It would have been at best awkward and at worst devastating if he discovered to whom her heart really belonged. Luke was beginning to know her so well and as they became closer she was finding it increasingly difficult to protect the distance she must maintain to not only write the poetry which was currently centred almost entirely on Jonathan, but also to enjoy her space to dream of and fantasise about him.

Jonathan was almost losing his mind, his jealousy torturing him relentlessly; the visions in his head of Melissa with Luke Scott disturbing his sleep as persistently as his previously untainted and blissful dreams of Melissa had done. He had begun to notice them huddled together talking animatedly in the Art room during breaks or over lunch time when they were allowed as Sixth Formers to access the room to work in. He also knew from his own life experience of both love and lust, knew without a doubt that Luke was very interested in Melissa and not just as a friend. Well he suspected that most of the Sixth Form boys lusted after her, but were intimidated by her intellect and self sufficiency and would never make a move on her. Luke Scott was not threatened by Melissa's intellect, for his was also formidable and he was, Jonathan admitted, a very good looking young man with an astounding talent in Art. He was a free spirit which was problematic because the preparation for and passing of exams, even Art, was to a degree formulaic. Unbridled creativity must ultimately be channelled and tamed somewhat in order to provide the examination boards with what was required in terms of the syllabus and for grading criteria to be fully met.

Melissa was more astute and despite her broad interest in the field, was able to work within the constraints of the syllabus to achieve her ends, a place in Art School. He genuinely admired Luke Scott's talent but feared his grades would not be high enough for him to progress to the course he was aiming for. There was still time and even though he was not in his own group for Art, Jonathan had tried to help Luke. He encouraged him to see the merits in completing homework as set and to restrain his digressive tendencies for the duration of this course. Ultimately once he was established in the future, he could enjoy a free hand. This was not the issue at the forefront of his mind as he drove home from a departmental meeting, called so that they could put the final arrangements into place for next half term's residency by Julian Long. The meeting had been swift and expedient, with no discernible problems encountered and now he should be hungry but food was the last thing on his mind.

He was a fool to think that she could possibly feel anything for him; he had deceived himself surely in believing she had reciprocated his covert love. He thought he had read the signs, sensed the unspoken tremulous passion emanating from her eyes, her voice. He remembered with absolute clarity the touch of her arm against his, irrefutably evoking a moment of the utmost eroticism between them. He had known he must maintain his distance but he had not counted on this turn of events which was the most unbearable and agonising form of purgatory. How would he cope with the trip to Liverpool tomorrow, he could hardly avoid her as there were only ten students and two teachers involved.

He recalled how he had spoken to Luke last week when he had found him in the Art room sitting alongside Melissa's easel, talking in subdued tones, when strictly speaking the session had been exclusively for his own group. "Luke, I see you are here again, to what do we owe the pleasure? I am sure you know that this session is not open to your group and whilst I can applaud you spending some breaks and lunchtimes working here, is there not a class you should be in right now?"

Affable as always and utterly respectfully, Luke replied, "Good morning Sir. I know that I shouldn't be here, but my French teacher is off sick today and our class has been cancelled so I came to keep Mel company."

"Well, Mel, I mean Melissa, should know better than to agree to your presence here Luke. We can't have open house or no-one would be able to concentrate." He avoided looking at her for he sensed she was actually amused by this whole incident and he did not want to lose face.

She replied quickly before Luke could speak and for years later she would question what encouraged her audaciousness and playful irreverence when she said, "But Mr Pritchard, Luke inspires me and I really need him here to encourage me to finish this piece. Please can he stay, just this once?"

Both Luke and Jonathan were completely taken aback by the response from a young woman who usually deferred to the authority of her teachers and was averse to openly questioning rules and regulations. Luke was encouraged by the words, 'he inspires me' and Jonathan was devastated by them. Melissa discovered an unanticipated, rather thrilling sense of power when Jonathan acquiesced and said that, on this occasion as they were both exemplary students, Luke could stay but there were to be no further flouting of the rules.

When he got home eventually through the thick fog and he poured himself a large glass of Chardonnay, he tried to rekindle those wonderful visions of Melissa he had so enjoyed before his errant imagination linked every image with Luke Scott. He placed a Beatles album on the turntable and wandered lethargically into the kitchen. The music irritated him tonight and no sooner had it begun that he went back into his living room and with undue and unnecessary force he pushed the stylus off the track, probably scratching the record, but he was unrepentant. His humour must improve before tomorrow as he needed a clear head and the utmost concentration for the trip. He poured another glass of wine, turned the light off in the kitchen and made his way up to his studio.

There on a large easel, almost taking up half an entire wall was a partially finished oil on canvas, the Pre-Raphaelite hair tumbling on to glistening white shoulders, the eyes intense yet accessible, molten, and the half painted smile seemingly meant only for the creator of this work. He spent an hour working on the delicate colour of Melissa's skin, bringing it slowly and now tentatively to life; his agony subsided but not completely, as he reluctantly embraced the plethora of uncertain thoughts that had woven an almost invisible web to ensnare his composure.

It was an excruciatingly bitter and unwelcoming day that saw at least half of the students, who had paid for the trip, fail to arrive and those who braved the problems of transport and motivation, seemed listless as they waited for the mini-bus. Jonathan noted with mixed emotions that Melissa had not arrived at the given time and wondered if, like the other non arrivals, there was a message from her mother on the school answer phone. There certainly hadn't been one when he checked earlier. It was fortuitous that the four students present would now benefit from the undivided attention and expertise of the two members of staff accompanying them.

They were about to set off and Mr Brown had instructed the driver, when he spotted a frantic and breathless girl frantically trying to get the attention of anyone on board who could see her. The doors were opened and Melissa threw herself in to the nearest seat, gasping for breath whilst attempting to thank Mr Brown for stopping. She loved the Walker Art Gallery and was furious that her alarm clock had failed to go off and for some reason Carol had forgotten that she needed to get away half an hour earlier today. Stuart had been roused by an irritated Carol, relieved of his striped pyjamas and appeared almost instantaneously, fully dressed but disgustingly unshaven, to save the moment and had driven her, rather swiftly Melissa had observed, to the school gates.

It was only when the person she was pressed up against said with undisguised humour, "Glad you made it Melissa, and when you have caught your breath perhaps you could remove that rather cumbersome folder from my right leg!" She recovered her composure and looked at Jonathan only to lose it instantaneously as he grinned innocuously and so endearingly, his eyes twinkling with amusement and palpable relief that she was there. She returned his grin, apologised for both misdemeanours, removed the bag and allowed him to help her off with her duffle coat beginning to feel for the very first time, incredibly relaxed and assured in his company. The other students were talking amongst themselves and Mr Brown was sitting in the front with the driver earnestly studying an opened map which rested on his knee; relishing the closeness of Jonathan and realising that conversation in this environment would be incongruous, she closed her eyes for the journey, her body becoming symbiotically drawn to his, fusing where they made contact. He reciprocated this blissful silence, speaking only to respond to occasional questions from the other students. Melissa wondered how the turmoil that had characterised the last year, could have abated instantaneously.

The visit was thoroughly enjoyed by all it seemed with the exception of David Ramsbotham who spent most of his time chatting up a giggling blonde cloud of a girl who willingly extricated herself from another group in order to float with undisguised intent on the edge of theirs. David was distracted, toyed with, encouraged, titillated and then when his hopes of receiving a tangible means of contact in order to pursue the feast of hormonal delight that had been all but promised, she giggled and simpered her way back to her waiting group without a backward glance! The traffic was congested, exacerbated by the foul weather conditions and the arrival time at the school which was the designated pick up point, was some half an hour later than they had expected. Melissa had said she would ring if she needed a lift and had told Carol that she may call in to see Susan on the way home, but in any case she had promised to let her know her movements.

The mini-bus departed as did all the students, most of whom had cars waiting to deliver them warmly and expediently to their homes. Melissa had so enjoyed the atmosphere and the relaxed mood that she could not possibly go home just yet to what was invariably an unpredictable welcome. As he drove out of the school gates, Jonathan spotted her fumbling in her bag for change to telephone Carol from the nearby phone box. He wound down his window, the bitterly cold air seizing its chance to invade mercilessly. "Is everything alright Melissa? You really shouldn't linger here in the dark you know, they say it might snow later and it's already freezing. Are you walking home or is someone coming to pick you up?"

He had startled her and she dropped her bag which landed on her left foot causing a sharp pain which made her cry out and, had she been alone, would have been accompanied by a string of guttural expletives. He leapt from his car as she struggled to retrieve the objects that had begun to slide about in the ice, but was of absolutely no assistance to her whatsoever as he slipped in his haste falling solidly and most unceremoniously onto his bottom! Melissa, momentarily forgot her injury and seeing him in such an ungainly position, proceeded to roar with uncontrollable laughter, which to her utter relief he reciprocated. They were still there in the freezing cold, laughing uproariously, her possessions strewn about the pavement, when a puzzled Mr Brown drove past a few moments later waving to his colleague as he did so.

"Get in the car for God's sake before anything else happens, or any other body parts get damaged!" He was still laughing but not so manically now.

Still chuckling, but having regained a little self possession, she managed to say, "But Sir, I need to phone my mother to let her know I will be going to see my friend, otherwise she'll go crazy if she doesn't know where I am."

"OK, leave your bag in the car, make the call and I'll drop you at your friend's house, unless you want to go straight home. It's entirely up to you, but I am not leaving you here in this bloody awful weather, I must make sure you get to wherever you choose to go safely, alright?" Her first thoughts were not about being alone in the car with him, something she had fantasised about for so long, but about that fact that he seemed so informal here away from the school environment, he had even said 'bloody'! She made the call. She got in the car and it was only then that the familiar feeling relentlessly invaded her whole body almost making her incapable of speech. "I like Holman Hunt too, very much actually," he said casually. He had noticed me looking at the Holman Hunt. How much does he see without me realising, how many times has he watched me, observed my preferences, my moods, my... oh! Oh God, what must he think when he sees me with Luke? What have his observations led him to deduce from our closeness?

She didn't openly question his knowledge, just absorbed it and began to lose some of her debilitating nervousness as she replied, "I don't know much about the Pre-Raphaelites as a movement yet, but yes I do like his work. His paintings whilst being so incredibly detailed and beautiful also seem to be symbolic, to be telling a story with a strong moral message. I like that aspect - it gives them more depth somehow." Then she added recklessly, "Its good of you to drop me off at Susan's, won't your wife or someone be worried about you?"

Why did she want to know? The tension in this car is unbearable, I can't be getting these signals all wrong can I? "Firstly I am gratified, no - more than that, I am delighted that you have already begun to look at Art in such a critically analytical way, and secondly no I don't have a wife or a 'someone' here Melissa. I do have some marking to do but really it's no trouble and I am in no hurry to get home." No hurry at all he thought, I have my Melissa in the car with me and it seems like the rest of the world does not exist. "By the way, remind me to show you some more paintings by the Pre-Raphaelites not only would you find their work and lives fascinating, perhaps even as stimulating as Gaudi or Gordon Craig, I also think you would be most surprised at how much you resemble the model Elizabeth Siddal, whose type of beauty they extolled." She found this remark thrilling for his voice exuded an unashamed, undisguised admiration for her and she was able to shake off, at last, the doubts that had been insidiously creeping into her consciousness over the last few months.

Jonathan trembled slightly, manifesting itself almost as a shiver of unease, with the realisation that something had changed fundamentally between them now. They neared the corner of Susan's street and he stopped where Melissa indicated she wanted to be. He never knew why he did it, it was not premeditated merely the spontaneous dictates of his heart unrestrained momentarily, but he took her hand, the shock of electricity almost making him release it immediately, and without either of them looking away from the windscreen he said "I think you are truly wonderful Melissa and if circumstances were different I would want to get to know you so much better. I would have loved for us to be friends in another life, but as it is it's just impossible." He gently let go of her hand and they simultaneously turned facing each other, the street light barely penetrating the darkness, yet their eyes met across a luminous abyss of palpable desire.

"Why? Why is it impossible? Surely it can't be wrong for you and I to be friends can it?"

"Yes it is wrong Melissa. For a start I am your teacher and could not betray the trust that is placed on me by the school and your parents. Secondly, even if I was not teaching you, there is a vast age difference between us and you know how that would be viewed, even if we were just friends."

"How old *are* you Mr Pritchard?" she was genuinely curious because the way he had said 'vast' made him seem ancient, which she was sure he wasn't.

He thought for a moment before replying; he did not usually divulge personal information to students, but he decided that as this was Melissa in whom he felt an innate trust, and as he had used it as a reason for them not to be together, he could tell her, "I'm twenty nine, so you see it really is a problem."

She didn't think so and chose to ignore it; she was grasping at the almost tangible possibilities he had strewn at her feet, "What if I came to model for you, would that be acceptable do you think? I have heard that you are often commissioned and you must occasionally need a model, even if the work was just for yourself. I would love to model for you, really I would, I am sure I could learn a lot from watching you work." She looked at him with such entreaty in her whole demeanour; he was almost overcome by the pleasurable wave of potential that flooded his reason. She was in earnest, waiting for his reply, waiting for him to acquiesce, for them to develop their friendship. They both knew it was more, so much more than that, but this was not the time to vocalise, to disclose, or to embrace the ecstasy of those visions that danced in their minds.

He made himself turn away and reached into the back for her bag and she knew the moment had passed and the possibility of them being alone together for any length of time thwarted; she felt bereft. The tears began to flow relentlessly as she gave way to the complexity of her misery, unable to understand the mores of a society that would frown upon two people following the inclination of their hearts. In her naivety, she had thought Jonathan would allow her to model for him, to visit him occasionally, what could be wrong with that if they were only friends. If they were only friends! They were not even that, she knew very little about him and it seemed to her at this moment sitting in a now exceedingly freezing car, in this dreary street, that it would never happen because he did not want it to. He was devastated by her crying, knowing he was the cause and knowing he could not comfort her as he dearly wanted to in case it obliterated, by its very action, the words he had just spoken.

"I'm sorry, Mel. God I am truly sorry. Try to understand please? Try to think that this is not just about you and me it has much wider implications. I could even lose my job. Mel? Mel? Please say something." He handed her the bag and she took it without physical contact and opened the door saying thank you as she slammed it shut, almost running now to the dubious haven of Susan's frivolity.

Chapter ten

He took the mail from his pigeon hole and settled at the desk in the still deserted staff room to open it. It was a new term, January 1970 and he hoped it would prove easier for him emotionally than the last couple of weeks of the autumn term, which had seen him torn between the polarised positions of duty and heart. It had seemed to him that in the couple of weeks after their car journey, Melissa had spent almost the entire time with Luke Scott which tore unrelentingly at his resolve, but did not dislodge it. To compound his misery and disquiet there had been a discernable atmosphere between Lydia and David when he went to their house to pick up Jack on Boxing Day and, although he couldn't say for sure, he felt it had something to do with what he now knew were Lydia's harboured hopes for reconciliation between them, her dreams of creating again the family unit that had once seemed so strong, so unsinkable. His mind had instantly conjured up the picture, which was locked vividly in his memory, of Lydia's attempted seduction of him last summer and he dearly hoped she had not revealed any of the events to David.

The residency of Julian Long would start in two days and the secretary had typed up a biography and fact sheet for the students which he must photocopy tomorrow and there was also a relatively flexible itinerary for the weeks ahead, involving some trips to the Lake District and some small group intensive sessions facilitated by Julian. It should prove a stimulating and hopefully rewarding half term.

Amongst the mail was a handwritten square envelope with simply

Jonathan Pritchard - Personal written across it. He opened it and discovered a card with Ophelia by Millais on the front, he gasped as he reaffirmed his opinion that Lizzy Siddal, the model for the painting, which he felt was one of the greatest masterpieces of Pre-Raphaelite art, could almost be Melissa. Clearly after their visit to the Walker Art Gallery and the disturbing aftermath, Melissa had thought the same, for the card was from her even though her name did not appear on it. He opened it and read:

IF

If I gave you my mind
in its nakedness,
would you clothe my thoughts
with wonder and perception?
Would you take my soul
dancing in the moonlight of realisation?
Or would you wander
the streets of my mind
in blindness.
Not thinking to knock
on the doors of illusion,
not needing to climb
the mountain of knowledge,
not wanting to see the light
in the valley of awareness,
but shielding your eyes
from the intensity of my being.

Jonathan just wept, unashamedly and copiously; thankfully his distraught, abandoned state was witnessed by no-one but himself as the school was empty except for a caretaker who had gone about his duties after unlocking the staff room for Mr Pritchard. He was besieged simultaneously by a combination of rapturous happiness, unendurable despair and a welcome sense of release from the months of turmoil as an embryonic idea was created and then lingered patiently until he was able to give it form and direction. Some time later with the precious card in the inside pocket of his jacket, he walked languorously to the Art Block and was determined to deal with whatever the day threw at him both professionally and as always with the utmost assiduous efficiently. Tonight seemed a lifetime away and the day would be interminably long. Thank God he did not teach Melissa today for it would have been the ultimate test of his resolve if he had to look at her, teach her and maintain an intolerable restraint after reading that poem.

But when at last Jonathan returned home that night he knew the tide had turned for them; they were bound in some way he could not analyse, didn't want to analyse, and he must grasp this moment or he knew with absolute certainty that he would regret it forever. He must ignore the ethical and professional issues that reason tried to push to the forefront of his mind. If he heeded those thoughts he would not be able to take this course; he would yet again be cast adrift, drowning for certain in the sea of misery that personified his longing. He would let her visit him and model for him, a platonic half way house; a compromise he felt he could justify. His love would not be denied now, it insisted on having its voice, its freedom to explore the object and source of its very existence; the physical manifestation of this love could and had to wait; in this he was most insistent.

Melissa had been so confused and miserable when she had rung Susan's door bell on the night Jonathan had rejected her despite admitting he had feelings for her. Susan took one look at her and went straight to her parent's drinks cabinet and made them both a stiff Vodka and Lime, took Melissa's coat, hat and gloves and led her to the cosy 'parlour' where they could talk. Her parents were out at the pub, even though the pavements were virtually sheet ice. What the bloody hell has that Luke Scott done to upset Mel like this, she thought simplistically. The Vodka tasted good but disappointingly for Susan it did not loosen her friend's tongue and there really wasn't any gossip to be heard. So she spent the next hour talking about Woolies and her latest 'Mr Right Now' because as she said to Mel it was taking some time to find the elusive Mr Right so she had wisely, in her own opinion, decided to enjoy the pleasures of the various and varied young men who asked her out. She kept back some of the more lascivious information at this stage because she knew how moral Mel was and she also knew she was still a virgin, God it was almost 1970 and next year they would be seventeen.

Susan was quite proud of the progress she had made since her disappointing initiation into sex by the nice but somewhat smelly Norman Bishop. God that seemed like years ago! At least she knew now that it could be fun, lots of fun and quite addictive! She did not know any other virgins of their age. Quite frankly it was bloody abnormal and was probably related in some way to Mel's other abnormal behaviour, like Vegetarianism, Leonard Cohen worship and reading! So what had upset her? If it was actually Luke Scott, she might ask Mel if she could ask him out herself. OK he was a turncoat and a weird Vegetarian too, but he was so bloody gorgeous she would love to get her hands on him! But only if Mel said it was OK. Friendship came first.

Melissa could never tell Susan about the events of this evening; she instinctively maintained a silence on any issues related to school in general and Art in particular just in case she inadvertently became transparent and Susan guessed that she still liked Jonathan Pritchard. Susan wasn't interested anyway, only in the gossip or in the ins and outs of who was dating who, but most persistently she tried to elicit information about her relationship with Luke and again Melissa managed to deflect the questions. No they were not questions; it was a bloody inquisition every time! Susan was incredulous that Mel could spend so much time with this paragon and not get his trousers off. Melissa found Susan rather crude and worried for her lately, worried in case she got VD or worse, became pregnant, both of which Susan assured her were impossibilities.

"I am careful Mel," was all she revealed. Before Melissa was to set off to walk the couple of streets back to her own house, she was subjected to an impromptu fashion show; Susan with all her new found 'wealth' since starting work had indulged her fetish for purple on a daily basis. It was unrelenting, how many shades, textures and shapes could purple come in? It all served to lighten Melissa's mood and when the telephone rang with Stuart's offer of a lift she uncharacteristically assented with some genuine enthusiasm. She was in imminent danger of a further deluge of purple as Susan had offered to show her the new, *purple*, coordinating bedding she had bought with her wages last week!

She was dreading Christmas with her mother whose recent state of equanimity had been short lived and, having endured the last two weeks of term with barely a word from Jonathan except what was required in relation to her work and its progress, she was also dreading the new term. She had made a mess of not only one hand, but both as her desolation precipitated simultaneous and ferocious attacks on the inviting skin around her fingers. She was almost too ashamed to reveal them they looked so terrible! How much longer could this impasse continue making both of them miserable and without a justifiable reason as far as she was concerned. Stuart had organised a trip to see a pantomime and generously bought an extra ticket for Luke who like her hated pantomimes with a vengeance, but it turned out to be quite an upbeat version of Cinderella and they even found themselves laughing occasionally with the rest of the audience.

For New Years Eve, Melissa had been allowed to go with Luke to a dance in a nearby town where a new local band was playing. Luke knew the brother of one of the band members and not only did he say they were really cool, but they were given a reduction on the ticket prices. Luke hoped it would help Melissa out of this malaise she seemed to have been drowning in for weeks now. Carol even agreed without a struggle, to Melissa staying over at Luke's house as there was a newly vacated bedroom since another of his sisters had left home and got a flat in Bootle. Luke's dad, Norman, was generously foregoing his alcohol consumption to pick up his cherished only son and this lovely lass he had taken up with.

Luke and Melissa needed to let their hair down; it had been a tough term and when this artist was in residency next year they would actually have extra project work to do. It wasn't even voluntary which Luke especially found unjust and undemocratic, mostly because he hated the constraints of what they had been told would be involved, and partially because he just hated wildlife paintings. Melissa was secretly relieved not to see or be aware of the presence of Jonathan; the release of tension was welcomed unequivocally. The dance proved therapeutic and both Luke and Melissa were almost abandoned in their enthusiasm and danced until they were exhausted and their feet hurt. They drank plenty of the cheap alcohol, Luke taking beer and Melissa sticking to her Vodka and Lime, she didn't want to feel drunk or sick like that time long ago now with Susan.

On the way home they talked and argued animatedly about music and the relative merits of this band and others that they had both seen in Liverpool and Luke's bemused dad wished he was young again and in love, as clearly his son was. Who could blame him either he thought, she is a rare lass, what with those looks and a brain to boot, prefect for his lad. When they got home they both declined the offer of cocoa or Ovaltine; imagine that in your stomach on top of the alcohol they both thought! Norman asked them to be quiet if they were staying up for a natter (or more than likely, a kiss and a cuddle he mused to himself) because everyone else had been in bed for an hour or more, after all it was two o'clock in the morning. It was cold but the fire in the front room was still glowing and they went in, closing the door securely behind them and curled up together on the sofa and, as usual when they were together, it wasn't long before Luke started to kiss her.

She enjoyed these kisses; she no longer berated herself and had come to realise that it helped her deal with and lessen the depth of frustration she endured because the man she loved was unattainable. She cared deeply about Luke and they were great friends despite their at times polarised views on certain subjects; tonight she felt so safe again and unbelievably relaxed that she did not stop him when he reached towards her breasts, having somehow undone the ribbon that secured the top of her dress. For the first time he kissed them, tenderly and alternately and the pleasure she felt caused her to sigh partially with desire but mostly with relief that he had initiated this.

It seemed to occur without her realising it, just as the fire flickered its last light she found herself taking his shirt off and allowing her dress to be removed and as it slipped to the floor she actually realised she wanted this to happen. Confusing as it was, and the fact that he was not the man she loved did not stop her feeling so incredibly close to him, trusting him and wanting to lose her virginity to him. All thoughts of saving this for Jonathan left her consciousness, she allowed Luke to lead her, to show her what to do although there was an intuitive response from her that excited and surprised him at the same time.

He knew she was sensuous and tactile but she had always held back, unable or unwilling to reciprocate. She trusted him completely with this moment and he did not fail her. He whispered again and again that he loved her, reassuring her it would be alright and she melted it seemed into him, savouring the warmth of him, the taste of his skin and when he gently entered her she felt only a little discomfort which was forgotten as she felt the bliss of her own sexuality, empowered now as she realised he was enjoying her so much. He interrupted the delightful experience for a moment and as he entered her again she realised he must have put on a condom and that thoughtfulness amidst his gentle, loving passion, sent her into a subtle yet discernable wave of pleasure and minutes later he clung to her in his own sated bliss. They lay there on the sofa in the now totally dark room for what seemed like hours and moved only when the cold forced them to make their silent ways to their respective rooms. He kissed her gently as they parted and as she lay in the unfamiliar bed she reflected for a brief second, before sleep overtook her, that she was very lucky to have made love for the first time with such a gentle and selfless boy.

Luke understandably assumed that their relationship would now be on a different level; they would be boyfriend and girlfriend and they would, he hoped continue to enjoy each others bodies as well as their minds. However, when he presented this scenario to Mel the next day as they sat in his room after breakfast cradling large mugs of tea, she said she didn't see why that should be the case. "Luke what is wrong with the way things are. I mean *we* both know what happened, it's special and private, but we are still close friends aren't we? If we try and force some superficial change, we may lose that and it frightens me. Luke you are my best friend and it really matters that we don't lose sight of that."

He was so visibly disappointed it tore at her conscience, she added "Luke, don't be upset. Please don't spoil this lovely morning and the time we can spend together before I have to go to my grandparents for lunch. I am so grateful to you for last night; you made me feel so special Luke, I'm glad it was with you." He didn't say anything just stared distractedly into his tea as if she had already left the room. "Luke, please look at me and tell me what I've done wrong, Luke please?"

"You *are* special Mel; do you remember what I said to you last night?" He was looking at her intently now and suddenly she realised the enormity of what had happened between them and she also realised that she was pivotal to his happiness, the responsibility of knowing her actions could cause him pain was overwhelming. What have I done? What did I start with that kiss all those weeks ago? He said he loved me and I do care about him so much, so very much and would hate to hurt him, but I am already doing just that without even intending to. I have been utterly selfish, giving him hope when I can't reciprocate his love in the way he needs me to. She chose her words carefully and for the first time for days her mind was suddenly filled with Jonathan's presence as if he was there testing her, watching her response, waiting it seemed for his own answer.

"Yes Luke I remember what you said and I care about you too, I always have. Surely you know that?" She put her mug on the bedside cabinet and asked him if he wanted her to choose some music for them to listen to. He nodded and seemed content for the moment as they sank into his cushions, wrapping themselves around each other, content with the tangible comfort each found in the other's physical closeness. Their thoughts as the morning gradually encroached on their ultimately transient yet currently impervious haven could not have been more disparate. Luke was hoping to see Melissa in a couple of days and be alone somewhere with her so he could make delicious love with her again, his misgivings about her need to maintain the status quo in their relationship slowly fading as he felt her arms about him. Melissa conversely was immersed in the frantic visual display her imagination was conjuring up; a dramatic juxtaposition of these two men, both of whom she needed in her life and, ironically, both of whom would probably vacate it.

She genuinely could not see Luke for a few days and whilst he was initially disappointed he acquiesced when she agreed to a definite arrangement for him to come to complete some Art homework at her house one morning, and after lunch they planned to go to the pictures which on this occasion he did not really enthuse about. He did however see the delightful potential of being together with her when both Carol and Stuart were at work. It was the day before he came over that Melissa took the poem, which she had written some months previously, to the school and somewhat recklessly delivered it to the caretaker who was clearly not having such a protracted holiday as the students and teaching staff. She was compelled to do this, she didn't question why, simply knew that although she had lost her virginity to her dearest friend, Luke, she longed for Jonathan even more and that she did not question either. It was just so. The delivery of the poem left Melissa with a feeling of such tangible relief; her whole being was imbued with a sense of calm, she had shared her innermost thoughts with him now and must wait for his reaction. It was with a tender and genuine affection that she responded to Luke's ardour on that grey, unwelcoming afternoon, indebted to him for his gentle ability to propel her towards the delightful discovery of her own sexuality.

When term finally started and after such a momentous two weeks break, Melissa found she relished the residency of Julian long, the diversity of work they were involved in enriched the curriculum without, she felt, being overly demanding. They worked with him for only one session a week, but nevertheless she felt renewed stimulation and realised her imagination had been somewhat stagnant for a time. The affairs of the heart she was discovering were not only time consuming but draining, and she invariably found herself in Luke's arms when they had the privacy to explore each other undetected by respective parents! But she enthused so much about the residency it caused tension between her and Luke. He felt the whole 'experiment' as he called it was a waste of his time and could see absolutely no relevance to their studies whatsoever. He said to Melissa he would have preferred extra time for Art History, which they both found fascinating.

She lost herself in the sheer enjoyment of her Art, was also discovering a passion for Shakespeare's anti-heroes and was almost obsessed with Macbeth, God she loved that play. She was in her tutor room one lunchtime about two weeks into the term, reading some critical analysis and totally engrossed in a section on imagery, when Jonathan asked her if she could call into the Art Block for a moment at the end of the afternoon's teaching, as he needed to see her. She thought perhaps she would be admonished about the poem, she dreaded to think of his reaction. She had thought many times since she had delivered it, that the poem may have got into the wrong hands, she really should not have done it and now he would rebuke her.

"Hello Mel," he spoke informally, they were completely alone and she sat down where he indicated, relieved to be able to do so as her knees almost buckled when she looked at him, he seemed even more adorable if that was possible. "I won't keep you a minute. I just wanted to give you this and to ask you if your offer was still open." He gave her an envelope and she could sense he was inhibited by the school environment despite the informality of his opening greeting, as he spoke in couched terms. What offer, she thought?

"Sorry Mr Pritchard I'm not quite sure what you mean." There was a stilted silence as she scoured her mind; then as she looked expectantly at him for clarification she saw the embryonic beginnings of a smile and she understood in an instant. He was asking if she still wanted to see him, to model for him outside school hours. My God! MY GOD! She mirrored his smile, fused in complicity now as both smiles became joyous yet tempered laughter. Melissa was overjoyed to watch his wonderful face almost transform with rapture as eventually and silently she nodded her head in assent and fixed her eyes on his, revealing her absolute, transparent delight. She grabbed a piece of scrap paper and scribbled her telephone number down and added a codicil, 'Say you are Susan's cousin, Brian, if someone else answers the phone when you ring!' They parted with no words, for it had all been said so perfectly without them and she felt able to wait until she reached the welcome familiarity of her soothing room before she opened the envelope.

There was a card, probably from the same series as the one she had bought, this time the print on the front was The Lady of Shallot by J. W. Waterhouse an artist she had never heard about; it was so incredibly exquisite she thought and she discerned an uncanny resemblance between the model depicted here and the model for Millais' Ophelia. Then she read what he had written inside in response to her own poem and it left her breathless:

TOTAL BEAUTY

*You cannot give me your mind
in its nakedness;
strip it of its garments of reason,
so delicately weaved with understanding
and laced with logic.
The thoughts that clothe your mind
are all part of your total beauty.
I wander through the deep labyrinths
knocking on the doors I see.
Some are opened,
for others I have yet to find the key.
Still I know there are more doors
deep within the endless corridors,
perhaps beyond the valley of awareness or,
at the very peak
of the mountain of knowledge.
These doors hold the secret of your soul,
they hide your innermost feelings and desires.
One day I will find them,
I will knock and they will be opened.
But till then I am content
to gaze at the beauty around me.
I do not shield my eyes
from the intensity of your being,
I love its warmth,
it permeates through to my very existence
and I know I am alive.*

Jonathan

Chapter eleven

Barcelona? Barcelona! There's a Sixth Form trip for Art students only and it's to Barcelona. Luke are you listening? My God I just cannot believe it, bloody hell I could see as much of Gaudi's work as I can take in a week if I go and what about all the Art Nouveau? God Luke isn't it wonderful!" Melissa threw the letter down on the bed and almost ran across the room to him and grabbed both his hands in hers trying to get him on his feet and off the cushions where he was lying rigid, attempting to elicit a response because so far he had been mute. Not the reaction she expected even though she knew he did not enthuse about the work of Gaudi, because Barcelona was supposed to be such an interesting city and she was sure he would want to go. "Luke what do you think? Why aren't you as excited as me I thought you would love to go?"

As soon as she had spoken the words however, Melissa became instantly aware that she did not want him to go. It was in fact the last thing she did want; the letter was signed by Mr Pritchard and Mr Brown and so presumably they would be the members of staff accompanying them. Jonathan, Barcelona – it seemed a delicious combination. The weather there would be great in June and besides, she had never been abroad, Carol did not fancy it and Stuart; well Stuart went along with Carol in most things. She couldn't wait to get home and see what her mother's reaction would be. Surely she would be allowed to go; she must be allowed to go. She turned her attention to her friend who seemed genuinely despondent and looked so forlorn it tugged at her heart, so she joined him on the cushions still holding his hands entreating him to speak.

Tides Must Turn

"No Mel I won't be going, there is no way my parents can afford it and if they did have money for a holiday abroad I would rather they spent it on themselves and went somewhere. They work so bloody hard and I don't think mum is very well, I've not said anything before but I am really worried Mel, I think it could be serious." When Mel started to think about Luke's mum, Brenda, she realised that she had visibly changed even in the time she had known her. She was definitely thinner and it made her look older, but the thinness was combined with a sort of listlessness which replaced the energetic good humoured demeanour she previously presented. Melissa always thought that Brenda was permanently happy; always bubbling with undisguised enthusiasm, unconditional support and genuine pleasure for whatever any of her children aspired to or achieved. She was the archetypal mum as far as Melissa was concerned; she felt so comfortable with Brenda and there were many times she had wished Carol could be more like her.

"Could you ask your dad about her Luke and see if he will tell you what is going on, surely they must tell the children if something is seriously wrong. You never know you may be worrying about nothing," although as she said this she did not truly believe it, "and it would be better to know for certain than to speculate and make yourself miserable with worrying." She cradled him now and he softened to this familiar and somewhat maternal gesture which exemplified their closeness which in other circumstances could almost have been the comfort given by one sibling to another. She kissed his head and moved his hair from his eyes which were moist and as she did so she felt a wave of pure guilt run across her mind like goose pimples on the skin, a shock of reaction, a visible anguish.

The last two weeks since her pivotal meeting with Jonathan had been a complexity of Art project work, History deadlines and a visit to see As You Like It which Melissa thoroughly enjoyed even though it was not one of Shakespeare's tragedies, which she preferred. She found the minimalistic, symbolic staging and the incredible lighting effects created an effortlessly appropriate milieu of fantasy which was how Melissa perceived his romantic comedies. So for its production values alone, she was glad she went to see it. Melissa's growing fascination with design and the ultimate realisation of what had often begun its life as a vague idea, was influencing her approach to her studies and the natural cross referencing from theatre to art energised and motivated her. She had also been invaded by the thrill of anticipation; the first meeting with Jonathan which would happen soon and was now a tangible if not yet actual delight. She had neglected Luke.

"I love you Mel, you always seem to know instinctively, how to make me feel better. I think when you have gone home I will ask dad and at least I will be doing something positive rather than creating these endless scenarios in my mind. You know when I actually think about the possibility of anything happening to mum I realise that she is our strength; I don't know what any of us would do without her Mel."

"Well you may not have to be without her. Just find out before you start thinking like that Luke Scott. Now I must go I've got behind with my background reading for Art History and I want it done before the weekend, I'd like to go to Liverpool on Saturday, I need a break from all this studying. I also want to buy some books and a couple of EP's. You OK now?"

"Yes I feel loads better Mel, see you tomorrow." He sighed as she left the room as he so often did because he had realised some time ago that she was an enigma, out of his reach even when they were having sex and he knew she was showing him genuine affection. He knew unequivocally that she was not in love with him and it was not his pride or vanity that questioned why, it was his reason. How could they be so close mentally and physically and yet not feel exactly the same about each other? She must have a very different perception of love to his own, even though she said she cared deeply about him and he was closer to her than anyone else, she still retained her other place where she would retreat without being fully conscious of doing so. He was more alone in those moments than he had ever been in his whole young life. He had to accept her as she was or lose her; this was his fear; he needed her friendship and although he desperately wanted to make love with her virtually every time he set eyes on her, he needed the friendship above even that. She had been right when she had said to him a few months ago that she was frightened of losing this unique friendship, for he reciprocated that trepidation and would do anything for that not to happen.

Stuart looked at her quizzically when she walked in to the gloomy living room where he was watching TV, although he remained in his chair and it was only a momentary glance, it was a new expression and Melissa registered the fact. "There is a phone number written next to the phone for you Melissa. Someone called Brian rang and asked if you could call him back. I'm sure neither your mother or I have ever heard you mention a school chum called Brian. Who is he?"

"Oh no-one you know," she said evasively, flushed to her core that Jonathan had telephoned, but making a mental note that it had been a mistake to ask him to contact her at home, it was too risky so they would have to find another way. "Did he say when would be a good time to call or was it just open?"

"I didn't quiz the young man Melissa, it's really not my place is it." She went to make some tea so as not to alert his suspicions that she was eager in any way to make the call and when she was sure he was engrossed in his programme and knowing her mother was in the bath for at least another half an hour, she tentatively rang. Her fingers trembled and she misdialled at first, but now it was ringing.

"Mel is that you? Thank God you got the message. I think we must find another way to get in touch with each other and make arrangements because that phone call was so nerve racking I almost hung up!"

"Hi, yes it's me and yes I agree totally, so we should arrange something quickly now if that was what you called about, and then discuss future arrangements when we meet up." God I can't wait, I wonder if I will always feel so ridiculously excited?

"Fine. How about you come round after school tomorrow evening, obviously I will have to drive you there as I live out in the country. Is that too short notice?" She noticed the discernible tremor of vulnerability in his voice and she realised he must be as nervous as she was. They agreed he should pick her up a couple of streets away from the school which was close to where Susan lived but as it was dark she was sure that no-one would see them, and in any case they would all probably be at work. She would spend an hour in the library after her last class, giving Jonathan time to deal with his admin and then it would be just the two of them. She told Carol she was doing some extra Art work after school and would then have dinner with Susan; she told Luke she was going to Susan's who was having a boyfriend crisis and needed her to confide in; she told Susan that if anyone called or asked she must say she was with her and that when they next met she would explain everything. Of course she could not tell Susan the truth, so in reality she knew that she had very little time to create a feasible diversion in order to satisfy Susan's inestimable and incessant ability to probe. Her meticulous planning was complete and the imperative of the liaison was of itself, constantly strengthening and replenishing her energy and enthusiasm.

They said little to each other as the car made its way gradually to the village where Jonathan lived, their breathing at times the only indication that there were two people present. Once they had driven down the main street of the village, Jonathan took a left hand turn next to a pub, his pub, and there it was at the end of the lane a solitary light above the door twinkling a forlorn welcome on this, one of the coldest nights of the winter. Melissa took it all in, the double fronted archetypal stone built country cottage, with its dark green door, the paint peeling a little from the weather and neglect; the lattice windows on either side creating the perfect symmetry which was mirrored on the top floor; the small front garden weary now from the onslaught of winter's harsh incursion, the shingle path leading to a solid slab of stone which formed the door step – it was idyllic, idiosyncratic and so right somehow for this man to live in such an exquisite place. His voice interrupted her reflections and she was suddenly aware that they had stopped and he was opening her door for her, offering his hand which was divest of its leather glove now. She took it gladly and they walked hand in hand to the front door which he opened deftly with his free hand and then guided her in to the dark hallway which was instantly illuminated as he turned on the light and then letting go of her hand he closed the door behind them.

It was bitterly cold and Jonathan began the lengthy task of creating some warmth, partially from electric fires and in the room he used most, when he was not in the studio, the kitchen cum dining room, he lit the coal fire. He told Melissa it wouldn't be long before they felt warmer and as he was cooking them a meal it would soon be quite cosy, really it would. This was unnerving for them both, Jonathan busying himself to avoid the pervasive image of the two of them locked in an embrace and Melissa as still as he was active and with similar inclinations which almost overwhelmed her, watched him intently. She needed to remember every second, every detail about this evening. She said, "Are you going to show me the rest of the house Mr Pritchard?"

He grinned at her and as he came to where she was standing, huddled in her coat and gloves, he said, "Mel, please can you start calling me Jonathan, or even Brian, I can't imagine how we can become friends if you persist in addressing me with such formality!" He came closer and she imagined for a second that he might kiss her, but he began to take off her gloves, slowly, tenderly and as her hands were revealed, he rubbed them gently with his own to warm them and then, she would remember it as the most erotically charged moment of her life, he pulled both hands towards his mouth and blew sweet warm breath into their conjoined palms. All she could do was gaze in to his eyes as if fused and he, who had not looked away from her eyes throughout the whole process, held her gaze and her hands until a wayward spark from the fire broke the spell. She took off her coat and Jonathan proceeded to show her the cottage, not quite believing she was really here at last and glad that he had covered the now finished portrait of Melissa which was securely stacked behind the landscape he was currently working on for his good friends Maggie and Jock in London.

Physically they could not have been more dissimilar; she was delicate with a willowy, sylphlike figure, her creamy, now flawless skin which had a tendency to become sporadically freckled in the summer revealed high cheekbones above which her large green, almond shaped eyes prevailed - intense and charismatic. Her hair, a totally separate entity, was almost beyond describing in mere words; wild almost pure red and defiantly long in its desire to grow unrestrained and untamed. Jonathan with his Latin skin, redolent with the timbre of summer's alluring song, taut and covering a taller, more muscular frame; his angular, chiselled face containing the dark pools of his eyes at once both sensual and innocent - a captivating combination he was not aware he possessed.

She adored his bedroom, its romantic white walls covered in paintings; a small old three drawer white chest on top of which a magical Tiffany lamp waited to be brought to life; the exposed floorboards covered only by two white rugs either side of the bed which was black iron framed, its high mattress covered with a patchwork quilt above which was a large framed print, not an original Jonathan Pritchard like many of the other wonderful paintings, but a print she recognised instantly: Ophelia by Millais! She was frozen, eyes fixed on its prominence when he walked in front of her and tenderly, with an endearing hesitancy, turned her face to his and said, "I have had that print for almost two years Mel. It's my favourite painting of the Pre-Raphaelite movement and I just had to frame it and hang it here in my bedroom. Can you imagine what I felt when you sent me the poem in a card which had the same print on the front? Can you also see from this larger image how uncannily you resemble Lizzy Siddal, but you my dearest Mel are really much more, so much more beautiful."

She sighed gently as his words of adulation found their home, and he noticed her sway slightly; he desperately wanted to hold her, to press her to him, to kiss her with all the latent passion he had suppressed for so long, but remembered in time the promise he had made to himself when he had decided to let her come to his home and so he took her hand and showed her the studio. Thankfully she did not want to investigate or move anything, she was too polite to do that he assumed. She said how much she would like to see it during the daytime after he had described the incredible light the room got, then they went down to the kitchen and he began to make a vegetarian meal for them. Melissa had only mentioned once some six months ago that she had become a Vegetarian and was so moved that he had not only remembered, but had taken the time to plan such an interesting meal when he had clearly been so busy yesterday; how had he found the time to buy the ingredients? She watched him for a time, his face endearing - a concentrated mask, moving only when he looked up from culinary tasks to smile and speak softly with her and as the gravity gave way to this captivating, acquiescent animation she could have sung her pleasure to the world.

She was very curious about the print of The Lady of Shalott which had contained the poem he had written for her so now she took the opportunity to ask, "Jonathan?" it was wonderful to say his name overtly and so deliciously unrestrained, "The artist John William Waterhouse who painted The Lady of Shalott, was he one of the Pre-Raphaelite Brotherhood?" Jonathan was delighted as always with her inquiring and intricately analytical mind and furnished her with some basic information which he knew she would develop and deepen until she was as conversant with the subject as she needed to satisfy her incisive investigations! He paused in his preparations as he answered,

"Waterhouse was painting in the late Victorian period Mel and although he was not part of the PRB which was actually formed in 1848, this particular work based on Tennyson's poem, does show how much he was inspired by Rossetti and Burne-Jones. But British artists in the late nineteenth century were somewhat conservative in general and took their lead from what was approved by the Royal Academy. Burne-Jones was also inspired by Tennyson when he painted what is perhaps his best known piece, King Cophetua and the Beggar Maid. If you have not read any of Tennyson's poems I can let you borrow a small volume and you can let me know what you think; he was the most popular of the Victorian poets." Melissa thought he had finished and was about to speak when he looked up suddenly and said with a grin, "Oh and did you know that your Holman Hunt also painted The Lady of Shalott although his painting depicts the earlier part of the poem when she was locked in the tower." He didn't want to sound pompous or patronising or too much like the teacher he wanted to extricate himself from tonight, so he returned to the final preparations for the meal and waited for her reply which was brief.

"Holman Hunt painted The Lady of Shalott? Really! I don't think I've seen it but perhaps you could show me a copy of the painting before I go, I'm quite intrigued. I've been studying the Romantic poets but I don't have an extensive volume of Tennyson's poems so yes I would love to borrow yours, thank you Jonathan"

Jonathan was making stuffed mushrooms using a mixture of nuts, pine kernels, chick peas and breadcrumbs all combined with beaten egg and seasoned with salt, black pepper, oregano and a sweet paprika. He had already made a ratatouille the night before which only needed heating up and the potatoes which he had partially cooked were already baking in the oven waiting to be joined for the last half an hour by the mushrooms. Melissa thought it smelled divine and told him so; she never got food like this at her own home although Luke's mum often made them tasty vegetarian meals without an omelette in sight! Jonathan had put the mushrooms in the oven and seeing that Melissa had finished the lemonade he had given her earlier (much to her surprise and consternation, did he really think she wasn't old enough to drink?) he now asked her if she drank or even liked wine.

"Well I've only tried it once at home one Christmas, mum and Stuart don't have alcohol in the house unless it's a special occasion, it was something German and too sweet so I usually drink Vodka and lime if I go out."

"Really! Melissa Johnson you do realise you are under age to be drinking in public houses, don't you?" He really does enjoy teasing me she thought as he grinned and went to the fridge and returned with a bottle of white Rioja which he opened and poured into two glasses.

"Try this and see what you think, it's dry but quite fruity and remember only one glass for you, I want you to remember our first evening together, so just sip it!" She smiled feeling relaxed and now ravenously hungry. God he could cook as well as being a talented artist, a great teacher and divine to sit and watch! As they ate their meal and they sipped wine, they began to share details about their lives and experiences, tentatively initially not wanting to inundate each other with too much factual information. As she had suspected he did have Latin blood and now she knew why he always looked so bloody gorgeous and tanned; he spent most of his holidays in Spain with his mother and she became hungry for more details, but that could wait for another visit, now she wanted to know about his marriage, his *marriage!*

"So you met Lydia when you were studying, you must have been quite young?"

"Yes I was, I was twenty and thought she was the most wonderful woman I had ever met, we seemed to gel straight away, but the strength of our relationship was, I felt then, based on the fact that we developed a close friendship before we became lovers." Melissa had never spoken with anyone in her life who openly used the term *lover!* It really was, she mused, rather bohemian! Jonathan continued, "But ultimately, despite all our hopes and plans, the relationship ended, but thank God we have been civilised about our son."

"You have a son?" Melissa was incredulous, she had never even remotely thought he had been married yet alone had a son! "How old is he and what is he called? How often do you see him? Tell me about him Jonathan."

"Well you know Mel I can hardly remember a time when I didn't have him, he really is the most important person in my life. I never thought being a father could be so amazing and so rewarding; Jack gives me so much pleasure but there isn't a day that goes by without me feeling terribly guilty about the break up of the family unit. I would have done anything to prevent him suffering; both Lydia and I try to make things as easy as possible for him and I get to see him as often as I want. Thank God he seems well adjusted; he really is a very happy little boy who is loved very much." Jonathan was animated and Melissa could see from his facial expressions and from the tenderness dancing on his tongue, his adoration of his son manifesting itself in the words that were imbued with unconditional love.

"Enough of me now, what about you Mel? You haven't told me very much about your life and I am so eager to know everything even though logic tells me we must take this slowly and savour each time we are together." He poured her 'just one more' glass of wine which she thought was lovely and they moved into his living room, which was warmer now and filled with the soft glow of two quite intricate and ornate Tiffany standard lamps. They sat on his large sofa and she curled her legs up underneath her, despite the school uniform she still wore making her feel restricted and uncomfortable – she would have to remember to bring a change of clothes for the next visit. As she began to tell him a little about her young life which she felt had been much less eventful and much more geographically restricted than his own, he took her hand automatically and looked intently into her eyes, every word she spoke was studiously digested. He was feeding off her closeness, gorging himself on her presence, almost choking on the proximity of her beauty and yet was savouring every gesture, every intonation, every facial movement as if he would never have her so close again.

"So why do you think your mother married Stuart? Do you think she was lonely Mel? Because from what you have told me the situation at home and the relationship between you and Carol was far better before he appeared on the scene."

"Well to be honest when I compare my relationship with my mother to the relationships most of my friends have with their mothers, I think it's always been dysfunctional. I am not sure why but she is unable to be tactile with me and finds it hard to relate to me, almost as if she has completely forgotten what it's like to be young. You know it has occurred to me that in some ways her behaviour seems like jealousy, but how could that be? She is my mother for God's sake she should be proud of me and enjoy my youth; it's not as if I have given her any real cause for concern, I mean I've never taken drugs or got into trouble with the police or given up on my studies, like Susan. The worst crime I think I have committed is to wear caftans, light joss sticks and to play Leonard Cohen's music too loudly in my bedroom!"

Jonathan smiled and silently went over to the turntable and a moment later the room was resonating to the words of *Bird On the Wire*. They listened, relishing the permeation of the words, his words, both thrilled as their mutual appreciation of this music fused their joint consciousness. The volume made Melissa feel abandoned, freely able to lose herself in the joy of the music as she could never do at home, for even though she played music when she was alone, she lived in a small terraced house and knew that the neighbours would complain to Carol if she played her music too loud. This was heaven, absolute heaven and he, Jonathan, loved Leonard Cohen too! When it finished and they looked at each other for a moment, their happiness reflected in the mirrors of the other's eyes, he told her that even though he thought this song was absolutely superb it was not his favourite.

"I know what your favourite song is," she said, and without a moment's hesitation she added, "*Suzanne*."

"How could you possibly know that?"

"Because it's my favourite Leonard Cohen song too."

They spoke no more as they both realised she must get home soon, but for a short time Jonathan played some Billy Eckstein and Sarah Vaughn for her, which to Melissa's surprise, she adored. Jonathan had wanted to ask her about Luke Scott but some innate defence mechanism prevented the words being formed let alone uttered; there would be time for the questions whose answers may unwittingly cause pain. All too soon they made their way out from the haven of discovery to the deluge of sleet, they had been blissfully unaware of, which was permeating the darkness outside; she could never recall being so happy and it was with a painful resolve that Jonathan delivered her without even the hint of a kiss to her street.

Tides Must Turn

But, as he watched her walk resolutely to her house, something started to rise inside him, slowly at first like the gentle simmering of a pan which is then turned up to full heat inadvertently and, before she reached her door, he recklessly obeyed its call and drew the car up alongside her. "Please get in Mel, just for one minute, please." She was in serious danger of being seen now as she neared her home but intuitively, and without real regard for that possibility, she got in and he drove a short way around the corner and pulled up. He turned the lights off and faced her.

"I'm sorry Mel and I know I really shouldn't be doing this, but I must say it or I'll go mad, I simply must tell you."

"What is it Jonathan, for God's sake you are worrying me now."

"I love you Melissa. I love you to distraction." He seemed like a young boy to her at that moment, his eyes pleading, hopeful for reciprocation and the comfort it would bestow. She sighed inwardly - glad he had not said anything ominous, had misgivings about seeing her or about revealing facets of himself to her so willingly. She was elated.

"I know you love me Jonathan, I know you do." She took his hand now, holding it firmly and registering the fear so clearly visible in his eyes, his vulnerability shining its presence. Her eyes met his with open affirmation and she said softly, "Don't you realise I love you too. I've always loved you, ever since I was fifteen. You must know that surely. Haven't I said it in so many ways, haven't you sensed it, felt it, just known that it existed?"

"I hardly dared hope; I've spent the last year or so on an emotional seesaw, never really knowing what you felt. Oh God Mel do you really love me or did I dream you just said that?"

"I truly love you. If only you knew the times I have hoped for and imagined this moment, this amazing surreal moment when you would tell me you loved me too. OK it wasn't in a car on a bloody awful February night just around the corner from my house, but I have so longed for it!"

He held both her hands, if he kissed her now they would both be lost, he knew that, so he explained, "I'm so relieved Mel, so unbelievably happy and, after what has seemed like a lifetime, I might finally be able to sleep tonight. But we must be so careful, you know that don't you? This really is something I could be sacked for, and I would never be employed in teaching again. I have explained this to you before, but we must both accept that there can be nothing physical between us whilst you are my student."

"Yes, Jonathan I suppose I must accept it even though I think it's crazy. I'll be seventeen in June so I think I am old enough to decide who I can love. I can appreciate the logic of it, but my heart tells me I want you, mentally and physically just as you want me."

"Oh God yes Mel, I do want you so much. Right now I am fighting an overwhelming urge to kiss you, but I know that a kiss would precipitate a physical relationship which could destroy everything for us and we have only just begun this wonderful and exciting journey of discovering each other, so please understand and be patient with me. You must go now my darling and even though it will be difficult at school, we have to behave appropriately. Te quiero mucho." The endearment spoken in Spanish excited her, she was deliriously happy and if the physical realisation of this love had to be postponed for a while then she would have to accept it.

Chapter twelve

Spring was spinning its magical, fragile web of colour and winter was slowly retreating, returning sporadically in its futile attempts to dislodge this familiar interloper. Melissa was looking at the Holman Hunt painting of The Lady of Shalott, she was ensconced in her room with Luke who was feeling marginalised by her somewhat obsessive preoccupation with the world of the Pre-Raphaelites. Luke was also distracted by the news he had received yesterday about his mother's health and was waiting for the appropriate time to talk to her. Once he started to open up about his feelings he knew he would break down and he must be with Mel when the vulnerability surfaced relentlessly claiming his fragile composure; this was where he felt safe, cocooned from pain and when the inevitable unthinkable event took place, he knew she would give him strength to cope. Now he became aware that she was reading something to him:

>'There she weaves by night and day
>A magic web with colours gay.
>She has heard a whisper say,
>A curse is on her if she stay
>   To look down on Camelot.
>She knows not what the curse may be,
>And so she weaveth steadily,
>And little other care hath she,
>   The Lady of Shalott.'

"Oh God Luke this is so tragic, so bloody unfair. Did you know that the Lady of Shalott was doomed to live in a tower weaving a tapestry which depicted the exploits of King Arthur's knights, and was only allowed to see the world reflected in a mirror; she was forbidden to look out of the window but when she saw Lancelot's reflection she disobeyed and turned to watch him. The tapestry began to disintegrate and the mirror cracked, but can you believe this Luke, she was condemned to drift down the river to her death; that is where the Waterhouse painting comes in, remember me showing that one to you?" She began searching through her book to locate the picture when she realised that Luke was in the same room but could almost have been in another country, he was so removed from her mentally. Melissa took her mind back to yesterday when they had been making love, secure in the knowledge they would be alone all day, and she had sensed then that he was distracted even though his body had been insistent in its need for hers.

Melissa had wondered if she should attempt to extricate herself from the sexual side of this friendship, was she being disloyal to Jonathan now they had spoken to each other of their love? She still enjoyed being with Luke physically, it comforted and pleased her although instinctively she was gradually becoming aware that there must be heights she might only reach with Jonathan. She felt so wonderful when she pleased Luke and whilst the lovemaking was not a completely altruistic act on her part it was the giving of pleasure which ultimately caused her own delightful but subdued climax. Luke had taught her so much, had led the way to the amazing discovery of her own sexuality, to the pleasure of touch, of soft words, of being loved; it was marred only by her own inability to utter those words of love he so needed to hear. How could she be hypocritical, false with Luke, it would be anathema to her; mutual honesty was integral to their friendship Why then had she had not spoken of Luke to Jonathan? Conversely and more importantly, why had she not talked of Jonathan with Luke, it was not as if she could not trust Luke, but it was much more complicated than that because Luke loved her; so the only way she could cope at the moment was to completely compartmentalise her life. Melissa often wished she could confide in someone, a close female friend perhaps, someone with whom she could discuss, dissect and analyse the emotional dilemma she was now faced with. For a few weeks she had managed to avoid contact with Susan but soon she would be located, confined, confronted and relentlessly cross-examined by her. Historically Melissa had instinctively avoided revealing too much to Susan, now she was genuinely frightened that if she knew about it, she would not realise how important it was to be utterly discreet about her meetings with Jonathan. In essence she was isolated in her emotional turmoil.

Last week she felt distinctly uneasy when Luke took her hand after they had been working on their Art projects together; Jonathan had walked past them and as their eyes met fleetingly she recognised the unmistakable pain of jealousy; the barely concealed sadness in his demeanour as he walked out of the Art Block filled her whole being with perplexity. She had asked herself why he should be jealous when he had so meticulously drawn up the ground rules for their relationship and must surely know that her love was his and his alone. They had been together the previous night and again she had been in heaven; each time they were together deepened and strengthened their love and as they laughed, talked animatedly, argued about theatre, art or music the vivid visual images of a tangible future with him were slowly pervading her whole being.

Melissa learnt to enjoy the creativity of preparing and cooking a meal – it became the sensual surrogate for the physical passion which was becoming almost impossible to suppress. She discovered an unadulterated pleasure in his art – the diversity of his talent and his refreshing ability to see beauty in what others might have dismissed as mediocre. Jonathan's enthusiastic utterly sincere praise of her own work gave her such encouragement and joy, underpinning her confidence and endorsing her resolve to apply for the very top art schools. These few hours in the week that they were together provided the sustenance they fed on greedily when they were apart; a fleeting glance of admiration during an Art class or a covert smile of transparent love in the corridor only reminded them of their desperate hunger. Melissa delighted in the way Jonathan stroked her hand as he revealed more about himself. He had even questioned her about the scars around her nails and had slowly kissed each finger in turn, especially the left index finger which was sore and had been the subject of a recent assault by her teeth. If he could kiss her fingers why could he not kiss her lips?

They had shared some of their own poems with each other, rapturous when the poems revealed the extent of their love for one another. Later

Melissa had read aloud her favourite W.B. Yeats poems for him and had noticed a discernible moistness in his beautiful, concentrated eyes as she finished *When You Are Old;* he had gone almost immediately to make them both some Earl Grey tea and when he returned to the room his eyes were red but neither of them referred to it. Jonathan was remembering the first time he had seen her and Melissa was relishing his close proximity as her face became flushed by a combination of the warmth of the room and his sheer physical presence which overwhelmed her always. The latter part of their evening was spent in the studio and Jonathan sketched her whilst she reclined on the chaise-longue still wearing the white cotton shirt and blue jeans she had brought to change into. It didn't seem appropriate clothing to Melissa, but Jonathan had said she looked perfect. She had not fastened the top two buttons of her shirt and the slight glimpse it afforded of the softness where her small breasts began to swell, was agonisingly erotic. Yet he observed and recorded her beauty as any professional artist would and detached himself from his growing inability to maintain a physical distance from her.

The previous visit had, somewhat unwisely, been on a bright Saturday afternoon and it was during a sitting in the studio that she had discovered the large painting Jonathan had completed months before she started coming to his cottage. "This is incredible Jonathan when did you paint this? God it's so flattering and so large, it must have taken you forever to complete!"

He had not wanted to reveal the extent of the misery that had at times engulfed him in a sleep deprived deluge of frantic nocturnal painting which had become therapeutic as his love for her had spun almost out of control. Now it was impossible to conceal his emotions from her; he had an insatiable need to bare himself to her, to let her know how deep his love was and the extent to which she had disturbed his equilibrium since the first moment he set eyes on her. "Often I couldn't sleep Mel. I was so miserable thinking that this incredibly powerful love I was feeling may never be reciprocated. Even when I had the slightest indication from something you said or a momentary glance that gave me some respite from the insecurity, it was always transient somehow. There was a persistent seed of doubt waiting to germinate and grow irrepressibly and I couldn't cope; the only solace I could find was to paint you from memory. You are wrong about it being flattering though because the truth is that it does not do justice to your beauty, both inner and outer, which far surpasses what I have managed to recreate here. It did take a long time but it was so soothing and I felt like I was making love to you here in this studio, willing you to love me back, desperately willing you to love me back." She had wanted to hold him then, to take away the pain of the past year but the firmly established, agonisingly frustrating rules he had laid down prevented her spontaneous action. Perhaps he had wanted her to take the initiative, to test the solidity of his resolve, to kiss him until he reciprocated with all the repressed passion she knew was only a touch away.

Melissa was brought back to the present when Luke gently closed the book of Tennyson's poems and placed it on the end of her bed. "Mel I need to talk to you about my mum. I know I am being bloody miserable but when I tell you what has been happening you will understand." He began to tell her slowly then, holding on to her as if she could alleviate the agonising pain he felt when he finally spoke the words he could not bring himself to completely accept. "The specialist said the cancer was too advanced to respond to any treatment, her body is riddled with it which is why she has become so awfully thin. All they can do is ease the pain as much as possible and then eventually take her in to hospital when she can't cope with it. She's dying Mel, my mum only has a few months to live and I can't do anything about it, I feel so useless and yet so bloody angry that this has to happen to her of all people – she is the most wonderful person who doesn't deserve to die so young. God Mel I can't do anything, I can't do anything, there's nothing I ………." She pulled him close to her and held him whilst he sobbed uncontrollably, her shirt becoming wet with his misery. Melissa could not speak any soothing words or lessen the pain; she functioned as a surrogate mother, just holding him for almost an hour the room becoming a small suffocating cell containing his loss of pride. He would be dignified everywhere else she knew; only with her could he become abandoned in his suffering.

Melissa for her part felt guilty about her other life, the other compartment – the meetings with Jonathan which would clearly have to be placed on hold as Luke needed her exclusively for some time to come. Poor Luke, to have such a fabulous mum and then to discover you are losing her when you are only eighteen. She couldn't begin to imagine his torment; her own mother had become more lenient with her, the inquisitions about where she went and with whom had all but disappeared. She had even agreed to Barcelona without even a murmur of protest about the cost. But Carol's irrational disapproval of her daughter's clothes and the now unveiled jealousy of the ease that had developed between her and Stuart had become intolerable to the point of Melissa wishing she lived somewhere else. Carol seemed to be permanently critical of Stuart who stoically persevered to the extent of being browbeaten; he attempted to calm her down when she was determined to argue openly and fiercely with him and, to Melissa's embarrassment, these arguments often contained allusions to their sex life. Really how could she complete her homework or find inspiration for her art when the prevalent atmosphere in her home was one of barely concealed animosity and Carol was in a permanent state of readiness for open warfare?

"Luke? ....Luke are you feeling a bit better now?" Melissa returned to her room after leaving him for a short time as she made some tea and went for tissue which would be superfluous now as Luke's tears had dried, their remnants staining his skin - a visible reminder of his sorrow. She stroked his forehead, moving his hair away from his eyes and then without saying another word she undressed him and guided him under the covers and after drawing the curtain on the inopportune spring sunshine, she took off her own clothes and joined him. They always found solace in each other's physical closeness and now she felt him relax finally, sleeping now - his breath warm on her breasts where he had laid his head as she held him tightly offering transient respite from the unbearable events that would transpire all too soon. When Luke left at about four o'clock Melissa was attempting to read a history text book but found her mind wandering aimlessly from its turgid expanse. When the phone rang she was so grateful for its intrusion she almost slid down the steep stairs in her desperate need to be distracted.

"Is this the young woman who likes Leonard Cohen?" Jonathan teased, "If this is Melissa Johnson she may be interested in the following information!"

Despite the emotional drain of the day, Melissa began to giggle and when it abated somewhat she answered, "Yes this is she!"

Jonathan was, she sensed, full of excitement and as he spoke she could feel his barely contained enthusiasm, "Hi Mel! How do you fancy seeing a Leonard Cohen concert next month?"

"What? Are you joking Jonathan? Where is the concert and how do we get hold of tickets he sells out very quickly you know!"

"Well Jonathan Pritchard and Melissa Johnson, if she will do him the honour of accompanying him, will be travelling to London to see the indisputable hero of the aforementioned lovely Melissa at the Royal Albert Hall in London on the 10th May."

"Jonathan, bloody hell!" she squealed, "My god how did you get tickets? Yes, yes I'd love to come. Thank you so much." For a moment she was lost in the immediacy of her amazement and the joy of possibility; to see Leonard Cohen live in London and with Jonathan - My God! Then Luke's plight and the suffering of this afternoon and his very imminent need of her support came to the forefront of her mind, forcing her to temper her mood and contain her response. "Listen Jonathan, I'm saying yes but I will need to check with my mum as it will be a late night I expect. Can we talk about it when we next meet?"

"Mel darling, I will not be able to see you for a couple of weeks as I am going on a staff development course in two days time; then I'll be spending a long weekend in Toledo with my mamma for my 30th birthday, and I am hoping Lydia will allow Jack to take two days off school and come with me." In some respects he was relieved that he could not see Melissa because he did not trust himself anymore when she was close to him. He felt that at any given moment he would follow his body's desperate craving to show her his love. It was becoming painful to restrict his fingers, his lips, to her hands or more recently her cheek when he dropped her off in her street. He was concerned about his occasional lack of professionalism when he observed his adorable Melissa with Luke Scott and if he did not ask her about it soon he would go crazy. He was very concerned about the lighter evenings and the fact that they may be seen going into the village. His landlady had just missed Melissa the other Saturday afternoon and she was, he knew, a dreadful gossip! It was dangerous.

He was perturbed by the phone call he had received last night from Lydia whereby she informed him that she was no longer involved with David. She hadn't sounded too upset apart from the fact that she felt worried about Jack who had become very fond of him. David had agreed to call round occasionally until the summer to ease the transition for Jack who had been used to seeing him quite regularly. Jonathan needed breathing space although he did have legitimate work to take with him; the most burdensome being a report for the Headmaster on the residency of Julian Long, which the whole department agreed had been an unqualified success. Right now he needed Jack, his mamma and Spain.

Melissa was disappointed by his news but it also gave her time to see if it was logistically possible to organise going to the concert whilst still being there for Luke. "Ok Jonathan, but I will miss you so much, will you be able to contact me if we arrange a time for me to pick up the phone?"

"I will miss you too, don't you realise how much Mel? I will try to arrange to call you but it could be problematic and I do worry when I have to call you at home, you know that. I must go querida, te quiero mucho"

"I love you too, Jonathan. Bye." When she placed the phone on its cradle she collapsed on the bottom stair and sat motionless, deep in thought until Carol arrived home somewhat earlier than usual. She spoke briefly to her daughter and seemed agitated as she went upstairs to her bedroom which is where Stuart found her some time later rummaging through his document drawer. Downstairs Melissa was diligently following her mother's instructions peeling potatoes and almost predicted the ensuing row, which she was sure could be heard throughout the street.

I am so bloody sick of this, she thought; I would rather be anywhere else at this moment than stuck in this dingy house with the sounds of World War Three upstairs and the prospect of another unappetising meal of potatoes, omelette and carrots. She wiped her hands, left her task and went to the telephone. Some half an hour later the row audibly escalating and with a note propped on the kitchen table telling Carol she would be home late and not to worry, she walked out of her front door, climbed into a black Morris Minor and was driven to her future.

Chapter thirteen

They lay on his bed, the room was filled with the sweet smell of Melissa's patchouli oil which she had smoothed into her skin after making the phone call and Leonard Cohen had been placed on the portable record player. His words now echoed their world; his voice soothed them as surely as Jonathan soothed her with soft innocuous kisses and surprisingly innocent caresses.

And you want to travel with him
And you want to travel blind
And you think maybe you'll trust him
For he's touched your perfect body
    with his mind.

"Mel………..Mel, come closer, let me make it better, darling, beautiful girl, try to stop crying, open your eyes and look at me Mel." She softened, became limp like a rag doll willing him to mould her, to shape her mood, to form her in any configuration he wished. She had abandoned herself to the pain of disappointment, the reality of disillusionment and the ever present burden of uncertainty which had all surfaced simultaneously stripping her of her usual stability. The day had exhausted her emotionally and although she did not fully realise it, for she gave of herself totally, she was finding it almost impossible to be all things to Luke. Mother, sister, friend and lover were part of the multifaceted Melissa that Luke unwittingly demanded. Melissa had no-one, no-one except Jonathan she now discovered, with whom she could break down, find respite and shed some of the domestic worries and stresses that were compounded by a gruelling sixth form schedule. Of course Jonathan had heard the row; firstly when Melissa had telephoned him, clearly upset, and further confirmed when he pulled into the street to collect her. Poor Mel, he had thought, she is such a wonderful selfless and caring girl, why should her mother be so selfish and self absorbed, putting her through that embarrassment on a regular basis. She was here now in his arms and he would soothe her troubles, hold her tightly till she felt safe and give her all the tenderness she both needed and deserved. He was able to repress the desire that she inevitably aroused in him; what she needed now was comfort. She seemed so small in his arms as she wept, her delicate white shoulders undulating to the beat of her vulnerability,

She opened her eyes the tears still falling unabated, and he reached over to his drawers and located a large antique bristle brush and as he propped her up he began gently and rhythmically to brush her hair. He took care with its copious and voluminous waves making sure he did not hurt her, pausing now and again to take up another section which he lovingly separated and smoothed; she sighed spasmodically, contentment replacing sorrow, slowly and delicately like petals unfurling in the heat of the sun. When he placed the brush back on the drawers he turned her to him and in the soft glow of the Tiffany lamp and with Ophelia in the corner of his eye his mouth located the salt of her tears and he licked away the traces of sadness. As she closed her eyes in pleasure he kissed each eyelid and slowly licked the residual tears from her long eyelashes, pulling her closer to him as he finished. He held her closely breathing in her unique smell and she felt safer than she had ever felt; she relished the muscular bulk of his body which encircled her small frame; she needed to feel utterly and totally protected and Jonathan had more than succeeded in fulfilling that need without any further words being spoken.

Then it happened: the kiss that would determine the next eighteen months of Melissa's life; the kiss that would propel their relationship towards a precarious, uncertain, yet unparalleled ecstasy. Her lips found his as they moved away from her moist eyelashes brushing her cheek as they made their journey back to the chaste distance of a few moments ago. There was no doubt about his response, how could he refuse, deny or conceal his suppressed need of her; he relished the flesh of her lips, her tongue as it traced the contours of his own mouth, her teeth as they gently nibbled at his lower lip, her hands in his hair, her sweet breath mingled with his and her breasts pressed so earnestly against his chest as if she needed to permanently fuse their bodies refuting any separate identity. He was euphoric, lost utterly in the moment knowing in an instant that he would never feel like this with any other woman; this indescribable rapture was not ephemeral; he had never experienced anything that even remotely compared to this kiss. He would be hers always.

A lifetime passed and when they moved away from each other they found themselves smiling with the sheer joy of loving each other and the relief that finally they had allowed themselves this happiness. Neither was concerned with the world outside that room; with propriety, consequences or with the existence of any other being, they needed only the sustenance of their love. "I love you Mel. God I love you so much, and I need you to know that I have *never* felt like this before, I can't tell you in words............ it's impossible – mere words just can't begin to express how wonderful you are. No woman has ever made me feel so intensely alive, so aroused and so happy." He drew her to him and kissed her hair and whispered again and again those words she needed to hear, those sweet words of love that made her feel quite dizzy. She wanted more now, needed to feel his body entwined with hers; she needed him to love her completely to be inside her where she could experience what she had longed for since she first saw him.

"Jonathan," she whispered, "make love with me, love me now.......... please – I want you so much." As she spoke she reached towards his shirt unbuttoning it and moving her lips to his for affirmation and to her utter joy he responded kissing her with unadulterated passion and a strength that almost made her breathless. They undressed each other with an urgency which had no respect for those frustrating devices which contained their bodies; ripping at shirts, underwear and anything else that thwarted their need to touch until they were finally at their goal flesh touching flesh. Was there any part of her body he did not touch, kiss, and marvel at? He returned intermittently to her lips, her tongue and yet again her eyelashes which were a source of sheer delight to him.

There were places he touched, kissed that she had never imagined would send such waves of sheer electricity throughout her whole body making her gasp then cry out alternately with pure ecstasy. She was lost in the beauty of him, his skin bronzed, satin and taut inviting her own fingers and lips to explore, his eyes conveying unadulterated, sweet love and his body trembling with lust as he watched her stoking, kissing and biting gently until he must be inside her.

Afterwards they lay exhausted, replete and with the happiness that comes from such harmony of body and soul, their whole beings affirming the sheer perfection of what had just transpired and sent them spiralling into simultaneous and consuming orgasm. Jonathan who was almost thirty and Melissa who was still sixteen were unable to speak – no longer defined by the roles of teacher and student they were equal in this reciprocal love; they clung to each other as if the world might end and rob them of what they had just found - which was so completely exquisite.

As Melissa lay secure in Jonathan's arms she knew she wanted this night to last for ever; the thought of going home made her shiver and intuitively her lover pulled her even closer stroking her soft willowy back and whispering love. She sought his eyes and finding them closed she kissed his cheeks gently and slowly and as he stirred she echoed the kiss on his throat, his ears and finally lingered near his lips until the imperative of his desire demanded her lips be locked with his. "Mel," he sighed as they stopped for breath, "wonderful, beautiful Mel – love me always ……….. love me always." As he spoke her whole body became pliant, yielding, willing him to be in control now, to unleash yet again the intensity of his desire. She moved away from him, only inches, but he couldn't bear it and followed her with his mouth, his eyes, his now deliciously visible lust and his arms as they lifted her up and onto him both of them crying out with the sheer joy of each other. And so began another delectable journey of discovery, of touch and response, of abandonment and smiles, of tears of joy and soft sighs of pleasure until they lay exhausted and sated as the light warm breeze of the early evening became the chill of midnight.

"Jonathan, wake up ……… wake up!" Melissa was sitting on the edge of the bed shaking him gently.

"What is it darling, what's wrong?" Once he had asked he knew immediately what the answer was and felt an overwhelming sense of guilt. How could he have been so selfish, knowing she should be back home well before this and realising instantly, that after only a few hours, the reality of their lives outside this room was already knocking on the door. "OK Mel, calm down and we'll decide what the best course of action is, come here and keep warm. What time would Carol usually expect you?"

"Well I did leave a note but I usually let her know if I will be this late and although it's not school tomorrow, she would at least need to know where I am."

She looked so frail, so vulnerable and so beautiful, he pulled her closer stroking her hair and said softly, "Could you call and say you were at your friend Susan's house or is it too late. I mean would it be best if I took you back now even though you will be late or could you …. could you possibly stay?"

"Oh God Jonathan I want that more than anything, I need to be with you tonight, the thought of going home is awful, but she may get worried and ring people and then I wouldn't know what to say – how to stop her finding out."

"Right darling, get dressed and I'll drive you home and then the worst thing you will have to deal with I hope is Carol's anger. We must hurry though just in case you are right and she calls your friends. I don't want you to have to go through that. We must be more careful next time or find a way we can be together all night, I want to wake up with you Mel; I'd like to show you the wonderful view from the studio at dawn and make love with you on the floor as the light begins to flood in and the birds sing their welcome to the new day. Then I'd like to bring you breakfast when you are back in my bed and make love again and again and………………."

"Stop it," she giggled, "Stop it at once Mr Pritchard you should know better!!!" Finally they were dressed and walked out to an inhospitable grey night. Jonathan watched as she turned the key in the lock of the completely dark house and as she silently mouthed the words 'I love you' and closed the door behind her he felt ridiculously close to tears. How could he be without her now – he wanted her with him - in his home, in his bed, he wanted her totally and yet he was unable to shed the heavy mantle that was reality, the invisible chains that were propriety. He had never dreamt such happiness existed, such physical ecstasy was unsurpassed and beyond description. Even in his widest most erotic imaginings he could never have predicted this heaven that manifested itself when their bodies were together and now he could not be without it – he wanted her again as he drove through the darkness that echoed his sense of loss. He would be so distracted when he went on the staff development course, Melissa's delectable image pervading his mind, but somehow he must restore equilibrium and behave in a professional manner.

Lydia had said that he could stay with her and Jack when he was on the course in London, but Jonathan had declined remembering the night last summer when he had almost been persuaded to make love to her. He had booked into a ridiculously expensive bed and breakfast in Victoria which was within walking distance of the venue and although his expenses allowance would not fully reimburse the costs he thought it was worth subsidising the accommodation for the sake of his peace of mind. As he arrived back at his cottage Jonathan Pritchard felt a sudden shiver of foreboding which lasted seconds but would be recalled many months later when he was faced with the most difficult decision of his life. Like an automaton he walked up the stairs to the bed with its rumpled reminder of the joy of a few hours ago and, without undressing, he lay down holding the pillow that was suffused with Melissa's presence.

Melissa had crept upstairs, grateful for the darkness and the faint sounds of sleep that emanated from her mother's bedroom and as she lay on her bed after cleaning her teeth but having been unable to wash her body and obliterate the wonderful residual hint of sex, she sighed in utter contentment. This was how it was supposed to feel then – this almost indescribable heightening of all her senses, this flame that had merely flickered gently when she had made love with Luke, was now a fire raging uncontrollably. She had been amazed at her abandonment, her instinctive animal need to touch and explore every inch of him, her total lack of inhibition and control; she had wanted to stay in his room for days, just the two of them making delicious love and nothing else. She was hungry only to explore further, to experience again and again the sensations he had awakened in her and to lie exhausted and exhilarated in his arms all night until the dawn brought renewed energy and reawakened their lust for each other with its seductive hues. She recalled the soft timbre of his voice as he whispered that he would love her forever, need her and cherish her always; she recalled the moments he spoke only in Spanish and how it had thrilled her to her core, heightening her sensations and precipitating the unstoppable journey to orgasm.

Now she remembered the intensity of his eyes as they locked with hers sharing with utter delight the final moment of their simultaneous ecstasy, unwilling to close or avert hers for a second, and expressing such love and joy she was unable to recall it now without her eyes filling with tears of happiness. Finally she slept, blissfully unaware of the furore that would be waiting to destroy the beauty of the warm day that would awaken her yet give her only momentary pleasure.

"So where were you Melissa? I suppose you thought you wouldn't get found out did you, creeping in this house at all hours thinking I was a complete fool and would not look at the clock."

Her mother looked awful, standing rigidly upright by the table in their tiny kitchen, her pretty face contorted with anger, her hair severely secured behind her ears and her hands firmly on her hips in a stereotypical expression of indignant outrage. Melissa was so worried she nearly keeled over, her legs protesting their ability to cope with this onslaught. Obviously her mother could not know where she had been and surely she must have read the note but in any case why was she making such a big deal out of last night? She had been allowed to come home late before now and had not even been questioned about it. How contradictory and irrational was that? What had happened to her mum's promise to treat her as a grown up? Actually, Melissa thought, it is me who should be angry here because if Carol and Stuart had not been so self obsessed and screaming at each other for the entire world to hear I would not have rung Jonathan and gone out anyway. Bloody selfish actually.

"Calm down mum for God's sake and let me explain will you?" In essence she was playing for time, trying to think of a plausible explanation that would divert her from the truth which she could not possibly know – absolutely not, no ……. no way could she know.

"Calm down, you have the nerve to tell me to calm down when you come creeping into my house at nearly one o'clock in the morning and without even a phone call to tell me where you were. And don't try and tell me you were with that Susan Posthlethwaite or poor Luke Scott because they both called to speak to you and I felt like a fool when I could not tell

133

them my own daughter's whereabouts. So come on Melissa I'm waiting for an explanation and an apology if you have the decency to offer one." She had not moved from the inflexible position she had moulded herself into as the altercation had commenced. "Well, don't just stand there, answer me," she bellowed.

Melissa was indignant now; what gave Carol the right to behave in whatever manner *she* chose and then turn round and give her daughter the third degree. Melissa wondered if Stuart would intervene; he was mutely reading his paper with his face almost making contact with the print, his hair visibly unwashed and unkempt, and his spoon sporadically lifting up copious amounts of corn flakes. He seemed strangely subdued for a step father who had often sprung to her defence; perhaps the argument last night may have some bearing on his lack of activity.

She found herself saying, "You've got a bloody cheek mum, and after what I went through last night listening to you two shouting and fighting without any thought for what I might be feeling down here. Don't you realise how upsetting it is for me to live with this bloody volatile atmosphere never knowing if you and Stuart will be making love or war and always on tenterhooks in case I say or do the wrong thing myself. God I wish I lived anywhere else at this moment rather than in this sodding mad house!"

She felt it without fully seeing or predicting it, the blow to her face so violent it sent her careering across the kitchen and as she lifted her hand to the painful point of contact she felt the blood pouring from her nose. Christ, Carol had never even slapped her before, even when she was naughty as a child, not once, ever. What was happening here? As she held her face and looked over at her mother in total disbelief and with what she would later recall as recognition - the recognition that her mother really did not like her at all, Stuart leapt to his feet. He gently pulled her down into a chair and gave her his handkerchief for the blood and immediately went over to his wife and said,

"How dare you take the spite and anger you feel towards me out on Melissa, Carol? How dare you? She left a note which I held out to you last night but you refused to even look at it because you were so intent on continuing to argue with me about my credit card statement. I tried to tell you then that she would be late, but you were determined to give her a hard time because her two friends rang and you felt foolish because you could not tell them where she was. But to hit her, that is unforgivable Carol, totally unforgivable." Throughout this Melissa remained seated and incredulous on two counts; her mother had hit her and Stuart had spoken more than three sentences at once! She would never feel the same about either of them again.

"Oh so you are taking the little madam's side again are you Stuart, I wonder why?" Carol was shaking and as the full import of her action sunk in she made to walk out of the room but at the door which she clutched to steady herself, she shouted, "I still want to know where you were Melissa and what's more important what you were doing till almost one in the morning and you will not leave this house until you tell me. What's more, it is not your place to comment on or make remarks about my relationship with Stuart and if I want to argue with my own husband in my own house then I will. Do you understand me Melissa?"

"Yes I understand you perfectly. This is *your house* and even though I am your daughter and trying to get through an A level course you can behave how you like, as selfishly as you like and with no thoughts for your daughter's peace of mind, because this is *your bloody house."* She was crying now, incredulous that her mother had turned her back on the relative leniency of the past six months, incredulous that she could look at her with such loathing and in total disbelief that the wonderful events of last night were being pushed to a small corner of her mind by this protracted and vicious onslaught. "If you must know I was with a girl from the debating society, we were preparing for the next session. I did not give you a ring because I was bloody upset, alright? You were the last person I wanted to talk to after listening to you arguing with Stuart for an hour." Carol seemed satisfied with that and with a quick glance at her daughter which on close scrutiny could have been interpreted as regret, she walked out of the room and with a slam of the door, remained in her bedroom for the rest of the morning.

Chapter fourteen

Bloody hell Melissa what happened to your face, Christ don't tell me you've taken up Karate or something else bloody exhausting and dangerous. You definitely didn't get that shiner sitting in your room listening to that dreary Leonard Cohen. You'd better come in out of the rain and tell me all about it." Susan was wearing purple suede trousers, purple snakeskin boots and a multicoloured shirt in predominantly purple and lilac tones which, if you did not know her proclivity for the colour, would have led you to believe she had been the victim of a petty criminal with a surfeit of unco-ordinating and garish stolen goods to offload! "Here have a Brandy and Babycham - I think you could do with it, bloody hell that bruise is even worse in the light. Sit down Mel my mum and dad are away at Blackpool for the week so we can drink everything in their drinks cabinet if we want to."

Mel was so tempted to tell Susan everything but, despite her sense of complete isolation as Jonathan was uncontactable and she had avoided Luke for a few days, she decided to go with the edited safer version. She was worried about the situation at school and the very real danger that her dearest Jonathan could lose his job, even his career. "I think my mum has totally lost it Susan; she's changed so much since she married Stuart. Sometimes she has been almost human for a while, you know letting me stay out 'til midnight, not going berserk about my clothes, that sort of thing but most of the time she's irritable and volatile and Stuart and I have to keep a low profile in case she creates a bloody scene for no reason at all. I wish I could leave, I really do; I've had enough, especially after yesterday morning when she did this to me. God I couldn't believe it Susan. I mean would any reasonable person, let alone a mother, do this to someone just because they came in a bit late?"

"Bloody hell Mel are you telling me that Carol did this and Mr Grey didn't even try and stop her?"

"Well to be fair he is in a difficult position so he just kept quiet when she was shouting at me. I don't think either of us could quite believe it when she lashed out, she's never been violent towards me before and he did get involved at that point. Actually he was quite sweet, giving me his handkerchief because my nose was bleeding, and then he really got angry with her telling her she had no right at all to hit me."

Susan poured them another Brandy and Babycham and was determined to find out where her friend had been last night; it was a mystery because Mel clearly hadn't been at her own home or at her house, and she also knew she had not been with Luke because he had rung to see if she was there. Susan's bloodhound brain was on the scent – it suddenly occurred to her that Mel had not even explained about that other time a few months ago when she had been asked to cover for her when Mel had gone out one night – and *that* had not been to Luke's either! "So, how have things been since yesterday morning? Have you spoken to Carol – not that I would if she had gone for me like that. Has she apologised to you or anything?"

"Yes she has spoken but only brief clipped sentences and she has certainly not made any moves to apologise, as I said I think she's lost it. Stuart is keeping a low profile yet again and quite frankly I feel sorry for him Susan, I mean mum is so irrational and I think he will leave before long – I know I would if I was him. He might be grey and boring but she chose to marry him and he's harmless enough and actually quite kind. You know I sometimes wonder why my dad left, I only had Carol's version of events which was skeletal really; she said he was unfaithful and they had drifted apart but there could be more to it than that couldn't there?" She took a large gulp of the Brandy and Babycham which was making her feel warm from the inside out and relaxed on the comforting expanse of Susan's parents' large threadbare but cosy sofa. If only her own home was so welcoming and familiar, a place she actually relished returning to in the evenings rather than the hostile discordant theatre of war that Carol had established over the last two years.

Susan joined her friend on the sofa and after giving her a warm genuinely affectionate hug, she said, "Mel, where did you go last night? Did you know that Luke rang me? He was worried about you, and after speaking to Carol and hearing her tone of voice, he sensed you would be in trouble. He really cares about you doesn't he Mel? You are so lucky to have such a bloody gorgeous sexy boyfriend who worries about you and everything. Did you go to the same place you went that other time you asked me to cover for you if Carol rang?" She took only a small sip of her drink, wanting to be fully alert for all the juicy details which she was sure were about to be revealed and gazed intently and sympathetically at Melissa!

"Susan, firstly I want you to know that Luke is not my boyfriend although I really feel deeply about him and we are very close. To be honest Luke wants more, you know for us to be official – a couple, but it's never going to happen because I love someone else so Luke and I can never be more than truly close friends." God perhaps she had said too much, she must be careful with Susan as this gentle questioning she knew was a smoke screen for her unswerving and relentless quest for detailed information on every aspect of her life. "I shouldn't have said that Susan, please promise me you won't tell Luke that I love someone else. Promise me please? It would hurt him so much and it's so important for us to maintain our friendship especially at the moment. He really couldn't deal with anything else right now, his mum is really sick."

Intrigued was not an adequate description for what Susan now felt, she was amazed actually, what a dark horse Mel was; bloody hell - a gorgeous bloke on tap who was really keen and here she was saying there was someone else! How the hell did she have the time for all this larking about when she always had her head in a book or was scribbling away for her art projects or worse - writing essays which had bloody complicated, boring titles? "I'd heard about Luke's mum, I'm really sorry for him it must be awful, really awful. I would never do anything to upset him Mel you should know that after all the time we've been friends. OK there was a point when I thought seriously about asking you if I could, you know, make a play for him if you weren't interested but since then you've been inseparable. I didn't realise it was *just* friendship though or I may have asked you again! Anyway I have some news for *you* actually Mel but that can wait until later when you feel a bit better. I've just had a thought though, what is the situation with Carol, you know will she go crazy if you are late tonight or what?"

Heartened by Susan's sympathetic response and feeling the glow of the strange combination of alcohol which she had never heard of but was, according to her friend, all the rage, she said, "Right now I don't care what my mum thinks. I've always towed the line and adhered to her rules but now I feel angry that she attacked me the first time I broke them. Did I tell you though, that I actually left a note – which makes it even more unbelievable doesn't it? But I really can't say anything about this other person, not yet Susan, you have to understand I must keep it to myself and I need you to accept it but help me anyway. Could you do that or am I asking to much?"

"Well you know me Mel I do like to know all the gossip, but if you say you can't tell me there must be a bloody good reason so I suppose I will have to be patient which is not easy for me is it?" she giggled and Mel softened. "But what I don't understand is that if you and Luke are just friends, why can't you tell him about this other bloke and share the problem whatever it is with him?"

"Because he loves me and because we have been having sex together for nearly five months."

"Bloody hell, I still thought you were a virgin! Well this isn't straightforward is it? I can see your problem Mel but why didn't you tell me about it before?" Melissa thought that it was nobody's business but hers and Luke's but was not about to say that now to Susan because she needed her help and because Susan would not understand anyone wanting to refrain from placing such private information into the public arena. She had trusted her with a fragment of information in order to keep her happy and prevent further cross examinations – for a while anyway!

"I didn't keep it from you deliberately, Susan, it's just that we haven't seen as much of each other lately what with my studies and your work and hectic social life, there just wasn't the opportunity. Luke needs me now more than ever until his mum, you know ....well until she has to go into hospital and .... God I can't bring myself to say it it's so awful. To think that Brenda will soon be gone – what the hell will that family do Susan? They are so close."

"I don't know - I really don't. At least Luke will have you. But what about the sex, Mel, do your feelings for this other boy affect that? I still don't understand."

"I think I must stop having sex with Luke but I don't know how to tell him without revealing the reason and hurting him. It's a mess isn't it? But nothing has happened between me and this other person," she lied. Melissa would never have sex with Luke again it was not in question, even though she did not know at this point how she would deal with the situation when Luke, as she knew he would, initiated their lovemaking. She didn't want to dwell on it now; it was painful and ultimately unfair to Luke. She regretted her actions on that night so long ago when she had kissed him passionately and determined the course their friendship would take. She had been so unfair and selfish. Now she would be causing pain to her dearest friend Luke when he really did not need the utter devastation of his life to be further compounded by her denying him the pleasure of their lovemaking "But I need you to say I am with you if my mum ever rings when I go to see this man. Will you do that for me Susan, God I would really appreciate it - you'd save my life really you would. Anyway I am feeling a bit better now so you can tell me your news if you want to."

Somewhat disappointed on the revelations front but clinging to the word 'man' that her friend had let slip, she had a fleeting thought that barely surfaced but would remain in her subconscious until events in the future sent it spinning to recognition. Susan with little encouragement became enthusiastic about the changes that were about to occur in her own life. "Well Melissa Johnson, you are not the only one to have an eventful life! I am leaving home and going to live with my new boyfriend Tom in Lancaster; he's got a really nice flat and as we work together we can travel in his car which is fab Mel - it really is! It's a Hillman Imp and he's teaching me to drive in it; I don't know if I'll ever get the hang of it but it's great fun."

This news was welcome distraction and Mel was anxious to hear more about the boy who had finally caught her errant friend's heart – if he had caught her heart at all. "Come on Susan, tell me more about him. What does he look like because I know how important looks are to you, and what's more, how do you feel about him? You did say you were happy with Mr Right Now if you couldn't find Mr Right – and you did seem to be having fun. So what is it about this Tom that persuaded you to settle down – bloody hell Susan are you really going to move in with him?"

"Can't wait actually Mel, then we can have sex all the bloody time even in the middle of the night. He's really good at it you know, not selfish like younger boys and he accepts me as I am which is great – he even likes purple. You know the first time I went to his flat just after the New Year I nearly died Mel, I really did – he had purple walls in his bloody bedroom! OK not on *all* the walls which I would have liked, but on two of them and he even had a purple shaggy rug next to his massive bed. Even now just talking about him makes me want to see him - I could bloody eat him he's so gorgeous!"

"How old is he then and where did you meet him and……why didn't you say anything about him before this?"

Susan was on a roll – information gushing forth furiously like a leak from a pipe, "I met him at a work's party, well actually met is the wrong description," she giggled, "we were drunk and had sex together at his flat! I thought that would be it you know he would think I was easy, a tramp, and we would never speak again. But when we met at work the next day, both with bloody stinking hangovers, he grinned and said he was sorry for taking advantage of my inebriated state and would I like to go to the pictures with him that night. Well once I had looked in the sodding dictionary to see what inebriated meant and realised it wasn't something kinky that had happened without me realising it, I let him know I would meet him!! The sex that night was even better especially because I wasn't drunk! Tom is twenty one and a trainee manager at Woolies – he's got really blond hair and tanned skin; you know the type Mel, looks like he should live in California or some other really exotic place. Perhaps it's early to be moving in, but well he asked me and I thought why not, we get on really well and I've stopped fancying other boys – well that's not quite true, but now I only look and don't touch! Also my bedding will really go with his walls and rug! So what do you think Mel isn't it great?"

Melissa laughed silently, her own worries falling to the ground like discarded clothes. Susan was maturing but was still the funny girl who made her laugh with her incorrigible approach to life. Now, after all the times Susan had been insistent that the better class of boy could be found in Woolies, it was in that very place that she had quite possibly found her Mr Right!. She's a survivor Melissa thought, and what's more will probably never suffer in the way I do – it's really not in her nature to let life defeat her in any way at all, she taps in to her reserves of humour and moves on to the next chapter, joking about whatever misfortunes have befallen her.

Melissa rediscovered the pleasure of Susan's company that night, despite their divergent approaches to life and their polarised intellects; they had a history of loyalty that surpassed those differences. Melissa thought for the very first time that one day she may be able to confide in Susan about Jonathan without worrying about her friend revealing the details to anyone else. It was illuminating to see Susan's enthusiasm for this Tom and the revelation also engendered an embryonic idea that she now voiced to her, "So Susan will it be OK if I sometimes say I am staying overnight at your flat? Do you think Tom would object to you providing an alibi for me?"

"'Course not silly, he'd think it was very exciting, you know, that a friend of mine was sneaking off to see her secret beau and we were helping the course of *true love* along its way! But if you are not having sex with Mr Mystery why would you want to stay out overnight?" Susan asked.

"Because I may want to get involved physically one day and because Susan Posthlethwaite you don't have to have sex to want to spend the night with someone you know! But really in a couple of weeks I want to go to London to see Leonard Cohen in concert and I can't pass that off as a school trip. Will you have moved in with Tom by then?"

"Well I am *gutted* Mel! You are going to see the fabulous Leonard Cohen and didn't think to invite your best friend!" she teased. They both laughed uproariously and as it abated Susan said she would be glad to provide cover and even though every cell in her body oozed curiosity she felt that one day Mel would confide in her or let some details slip, one or the other, so she would try and be patient until that day of revelations!

Melissa Johnson did not see Leonard Cohen in concert at the Royal Albert Hall on the 10th of May; she attended the funeral of Brenda Scott and held on to her dearest friend Luke who coped only because his wonderful Mel was with him, supportive and understanding as she always had been since the day he met her. The church was full to overflowing and the service was so moving very few of those attending could hold back the tears; Brenda had been much loved in her community even though she lived amongst them for less than a year. It was such a tragedy everyone said and those who travelled some distance to attend, who had known her for much longer, echoed those feelings with the intensity that came from a shared history. Luke's sisters were amazing, organising everything because both Luke and his dad were rendered incapable so overwhelming was their grief for the woman who melded the family together. Their own grief was no less intense yet they found the reserves needed to deal with organisation, announcements, food preparation and paperwork and at the same time supported their father and brother who had so relied on Brenda's pivotal role in the family.

Melissa had somehow managed to be with Luke and show him she that cared deeply and would support him through the difficult times ahead without sharing her body with him. Two weeks ago he had visited her in tears saying that the cancer had really taken hold and Brenda could not cope with the pain and its management outside hospital so had been admitted that day; she had held him tightly and spoken to him of his mum trying to encourage him to focus on the positive. It was virtually impossible for Luke to do that - he just wanted his mum back, to be well and happy and for things to return to how they had been before she became sick; Luke wanted to turn back time – to see her smile, hear her laugh and watch her cuddle his dad in her openly tactile way. He even wanted her to shout at him and tell him to get his act together when he wandered off course sometimes as was his artistic wont. Now he held on to Mel as if she had the power to reverse the events of the last few months, as if she was the giver of life itself; he felt she could filter her vibrancy, her energy through him to Brenda so she could find strength and recover. His intellect told him it was fruitless but his heart propelled him to seek solutions, find hope from the impossible. Her body was his solace and he sought it with a fervour that was borne of a desperate need to obliterate reality, to forget the pain of loss, to feel warmth and joy with the girl he loved.

Melissa had managed to kiss him, stroke his face, hold him so he felt safe and had somehow been able to divert him from his ultimate goal which was so clearly visible despite his misery. He had sought her breasts, gently moving his face towards them as he untied the drawstring on her cheesecloth blouse and she had allowed him a moment of peace, watching him as his mouth found her nipples and then like a baby he had nestled there for an eternity whilst Melissa tried to imagine if Jonathan would understand. When he had moved away slightly, whispering that he wanted her, and his hands had reached under her skirt softly stoking her thighs she had stopped him and gently persuaded him that he must go home to comfort his dad. He had a hurt uncomprehending look in his eyes, but within moments he was thanking her for being so understanding and encouraging him to think of others who were also enduring this interminable pain. She felt only maternal and loving with Luke and the stirrings of desire he had once created within her had been surpassed by the amazing, abandoned and truly rapturous passion she had discovered with her beautiful Jonathan.

Chapter fifteen

Jonathan and Jack had arrived at Maria Luisa's village in the little red Seat car he had hired for the four days they would be staying, and were amazed to be greeted with what appeared to be the final stages of wedding preparations. His mamma greeted them with her usual gusto – a combination of squeals of delight, tears of joy and wet kisses all over their faces finished off with crippling hugs and unbroken sentences of her own special Spanish endearments some of which Jack did not understand! His abuela seemed to be even more excited than she had been the last time his daddy had brought him; he wondered if perhaps she had discovered a new flavour of ice cream and couldn't wait for them to try it tonight after dinner. He was always allowed to stay up late and eat with grown ups when he was here in Spain, it was great fun listening to them talk and laugh so loudly and being given so many hugs and treats! Well it had to be something as important as ice cream anyway, or why would her eyes be sparkling more than ever and why was she going about the house singing and humming as if she had a very nice secret that made her happy?

Grown ups were like that, he thought, they kept surprises from you as if waiting made them even better, but Jack thought that it was silly really because if there was something exciting like a trip somewhere nice or even a special treat, he always wanted it straight away. It was never better when he was made to wait and guess what the present or treat was and watch his mummy, his abuela, or even Daddy who was not *so* guilty of this strange grown up behaviour, smile to themselves imagining you did not notice. Oh well he was happy to be here with Daddy and would wait for the ice cream treat patiently as his mummy had taught him to do.

"You're getting married, *you're getting married* mamma?" Jonathan was in disbelief despite his previous suspicions that his mamma was perhaps involved with Mario the ageless carpenter, it had never occurred to him that she would remarry one day. He always pictured her as a contented old lady living with her cats in her idyllic house with her friends calling and their infectious laughter echoing in the surrounding hills. Never in his wildest imaginings did he think this would be happening. God what a surprise! His mamma with her amazing predilection for celebration and fun had organised her own wedding to Mario to coincide with the day her beloved niño had his 30th birthday! This was just the beginning of an eventful weekend containing revelations which would shake his accepted knowledge of his mamma and question his own identity.

Much later that night after consuming unprecedented amounts of tapas and red wine and being questioned enthusiastically by Maria Luisa about his love life, school, art and yet again his love life, he lay in bed with delicious memories of his sweet Melissa for company. He hoped she had not been discovered arriving home late on that unbelievable evening just ten days ago when he had dropped her off after the joy of discovering each other sexually. Jonathan had become only too aware from what Mel had told him, that Carol was very volatile at the moment. He felt responsible for her, protective and so amazed still at the passion they had shared – he had not thought such physical heights of sensation possible, nothing could have prepared him for the ecstasy of loving her or the emptiness of his bed, his home and his heart when she had left. He fed on the vision of her now, of their bodies fused together, of her fingers and mouth on his skin, of being deep inside her and watching her beautiful face as she moaned with pleasure and seeing pure unadulterated love in the fathomless depths of her eyes.

He wanted her here with him, to share this corner of Spain and meet his mamma and her friends; circumstances made it impossible even though in his heart he knew without a doubt that his mamma would adore her. As he lay listening to the comforting Spanish countryside imbued with the sounds of an embryonic summer, Jonathan thanked a God he was not so sure he believed in, for bringing him the unsurpassed joy of Melissa. His sleep that night was overflowing with erotic dreams of her which served only to exacerbate his frustration as he woke intermittently with an almost permanent erection, in disbelief that he could not reach out for her, touch her slender body and whisper his love as he drew her to him. So he fantasised and hoped she was missing him and looked across the room at the empty bed his son usually occupied; Jack had been allowed to sleep in his abuela's room for the last time tonight for after tomorrow her new husband, Mario, would be installed in there.

The following day was a non stop carousel of celebration, a birthday breakfast and a wonderful wedding in the village church followed by such eating, dancing, animated conversations, cava and to Jack's delight, copious amounts of ice cream! Mario had given Jonathan such hugs and talked endlessly with him as if he was his own father. A huge smile had been on his face all day - a signifier of his happiness that at last he was marrying Maria Luisa, the only woman he had ever loved and with whom he could be happy now as he grew old with her. He could not speak of the past with Jonathan, or Antonio as he preferred to think of him even though Jonathan's middle name was recorded officially by its English equivalent – Anthony. He was not allowed to speak of anything until Maria had spoken with him herself and he was somewhat anxious about the reaction to the story which began so long ago with heartbreak and ended here now today with the beginnings of true happiness. Maria Luisa had decided to speak to her dearest boy during that evening when guests were enjoying the makeshift band that the villagers had formed for this special day and Jack was playing happily with local children, his Spanish improving continuously from necessity.

Jonathan knew his mamma had something very important to tell him, but was not prepared for the magnitude of a story which had begun some thirty years ago before he was born. "Cariño mio, I want you to let me tell you the story before you be interrupting me with your questions, promise me you will let me say without the interruption, querido."

"Sí mamma, claro." Jonathan was nervous as she began to turn his world upside down. Maria Luisa spoke without interruption and with fleeting tears in her eyes which were replaced intermittently by smiles of joy. She had loved Mario since she was a young girl and he had lived close by her own family in Madrid. As they grew up and went to the same schools they became inseparable much to the dismay of Maria's parents who were middle class and wanted their daughter to aspire to a university education and a profession. Mario's family were craftsmen and had a small carpentry business; but even the fact that they owned their own family company did not make them socially acceptable in the eyes of Maria Luisa's parents who were voracious snobs. She was told she could not see him and that soon they would be going to live in England where she could further her education and perhaps, once she was fluent in English, develop a career there. Of course a major factor which contributed to her parents moving to England was Franco's victory in the Civil War, which had precipitated a mass exodus of Spaniards. In 1938 the Republican government had fled Madrid and sought refuge in Barcelona. Her father had of course been a Republican and would have been worried about the ensuing war tribunals that Franco's regime was sure to establish at the end of the war. Being an astute man and realising the economic devastation that would inevitably follow such a war, he had managed to filter most of their assets out of Spain before the move was completed.

They had taken her on short and occasionally extended visits to the part of Lancashire where her father had business connections and had been offered a prestigious position. They said it was too familiarise her with the new way of life and culture she would be part of once the move was finalised. They were insidious in their resolve to introduce her to suitable British young men as she was almost eighteen and hoped she would be engaged when she went to University as they insisted she must. Maria Luisa resisted continuously and began to see her Mario secretly as often as she was able to get away from her house undetected, even occasionally skipping school to spend long days with him in the countryside or the exciting streets and cafes of Madrid.

On one of the summer visits to Lancashire she was introduced to the man she married one year later when she was pregnant with Jonathan; Donald Pritchard was a very gentle and sensitive man who adored this petite exotic Latin beauty his parents were so keen for him to court, despite her fiery temperament. Eventually and despite the fact that at that time Maria Luisa had love only for Mario, she consented to an engagement even though Donald had not even kissed her; she assumed that the British were not passionate after all they lived in this cold damp place with little to brighten their lives so passion she thought was reserved for the bedroom – if it actually existed at all!

She explained to her son that the engagement served only to appease her parents who had made her life so difficult regarding Mario and she began to grow fond of Donald, but consenting to the engagement gave her leverage to resist university which she knew would be a struggle as she really was not academically inclined – not at all! Mario was enraged and threatened never to see her again which was a distinct possibility as his family were relocating the business to the village near Toledo where he would live out the rest of his days. This village had been the childhood home of his parents and as Mario was going to take over one day, they felt he would gain more standing and become established more securely in a small village setting. There was too much competition in Madrid and times had been very tough lately as the war drew to a close.

Then she revealed the most shocking fact to her son; his biological father was Mario! Without too much detail which would have been inappropriate, she told him that she had become Mario's lover when she was nineteen shortly after her engagement; he had been so upset thinking she did not truly love him and would soon disappear to a life in another country and he would be totally forgotten. He expressed his eternal love and told her he would never love anyone else – and he never did, remaining a bachelor until this day. Her parents kept watch vigilantly and as their move to England became imminent and the house was packed up and sold, she still found ways to see Mario and enjoy her last moments of his love. She explained that times were different then and perhaps if this was happening now she might have had the strength to resist, but she respected her parents and could not face the isolation that disobeying them would have precipitated.

When she left Spain for the last time and travelled to her wedding day thirty years ago, she was just twenty years old, pregnant with Jonathan and utterly bereft. She could not possibly tell Mario who had said that if she went to England he would never speak to her again; she could not possibly tell Donald whom she was about to marry; she would die rather than tell her rigid parents and so she kept this secret until some years ago when she re-established contact with Mario and told him the story. Donald had thought his son was premature and Maria maintained the façade, believing it was important to prevent anyone being hurt. Maria

Luisa explained to her son that she had grown to love Donald deeply, if not as passionately as she loved Mario; she had felt fiercely loyal to him and had been devastated when he died so young leaving her in no man's land, neither familiar with Spain anymore or totally accepted in England. But she had been determined to carry on her life in England until she was in a position to make unencumbered choices. Her first priority had been Jonathan and his schooling and now she revealed that Mario had been sending a little money each month which had helped her enormously. So Jonathan Pritchard discovered on his mother's wedding day and his own thirtieth birthday that he was completely Spanish, had a father he had never met until a year ago and his dearest son Jack now had an abuelo here in Spain as well as a granddad in London.

That night Jonathan slept in the little room with Jack and once his son was breathing deeply after his exciting and exhausting day; he lay deep in thought about his mother, family and life. How often were impossible decisions forced on us without the tangible possibility of choice? He realised his mamma was much stronger than he had previously believed – to have obeyed her parents, left Mario and married Donald was not weak but a manifestation of her capacity for survival. She had taken the route which would provide the most security for her unborn child; he admired her immensely with a renewed respect and resurgence of pride that she had brought him up so successfully on her own, without recourse to retreat back to Spain when times were difficult. Suddenly he recalled a very vivid and disturbing dream he had had a year ago when he was having difficulty sleeping – it was at a time when his longing for Mel had been unbearable. When he evoked the detailed images from the dream which was as clear today as it had been then, he realised he must have had a subconscious knowledge of his tangled background, and that his state of anxiety must have precipitated that intolerable night of turmoil.

Jonathan had taken leave of his mamma and Mario who now kissed him enthusiastically on both cheeks (he could not bring himself to call him pappa yet but hoped to be able to one day soon) and was content in her very visible happiness and security. Jack kept repeating "Adíos abuela y abuelo, hasta la próxima" over and over again, more from a sense of novelty than a need to reiterate the fact that he would indeed see them next time! So they began their journey home after such a momentous

Tides Must Turn

visit and Jonathan was consumed with guilt as his son sang along to the Spanish songs on the radio and emanated a radiant innocent happiness which made him wish he could consolidate the journey's end with their return to a complete family unit.

How could he resolve this dilemma in his tortured thoughts when one woman and one alone had made him so supremely happy? This was one of the imponderables of life which had the potential to drive him almost insane, for this covert rapturous and consuming love for Melissa would have to remain that way for at least a year until she left school. She must in essence be marginal to the socially observable element of his life and yet it was Jack, singing enthusiastically now, and Melissa who were the very source of life itself to him. The moral stance of society therefore determined he love them in isolation, a disparate game he must play against his will; constantly torn between his responsibility as a teacher and parent and the need to proclaim his undying love for Melissa from the rooftops.

Lydia wanted to try again, she had now voiced her hopes that had precipitated her attempt to make love with him last summer and this added layer of complexity unnerved Jonathan. It was so clearly evident whenever he picked up Jack and he did not have the wherewithal to deal with it so he avoided protracted talks or offers of dinner or simply a coffee. In this way he could avert upsetting either Lydia or more importantly Jack who was very susceptible to atmospheres. But Lydia was blocking the divorce and so Jonathan Pritchard was, in the eyes of society and the law, still a married man and that disturbed him tremendously for it placed his wonderful Melissa in the role of mistress.

He arrived back at his cottage later than he had anticipated and although his desire to call Melissa was overwhelming he felt that eight o'clock was far too late to call and attempt to arrange a meeting for tonight. He heated some of the vegetable soup that Maria Luisa had insisted he brought home, cut two chunks of crusty white bread and poured a large glass of smooth, mellow Tempranillo and was half way through when the phone rang.

"Darling - thank God you're back safely, can I see you?"

"Mel ……………Mel, it's so good to hear your voice cariño. Is it possible tonight? I can't think of anything more wonderful, I've missed you so much. I need to talk with you and most of all at this moment I need to touch you……..all over."

"Come to the end of the next street in half an hour. I've told Carol I am staying at Susan's tonight because I really hoped we could be together when you got home. Jonathan I can't bear it when we are apart, it's been sheer torture and I've been so longing for you all day, I have to be with you. Say you are not tired, say you want me, say anything and I'll believe it."

"I want you Mel, I want you always." He finished his soup but left the wine for later and without even locking the door he drove to meet his Melissa. When he saw her waiting his heart missed a beat and recklessly stopped the car with a skid almost. He left the engine running and ran to her, lifting her clear off the ground, squeezing her until she begged him to stop. Amidst scattered kisses and whispers of love, each closely scrutinised the other; hands touched faces as if the remembered beauty had been a trick of the mind. Then he noticed the faded yet discernable bruise as he helped her into his car and asked her about it as they drove speedily to his bed. They did not make it.

"Stop the car Jonathan, I can't wait to get to your cottage I want you now. Stop the car anywhere." He obeyed, his body determining the action rather than his reason, for it was a light evening - a scattering of fleeting clouds abetting the moon as she created a fluid landscape of dancing shadows. He found a small track fairly close to his village but for Melissa and Jonathan the cottage was too far away, they must touch now. They flung themselves out of the car and into each others arms, kissing so deeply and hungrily they could have been apart for months not several days. She leaned back against the car, pulling him towards her and telling him over and over again how beautiful he was and how much she wanted him.

His kisses were not tender but imbued with a hungry unbridled passion which Melissa returned almost bruising his lips with the strength of her own raw desire. Frantically he pulled at her dress which was sent careering to the ground and as he found her breasts he gasped out loud. Melissa may have worried for a second that they might be heard but did not heed the stirrings of caution – how could they stop now? Whatever was occurring in the world at this moment was of no consequence for they would follow love's insistent directive. He lifted her up whispering his love in Spanish now "te amo, te amo siempre mi amante" - which amplified her desire; she wrapped her legs around him and very quickly they were frantically propelled to incredible levels of ecstasy. Afterwards they clung to each other breathless and trembling but minutes later collapsed onto the ground laughing at the sheer intensity and absurdity of it.

They put on the items of clothes they had discarded and still laughing they made their way to his home where they shared a fragrant hot bath and then he kissed her more tenderly and introduced her to Tempranillo – a large glass! They went to bed, the room illuminated only by candles which were scented with vanilla, Melissa's favourite, and sat talking for hours, occasionally kissing, occasionally stroking each others faces, and occasionally whispering love and reassurance. Melissa reassured Jonathan when he expressed his concerns about Jack and his own ability to be a good parent when he saw him so infrequently. After he had told her his mother's story she encouraged him to see the positive side to Mario's new status in his life. To have lost a father when he was so young was absolutely tragic, but to then find another when he was thirty was surely wonderful. She thought this especially true for Jack who would have an extra person to spoil him and make him feel loved. Surely that would help Jonathan feel less guilty that he lived apart from his son? Jack was so lucky really to have all these people in his young life who loved him dearly, so Jonathan should not unfairly burden himself with so much guilt and self deprecation. She understood his frustrations about having to keep their love secret but reminded him of the words he had used some time ago when he had told her they must not even think of embarking on the physical side of the relationship until she had left school. "Now look at us!" she smiled. He returned her smile then and drew his wise and understanding young lover to him, gently removing the tendrils of her hair from her face and kissed her so softly it was as if a butterfly had brushed her lips with its wings.

Jonathan in turn reassured Melissa about her problems at home and her concern that she had never lied to her mother in her whole life, but would now have to do so in order to be with him. She told him that her friend Susan was now living in a flat in Lancaster and even though she did not know who Melissa was seeing, had promised to give her an alibi whenever she required it. He encouraged her to see that she was only telling white lies and perhaps if Carol had not become so irrational they could have found a way to be less deceptive. He abhorred the violence Carol had inflicted on his wonderful Mel and reassured her that if anything similar occurred again he would help her find an alternative solution to living in that disturbing environment. He had absolutely no idea what form it would take but he wanted to protect her and keep her safe; years later he would reflect on the irony of these feelings. Then he asked her about Luke Scott.

"Mel, will you tell me please about Luke? I suppose you could tell me it's none of my business but I have wondered about it for so long now and what's more I confess to jealous feelings. Actually sometimes in the months before you and I became closer and then when we *were* seeing each other just before we began making love together, I was crazy with jealousy."

"I know you were jealous. I remember that forlorn little boy lost glance you gave me when I was with him one day in the Art block. I also recall thinking that you had no reason to be jealous as I had told you that I loved you and we had been spending time with each other here."

"Jealousy is not always rational Mel, otherwise reasoned argument and logic would dispel it and that is very rarely the case is it? It was not out of control though and I don't feel jealous now, well I hope once we are back at school it doesn't manifest itself, but that depends to a certain extent on what you tell me and what I see there. I'm aware of his mum being seriously ill and know you will be spending time with him – I don't have a problem with that so long as you are just friends. I don't know how he will cope; he really is such an unusual and talented young man and very close to his family especially his mother." He held her hand and kissed and gently licked the two sore fingers; he had given up trying to dissuade her from attacking them a long time ago so he soothed them instead. Then, a little frightened of what she would tell him, but needing to know anyway, their eyes melded and he listened quietly and patiently.

"................So we became lovers on New Year's Eve, well *day* actually as it was in the early hours of the next morning. I was waiting for you, that was what I had intended, but after you rejected me in the car towards the end of that winter term, I was confused. I thought you had absolutely no intentions of ever being involved with me, even though we both loved each other although the words had not been spoken. I needed him Jonathan. But now I realise I was selfish, because although I care about him deeply and he really is my closest friend – well *was* until you, I do not love him."

"He loves *you* though doesn't he?"

"Yes." This was getting difficult Melissa thought because, although she had avoided sex with Luke, she had cuddled him and then there was the last time she saw him when he was so upset and he had lain at her breasts until she sent him home. She hadn't wanted to hurt him when he was so vulnerable. It would not be wise to mention that incident to Jonathan.

"So Mel, I shouldn't ask because I know the answer; every cell in my body tells me you love me completely and I don't doubt that for a second, but have you managed to extricate yourself from that side of the friendship? I imagine Luke would desire you every time he saw you as I do"

"Yes I have managed and no we have not had sex since you and I have been together sexually but I have been comforting him and cuddling him. He is having such a difficult time and he needs physical comfort more than ever. I have to be careful not to make his pain worse if that is possible and of course there is the real problem of explaining why I can't make love with him anymore. I don't know what I'll say." Jonathan sighed in relief but he admitted to her a small sliver of jealousy which he hoped would slip away to nothing once she had spoken with Luke properly. He would have to be patient and he did feel such genuine sympathy for Luke; to lose a mother was possibly the most unendurable pain of all.

Much later after tenderly and slowly loving each other in the studio, where the now clear night allowed the moonlight to penetrate the flimsy voile curtains, Melissa and Jonathan lay naked on the single white rug on the floor. Their breathing was harmonious as they lightly slept; Melissa's slender body was totally enclosed by his arms and his legs as they kept her moulded to him, her head rising and falling on his chest as though they breathed as one. He woke first and lifted her in his arms carrying her to the bed and laying her down. He stood above her for a moment marvelling at her beauty and recalling their tender love of an hour ago, the sensations she had aroused as she explored him and asked him what he liked; the way they talked, asked questions, seeking always to please the other and give joy, was exquisite and so very erotic. He loved her more than he could ever express in his poems or even with his body, although his intuition and the heights they reached, told him otherwise. He was consumed by it; this love. He could very well have woken her now initiating another sensuous journey with a touch, a kiss or a whisper; he knew she would yield, respond with a passion that matched his own. But now he got into the bed beside her and was content to watch her sleep, until finally he curled up in her shadow and instantly joined his Melissa in her dreams.

Jonathan Pritchard did not see Leonard Cohen in concert at the Royal Albert Hall on the 10th of May, he attended Brenda Scott's funeral; he was one of two staff members representing the school. He watched Melissa three rows in front of him, watched as she enveloped her friend Luke, occasionally brushing strands of his hair from his face and eyes, watched and was disconsolately jealous. She managed to speak to him briefly, before she left with the family for the small gathering of close friends and relatives at Luke's house which Jonathan would not be attending. Yes she would see him tomorrow night; yes she loved him desperately; yes she knew he was feeling fragile about the amount of time she was spending with Luke.

Melissa felt torn, because she needed Jonathan to understand, after all he was thirty years old he should not be feeling so dejected and vulnerable – could he really love her that much? Sometimes she saw the gauche boy in him and it was endearing. Sometimes when they were in the formal setting of school and their eyes met, she felt her whole body become suffused with desire. But the denial of it which was often protracted, days going by until they could make love, was excruciating. Then sometimes he would be able to give her a lift to Susan's and they would sit round the corner and kiss, clinging to each other as if it would be their last moment together while destiny lingered on the horizon, waiting with malevolence to test their endurance.

Chapter sixteen

"But Mel I don't understand any of this; I thought you enjoyed making love with me? I was sure we would be close again in that way after, well, after the funeral." He had a lump in his throat but acknowledged the vital role Mel had played in his gradual recovery; his ability to function on a daily basis and return to school although his concentration level was low, was entirely due to Mel's unfailing support and encouragement. His dad had gone to pieces and there seemed a real possibility that he would lose his job. Mel had gone to the other place now; he could not decipher the look in her eyes or read her face, she had travelled beyond the confines of this room. They were lying on the cushions listening to Colloseum and he felt lost and rejected because now she wouldn't even kiss him and fended off his attempts to touch her. The trip to Barcelona was next week and Mel would celebrate her birthday there and he wanted tonight to be special, for them to resume the wonderful sex which had obviously been impossible in the aftermath of the funeral. She was adamant though that nothing closer than cuddling would occur and even the cuddles had a detachment he had never experienced before.

Melissa knew it was the right time to tell Luke that they could no longer be lovers as well as friends. How could she do that without mentioning Jonathan? How could she do that without hurting him and damaging their friendship irrevocably? She had to try and yet she was procrastinating thinking of ways to deflect his question and change the subject, but his eyes which now found hers, as she returned to this familiar haven of a room, insisted on an answer. "Luke, you know I need your friendship so much but I can't be your lover anymore, it's impossible. Can't we return to being just close friends without sex?"

"I need to know why Mel. I love you, so for me it's more than friendship but I've always known you didn't feel the same way. You've never deceived me and you've always been totally honest saying you care for me deeply but never saying you loved me. Just keep being honest with me Mel, please, just tell me why?"

"Because I love someone else Luke. I'm really sorry if this hurts you because the last thing I want to do is to hurt you. I suppose I want it all don't I? I want to be your close friend even after I have rejected you physically, but I appreciate that it may be impossible for you to stay friends with me. If that is what you want I will have to go along with it, but I would be devastated to lose what we always had from the moment we met, which is an amazing special friendship based on truth."

His voice was angry now, hurt, "Bloody hell, when did all this happen Mel, have I been blind or what? I mean who is he and when did you meet him and are you lovers and……….I can't stand it Mel. To think of you with someone else - it's bloody awful. Christ I never really thought this would happen you know, I assumed we would continue as we were and hoped that one day you would discover you really loved me."

"I'm truly sorry dearest Luke, I really am but there is no way I can avoid hurting you and that makes me unhappy too. I can't tell you who it is, I just can't. One day I hope you will understand and perhaps forgive me, but if you want me to go now I will OK?" She moved away from him but he stayed listless on the pillows, his heart was in disbelief and he knew he should say something, rescue the moment, assure her that they would still be friends, but he couldn't speak, no words formed, no contact was possible. He let her leave without looking up or speaking and once he heard the front door close he felt a finality that utterly unnerved him and the shock was so deep he was even unable to cry.

Carol had been prescribed tranquilisers by her doctor and told Melissa and Stuart that he had told her she was suffering from stress and anxiety. God, thought Melissa, what the bloody hell has she got to be stressed about? She has a long suffering husband who she treats like a bloody doormat, and a daughter who works hard at school and has never given her real cause for concern like some modern teenagers give their parents. Perhaps this turn of events would be the precursor to a more predictable phase in their lives. God anything was better than the last few months. She barely communicated with her mother and even though she was allowed to stay at Susan's overnight occasionally, Carol still made life at home difficult, constantly criticising Stuart, disproving of her clothes and showing absolutely no interest in her studies. Sometimes Melissa reminisced and thought back with nostalgia to the days when it had just been the two of them; she longed to conjure up the mother of her memory to replace the monster she had become.

It was a week before the Barcelona trip and Melissa was so worried she asked Jonathan at school if they could meet just for half an hour at lunchtime. This was so unprecedented that he also became concerned and found it difficult to concentrate on his classes for the rest of the morning. They had arranged to meet some two streets away from school and Jonathan initially thought he might not be able to make it because he had arranged to discuss the results of the mock exams with Mr Brown who didn't take kindly to arrangements being changed. However, when Jonathan told him he had to hurry home to meet the plumber who was coming to mend a leak he had discovered only that morning, he couldn't have been more understanding. He left promptly and picked her up and took her to a café some short distance away and when she had her preferred cup of tea and he had a large mug of coffee she told him.

"I am three days late Jonathan and that's never happened before. I am worried sick."

"God Mel are you sure, I mean yes I know you must be sure, but……" he garbled.

"Yes of course I am, but I don't know much about this sort of thing. I thought you would know more. It doesn't always mean that someone is pregnant does it?" She looked tired, drawn and he felt culpable. He should have spoken with her about contraception; he should have been less consumed with passion and behaved more responsibly – thinking about it in this stark, unwelcoming place he couldn't quite believe they had risked pregnancy.

"Darling girl try not to worry, it could be the stress of the exams, or it could be your body's reaction to all the problems you have had to deal with at home or even the worry about Luke. It could be any of a number of things and I really think you should give it a few days or so before you start panicking." He took her hands from the cup where they had stayed unmoving since they arrived and pressed them to his lips. "Look at me Mel. Please?" When she responded he continued, "If this is a false alarm and I dearly hope it is, then we must sort out some form of contraception. I want you to forgive me Mel, for being so selfish and not thinking about this before. I don't really know why that happened and there really is no excuse."

"Jonathan, why should it have been down to you to think of contraception? There were two of us making love, not just you. I know that I preferred not to use a condom." She looked around to ensure they were not overheard before she said, "It is beautiful that way, to really feel you inside me. It's the most amazing way to love and I don't even want to consider using condoms with you. There will have to be another way. But well, it may be too late. Bloody hell what will we do if I am pregnant, Jonathan, I'm not even seventeen until the end of next week and I have a whole year of studies left to complete?"

"I really don't know my angel. All I know is I love you to distraction and I want you to stop worrying for a few days and then as arranged we will meet up and go to my house for dinner and sort everything out then. OK?" He leaned over and kissed her downcast eyes on the lids and was as always so tempted to lick her eyelashes but stopped himself in time for he would want her then as always and he had 4b in fifteen minutes! They parted with a hug and he kissed her lightly on the nose before returning to school. If Miss Jones the Maths teacher who was walking past on the other side of the street thought there was something unusual in Mr Pritchard getting into a car with young Melissa Johnson, she dismissed the thought as soon as it surfaced. He had probably taken her to an Art shop to collect materials or buy books; Melissa Johnson was known for her avid reading and her great love of Art. Some members of staff had commented on how she spent more time over her Art projects than her other subjects, but that was perfectly understandable, she wanted to go to art school didn't she.

The very next day two amazing things happened: firstly Melissa received the results of her mock exams and was incredulous at her predicted grades – A for both Art and English and B for History! Not long after receiving this gratifying news she discovered she had started her period and once she had cried with utter relief she called Susan and arranged to see her to celebrate! Susan was sceptical – when did any sane woman want to celebrate her monthlies for God's sake? Melissa was still a strange girl! However when Melissa told her she had been having sex without taking any bloody precautions whatsoever and her period had been late, she went berserk at her friend. Susan could not believe a girl with such a clever brain could be so stupid and she made her promise to go to the family planning clinic with her tomorrow evening after she finished work. Melissa was going on the pill she told her - and no bloody arguments! Disappointingly though for Susan Posthlethwaite, the name of the said partner in crime was not forthcoming despite her persistent questioning and intermittent pleading! Sixteen years old and on the pill! Despite its supposed side effects, the pill had been hailed as the marvel of the sixties, the breakthrough that gave women control over their own bodies and more sexual freedom than women from previous generations ever imagined possible. For Melissa though, it was not for the benefit of countless partners but for her own peace of mind so she could be with her one beautiful lover and share the joy of him without worry.

When she told Jonathan he was relieved on both counts. She had been so sensible going to the clinic and he would willingly have gone to support her if she had asked. Now they had arrived at the cottage in daylight and he was sure people in the village had seen them drive through, but he would not be certain until his next walk down to the pub for Sunday lunch because if someone had seen him with a gorgeous young woman in the car he was sure to be quizzed about it! Melissa wanted to talk about Luke, about the Barcelona trip and about lots of other things she was animated about. She asked for a hot water bottle for her tummy and after he had massaged it for a while and given her some aspirin, he brought it for her and they settled down on the sofa to kiss, touch, gaze, talk and reaffirm their love. He even brought the food in there which was a simple supper: a selection of cheese, some ripe tomatoes and some chunky white bread which was as always accompanied by some delicious wine. Melissa marvelled at the fact that, until a few months ago, she had only tried sweet German plonk!

"I love you Jonathan Pritchard."

"And I love *you* my Melissa."

She showed him the guide book she had bought for Barcelona which had some great walking tours and they looked at it together, their excitement about the trip escalating the more they read. "Have you been to Barcelona before Jonathan?" she asked.

"No I haven't, although my mother is from Valencia which is further south along the coast and I have often thought about taking a car and touring right along that stretch of coastline, perhaps ending up on the Costa Almeria. I did think I would go to Barcelona last year when the department decided to organise a trip for last years Sixth Form, but it didn't materialise. Although we all agreed it would be a beneficial place to take Art students, no-one at that stage was able to take on the responsibility of organising it. I suppose the fact that I was a relatively new Head of Department meant I didn't have the time to organise it myself because I was being pulled in too many directions and was attempting to settle in. But this year Mr Brown, who has a tendency to be rather pedestrian, has come up trumps and we got the whole thing off the ground. So you and I will be seeing the place for the first time together." He looked wistful as he laid his head back and inhaled deeply as if the very air and warmth of Spain was pervading the room.

"Do you think we will be able to be alone together or will that be utterly impossible? I know I have this assignment to complete when we are there but on the itinerary it does mention free time – how free exactly?"

"Well Melissa Johnson, as you will be in the care of Mr Brown and myself and as there will be a curfew, you will be expected to be back in the hotel by 11 pm and no exceptions!" he teased. After giving him the inevitable whack in the side, Melissa moved closer to him and he put his arms around her and said, "We may manage to be alone at some point darling, but I must be so careful. I would have thought there was absolutely no chance of us being able to make love, as I share a room with Mr Brown and you will be in a room with two other female students – it's much too risky. We will play it by ear and hope we get an afternoon or evening to eat together, take in a museum or two that are not on the prescribed list and perhaps even kiss in the sunshine up in Parc Guell. We can make up for lost time on the lovemaking front when we get back!"

"You know I really can't wait to go even though the journey there and back in a coach won't exactly be fun. Missing the concert by Leonard

Cohen was disappointing, even though it was good that you managed to sell the tickets at so short notice, so this trip will be a great treat. I need to try and see Luke before we go, I must know if he still wants to be my friend – he really is very important to me; if I go to Barcelona without seeing him I would feel awful. Can we talk about Gaudi some more now Jonathan and can you show me that other book you bought? Oh and don't forget you were going to teach me some basic phrases in Spanish!" She looked up at his face now and saw a glint in his beautiful eyes which she recognised as the delight he took in surprising her and she knew he was about to do just that. He walked over to the sideboard and brought a small wrapped package to her and watched her intently as she opened it with all the childlike impatience and curiosity he so loved about her.

"It's a tape. It says *For Mel*. What is it Jonathan?"

"Lets put it on shall we and I will get you another glass of wine and we'll turn off one of the lamps." He put it in the machine and pulled her onto his lap, together with the hot water bottle which remained almost permanently attached to her aching stomach. He moved her copious waves towards the back of her head so her face was made available to kiss and stroke and then he watched her reaction as she listened to the tape he had taken days to compile. He had found and copied every one of the songs that Leonard Cohen had sung at the Royal Albert Hall – he had done that for his beautiful Mel who had so selflessly supported her friend Luke and had not once complained about not being able to see her beloved Leonard Cohen.

"Hi Mel, can I come in?" Luke stood at the door; his eyes briefly locked with hers and in that instant she experienced the depth of his pain.

"Of course Luke, don't be silly, you are always welcome here you know that." Melissa led him upstairs to her room and they sat on the bed and she waited for him to speak, the unfamiliar tension enveloping them like a thick and damp winter fog. She made him look at her when the words were not forthcoming, tilted his head up so she could convince him it was OK; she was Melissa, his friend and he could say anything to her and she would still be his friend, always.

"Mel, I couldn't let you go away tomorrow without making everything right between us," he spoke hesitantly and the tremor in his voice made her feel such overwhelming guilt, it tugged and twisted somewhere deep within her stomach. "I know you didn't want to hurt me, you were just being honest and I love you for that. I love you anyway, it's not something I can switch off and who knows I may be destined to feel this way about you for ever." He smiled and tried to make light of it, but Melissa knew Luke, knew he was suffering, and knew without a doubt that he was utterly sincere about what he had just expressed. She took his hand and squeezed it affectionately, willing him to continue, to say all he needed to say until he was purged of the intensity of this pain.

"Luke, what I want more than anything is for us to be friends and for you to be happy. I wish there was something I could do to make you feel better. Perhaps when I come back from Barcelona we can begin to renew our friendship and hopefully you will not feel so awful seeing me. I am still your Mel you know; I will always be your friend Luke. Please believe that......please. You mean too much to me for us to give up on the friendship; we know each other too deeply for us to let it go."

"I know that Mel. In my head I know that; the problem is in my heart. I will try to deal with it though, find a way to rescue the friendship from all this, and when you get back from Barcelona we can meet up and maybe by then I will know if I can cope. What you say is so true, but I *love* you – it's as simple as that. I'll always be grateful for what you gave me, especially the way you supported me when my mum was ill and then giving up the chance to see Leonard Cohen to be at her funeral. I'll never forget that Mel." He hugged her tightly and moved towards the door.

"Luke, just remember that my feelings towards you are still exactly the same; I really care about you. You will always be so special to me Luke in so many ways, and I will always be grateful that I lost my virginity to you, there really could not have been any one else." Melissa now realised that the pattern of her life was exactly as it should be, she was meant to have known Luke physically, meant to experience his tenderness and love. He had so sensitively opened the gates to her own sexuality, through his sweet love making she had slowly begun the flight to the heights she now soared to with her darling Jonathan. How she wished she could be open with Luke and tell him everything, but it was intrinsically impossible

Some time later Melissa went downstairs to brave the ordeal of the 'family dinner' and saw a card and small gift bag on the telephone table. She recognised Luke's writing instantly and even though it wasn't her birthday yet she was curious and must open them but would do so in the privacy of her room. His card was poignant the words expressing his love and the picture on the front depicting a Mediterranean scene which he must have taken so long to find. What humbled and surprised Melissa was the present; Luke had bought her a copy of Beautiful Losers by Leonard Cohen and he had done so with the knowledge she did not love him, with the knowledge they could no longer share their bodies as well as their minds, done so despite the impediment of his still very tangible distress. God he was an incredible human being, she thought, life would have been so much more straightforward if she had fallen in love with dear, sensitive and beautiful Luke. She shivered as she secreted the book in the depths of her bookcase, not a book Carol would approve of, and she felt the chill deepen as a sense of foreboding tore relentlessly at her equilibrium. Tomorrow she would be taking her first trip abroad; tomorrow she was involved in adventure and anticipation; tomorrow she would begin the journey to the wonderful city which was rich with Gaudi's presence and which she knew would inspire her to a level of creativity her art had never known. But that was tomorrow and today must be lived with all its uncertainties and sorrows and regrets.

Chapter seventeen

Their basic hotel was right on the edge of the Barri Gotic, the Gothic Quarter, with its myriad of narrow alleys, evocative medieval buildings and churches; once entirely enclosed by Roman walls – the crumbling remnants of which remain as a testament to their former fourth century glory. The centre of the quarter, the Placa de Sant Jaume, Le Seu – Barcelona's magnificent Gothic cathedral and La Rambla were all within a short stroll from their well chosen hotel. It was magical and Melissa was in awe; not only had the journey been so thrilling she had been unable to sleep for a minute, anxious not to miss anything, but she found this city more magnetic and exciting than anything her imagination had been able to conjure up. She felt so impetuous and wanted to explore immediately, but other plans had been made for the group that day, clipping her wings and preventing her soaring to the heights her enthusiasm and love of Gaudi strained to reach.

The group, consisting of fourteen students and the two members of staff sat down in the designated area of the compact breakfast room in the hotel and various maps, hotel phone number, basic Spanish phrase lists and assignment sheets were handed out. It was made clear that the rules issued before they left the UK must be adhered to and the curfew of 11 pm was not negotiable under any circumstances – students flouting any of the 'reasonable guidelines' would be dealt with severely. Melissa wanted to ask impertinently if that meant that Mr Brown or Mr Pritchard would have to deport the misbehaving student, but being the young woman she was it remained unspoken in her mind making her smile to herself! There were cafes and small inexpensive restaurants circled on the map, most of them close by and on the last evening before the protracted, arduous coach journey home, they would all be eating together in the nearby picturesque, Placa Reial amongst the magnificent palm trees and the ornate iron lampposts decorated by the young Gaudi. How thrilling, Melissa thought, and what a wonderful last image of a warm Barcelona evening to take back to an unpredictable English summer. Jonathan hadn't mentioned this arrangement to her, but she supposed he must edit and curtail what he revealed about school, the staff and other such detail when they were alone together, for the sake of professionalism and propriety. As she looked over at him now speaking to a waiter in his fluent Spanish she felt she must touch him or she would not be able to get through this day, despite her excitement and barely contained adulation of Gaudi!

Melissa was the youngest in the group, her birthday being in two days time when she would reach the advanced age of seventeen! Despite this she found the two girls she was sharing a room with, most immature and despite making an effort to discuss the city and Art Nouveau and even Gaudi with them, she got very little response. It would seem that they looked upon her enthusiasm for school, the strange architecture of Gaudi and her attitude to the hideous assignments they had been given with scepticism and overt disdain. So why had they come on this trip, she thought, as Barcelona was incontrovertibly linked with the architecture of Gaudi and Art Nouveau. Melissa was also quite upset and felt affronted by their comments – why was it so wrong to enjoy your studies and feel so privileged to be in this fantastic city. Carol and Stuart, who were having one of their 'close' evenings just before Melissa set off, gave her enough money for food and a little for her to 'enjoy herself'. She also had some birthday money and was looking forward to buying some prints and anything authentic, but not tacky, relating to this city and Gaudi. These girls wanted to get the assignment work completed quickly and were planning to try and meet gorgeous Spanish 'lads' and buy clothes once the laborious tasks set had been dealt with. Melissa agreed with one sentiment obviously, that Spanish men were gorgeous - for didn't she have one of her very own sitting just across the table.

Transiently, Jonathan and Melissa found each others eyes and fleetingly each felt a smile of unadulterated happiness burgeon and remain fixed for just a second before they must avert each other's gaze. Their eyes had spoken much in that second: they had reaffirmed their love; proclaimed their need to be together for ever; sung the unmistakable song of absolute desire and told each other that no-one else existed in the world to compare with the other. So, as they were all despatched to their respective rooms to collect sketch books and whatever else was required for the day, Melissa sought strength and solace from her lover's eyes and was able to detach herself from the unpleasantness of her companions in the shared bedroom. She had a compact backpack which contained her sketch book, guidebook, Spanish phrase book and various other items which went with the territory of being a woman!

Jonathan had told her about Franco's attempts to suppress Catalan which was the form of Spanish spoken in Catalunya for over 1,000 years; it was still banned on TV and no longer taught in schools. He was not so familiar with it and found it more guttural than his own more widely spoken Castilian which most people here would happily respond to. So Melissa was determined to try her Castilian Spanish and felt confident enough to ask for things in bars or shops; she had been heartened when Jonathan had kissed her fiercely after hearing her tentatively speaking his language, telling her it was the most endearing accent ever. He loved her soft Lancashire intonation infused with the Latin cadence of the Spanish – he said it was sexy. So now she could see if other Spanish men reacted the same way. Perhaps she was about to be kissed all over the city when she spoke their language! She giggled at that ridiculous thought and ran to the stairs eager to go to their first place on the itinerary – the Sagrada Familia.

They were using public transport to see most of the prescribed places on the itinerary and they all marvelled at how cheap and efficient it was. When they were on the bus Melissa managed to place herself next to Jonathan who seemed a little unnerved, and under the cover of her backpack she found his hand on the seat next to hers and squeezed it. She laughed quietly when he glanced around furtively to see if anyone had suspected anything! The others were not even close to them and Mr Brown as always had his head in a guide book or some other informative piece of literature. She felt him relax then and stroke each finger in turn, occasionally stopping at the damaged ones to smooth the broken skin.

Then she felt the most exciting, delicious feeling flood from her hand like a transfusion of molten heat reaching every part of her and finally centring around her groin almost making her squirm with desire. For he had turned her hand over and was stroking the palm with one finger, his touch so delicate and slow, moving in circles and then across alternately – it was so light it was barely discernable but unbelievably erotic. How bad of him to tease me this way when I am unable to respond she thought; simultaneously she caught a boyish grin appearing on her lover's face and knew she was complicit.

They arrived in the 'modern' extension to Barcelona begun in the late nineteenth century after the old city walls had been demolished in order to accommodate a growing affluent population. The area known as Eixample, literally extension, had become a fashionable area in which to live and had attracted *modernista* architects whose work soon became desirable status symbols and were bought by the wealthy middle classes now populating the area. Melissa had read about many of these architects and their work but now she was about to see Barcelona's most famous and still unfinished landmark, the Sagrada Familia, Gaudi's most famous work. As they alighted from the bus and she looked towards its indisputable awe inspiring spires, she let out a gasp of utter incredulity; nothing had prepared her for the scale of it, the magnificence and the sense of spirituality it engendered within her even though it was still some distance away.

As they walked closer she knew she was virtually alone in her reverence as others in the group were talking or giggling and seemed less than impressed. The only exception apart from the teachers was Mathew Daw, a quiet and diffident boy who, like herself, seemed to be a loner in the Lower Sixth; Melissa noticed him stop dead in his tracks and whistle to himself, perhaps he was a kindred spirit in terms of admiring Gaudi she thought. Mr Brown had brought the group to a halt and was giving factual and historical information about the cathedral and despite his somewhat droning tone she listened intently. She still found it amazing to hear him reiterate that although only eight towers had been built the original plan was for eighteen: twelve for the Apostles, four for the Evangelists, one for the Virgin and a massive 558-ft spire topped by a lamb symbolising Jesus.

They were taken to the entrance and told they had three hours here to complete the work that had been set and would meet back at this point for further instructions (*and* lunch, Melissa thought, I am already incredibly hungry). Melissa, who decided to walk around and sketch on her own, even managed to climb the twisting 400 steps to be rewarded with a magnificent view of Barcelona, although she felt somewhat dizzy and had to make a hasty retreat before she keeled over! Later she took her sketch book outside to make detailed pencil drawings of the Nativity facade and found herself a short time later joined by Jonathan who, without saying anything a word sat next to her and began sketching loosely and prolifically with pencils and charcoal.

After half an hour or so, they seemed to come to an impasse, both resting their pencils and putting the sketch pads down for a moment and as she closed her eyes and turned her face towards the sun, basking in its warmth, he said, " Well my beautiful, are you happy. Is this first morning here as inspiring as you thought it was going to be?"

"God yes! More so in fact, I wish we had longer here so I could relax a little more and really *taste* the atmosphere as well as feeling it. I was just thinking about Gaudi's obsession with this project and the dedication that drove him to live here on the actual site until his death. God that was ironic wasn't it? You know to be hit by a bloody tram and take two days to die with no-one recognising who you are initially when you go into hospital! Just imagine if he had lived to finish this, Jonathan? God what a vision of sheer genius; I wonder if he would approve of the work they have completed since he died?"

"You are wonderful, do you know that." His eyes drank in her beauty and animation; for a brief, foolish moment he was tempted to bury his face in her hair, run his fingers around the contours of her face and kiss her until they were both breathless. But, it was a fantasy and he must act with decorum and propriety despite the unmitigated desire that her very presence, let alone such close physical proximity, aroused in him. So he continued. "Try and write whilst you are here Mel, you may find this whole experience conducive to poetry, prose or even a type of diary of your emotional journey. By the way, try not to touch me on public transport, you incorrigible woman or I may have to deal with you 'severely' I am certain it is against the prescribed rules for this trip; molesting the staff

– whatever next!" He smiled his love and then as he spotted Mr Brown and made to join him he recommended the museum for a brief visit as their time here was almost up. Before he left he added, "I will bring you back here my darling. We will come back and enjoy this city together and when we return to England we will be utterly exhausted, from walking, sightseeing and more importantly from making endless love together on hot Mediterranean evenings." With that he left motioning to Mr Brown that he had seen him, completely unaware that Mr Brown had been there for some time watching the young teacher and the stunning student, watching them with some concern.

After lunch which Melissa took in a small bar with Mathew Daw and a girl called Sally Jones from the Upper Sixth, they set off as a group to Parc Guell. Some of the students complained it was too hot to walk around and if they were forced to do so they might even get sunstroke! Melissa and Sally glanced at each other in disgust and set off to complete their work with enthusiasm and gratitude that they were in a land where the sun seemed to shine endlessly and parks seemed so inspired. Melissa liked Sally intuitively and they conversed easily as they sat sketching on Gaudi's fabulous wave bench. They marvelled at the intricate mosaic and the views of Barcelona and they laughed together when Melissa told Sally about the intentions of her room mates and how they had scorned her love of Gaudi. Sally confided that she had no patience with people who squandered what she termed as life's gifts.

"For instance," she had said, "it's a privilege that we have actually been able to come here and to be deliberately blind to the beauty around is indefensible." Later she told Melissa that she wanted to be an architect, but she still felt it was much more difficult for women to be successful in certain fields; an uphill struggle she had called it, but was nevertheless determined.

They went into the house in the centre of the park where Gaudi had once lived, although he had not designed it, and both expressed disappointment; it seemed somewhat austere for such a talented and creative man to have called it his home. However, Melissa tried to touch as many of the surfaces as possible believing, somewhat romantically, that Gaudi had once touched these very objects! Just before they had all arranged to meet with Mr Pritchard and Mr Brown the girls went back to make more detailed sketches of the impressive entrance to the park with its multicoloured dragon and steps leading up to the market place. Before they boarded the bus Sally said, "I'm really glad we got talking Melissa, or can I call you Mel? I've seen you around, well you are really distinctive actually, so beautiful and all that incredible hair – what I wouldn't do for hair like that! I thought you might be a bit stuck up actually, but talking with you today has taught me yet again not to jump to conclusions; I have a tendency to do that sometimes – judge people before I really know them."

Melissa thought that Sally was also good looking; she had fashionable short glossy blonde hair, cut so precisely it looked as if a tape measure had been used to ensure all the angles and points were symmetrical! She was slim like Melissa but some inches shorter and had breasts that seemed to have been destined for a much larger girl, as if they appeared on her by mistake and yet had been determined to stay put! Melissa envied them because just like Susan Posthlethwaite, Sally seemed to carry herself in a manner that amplified their already generous proportions! Although, as Melissa was thinking about breasts, she also acknowledged that in all other respects the two girls in question could not have been more different.

Melissa joined Mathew and Sally for dinner that night in a little tapas bar/restaurant on La Rambla and her companions were very impressed when she ordered beer and tapas in Spanish much to the delight of the waiter. Sally said he was gorgeous and Melissa agreed whilst Mathew played with the food attempting to discern what exactly it was. The girls were more adventurous, and of course Melissa had been introduced to such Mediterranean delights by Jonathan. She wondered where he had gone this evening; he had winked at her briefly once the group arrived back at the hotel late this afternoon as he made his way to join a somewhat taciturn Mr Brown as he headed off up the stairs to their room.

Sally's mum, they discovered had been a singer with a jazz band back in the early 'fifties and had made a good living together with Sally's dad who was the saxophone player. As the evening wore on Sally told them many fascinating and at times hilarious tales about her parents and the life she had led until she was about ten. At that stage her mum had decided she wanted a regular and reliable form of income so incredibly, according to Sally, she went to work for Marks and Spencer! What also intrigued

Melissa was the revelation by Sally that she was a feminist – she couldn't wait to speak with her again and glean more information, she certainly was a very interesting young woman.

When Melissa reciprocated and told them about being a Vegetarian and the endless omelettes her mother had assiduously provided with a variety of accompanying vegetables, they giggled complicity. Without mentioning Jonathan obviously, Melissa told them that a good friend had introduced her to much more interesting and appetising food. She said she really enjoyed pulses, varied fish, garlic and pasta; she hoped to try the local dish, *Espinacs a la Catalana* – spinach with pine nuts and raisins, whilst she was here. Tonight they had already been served with another local starter – crusty bread rubbed with tomatoes and olive oil and then for main course Sally had eaten fish whilst Melissa had a hot pot made with tomatoes, onions, aubergines and peppers but she was not sure what it was called! Sally thought she would enjoy the spinach dish as well and so they decided to have dinner together tomorrow night too. Unfortunately though it seemed that Mathew was not altogether enjoying his food and would more than likely search for sausage and chips alone tomorrow night!

Jonathan passed an altogether different evening in the company of the serious and rather tedious Mr Brown, or Timothy as Jonathan knew him. They had a pleasant meal in a restaurant in the vicinity of the Picasso Museum and although Jonathan sensed he had something of import to say, Timothy kept his colleague in suspense until their coffees arrived. He cleared his throat noisily before warning Jonathan, who he knew was much younger than himself and would benefit from his years of experience, of the dangers of teenage crushes. He himself had often been the subject of such attention when he was younger he told him, but it had to be approached with great delicacy, tact and firmness. Jonathan listened attentively whilst Timothy continued in this pompous and somewhat ignominious vein, stating that he felt the admittedly lovely Melissa Johnson had such a crush on him. Jonathan must avoid the type of contact he had witnessed himself this very afternoon - actually sitting in isolation with a student who displayed all the signs of a serious crush was tantamount to encouragement he said with self satisfied sagacity. Jonathan merely nodded with a rigid mask of seriousness, for he had not been given the opportunity of speaking!

Jonathan was torn between absolute, abject fear that Timothy suspected something, and incredulity that he was the recipient of such a pompous and obviously patronising lecture. He wanted to both laugh and cry at once and then when he calmed down on the walk back to the hotel and the dubious delights of sharing a room with a man who Jonathan knew without doubt would be a snorer, he wanted to run. He wanted to run to his Melissa and tell her he would give up his job, change career so they could be together without all this bloody awful subterfuge and hypocrisy, without the need to keep their love for the hours of night, secreted and hidden from the world and without the need for self righteous colleagues to 'warn him for his own good'. He didn't run, he walked back to their hotel to face a night of spasmodic sleep which as he had guessed was punctuated by strident and relentless snoring from Timothy's side of the room. Of course, as he had also predicted, his colleague awoke the next morning and professed to have had a wonderful night's sleep!

They had an early start the next morning and were taking the metro to the Passeig de Gracia and taking a walking tour of this elegant area, which contained a wealth of extraordinary architecture. Jonathan avoided walking anywhere near Melissa, in the hope that Timothy would think he was heading his advice and seeking to discourage her schoolgirl crush. He watched her though and saw the admiring glances from passing males of all ages; her tight jeans and sleeveless, semi-transparent white cheesecloth top balanced tentatively on her delicate shoulders, as if just a slight breeze would dislodge it, was so tantalising to him. He watched her walking and saw that she was oblivious to all the male attention, her eyes scouring the buildings for interesting hallways to dart into and feast on; Jonathan found it so endearing. In fact one man was so taken by her he virtually turned full circle, and was then so disoriented as Melissa walked on out of sight, he crashed into a lamppost!

It was an exhausting walk on such a hot day, but well worth suffering the heat for. Even the entrances and hallways were incredible when the rest of the building was closed to the public. They saw, photographed and sketched the Mansana de la Discordia: three incredible buildings which included one of Gaudi's most famous – the name deriving from the very discernible differences in style between the Casa Lleo Morera, the Casa

Amatller and the Casa Batllo. Next door was the perfume museum which some of the girls wanted to see as the entrance was free. They continued the walk and found the impressive Casa Montaner i Simon, an amazing building topped by a tangle of barbed wire on the top and designed by Antoni Tapies whose controversial and experimental designs are open to interpretation. Mr Brown expressed his view that the man had no coherence, lacked depth and merely utilised his art form to make confused political statements; Jonathan could not have been more divergent in his own assessment of the architect, admiring his originality and ability to experiment with unusual and diverse material. The morning continued with a range of architecture including the incredible Casa Mila, the apartment block, which for Melissa was the epitome of the unique and incomparable fusion of Gaudi and Art Nouveau. As she marvelled silently, the aesthetic pleasures of this city became indelibly etched in her imagination.

The afternoon was designated for the Picasso museum and most of the students were quite grateful that they would not be walking for hours in the hot sun. Melissa loved the sun and would have continued walking after lunch even if she had no idea where she was headed; it was the joy of discovering this beautiful yet busy city, randomly and without prescription that thrilled her. She would love to have Jonathan to herself to delight in its fascinating streets and unexpected visual delights. She was no admirer of Picasso but was, as always, hungry for knowledge and open to learning and the potential for changing her opinion; so now Melissa was becoming quite excited as they neared their destination. The museum was relatively new as far as museums went and was housed in a specially converted medieval palace which was in itself stunning. Gratifyingly for the teachers, most of the students seemed to enjoy the visit and one or two actually displayed visible enthusiasm! Melissa found it fascinating to see the range of styles representing the phases of the artist's work from his youth to his later period, but although she could appreciate his indisputable talent, she remained unmoved by him.

That evening Melissa and Sally went to Es Quatre Gats, a bar that had been frequented by many of the city's architects, poets and artists during the late nineteenth and early twentieth centuries, including Picasso himself. Later they went for dinner in a little restaurant they had seen in the same area of the Gothic quarter and tried some of the authentic local food they both seemed to enjoy. They talked animatedly and Melissa found herself thinking that Sally was much more unconventional and adventurous than she was herself.

As she talked about her ideas, Melissa found herself thinking of Isadora Duncan especially when Sally revealed that she did not believe in marriage. Isadora had many lovers, but those to whom she bore her two children – Edward Gordon Craig and Paris Singer – were surely her great loves? Melissa thought it was painfully tragic that both Isadora's children died when the car they were passengers in plunged into the Seine in 1913. Apparently Isadora had never recovered from it; her own death in 1927 followed the same pattern of tragic accident when her scarf became tangled in the wheel of a car in which she was travelling, and strangled her. She was about to discuss this when Sally said proudly, "My mum and dad are still together and very happy, *but they never got married*."

"Really, wasn't that very unusual when they first got together Sally?" Melissa asked, enthralled by the flouting of convention and the brave stance of Sally's parents.

"Yes it was but my mum is a very unusual woman, Mel and I admire her tremendously. It is because of her encouragement and belief in me that I feel able to attempt to make it in what is still a male dominated profession. God I think I could even try and break into even more staunch male bastions with the strength I get from her tremendous belief in my ability. My dad is great too though, I mean he is so unstereotypical – he has always shared the housework and the care of me when I was young; he's also not afraid to be seen crying, which I think shows strength not weakness. I know there are extreme feminists, who seem to detest men and blame them for the repression of women over the centuries, but you know what Mel, I think that men are victims of gender stereotyping as well. I mean women are also mothers and bring up both boys and girls and so they have a tremendous responsibility for the outcome. In a sense they often have more influence over children than the fathers because in most cases it's still the women who stay at home to bring the children up – even if they eventually go back to work."

"I agree with that Sally, I hate the artificial categorisation of men and women too - it's so restrictive. In fact I know two men who are just like that, caring, sensitive, artistic and yet not what anyone could define as wimps or effeminate." As she spoke one of those men walked into the restaurant with his companion a grim faced and somewhat over dressed Mr Brown, who seemed to be having great difficulty smiling or showing any form of enthusiasm whatsoever as Jonathan spoke to him. They found a table and, as she knew he would, he sensed her presence and looked over smiling genuinely at both girls. After they finished their food they sat with a glass of wine and talked some more about art, Isadora Duncan, (who Sally had never heard of but she would borrow one of Melissa's books when they got back), architecture and Melissa's interest in theatre design.

Sally said she was sure Mr Brown would not approve of the alcohol, but she was already eighteen so he could 'get stuffed'; then she added that she thought Mr Pritchard was not only gorgeous, but being an artist she was sure he was in touch with his feminine side. Melissa merely nodded her agreement and her inner pride knew no bounds – he was her lover and to her this praise from such an attractive articulate young woman was so gratifying. How she longed to be alone with him, it was becoming unbearable having him in such close proximity and not being able to even kiss him – yes, a kiss would suffice at the moment.

Melissa awoke on her seventeenth birthday to the discordant sounds of this Mediterranean city, redolent with a myriad of morning fragrances which combined to imbue her with a sense of anticipation and unequivocal delight. Everyone sang Happy Birthday to her at breakfast and there was a card from all the students which was a surprise. She knew that Jonathan had a present for her at home, some sort of surprise he had not revealed the details of, and she had a card from him which she had not brought in case someone saw it. He had written his own poem in the card and it was incredibly sensual and every word imbued with his love. As they all filtered out of the room, she felt a piece of paper being slipped into her hand and knew it was from him, hopefully he had extricated himself from the boring Mr Brown and they could spend this free day, her birthday, together. She told Sally she was spending her day alone, which Sally found perfectly acceptable as she also had plans and she deflected intrusive questions from her awful room mates who found it bizarre that someone would want to spend the day 'alone'. Some time later she found herself en route to Sitges along the coast with Jonathan in a hired car! He

177

said it had been difficult extricating himself from Mr Brown, but after all it was a free day for all and students had clear instructions in case of an emergency and so Mr Brown was on hand until three o'clock and he would be back to take over from that time.

"I had thought about driving us somewhere more cultural, but I expect we have both had enough of museums, architecture and even art for the time being. Apparently though, the old part of Sitges is wonderful and atmospheric to saunter around and to gently work off the excesses of lunch. If you really insist there is a small museum which I believe has some work by Picasso and my own favourite El Greco. But really all I want is some time with you my darling Mel; to hold you, walk along a beach in the sunshine and gaze into your beautiful face over a long lunch by the sea. Happy birthday my precious." She placed her hand on his thigh as he drove and in silence they enjoyed this time to relax together and look at the scenery, they were just two tourists incredibly in love and looking for a romantic place to have lunch and isolate themselves in each others eyes.

They walked along the beach and held hands so tightly they would discover red marks when they released them, and as soon as they left the sunbathers behind they clung to each other, bare feet in the warm sea, and experienced their first long languorous kiss in the hot sun of Spain. Melissa's desire soared with that kiss and she wanted more than anything else to find somewhere to make love with him and she told him so. Jonathan didn't see how it was possible when they hadn't yet had lunch and had to get back by two thirty so he could return the car and they could arrive back at the hotel separately. But he looked at her now and knew they must find a way to love each other on this beautiful day; he craved the taste of her body. The irrefutable hunger he felt for his darling Melissa far surpassed any need for food. So he booked a room in a small hotel and although the staff may have been somewhat surprised at the attractive couple who almost ran up the stairs devoid of luggage, they were circumspect enough to know that in the tourist business nothing was so very unusual!

They opened the curtains and the sun shone directly onto the double bed which soon bore witness to the most impassioned and uninhibited lovemaking Jonathan and Melissa had ever experienced and when Melissa found her whole body verging on the most intense and delicious orgasm, she drew her lover in to her even more deeply and their cries of joy so were so loud they thought the Guardia Civil would be summoned! They lay happily sated and totally amazed at the ferocity of their need for each other. The crumpled bedclothes on the floor, together with their clothes strewn about the place, made them reach for each other and laugh as they realised they had only been in the room for an hour and yet had managed to create such an appalling mess!

Jonathan led her to the bathroom and ran a deep bath for them, using the hotel's cheap sachet of bubble bath and as they lay facing each other he said, "Mel, I have never been so happy in my whole life and I want you to remember always, that you are the only woman I have *truly* loved – there will *never* be anyone else." It made her cry but he knew her tears were borne of their happiness. Now she looked so intently at him he felt she was boring a hole directly to his heart when she eventually whispered,

"Jonathan, say it will all be OK, we will get through my year in the Upper Sixth and then be together without all this secrecy. Say it will happen, tell me we will be together always. I need you so much and sometimes I feel frightened we won't make it."

He reached for her hand and placed the soapy fingers in his mouth, never taking his eyes off her for a moment, nibbling, almost biting them and as she moved towards him her still moist eyes appealing from their endless green depths, he said, "There is nothing, *nothing* I want more than to wake up and see your beautiful face next to mine every morning; there is nothing I want more than to love you and make you happy always and there is no-one who can part us my darling, not ever. Remember Mel - te amo siempre, I love you always." He motioned to her to turn around and as she came closer he encircled her with his legs. Then with her slender back to him he began to wash her, taking care not to wet her hair which she had twisted up on top of her head; as his hands reached around to rub the soap on her breasts and he simultaneously kissed the back of her neck their desire was again inflamed. They gently made love there in the suds of the warm bath and then as he wrapped her in the large white towel and carried her back to the bed it continued; rapturous, all encompassing and exquisite. They stood on the balcony for a time their arms wrapped around each other and looked at the sun dancing on the barely discernable ripples of the Mediterranean, creating an iridescent, transient latticework; the reflected light that captivated them was synonymous with their happiness.

Chapter eighteen

Jonathan Pritchard was becoming a very sought after local artist, but was totally unprepared for the commission he successfully negotiated on the Sunday after he returned from Barcelona. He was being served a veritable feast of tasty cholesterol, cooked as always by the inimitable Marian and served proudly by Bob in the garden of the village pub, when he was approached by a capacious, red faced middle aged man with a disarmingly charming smile. His manners, Jonathan supposed, had been subverted by the superficial and magnetic charisma he so obviously thought he possessed; furthermore he clearly thought it appropriate to enter into negotiations with an artist when he was about to play a game of Russian roulette with his heart! The aforementioned person who gave his name as Mark Beardsley, sat in such close proximity to Jonathan he could almost have masticated the food for him! Jonathan understandably was unnerved by him and, as all that had been exchanged so far were names, he wondered about the dubious intent of someone who could watch him eat with such concentrated fascination.

He spoke now after Jonathan had spent an uncomfortable fifteen minutes attempting to eat his food in a nonchalant manner, occasionally glancing with disbelief at this outrageously preposterous interloper. "Eh lad I bet you enjoyed that wholesome food, I say what you having for pudding – I might just join yer." Bloody hell thought Jonathan, what audacity, who does he think he is, purporting to be on such familiar terms with me. I am positive I have never seen him before in my life either in this pub or anywhere else and I think by now I know most of the locals. Yes, he knew the locals, for hadn't they teased him mercilessly after word had spread about the beautiful redhead he had taken on numerous occasions to his cottage. Speculation and supposition had been rife and he had been cornered about it and had reluctantly revealed that the young woman, who he would not name, was his model. Eyes had been cast heavenward, knowing glances had been exchanged between the men, and women had gossiped discovering an element of jealousy in their interest; for who wouldn't want to model for the gorgeous Jonathan Pritchard and him such a gentle and good mannered young man! Some even said they would willingly take off their clothes and model in the buff if he asked – many of those expressing this risqué view were well into their sixties!

Miss Glossop who did not frequent the public house had learnt of the growing celebrity of her tenant with pride; she knew he would not disappoint her – life drawings and a veritable bohemian lifestyle to boot! She would have to ask him to show her some of these nude drawings and paintings, perhaps she would be able to deduce from them who was modelling for him. She knew of course that his model must be his lover for it went with the territory didn't it, raw passion and then tragedy, hadn't she read it over and over again? No good ever came from being an artist's model, the prospects were poor to say the least – unwanted babies, drug addiction or agonising suicides seemed to be the norm!

"Do I know you Sir?" Jonathan asked politely.

"No lad but I know you, well I know *of you* let me say."

"So in what capacity do you 'know of me' and what can I do for you? I usually come here to the pub for a quiet Sunday lunch and then a read of the Sunday Times, it's one of the few relaxing days I have," he replied pointedly.

"Well, I have a factory near Manchester, handed down to me by me father and so I want you to know I'm not short of a bob or two. OK lad?" He sat up now as if someone had pushed an iron rod up inside the back of his jacket, a ventriloquist's dummy rigid with pride. "Aye I have a bit of brass and I want to give some of it to you lad."

Jonathan continued to be mystified at this eccentric behaviour; he had absolutely no idea what this man was inferring. So he waited patiently for the explanation which he assumed would be forthcoming or he would get up immediately and take his paper back to the garden of the cottage and read it in peace with a glass of beer.

"Aye lad, you see I have a fancy for a painting for me and the wife to hang in us bedroom; you know lad a bit saucy– spice up the old love life eh? I have a photo 'ere of what we want, it's from a magazine, you know a bit high brow an all that!" He thrust a crumpled copy of Goya's *The Naked Maja* at him and Jonathan's opinion of the man changed in an instant. OK he was not sophisticated and called the wonderful painting 'saucy' but in fact that was exactly the colloquial term which may have been used when Goya presented it in 1800. In Spanish art few nudes were painted before this and most certainly none had been so obviously sensuous. Goya had even been questioned by the Spanish Inquisition about both this and its sister painting *The Clothed Maja*. "So what do ye think lad?"

Jonathan was very interested in the commission and was curious how this Manchester business man had heard of him. Mr Beardsley said that apparently the young artist Jonathan Pritchard was getting quite a reputation hereabouts and even his own cousin who lived in-between here and Manchester had seen some of his work in the local library and indeed in this pub. As he had called at the pub a few times on his travels and seen the work for himself he had been 'right impressed' and now that he knew Jonathan painted nudes, well he had found his man 'so to speak'. Jonathan said he would be happy to take the commission, they discussed terms and further details and Jonathan made copious notes. After exchanging phone numbers, addresses, a retaining cheque and other essential information, Mr Beardsley left giving the disarmed Jonathan a hearty thump on the back. One thing Mr Beardsley was disappointed about however was Jonathan's strict rule about his working regime, under no circumstances would he be allowed to watch the artist at work and see the young model.

So for the month of July at least he would have more than one night a week with his darling Melissa and a bonus was the four Sundays they would spend together whilst Melissa modelled, before Jonathan went to Spain for a month with Jack. Jack and Melissa, Melissa and Jack – he thought endlessly and inconclusively about his dilemma. The two most important people in his life, together with his dearest irreplaceable mamma of course, and yet he must continue this polarised and draining compartmentalisation for another year or so. Jack who would adore Melissa and vice versa must be kept isolated for the sake of propriety and in order to protect his career. He knew the month away would be almost unbearable now he had won his Mel, loved her so wildly and so utterly – how they would survive without each others symbiotic presence he dared not ponder.

He knew she was going to be working in Woolworths for the summer to develop some financial independence from Carol who seemed on the edge; he worried about the mental state of Melissa's mother. He also worried about the attention she received from young men of her own age. Perhaps she would decide it was all too fraught, too complicated this loving an older man whom she had to see clandestinely. He worried that she would be courted by Luke again. He just worried – his insecurity at times so unnervingly transparent.

Melissa was modelling for the Goya commission and he thought she looked incomparable as she assumed the pose of the original model who was shorter and not as slender as Mel. He had spoken at length to the inimitable Mr Beardsley and described the physical differences between his own model and Goya's and it had been agreed that Melissa's long voluptuous red hair would be left loose and flowing but would not obscure her breasts. They were talking now, the artist and his model, about their trip to Lake Coniston which had been the 'birthday treat' Jonathan had organised; they had stayed overnight, under the guise of Susan's flat, and spent two romantic days walking, sketching, enjoying long languorous lunches and making love, both in the hotel and in pretty secluded woodland they had stumbled across. The rain had held off despite the brooding skies and it had been surprisingly warm as they delighted in their stolen and enchanted time together.

Melissa spoke without moving position, something quite difficult for a young woman who was inclined to gesticulate animatedly when speaking, "Darling, I have been seriously considering the direction I want to take with my art when I go to college and I am firmly set on design. My dream I suppose is to become a theatre designer despite the precarious nature of the business; I suppose it's what I have been leaning towards since the end of the fifth form. Do you think it's too risky or do you think I have good chance of making a living in that field?"

Jonathan continued painting as he replied, "In all honesty Mel I don't think it's any more uncertain working in the theatre than it is in any other art form. For instance if you decided to become a fine artist or a free-lance interior designer do you think you would be in work all the time? I think whatever you choose to do unless you restrict your creativity, you will have times when you worry about paying the bills and finding the money for the next meal. If you are lucky you will land on your feet and never experience those privations, but that is unusual. You have an incredible talent and the mental capacity to assess the requirements of the field you choose to work in and I know without doubt that you will succeed; it may take some time to establish yourself but I believe you have the right approach and that is half the battle." He smiled across at her now and asked if she needed a break or could he continue for just fifteen minutes more and then they would make some lunch.

"I'm fine Jonathan really, we can go on for a while longer, I wouldn't want to stop the creative flow!" Then she asked him if he would look at a sketch book she had been compiling which was purely based on designs for play sets. She explained that she had been building up this portfolio for about six months and had not shown it to anyone yet. She had written a fictional director's brief, or vision, for each of the plays she had created designs for, and then she had made scale drawings of the sets and sample stage furniture and scenery.

There was one play, *A Doll's House* by Henrik Ibsen, written in 1879, which had fired her imagination so much with its associated contemporary controversy and its very modern themes, that she had tentatively created a scale model from her drawings. She told him she had been inspired by Gordon Craig and another director/designer she had discovered, Vsevolod Meyerhold. "Even though the play was in essence naturalistic, a 'drama of contemporary life', as Ibsen had called it, when I worked on the designs, I really felt that the symbolic set I eventually created amplified Nora's growing realisation that she did not have a tangible marriage and must leave both her husband and her children." Jonathan was intrigued and asked her to bring them next time, but also said she should show them to Mr Brown, her personal tutor, and ask him to assess whether or not they should form part of the overall portfolio to take to her interviews for Art School. He asked her about the play and why it was controversial in its day and she told him:

"Well Ibsen's character Nora ultimately makes a decision to leave not only her husband, with whom she feels she has had a meaningless marriage, but her children as well. At the time it was considered a scandal. Of course society thought that a woman would never leave her children it 'went against nature'. In fact Ibsen was persuaded to write an alternative ending for its performance in Germany whereby Nora was led to the children's bedroom by her husband Torvald and when she saw them sleeping she relented, declaring she could not desert them. I still think society looks more unfavourably on a woman who leaves her children than when a man makes the same decision; what do you think Jonathan?"

"Yes you are right Mel, but I think in some ways it does seem unnatural for a woman to leave her children because unlike a man she has carried them in her womb and then endured the pain of giving birth and so must have a much stronger bond than a father. Even though I have just said that, I could not feel closer to my son and yet *I* left didn't I?" He looked forlorn as he spoke, his eyes and voice projected his regret and Melissa began then to talk of other things, for soon her Jonathan would leave her and she wanted each moment they spent together to be happy ones.

So as she lay naked on the chaise-longue, posing for a painting that would eventually adorn the bedroom of a portly Manchester businessman and his invisible wife, she gently recited a poem for her lover. She caressed him with her voice and entered his soul with her eyes as the room filled with Shakespeare's words and those that echoed and etched themselves in Jonathan's psyche would be recalled again and again throughout his life:

> ....*Love is not love*
> *Which alters when it alteration finds,*
> *Or bends with the remover to remove:*
> *Oh no! it is an ever fixed mark,*
> *That looks on tempests and is never shaken*........

July seemed to pass by far too quickly for Melissa and Jonathan; both working hard, Melissa at Woolworths and Jonathan at school completing admin and forward planning. Before they knew it he was setting off for London to pick up Jack and leave his beloved Melissa for a whole month. The last time they made love was two days before he left and they lay on the white sheets of his bed naked, warmed by the soothing air of a balmy July evening. Both were crying softly, their tears mingling as they kissed a sea of regret: regret that they could not share Spain together, regret that the subterfuge must continue for another year and regret that they would not experience the exquisite rapture of their passion for each other for so long. So as Jonathan took his Melissa back to the uncertain atmosphere of her own home and their fingers caressed each others features, they kissed one last hungry time, blissfully unaware of the import of the events which would occur this August in Spain.

Jonathan and Jack were not flying from Manchester's Ringway Airport this summer because it had been impossible for Lydia to bring Jack up to Lancashire as her current gruelling work schedule precluded any flexibility. Jonathan had booked them return flights from London and had no option about overnight accommodation; he would have to stay with Lydia. He dearly hoped he could divert Lydia's disconcerting sole topic of conversation and persuade her to talk about Jack, the holiday, her work, his work – anything really except her hopes that they could give their marriage another try. Jonathan was exhausted when he arrived at the house and in some respects was grateful that his son was asleep, even though Lydia told him that Jack had begged her to let him stay up and although she had acquiesced he had not managed to stay awake. Lydia had carried his sleepy little body upstairs and now she motioned for Jonathan to go up and kiss him before sitting down to the light supper of fresh bread and an avocado and prawn salad, accompanied by a good bottle of chilled Soave.

Lydia had placed the supper on the table in the kitchen and when Jonathan entered, after gently kissing his precious boy goodnight, he was shocked immeasurably when he saw her face fully illuminated by the somewhat stark fluorescent light. She looked so ill; he did not recall her mentioning any illness the last time they had spoken. He had not actually seen her for some six weeks or so because the last time he had been with Jack he had stayed at their friends Maggie and Jock's house for the weekend and Maggie had generously collected Jack from school. Maggie and Jock saw Lydia much more frequently than Jonathan and had managed that most difficult of diplomatic feats – to stay friendly with both parties when the relationship ends.

They were genuine and sensitive people whom Jonathan had met when he was nineteen and training to be a teacher, shortly before Lydia had entered all their lives seeming like a breath of fresh air at the time. They had effortlessly fused as an inseparable group, enjoying the vibrancy and excitement of this wonderful city which Lydia proudly showed them in all its burgeoning chic which would be unveiled with an unceremonious flourish in the next decade. So they had remained friends throughout the sixties when London had become a magnet to hordes of young people who came seeking a magical elixir which would transport them to their own ideas of heaven. As Jonathan, Lydia, Jock and Maggie so often observed though, the well packaged fiction of London crumbled effortlessly when reality in all its unpalatable manifestations invariably took hold.

He must speak now, because even though Lydia was managing to smile and beckoned him to sit down and eat his meal, he knew without doubt that there was something seriously wrong. If she was ill why hadn't Jack mentioned that his mummy was poorly when they spoke on the phone last week and, furthermore, why hadn't Maggie or Jock told him she was so unwell? He needed to tread carefully especially after recent meetings and more pointedly his manoeuvrings to avoid such meetings, because he knew how sensitive she had become. Jonathan also recalled those awful times when they had argued almost continuously just prior to their separation and he had no wish to revisit that unpleasant terrain.

He spoke softly, "Lydia is everything OK at work? I ask because you used to be able to organise some time off just before I took Jack away during the summer, even if was only a day. It seems that you have a much more stressful workload now and there seems to be much less flexibility for staff who have children, let alone those who have sole care of those children. I know its been difficult between us over the last eighteen months or so but I do care about you and to be honest you do look tired – actually you really don't look so well." He was so unprepared for what happened next it made him speechless. Lydia slumped onto the table knocking over the plate of salad and just missing sending her glass of wine careering to the floor and sobbed uncontrollably, each shudder permeating her whole body like a series of mild electric shocks. As the sobbing escalated Jonathan was overwhelmed with pity, he had never witnessed such crying and lack of control in Lydia since the day she had smashed their crystal goblets in an argument many years previously. He moved over to her, took her in his arms and just held her for what seemed like an eternity until very slowly the weeping subsided and her breathing was imbued with the shuddering spasmodic aftermath that remains after such a deluge of sorrow.

She was barely audible when she managed to whisper, "I'm sorry, so sorry Jon."

"Don't be sorry, why should you be sorry? Something is worrying you or clearly upsetting you deeply so you have every right to cry - come on Lydia take this tissue and wipe your eyes." She seemed unable to move and remained frozen in the moment utterly forlorn like the person out of focus in a badly composed photograph. Soon she began trembling perceptibly, her face ravaged from the onslaught of tears so Jonathan lifted her face up and wiped her eyes and then her nose and led her into the living room where he sat her like a child on the sofa and placed himself next to her. Something he had realised as he had held her in the kitchen was now patently obvious, Lydia had lost so much weight she was physically frail; her previous robust health and curvaceous body, seemed to have wasted away even since he last saw her. What was happening? He worried amidst this unexpected crisis, worried in case she misunderstood his kindness and concern, because even though he had made it blatantly clear that they would not be getting back together, these actions could be misconstrued and so he sat next to her but did not hold her now.

"Lydia tell me what's wrong – please? I don't want to seem intrusive but we have always been friends, haven't we? We started off that way and I want to be your friend now and help if you'll let me. Please Lydia, I'm worried." He took her limp hand hoping it would encourage her to confide in him. God how could he go away with their son and leave her in this awful state?

"I really don't know, Jon. I feel tired all the time and weepy and well…… well if you really want to know, I feel like a failure." Lydia's tears began to flow again and Jonathan would have been less than a friend, less than the sensitive man he clearly was if he had not held her now, softly stroking her face which was soaked with her tears.

"You a failure? You Lydia are one of the most successful women, no people, I know. You have held down a very responsible job and cared for our son alone since we broke up. You are beautiful and talented and more importantly you are the best mother any child could have, so how you can say you have failed I really don't know."

"Well, it's just the way I feel, I really don't think I am being good at either of my roles at the moment; I am like a zombie at work because I feel so tired and I don't have any patience with our lovely Jack. I didn't even manage to keep you or David, so I am pretty much a failure with men as well aren't I?" She searched for the tissue which was disintegrating in her hands and Jonathan passed her a new one, still feeling rather uncomfortable with this physical closeness after last year's events at his cottage. But he cared for her and she needed his comfort; she was the mother of his wonderful son and she was clearly beyond the first stages of stress from what he knew of the condition. He thought she was very run down and depressed and he asked her if she had been to the doctor.

Lydia sniffed ineffectually as her nose continued to run in pace with her tears, so she gave up trying to resist and just dabbed at the various fluids invading her face. She looked up at Jonathan, love so clear in her eyes it shocked him with its audacity, its ability to make her so transparently vulnerable despite her evident distress which should take prominence in his thoughts. She spoke with more control, "When do I get chance to go to the doctor, Jon? I barely find time for everything I need to do each day as it is. Since my promotion I seem to have almost double the amount of admin to deal with and I don't need to tell you how difficult it can be managing a team of very diverse and occasionally volatile staff. I don't know, I just feel like I need a break and I am sure that would sort everything out. I expect I need a tonic or something from the chemist." Her body became limp, fragile and almost folded into his as he held her like a child who needed firstly comfort and then firm guidance. For although Jonathan respected Lydia and her abilities he sensed that what she really needed now was someone to tell her what to do, to take her by the hand if necessary and make her help herself.

"Right, firstly as Jack and I don't fly until tomorrow evening, we are all going to the doctor's in the morning and Jack and I will wait in the waiting room, but I am not taking no for an answer Lydia. Secondly I want you to tell me honestly why you have lost so much weight and I mean honestly Lydia; God I have never known you to lose so much weight even when you went so thin for a time after Jack was born. When you have told me, I want you to promise to say exactly the same thing to the doctor tomorrow. Lydia, *Lydia*……..look at me and just nod if you cannot talk just yet; just nod Lydia and promise you will tell the doctor everything." She nodded and he sighed with as yet circumspect relief.

Jonathan warmed some brandy for her whilst she went for a shower and when she was ensconced on the sofa with him she revealed that she was not eating properly although it was not a contrived or premeditated act it was a by product of her long days. She said that once she had collected Jack from the after school childminder and fed him, given him some attention and love, she really did not feel like food. She was too tired to make the effort to cook or even make some toast, so she went to bed early but invariably could not sleep because work associated problems invaded the peace she fruitlessly sought. She also worried about the effect her long hours were having on Jack especially after her relationship with David ended because they really had got on so well and David took the trouble to take Jack out if she was too busy at weekends. One thing she admitted about David was his ability to actually persuade her to leave the work and enjoy at least one outing with him and Jack every weekend, he had said it was essential or she would be a 'slave to the job'.

"Lydia why did you split up with David then if you had such a great relationship and he was so obviously fond of Jack?"

"Because he asked me to marry him and I told him I couldn't." She gazed fixedly into the depths of the brandy glass and as Jonathan's mouth opened to form the words he could have replied for her before he even asked the pointless question.

"Why couldn't you have married him once the divorce came through?"

"Jon you know why: because I still love you and I don't want a divorce, I want us to be a family again." She was clearly embarrassed but met his eyes as she added "But even though I realise now that you don't want that to happen, I couldn't keep seeing him after he proposed and discovered my feelings for you. It would have been dishonest. I still feel like a failure though because I am clearly not moving on as you seem to be. The sad thing is that we are not best friends anymore and I know it's my fault Jon, I know it and I miss us being friends." She moved away from him now as if the words had by their very utterance, demanded the establishment of demarcation zones. Jonathan who was feeling decidedly hungry actually felt relieved, relieved that she was able to talk about what was troubling her and relieved that he did not feel so angry or even uncomfortable as he had felt only months ago. A vision of his wonderful Melissa danced across his imagination and he found solace in her strength and beauty and knew instinctively that she would feel empathy with Lydia, for one of Melissa's most endearing qualities was her innate compassion.

The doctor said Lydia was anaemic and suffering from exhaustion and unsurprisingly he also told her that she was severely underweight. She must take time off work, he insisted even though she protested her indispensability which he countered by saying that no-one, not even he was indispensable and that a sick manager was of no use to anyone. She would not improve her health whilst continuing to work, she must take two weeks off initially and he would see her again and assess whether or not he though another two weeks sick leave were appropriate. He had prescribed various medications but had also given her a special diet sheet after she had revealed what little she had been eating over the last few months. She must gradually build up her strength and could not suddenly attack her body with copious amounts of inappropriate food.

Jonathan was relieved and Jack, who had clearly been worried about his mummy but not wanted to bother Daddy who lived too far away to help, told her he would bring her back a special edible present from his abuela and new abuelo who knew the right food for sick people! She promised to rest and Jonathan in turn promised to call to check she was indeed following instructions. As she drove away from the airport she could barely see the road for the tears that once again careered relentlessly down her face.

Chapter nineteen

"Cariño it is for you - the telephone; it is the cold fish, she cry so much I hardly hear her words. Come cariño take the phone I must go back to my kitchen." Maria Luisa wiped her hands on her apron, handed the phone to Jonathan and went back to her favourite and sacred domain, her kitchen, where Jack was waiting with earnest anticipation to help abuela make the ice-cream! It infuriated Jonathan when his mamma called Lydia 'the cold fish' because it was so far from the truth; Lydia was sensitive and caring. Now she had said that this very same 'cold fish' was crying which was such an obvious contradiction in terms he was amazed she didn't realise it as she spoke!

Jonathan and Jack had been in Spain for almost two weeks and Lydia did not seem to be improving at all; in fact the two calls he had made to her had been disturbing for him and positively upsetting for Jack. Usually Jack was so carefree and blissfully happy when they came here and indeed the first few days when he was under the assumption, presumably, that his daddy had sorted his mummy's problems out, he *was* euphoric. He was being given more copious love and affection than ever, his new abuelo surprising them all with his ability to give Jack undivided attention, make him laugh with his somewhat outlandish humour and indulge him as if he was the only child on earth. Jonathan presumed he was making up for not being given the opportunity to be a parent to him when his mamma went to England and denied him, not only the chance to be a father but, the very knowledge that Jonathan was indeed his own son. He was beginning to understand and like this straightforward, occasionally diffident, man who had loved his mother and only her for all these years, and he was overjoyed at how much more fulfilled and youthful his mamma seemed since the marriage. Watching them as they shared their undisguised physical affection for each other, being openly tactile and so obviously passionately in love, served as a testament to the power that love, in all its manifestations, had over all other aspects of life. He felt the same elation when he thought of his beautiful Melissa whom he had spoken to only once since he came; the logistics of organising to telephone when she would be by the phone to receive the call had proved almost impossible so they had arranged for her to be at Susan's flat for the next call and Jonathan couldn't wait to hear her voice and her unconstrained words of love.

A few days ago Jack had asked quite innocently if his mummy could come to Spain and get well here in the sunshine with them. Jonathan envied him his wonderful naivety, his ability to be straightforward and utterly frank, untarnished as yet by the complexities of adult relationships. How he wished he could just answer in the affirmative, knowing Lydia would accept the gesture as one of simple friendship and knowing he would not hurt Melissa by inviting his estranged wife to Spain where she was precluded. It was incongruous: it was perfectly acceptable for Lydia to visit and see her son even though Maria Luisa did not like her, but Melissa whom both she and Jack would adore, was denied this pleasure because of society's hypocrisy. If only Melissa had been at another school, he had the instinctive feeling that his mamma would not mind the difference in their ages, especially since she had revealed her own remarkable love story. Now, after placing the phone back on the table, he had no option but to ask his mamma and Mario if Lydia could visit, because he was seriously concerned for her and did not want her to be alone in her struggle to regain her health. Jack wanted it too and he knew it was the only conceivable choice to make. Was he betraying Mel? He hoped she would understand as he had eventually learnt to accept her need to comfort and care for Luke when he was suffering.

Maria Luisa was not enamoured of the arrangements but knowing how loving and forgiving her son was (for the break up of the marriage was surely the fault of the cold fish who did not cook and was not attending to her cariño in the bedroom), she began to organise the little house with her characteristic gusto. Without questioning Jonathan, or Antonio, as her wonderful Mario insisted on calling his newly acquired hijo, she moved Jack into the small living room on the sofa bed so that her son and his wife could be alone. OK she never like her, that one with her take away meals, her cold eyes and her dark temper, but she was sick and must be cared for, eat plenty the home cook food, and also her handsome boy he need a woman. After all, she introduce him to the most beautiful local girls and he never show any interest – not at all, and he never mention the love with another woman, so he must still love this cold English fish – this Lydia. She knew her dearest Jack he always talking in the kitchen when he help her with the cooking, how he want his mummy and daddy to be together again, so maybe this way she help. This way, Lydia she get better and be a good woman to her boy, even learn the cooking in the Spanish way.

Jonathan was stunned when his mamma revealed the bedroom arrangements and yet he could not openly say anything to upset her because she had so obviously tried to do what she thought right and was making an effort to be nice to Lydia. He saw how shocked she was when he brought Lydia in from the car and when they spoke privately together Maria Luisa said she thought Lydia needed more than another two weeks off work to get better, "She no more than a vine twig now, it will take very long to get her plump and beautiful again so she be the good wife to you cariño. Maybe she learn from me now – to cook and have the even temper and then soon you have the good time in the bedroom and my lovely Jack he get the brother or the sister."

Jonathan could not help smiling at his inimitable mother's perverse logic and as he went into the bedroom he now shared with Lydia he was still smiling when he found her asleep on Jack's bed, which had been moved by Maria Luisa to lie directly next to his. She looked a little better already he thought as he lightly covered her with a sheet, nothing else was necessary as it was unbearably hot outside but the design of the old house ensured the bedroom was relatively cool. He would have to cope with his already burgeoning guilt, because it really would be difficult to explain to Melissa the necessity for Lydia to be sleeping in the same bedroom and, until she met his mamma, she would probably view the arrangements with incredulity. He would wait until he got back to England to explain because the distance and the longing that lay between them would make her feel insecure, as he himself would undoubtedly feel if the situation was reversed.

As Lydia gradually improved and Jack delighted in showing her everything and introducing her, in Spanish, to everyone in the village, Jonathan discovered he was having a pleasurable time. He saw Lydia improving day by day; his son was thoroughly enjoying having both parents together here at his special place for the first time; his mamma genuinely concerned for her daughter-in-law's health was taking Lydia under her wing and Lydia herself raised not a single objection. It was as if she was coming home he thought with utter surprise; he had imagined the Lydia of old becoming irritated by his mother's at times suffocating but well meaning ministering but astonishingly the sick Lydia seemed charmed and incredibly relaxed. She had told him that the doctor had signed her off work for a month and despite her disappointment, because she genuinely wanted to go back to work to ensure her department was running efficiently and to deal with the presumably mounting paperwork, she had accepted that she really could not recover if she did not heed his advice. Her store, a large department store in central London where she had been working for four years since leaving Selfridges, had been extremely understanding and the Personnel Manager had even told her that he had felt she was overworking and had noticed a marked deterioration in her physical appearance. He had even apologised and said it was remiss of him not to have offered her help prior to this crisis, her job was of course safe and she must take whatever time she required to get fully better, the store valued her greatly as an employee.

Jonathan sat outside on the terrace a few days before the holiday was to end and as he watched Lydia now, sitting in the garden shaded by a large imposing old cypress tree, he found himself experiencing an unexpected surge of tenderness towards her. Jack had placed her in between himself and Mario and was enthusiastically and simultaneously acting as both translator and teacher. Jack had proved to be the tonic Lydia had supposed she needed to get better, and now it showed in the embryonic glow subtly returning to her cheeks. The sun kissed her skin and warmed her to the core, the multifarious chorus of summer's sweet song diminished her stress, and the perennially blue skies opened up her heart to all those who were so assiduously caring for her. She went on long walks with alternate nursemaids, himself included, and had not once made him feel uncomfortable or worried that she might raise the subject of their marriage once again. She was becoming a great confidant of his mother and they were often ensconced in the kitchen for hours talking animatedly and occasionally giggling. Maria Luisa's only comment when Jonathan asked about their talks was, "You see cariño mio if you listen to mamma all that time ago and you bring your Lydia to my country she be thawed before now. Now she lose her fish scales, her skin grow golden and her blood it become fire in the Spanish sun; maybe your heart find the passion again for her querido? You make Jack very happy if you be together again with her and Jack you know is the most important one of all, sí cariño?"

The last night of the holiday was a hedonistic fiesta in the garden of his mamma's house. Despite the lack of a Saint to rejoice or a reason other than the sheer enjoyment of each other and the celebration of life itself, many of the villagers filtered in and stayed for varying lengths of time. Old Jamie the local gardener was still there when the first cock crowed the next day. They found him lying slumped on the terrace, his face and clothes endearingly crumpled; he was sleeping like a baby but snoring discordantly as only an inebriated man could! Jonathan was amazed that he had managed to sleep for hours whilst still clutching his half full bottle of rough red wine! His mamma laughed as she said, 'Don't worry cariño; he will finish it with his breakfast!' There was impromptu music and much dancing; Jack was almost sick from eating too much ice-cream but although Lydia swore he looked a luminous green about his face, he would not desist from his attempts to eat more than his friend Paco from the village.

Jonathan was delirious about his return home to his Melissa and had thought of nothing else all day; her smile permeated his field of vision. Whenever he had been alone sketching or walking in the hills, he had felt he could almost reach out and touch her; images of her mercilessly invaded and then toyed with all his senses amplifying both his mental and physical frustration beyond endurance. Even when he had spent a day painting in Toledo it was not the atmosphere of the city, redolent with the history of thousands of Jews, Moors and Christians or even the magnificent El Greco, but Melissa herself who was his Muse. At night he longed to have her by his side and although he was more than gratified that Lydia's health was so visibly improving, it was torture to have the woman he wanted only to befriend lying next to him, in place of the woman he wanted to make love to all night.

The surprises spewed forth like the froth from the sparkling cava which had been flowing all night: Lydia was to spend the next two weeks here with Maria Luisa and Mario; Jack had told the whole village that his mummy and daddy were properly married again now because they went to sleep together – all this said with various flavours and colours of ice-cream smudged around his happy little face; Maria Luisa had hugged Lydia and said to her face that she was wrong, Lydia was 'not the cold fish, she just a bit too reserved in the English way but getting more Spanish all the time and like the proper daughter'; Lydia danced and laughed more than Jonathan could remember in years; Jonathan had called Mario 'pappa' for the first time and both of them cried like babies before they drank a toast to each other! All this occurring amidst Maria Luisa's squeals of happiness and declarations that her life had never been so *perfecto!*

It was warm and still when finally Lydia and Jonathan went to their bedroom and after undressing some distance apart and climbing into their beds, the hypnotic lullaby of the Spanish countryside penetrated through the open windows inducing sleep. Lydia said simply - her voice a barely audible sigh of happiness, "Thank you Jon, I will be grateful always." He knew without hearing her cry that there were tears on her face, he saw without looking that there was unconditional love in her eyes and he knew without any doubt whatsoever that he had caused her health to suffer and the pain to linger in her heart impeding her recovery. He lay in deepest thought, sleep eluding him as he took himself back through the years and watched the movie of their relationship playing without intermission. He found himself wondering why they had not tried to heal the wounds of their once solid marriage knowing they had the responsibility of this wonderful and fragile child's life in their hands. He knew he had never felt about Lydia the all encompassing passionate love he now experienced with Melissa, but they had once been happy, so very happy.

Now it was Jonathan who felt lost, he had disturbed the still waters creating a deluge of unwanted feelings; guilt and regret poured from his eyes in torrents and he was absolutely incapable of containing it. She woke and held him, rocked him until the crying ceased and asked no questions; she was discovering now that there were tangible demons in all their lives who tore at their respective equilibriums without mercy. There were sorrows buried so deep that even the most joyous and ecstatic moments could not obliterate their need to rise to the surface occasionally. They served to remind us that the very source of the current happiness was also that which had caused our pain; the two were not the antithesis of each other but incontrovertibly bound. Without contrivance, or even a frisson of sexual intent, they gently kissed each other and, without expecting anything in return, she told him she loved him and always would and she would wait, wait with their son Jack, for him to come back to them. Jonathan looked deep into her eyes which shone their sincerity in the darkness and stroked her face as he was about to tell her he loved someone else and could not come back. But he knew he could not hurt her with these words and diminish her need to hope; Lydia had endured enough pain and now she must get well. So he kissed her cheek and they fell asleep in each others arms, which is where Jack found them the next morning when he brought them their coffee.

Jack thought it was as if Christmas and his birthday had come at once when he woke his mummy and daddy who were sure to be living in the same house together again very soon. He loved it when Mummy smiled and especially when she giggled, it made him feel really happy and now Daddy and Mummy were not arguing and seemed to be such good friends so maybe Daddy would come back to London, because Mummy had such an important job she *must* stay there. Daddy could go back to his old school to teach and they could all go to the park together and on the bus into London to the museums and have ice-cream when they finished being serious. Mummy had said it was *not* OK to run around and laugh loudly or disturb other people when they went to museums, or sometimes to art galleries when Daddy had been with them. So when they were at last allowed to be normal again she often bought him the ice-cream of his choice; once she even laughed so loud he thought she would collapse from it and fall on the ground because she couldn't stop! When he asked why his mummy was laughing so much she told him he must be the only little boy in London who wanted an ice-cream when it was so cold; she said something about it being almost freezing or something. But it was always good to have ice-cream wasn't it? If they sold it, it must be OK and why could a boy not have his ice-cream just because he was wearing gloves and a scarf and his thick winter jacket?

When Lydia dropped them off at the airport, retaining the little car Jonathan had hired, her face seemed transformed; she was resigned to wait and Jonathan sensed that she believed without doubt that he would return to her. She was stronger now thanks solely to his mamma and Jack whose unwavering love had soothed and healed, and so she lifted Jack clear off the ground and swung him round until he was dizzy. Lydia thought that perhaps she had overdone it as she saw the airport departure terminal spin even after she had placed Jack firmly on the ground! Jonathan caught her as she began to keel over and they both laughed as Jack looked on bemused and then for Jack the most wonderful thing happened; his daddy picked him up and they all hugged together, encased with love, like a proper family and Daddy even kissed Mummy's cheek. He knew it – they really *were* a family again and the best thing about Mummy staying in Spain to get better was that he would be living with Maggie and Jock for a while and they always had nice things in their fridge and let him stay up half an hour longer than Mummy did. So it *was* like his birthday and Christmas had arrived together!

On the plane journey Jonathan was deep in thought as an exhausted Jack slept against him; his thoughts were solely about Melissa and whether or not she would understand if he told her he had kissed Lydia. He was certain she would understand the need for Lydia to be in Spain because she was a remarkable young woman with an unequalled capacity for compassion. Should he tell her about the events that occurred in the middle of last night – explain his remorse, his relentless guilt for causing the break up of his family and thus making Jack vulnerable? He knew now that Jack had been insecure, even though all the outward signs had refuted this supposition, the transparency of Jack's plight had been so obvious on this visit to Spain. He was an intelligent and sensitive boy who desired to please both his parents and knew they both loved him deeply even though they had parted; these attempts to please meant he had concealed his pain and silenced his voice. Had they both asked he would have sung his hopes of reconciliation to the rooftops, he would have revealed his pain and then he would have asked his daddy to come back.

Jonathan knew that now; when he had left London and both he and Lydia had made huge efforts to compensate and ensure their son was well adjusted – they had utterly misinterpreted his reaction. They thought it was working, this modern approach. But their ability to be friends and speak civilly to each other was as painful sometimes for Jack as if they had become enemies, never speaking and avoiding all contact. They had kissed - Jack's mother and father – kissed as ex lovers expressing their regret for the pain, offering comfort when the darkness amplified their tangled emotions. Jack's mother found in that kiss a tangible thread of hope and Jack's father found confusion and torment.

Chapter twenty

Melissa was feeling rather drunk! She sat with Sally and Luke in the Eagle - a pub with a vast inner cobbled courtyard, where hordes of young people gathered at weekends, and a place well known for its seeming leniency regarding under-age drinking! The leniency stemmed more from an insufficiency of available and diligent staff, rather than from a positive policy to break the law. This veritable magnet with its vibrant and carefree atmosphere had drawn in the three friends and although they were all laughing and relishing each other's company, only one of them laughed with her eyes. Sally was not, unlike Melissa, desperately missing an older and clandestine lover; Sally was not, unlike Luke, concealing a yearning for a friend who was also once a lover. Both Melissa and Luke were astutely and successfully concealing their respective dilemmas and for the moment Sally was utterly ignorant of either of her new friends' emotional entanglements.

"I've decided to take a gap year before I start my course at university," Sally now said soberly. "I need to earn some money to supplement my grant and also I have managed to get work experience on Fridays at a well respected firm of architects in Manchester. But they will not be paying me, although they said that if I work out they may be able to give me the train fare! So in effect I will be working all the time, with Sunday being my only rest day. Do you know what? I'll probably slob out all day, not even get dressed and watch crap on the telly until the evening and then perhaps I'll meet up with you two and get totally drunk! Only joking – after all I will have to get up for bloody work at the crack of dawn and you two will still be at school! Saturday should be the night when we meet up, it's more logical as we can all sleep-in the next morning and take the whole day to recover!" Sally liked a drink especially with these two new friends, and now she was discovering she really liked Luke; OK she had always thought he was very good looking, she'd seen him around the Sixth Form, but now she knew him better she found she adored his mind. He was so in touch with his feminine self, so sensitive and yet very strong, artistic and really rather rugged. For Sally he had the perfect combination of sexuality and sensitivity combined with an astute and almost innate empathy with girls.

Melissa was forcibly dragged from the delicious, slightly inebriated, reverie of her and Jonathan having passionate sex, by this need to converse and was gratified because her very palpable frustration was becoming unbearable. It would be over a week before they could be together; she would have started in the Upper Sixth and from what she had observed it was going to be tough and even more demanding than the past year had been. It was not the thought of hard work that disturbed her thoughts now, but what she sensed had not been said when Jonathan rang her last week. It was difficult to rationalise because to all extents and purposes the call had been wonderful; they reaffirmed their need for each other and spoke of the power their respective voices had to induce pleasure and longing. But Melissa trusted her intuition, it had served her well and she was able to tap into its vast resources and never find it wanting. She knew intuitively that her next meeting with her dearest, darling Jonathan would contain inherent pain despite the sheer joy she knew she would fundamentally experience.

Luke watched her and knowing her well he sensed she was troubled and distracted. He wondered if it was related to this boy she had said she loved and who was the cause for the cessation of their beautiful lovemaking. He decided it must be and harboured a selfish hope that, if it did not work out for his dearest friend Melissa, she might re-establish their relationship on its previous footing, with all its associated joys. He had to admit though that once he had arrived at the decision to retain this friendship, Melissa had been amazingly understanding and had proved to be as steadfast in her feelings for him as she had promised she would be. He knew they would always be friends and what was even more surprising was the fantastic company of this girl, Sally, who Melissa had befriended in Barcelona in June.

The three were so at ease with each other; he felt like he could talk to Sally almost as freely as he could with Mel. Sally was pretty in a paradoxical way; her hair was short and what he considered to be boyish, but her body was so feminine and sensual he occasionally found himself feeling attracted to her. She was exceptionally intelligent and had strong views; she spoke at length about the inequality of men and women, particularly with regard to job opportunities. Luke found himself thinking about what she had said especially about what Sally called 'gender specific career paths'. After all why weren't there more male nurses and for that matter when had he last seen a female collecting the rubbish or fighting fires? Most of the boys in his form, albeit younger than him, scorned any male who overtly displayed emotion or even admitted to helping at home with house work; God since his mum had died and his dad had fallen apart, Luke more often than not made dinner *and* undertook most of the cleaning around the place. Now though was not the time to ask Mel what she had been thinking about so he entered the conversation as he took a long swig from his beer.

"I'm not sure if I'll be able to go straight to University either Sally, my dad needs support and the place I really want to go to is in London, so I'll probably do the same as you and wait a year until dad is on his feet again." Even as he spoke Luke doubted that his fabulous dad would ever be the same again; it was as if a large part of him had died with his mum. His inimitable humour and sparkle had been buried with her and it would take a miracle for it to resurface. "What about you Mel, I know you will be glad to get away from here and I am certain you will be offered a place with your first choice Art School? Do you think anything could tempt you to take a year out?" He was fishing inexpertly without any hope whatsoever of catching anything!

Melissa extricated herself from her amalgam of thoughts all centring around the next meeting with her lover and looked up to see two pairs of bemused and expectant eyes firmly fixed on hers! "What?"

Sally said with a glint of humour in her eyes, "Are you drunk Melissa Johnson – and you a mere seventeen and never been kissed!" Strange, she thought, she could have sworn that a brief conspiratorial look was exchanged between Mel and Luke, but maybe she was mistaken. Sally giggled and drank some more of her pint of Guinness, which she apparently enjoyed better than anything even wine, which was her second favourite tipple. In any case she, informed them, Britain's pubs were so far behind the times compared to the Continent - especially here in a small northern town; it was hard to find one which stocked wine let alone decent wine!

God, Melissa wished she could open up and confide in someone. At this moment she could almost have told anyone and everyone about her love for Jonathan Pritchard and how much she had missed him this last month. She decided she had had quite enough to drink, in fact she couldn't recall ever drinking so much and yet she had not intended to do so. She had blatantly refused to eat yet another one of Carol's awful meals before she came out and had only nibbled half the contents of a bag of cheese and onion crisps since then! Melissa had been rather incensed that her mother repeatedly turned down her offers to undertake the cooking. Carol had asked her what she would prepare and had been affronted by some of the 'strange concoctions' her daughter had described. Stuart who had recently returned from a 'little break' had actually seemed rather in favour of some variety on the food front. Melissa had actually been surprised that Stuart returned at all after the most recent of her mother's jealous outbursts when she actually threw some of Stuart's meagre possessions down the stairs. Melissa had made a hasty bid for freedom and shouted up the stairs that she would be at Susan's if anybody cared to know, and was gone before the war, in all its ugly and idiosyncratic manifestations took place proper. She couldn't help thinking to herself what sort of bloody tranquilisers her mother was taking if this behaviour was not being suppressed. Melissa realised now that she was supposed to answer Luke and managed to say, "I'm not sure."

Luke not gleaning any useful information from this obtuse and brief reply countered, "You're not sure you will take a year out or you're not sure ......well what exactly?"

"You know, you *both* know my situation at home, it's bloody intolerable so how can I possibly be left with any choice? I would like to travel, take some time before I go on to study, but I won't have enough money."

Luke persisted, "So when you say you are not sure, what do you mean then Mel?"

"What I mean Luke Scott is that I am not sure if I will move out and say get a job for a year, or travel and work, or just get the hell out of that madhouse and go to an Art College as far from here as possible. Well my first choice is the same as yours in London, so that's pretty far!" She recovered well, because despite the effects of the alcohol she managed to divert Luke's question. Her real dilemma involved putting such a great distance between herself and Jonathan Pritchard because even though he came to London to see his son, she would not be his primary reason for his trip. Or would she? Why was she feeling so bloody insecure? They left the pub arm in arm with Sally neatly positioned between them, thoroughly enjoying the close proximity of Luke Scott! Luke was thinking that for a Feminist, Sally was really rather nice about men! Melissa was thinking that if she didn't get back to Luke's spare room, or more importantly Luke's bathroom, soon, she would be sick!

Melissa was so desperately in need of someone to confide in she decided she would tell Susan about her relationship with Jonathan and ask her to keep every word she uttered secret. Then some hours later she would completely change her mind thinking there was absolutely no way Susan would be able to keep such juicy gossip to herself; she knew Susan Posthlethwaite well and remembered many occasions when she had revealed details that other misguided girls had told her in 'confidence'. Events precipitated the unveiling of Melissa's covert work of art however, when Susan revealed that she had discovered the name behind the voice of her friend's mysterious lover. The last time he had called as arranged to speak with Melissa, Susan had picked up the phone as Mel was in the kitchen and she recognised the timbre of Jonathan Pritchard's voice. For a few moments she had struggled to decide if this could actually be the person Melissa was having a love affair with; thinking back to the fifth form and Melissa's crush on her Art teacher, it seemed to slot into place somehow. It was incredible, Susan thought, and only happened in those true life type magazines, the Sunday papers her mum and dad read or in America where it happened all the time, not here in bloody Lancashire! How could a teacher do such a thing, I mean didn't they sign something or swear an oath not to have sex with students or something? What was worse he was so bloody old!

Susan confronted Melissa shortly before term started again and her boyfriend was out of the flat having a few beers down the pub with his friends. The two girls were drinking Vodka and Lime much to Melissa's consternation as she now preferred to drink wine, but Susan 'hated the bloody stuff'. The conversation began innocently enough with a discussion about Melissa's time at Woolworths which had now come to an end although she had decided to keep working on Saturdays throughout term time. Suddenly, like a starved lioness scenting food for her pride, she went for the kill!

"So how long has this thing with the ancient Mr Pritchard being going on then Mel?"

Disconcerted, but deflecting with expertise, Melissa said firmly, "You are joking aren't you Susan, I mean whatever could have drawn you to that ridiculous conclusion?"

Undeterred and now sensing very tangible intrigue, Susan said, "Come on Mel, it was me who answered the phone last time. Did you think I wouldn't recognise the voice of the man whose lessons were such bloody purgatory to me for a year?" There was no response so she continued, "Why the hell didn't you tell me for God's sake Mel, didn't you think you could trust me after all the years we've been best friends? I mean I agreed to let you use this place as an alibi when you bloody well met up with him didn't I? And I didn't tell a soul about that."

Palpably relieved yet retaining a guarded reticence, Mel countered, "Susan you have the worst reputation of any girl I know for revealing confidences so why would I have told you about it, if it was actually *true* I mean." Susan grabbed her friend's hand as she attempted to take a sip of her drink unsuccessfully asserting an air of nonchalance, and added with authority:

"You're bloody well bonking the Art teacher aren't you Melissa Johnson, admit it now or I'll never speak to you again."

"OK, OK yes I am bloody bonking the Art teacher as you so eloquently put it!"

Veritable squeals and waving of arms and other such histrionics followed, which Melissa deduced were precipitated by the magnitude of the gossip on Susan's own personal scale and so warranted such a theatrical display! Then Susan became calmer and said, "Bloody hell, so you ditched gorgeous, sexy, Luke Scott for someone old enough to be your father and a sodding teacher as well? How long has this been going on Mel and how did you manage to keep it from everyone especially bloody hawk eyes Carol, the mother from hell, and her dreary accomplice Mr Grey?" Susan seemed genuinely intrigued and utterly disbelieving that such a lovely young girl could be even remotely interested in an old and strangely foreign looking teacher!

"Susan, before I say any more and I will not give you *every* detail because ....well because my relationship with Jonathan is private, you have to swear, really swear that you will not tell anyone about this. It could lose him his job and I only have to keep seeing him secretly until next May when I go on study leave and in effect cease to be a student at the school, then we can be together openly. Promise now or I will deny any knowledge of a relationship with him. Promise?" Melissa looked at Susan with such pleading, her face set rigid, a sculpture of unadulterated gravity. Susan promised with a reciprocal level of sincerity and Melissa needing so much to offload the burden of secrecy, clutched at this unexpected hand in the dark. She gave Susan a meticulously edited version and hoped the ensuing and inevitable cross examination would not reveal any glaringly obvious flaws in her evidence! Susan she knew would relentlessly probe until she was satisfied that every last detail had been revealed, dissected and checked thoroughly for authenticity!

"Bloody hell! So no sooner had you lost your virginity to gorgeous Luke Scott you jumped into bed with Jonathan Pritchard? But let me get this straight, at first you were going to his cottage to see him, but although you fancied the bloody pants off him you just ate food and talked? *Talked?*"

"Yes, we *talked* Susan, it was incredible discovering that we had so much in common and learning from him about art and music. I discovered that I loved wine and he showed me so many ways to make wonderful vegetarian food and then when we became lovers, I never knew such pleasure was possible. I love him Susan but I have such a bad feeling just now, as if something beyond my control has taken him from me. God I have missed him so much and all this time I have had no-one to talk to, no-one. The worst part was when I realised I loved him and had to see him every day at school, knowing eventually that he felt the same way even though words were never spoken. What the hell am I going to do

Susan?"

Not for the first time, Susan Posthlethwaite thought her friend Melissa Johnson was strange. Luke was sure to be snapped up and then Mel would be sorry because she would definitely get fed up with this Jonathan who seemed a bit boring really. I mean who wanted to sit and talk for hours and then after that go into the bloody kitchen and cook. God she would rather have sex and then get fish and chips from the 'chippy'- cooking bloody food took up too much time! How Mel had the patience to sit in the buff and model for his paintings was beyond her, and what real man could see his girlfriend naked and not want to bonk her, that was just too weird! But it was when Mel had told her that Jonathan Pritchard also loved the wailing Leonard Cohen that she knew for certain they were both as loopy as each other! Imagine willingly sitting listening to bloody funeral fodder and getting depressed with someone you are supposed to be crazy about, I mean that *was* abnormal wasn't it?

"Well I can see now why you couldn't talk to Luke about it and I suppose you don't know this new friend Sally well enough to tell her do you? So in a way I am glad you told me even though I think you're bloody crazy and just asking to get hurt. It's too bloody complicated for my liking; I mean he has an almost ex wife and a six year old son, you have to sneak around to see each other, he is your teacher and he is almost twice your age, how many more complications could there be? But you say you love him, God knows why but you do, but I have to respect that because I think I love Tom, anyway I just know he's the sexiest man on the face of the earth so I suppose that's love! Anyway back to you, do you think you can keep it secret for the next eight months then?" She poured more Vodka and Lime and waited for Melissa to answer.

"I hope so Susan, because I can't bear the thought of losing him or causing him to give up his job, he's a bloody brilliant teacher despite what you thought of his lessons. I wish I could stop feeling so pessimistic though. I've never felt like this before - it was just the last phone call, there was something I couldn't put my finger on, something unsaid. I don't know, perhaps I'm being paranoid; give me another drink please Susan and then I really must get back.

Chapter twenty one

Mr Brown had told Melissa he thought her set designs were inspired, he had also been surreptitiously watching her during the first few weeks of term to make sure she was not still harbouring her crush on Jonathan Pritchard. So far he had seen absolutely no signs of misguided teenage devotion and apart from what was required in teaching terms, he had not observed any inappropriate one to one discussions or 'private' huddles. Thankfully then the young teacher, despite being his line manager, had heeded his advice and would be more vigilant in the future where young girls were concerned. He had to admit to himself though that this Melissa Johnson was one of the most mature and beautiful young women he had ever come across, so he could see how Jonathan Pritchard may have been flattered and misjudged the serious implications of the infatuation. He was, however, certain of one thing where she was concerned and that was her acceptance into her first choice Art School; they would be foolish not to offer a place to such a gifted and imaginative young artist.

The October half term was only two weeks away, Jonathan was going to London to be with Jack and Melissa was going to Windermere in the Lake District for a long weekend with Luke and Sally. Both friends had respectively organised a couple of days off work and were going with Melissa to stay with a close friend of Sally's, Steve, who worked on a farm and had a small tied cottage. He was apparently very bohemian, a Vegetarian like Melissa and Luke and actually grew Pot in his garden. Sally had said it was no different growing Marijuana to growing say Parsley or Mint and although she had occasionally partaken of it with friends, she was not bothered about it really and she knew, Melissa and Luke were adamantly against anything they considered altered the state of the mind. It would just be so much fun to let their hair down and have a break with no pressures from either work or Sixth Form.

For Sally this would be an important and hopefully significant weekend because she had become closer to Luke and had seen him on his own a couple of times; on the last occasion he had kissed her and it was absolute heaven. She wanted to take it further but sensed there was something he was keeping from her even though he opened up about so many things especially about how much he missed his mum. Sally thought she would have really liked Brenda and embraced the pain of Luke's devastation. She hoped that she would never have to experience anything so inconceivably tragic. She knew Mel was seeing some-one but for some reason she was unable to reveal either to her or to Luke, whom she had known for much longer, who it was. Sally believed in personal space and respected Mel's wish to keep the identity of her lover secret, but she astutely recognised a layer of latent turmoil lying beneath the surface of Melissa's overt happiness.

She was grateful to Mel for introducing her to Luke, the ideas of Isadora Duncan and the views and words of the playwright Henrik Ibsen. Sally thought he was a Feminist ahead of his time, for in the late nineteenth century his standpoint on women and their rights was certainly unorthodox. She also admired his ability to include other controversial issues in his plays such as the sexually transmitted disease Syphilis. Her favourite Ibsen plays were those Melissa also loved, *A Doll's House* and *Ghosts*; they had managed to see a performance of *Ghosts* in Manchester but as her friend pointed out, *A Doll's House* was infrequently performed. God she adored Melissa, she was one of the most incredible people she had ever met and yet she was so self effacing, often deeply insecure and totally unaware of her own delightful uniqueness, a quality which Sally often said to Luke was so utterly endearing.

Melissa had been so overjoyed to be with Jonathan again she suppressed her insecurities and expunged her doubts and, after drinking in the beauty of him as they entered the subtle romantic light of his cottage, she luxuriated in the bliss of their lovemaking. That first time they had been alone after he returned from Spain had been an intoxicating combination of the sensual and the spiritual, consummate lust and tender love, soft honeyed words and cries of unrestrained ecstasy. They had experienced an unparalleled joy in rediscovering each other and had even managed a whole weekend at Jonathan's cottage without being discovered by the ever vigilant village gossips.

The Goya commission was finished, Melissa presented her lover with a Crosby, Stills, Nash and Young album which he said was amazing, and Melissa revelled in the painting of Toledo's Gothic cathedral which Jonathan had finished in Spain and framed for her here in Lancashire. He also presented his darling Mel with a series of miniature watercolours, all featuring her in various poses and in a myriad of settings; her favourite was a nude where she was depicted in post-coital repose, draped across his bed with her hair loose and an enigmatic smile on her face. Rogue tendrils of hair invaded the space between her breasts and danced on her cheeks, but the remainder hung like a rich red velvet counterpane over the edge of the bed. Do I really look like that after we have made love, she thought?

Now as half term drew near Melissa felt the resurgence of her doubts and was in a state of near hysteria; the deceptive outer calm she struggled to maintain was the effective antithesis of the chaos that reigned tyrannically within her.

"Tell me again, darling Jonathan, tell me again."

"I adore you Melissa Johnson, and I will love you until the day I die. Come closer my precious darling and let me love you again and again." He drew her to him and kissed her so tenderly and softly her response was the delicate tremble of a leaf as a light breeze merely passes across the surface. She felt malleable, willing him with her flutter of desire to love her now with tender precision, exploring every sensation slowly and responding with quiet expertise to her transparent adulation. Melissa wanted to relish this lovemaking, lose herself in the moment and she wanted it to be protracted; for every blissful kiss and touch to be imprinted indelibly in her memory. And so it was as she wanted it to be; they relished each other as the chill autumn air slowly pervaded the room and yet they were blissfully isolated from this remorseless opponent, insulated by the intensity of their delectable journey to mutual ecstasy. Time had indeed been their willing ally and the soft glow of the lamp on their skin as they found that ultimate joy in each other was the only signifier that it was now dark outside and two hours of intense lovemaking had taken place.

Melissa watched him as he lay on the white sheets, his beautiful bronzed and muscular body supine and she knew she would never love anyone so intensely, in fact at that moment she knew she would never love anyone else at all. He had told her about Lydia and her health problems which had necessitated her visit to Spain and now she realised why his last phone call to her had made her feel so uneasy. It was the fact that they had slept in the same room that really unnerved her, eventually sending her on an unremitting roller coaster journey - hurling her mercilessly between jealousy and trepidation. She knew Jonathan would never have been sexually unfaithful to her. But when two people who had once been married slept closely together, there was an implied intimacy which was more threatening and disturbing to Melissa than any sexual infidelity could be.

She *knew him*, she knew Jonathan Pritchard and he was being drawn away from her, even though he denied it and their time together was as wonderful as it had always been. They continued to delight in each other, body and soul, but there was a small fissure in this delicate porcelain that contained their illicit love and she knew it would become an irreparable crack when the inevitable pressure was placed on it. He had not said Lydia wanted him back, but Melissa knew she did. So she waited, grasping every moment with her lover as if it was the last and yet never voicing her fears to him just continuing as always to cherish him.

Jonathan's future was being orchestrated by his love for Jack and his growing remorse for the pain he felt he had caused Jack's mother. His path was being laid and he knew he would walk along it, despite this incomparable happiness he had with Melissa. His love for Melissa would never diminish, he knew this a surely as he knew he must be a true father to his son. He was not in love with Lydia but he cared for her; he did not feel the intense passion for her that he felt every time he glimpsed or even thought of Melissa, yet Lydia was patiently waiting with his son for their journey to begin again. In her hands she held out the possibility of a future for their family, and each time Jonathan had seen her since they parted in Spain, she had subtly drawn him closer to his destiny. She began to glow with health and with hope; Jonathan himself had unwittingly become her physician and their beloved son Jack was the catalyst.

Jack knew without any doubt whatsoever that his daddy would come back and he was already making plans for their weekends together; most of these plans featured ice-cream in one form or another!

Jonathan asked himself how he could give her up, the woman who in any other circumstances would have been by his side for ever, the woman he loved from the first moment he saw her and for whom he waited so long. How could he envisage a future without hearing Melissa's voice animatedly talking or softly whispering endearments; how could he be without her touch, be without her body as it melded to his in ecstasy and how could he live without the reflection of his love in her eyes? Could he wrench himself away from the perfection of her, could he live with Lydia who could never give him the spiritual or physical joy he so effortlessly had found with his wonderful Melissa? He analysed, procrastinated, relented, resolved and then ultimately procrastinated. He knew Melissa would recover, she was talented, young, had such strength of character and although she said she needed him, unlike Lydia she would never be dependent to the extent of becoming ill. November punctuated his dilemma with visual reminders of winter's remorseless onslaught. Jonathan was caught up in its ignominious and ironic signposting of his relationship with Melissa. They had first confided their love for one another in the harsh cold of a February night and now, as winter yet again asserted supremacy he would willingly cast her into its inhospitable abyss.

The journey to visit Jack was becoming precarious, exacerbated by Jonathan's inability to concentrate on the road when his mind was a whirlpool of indecision. Jack asked continuously if Daddy would be back by Christmas, Lydia hugged him with expectancy and Melissa continued to delight and fulfil him. He must make a decision and he must make it soon or he would continue to compound the inevitable pain he would cause both himself and Melissa. When he had seen her last week they had walked for an hour in the cold and dark night, bracing the weather almost from defiance, both knowing it was symbolic of the imminent anguish he would bring to their lives. Now it was mid November and Jonathan Pritchard handed in his notice; by February half term he would no longer be Head of Art at Melissa's school.

She *was* hysterical now, it controlled her and she willingly gave way to its invasive insistence as she screamed at him, "OH MY GOD! NO,

NO……………………….you don't mean it Jonathan , *you can't mean it*! How can you give up what we have? You said you would love me forever, you said that only last week! Were you lying? *No you weren't lying*……… I know you, I love you. *You love me*, we are *supposed* to be together…………Tell me you have not handed in your notice. TELL ME IT'S NOT TRUE……….*TELL ME*…….." she was screaming now and it depleted her strength and she couldn't continue. Melissa Johnson was suffering a pain she never imagined existed. This knife which stabbed repeatedly at her heart and simultaneously made her feel physically sick, knew no limitations; it continued even when she thought she would curl up and die from its excruciating onslaught. She was as abandoned in this agony as she had been in their lovemaking. When Jonathan had spoken the words she had been waiting to hear for two months she had nevertheless listened in disbelief, each word registering its wound with precision.

Now they were both sobbing and neither could bear the distance of the empty space that lay between them in this room. This room that had witnessed their tenderness, their laughter and their passion; this room which now enveloped them with suffocating reminders of love seemed too vast a playing field for this brutal game. He moved quickly to her lifted her quivering body into his arms and placed her on the bed. He lay now entwined with her, his dearest love, her body convulsed with the pain he had wrought and it seemed to him that there would never be true happiness in this world ever again. Inexplicably they felt desire through this turmoil and inevitably they gave way to its call; loving each other with creative despair as if they were writing an epitaph for their relationship.

They had sought and found refuge *from* each other *in* each other and it had assuaged the pain momentarily and now as they clung together under the warmth of the covers he spoke softly, gently holding her face towards his, their eyes locking, "My darling Mel, how can I really explain without hurting you further? How can you, who have no children and are so very young, know the torture of being apart from a child who suffers even when they smile with you? I can't go on like this, selfishly being with you – taking my own happiness at the expense of my son's. I just can't do it Mel, even though I need you desperately and you have given me a happiness I could never have imagined existed. It's killing me too Mel, please see that. I am not convinced I can bear it and I certainly couldn't bear to be here near you and not have you – so I must leave – please understand ……..*please try* - my beautiful Mel."

To speak was almost an impossibility but she found some words from the depths of her disbelief; they formed the question that she knew would be the hardest to answer, "I can understand this love you have for your son my darling, of course I can, but why, *why* do you have to go back to Lydia?" Tears were falling now as she waited for the answer that would precipitate more fathomless pain.

"I have to go back to Lydia because my son needs a family; he needs us to be together in the same house and his needs really must come first. I have been utterly selfish and that is not fair to him. He didn't ask to be born and Lydia and I made a commitment to our futures when we had Jack but I was the one who left without really trying to heal the wounds of our broken relationship. Do you remember when you read out that Shakespeare sonnet to me back in July?" Melissa nodded, fully resigned to what he would now say. "Well, the sentiments haunted me, they still do. I loved Lydia once and we had some good years before we started to have problems, but I wasn't steadfast enough; when the relationship or Lydia if you like, became difficult and 'altered', I gave up on it. So essentially it was me who failed Lydia and walked away from our family without fully trying to see beyond the problems and rediscover our love for each other. Mel I am so sorry to say these words, but I do feel love for Lydia and although it does not even begin to compare with what I feel for you, I owe it to her and to my son to try again. If I don't do this I will be denying that there ever was any love between us."

Melissa knew she was beaten by this, she could not argue with his logic, his need to be a good father to his son but she would always question why he needed to be with Lydia to effect it. She felt as if the last two and a half years were being crushed from her; the covert pleasure of loving Jonathan from a distance and then the unparalleled joy of their last nine months draining the very essence of her being. How could she continue to function, go to a school where she would be tortured every day by the presence of the man she loved more than life itself. So it seemed to Melissa as she went to her room that evening and so it remained for days, the pain asserting its right to deplete her of the will to even get out of bed.

Carol did not know what to do. Even though she had been so self obsessed to the point of barely acknowledging her daughter over the last six months or so, she knew without doubt that whatever was wrong was serious. Stuart said they should call the doctor, but when he came he said there was absolutely no physical reason why Melissa could not get up and go to school. Perhaps she was upset about something and a little depressed, loving care and some hearty food should do the trick. Stuart, more sensitive now than Melissa's mother to her moods, told Carol that he thought she was suffering because of the break up of a relationship. Carol dismissed this view, just as she dismissed all his ideas and thoughts, as ridiculous. Surely she would know if her own daughter was having a serious relationship with someone? In any case she knew that the crush or whatever it had been on Luke Scott had been over for some considerable time; they were just friends she was sure of that. Melissa had never mentioned anyone else, although her daughter hardly ever conversed with her anymore – always staying at Susan's flat, or going on trips or, even worse taking part in that debating society which Carol thought was not acceptable behaviour for a young woman. She thought that sort of activity was a male preserve and the vision of her own daughter vehemently professing her views with an audience present was most undignified. If she *had* been involved with someone, then Melissa had managed very successfully to keep it secret.

Melissa stayed in her room for two weeks, listening to music, sketching and writing endless poems about her love for Jonathan; there was absolutely no way she could be persuaded to go to school her usual thirst for knowledge and the stimulus of the classes, now an anathema to her.

> ....*so love me now*
> *before the winter comes*
> *and afternoon loving with you*
> *becomes afternoon dreaming alone.*

She had written the words in September; prophetically she now realised. Melissa had never given way to self pity of any kind; she had always sought solace in her studies, in music and in art. She detested herself for behaving so pitifully but she was incapable of action, frozen in her anguish with no impetus to seek respite or relief.

Jonathan had been so worried when she had failed to attend school that he had telephoned Carol, who did not register the fact that it was usually a student's tutor who made such calls. She told him that Melissa was ill and would return to school sometime before the end of term; Carol said the words without any certainty whatsoever that they were true. Melissa refused to answer any questions about returning to the Sixth Form and Carol did not have the time or frankly the inclination to pursue it, she was far too inundated with pressure at work. Dealing with emotional teenagers did not figure very high on her list of priorities. She also had to contend with Stuart who she was sure was seeing someone else as he had not even attempted to initiate sex with her for well over eight months now; she was glad of course but she couldn't help thinking he was seeing another woman.

Most of their rows were about her obsession with his movements or his spending and occasionally about his interest in Melissa which Carol still found suspect. Even though he denied any wrongdoing, Carol was as convinced of his infidelity as she had been of Jay's. Stuart, who had never dreamed of seeing another woman and who was far too diffident to embark on that path in any case, could not win. He was damned anyway by his wife and found himself occasionally wishing he was the sort of man who *did* have affairs, at least then he would deserve the horrendous lambasting he received regularly from Carol.

There were only two weeks left of term before the Christmas break and Jonathan had not slept at all for days. He was crazy with worry for Melissa and constantly wondered if he had done the right thing. OK Jack and Lydia were blissfully happy that he was going back even though he had told Lydia that he did not want to resume the physical side of the relationship until he felt they were settled and he was ready. He had once enjoyed her body, but in his heart he wondered if he ever could make love with Lydia again after knowing the sheer ecstasy of his darling Melissa. He had told her that coming back to London had meant giving up a relationship which had made him really happy; when Lydia had pressed for more information he had told her he could not talk about it and made her promise never to ask. They had to wipe the slate clean and start again without recriminations or reference to the respective relationships that each of them had been involved in. Lydia saw the sense in that and whilst she hoped Jonathan was coming back as much for her as for their son, she was sensible enough to realise that this wasn't the case. He would grow to love her in the way he had when they were first together through a solid friendship, of this she felt certain.

Luke and Sally, who were now officially an item much to Melissa's delight as she thought they were perfect for each other, failed in their gentle attempts to get her back into the world outside her bedroom. Sally hoped that one day Mel could confide in her, because she sensed that this devastation had been brought about by the break up of the relationship her friend had been involved in. Succinctly she had assured Melissa that she would be there for her if she ever needed to talk anything through. Luke, who had confided in Sally about the extent of his past feelings for Melissa whilst refraining from revealing the fact that Melissa had broken up with him because she loved someone else, was very worried. He had never seen Mel so absolutely crushed by anything since he had known her. He was sure it was this boy who had caused her such unwarranted misery and, whilst he no longer harboured hopes of winning her back, he wished he could make it all better for her as she had for him when his mum died.

It was Susan Posthlethwaite who managed to get Melissa back on track. She came into the bedroom like a continuous blast from an aerosol whose nozzle had stuck! She opened the curtains despite Melissa's protestations, switched off Leonard Cohen and gave her friend no choice but to tell her 'every bloody thing' from the beginning. She made Melissa go and have a bath first and then she went downstairs and made chip 'butties' with the chips she had brought from the chippy. She poured Vodka and Lime – the Vodka in much larger proportions than the Lime and knew that this was what her friend needed. What was more comforting when some man had been a bastard to you than chip butties and a stiff drink? Susan was without any doubt that Melissa had finally found out how boring and old Mr Pritchard was and, even though she was suffering now, Susan was sure Mel would be grateful for the break up in years to come. Pity the gorgeous sexy Luke Scott had been taken though, but she had known all along that Mel would lose out there because he was too yummy to stay single for long! Melissa reappeared obviously clean, probably soothed by the bath water, but still looking bloody awful in Susan's opinion.

"Here Mel get this chip butty down you and take a good long swig of this." She proffered the enormous butties and a tumbler full of Vodka and a hint of Lime and sat her friend on the bed next to her. Seeing Mel grimace when she took a sip of the alcohol, Susan told her firmly to take a large gulp and eat one of the butties before even attempting to talk. Melissa actually enjoyed the butty and although she found the drink most unpalatable she did as she was told and within fifteen minutes she had finished the drink and was clutching the next one when she told Susan what had happened.

"Christ he's gone back to his wife and yet he told you he will always love you! God what a bastard, the least he could have done was to tell you he had fallen out of love with you! You could have coped with that, you know - been bloody miserable and not believed it for a while and then eventually hated his guts forever. Bloody hell I thought he saw his son lots I mean he was always in bloody Spain with him wasn't he? Are you sure he's not sodding well sleeping with this woman, this Lydia?"

Melissa said simply, "Yes I am positive, Jonathan would never do that to me Susan."

"It seems to me that she has bloody well wanted him back from the moment he left and I wouldn't put it past her to have used her son to make him feel so guilty he had no choice but to go back. Don't get me wrong though Mel, I still think he is a bastard and I for one will never look at art in the same way again, he has turned me right off it!"

"But you hate art Susan."

"Well that's beside the point. God, GOD - I can't believe he has given you up when you are so bloody gorgeous, and you could have any boy, or man, you wanted. What's more he's old and you are really young and so fabulous – everyone thinks so. He'll be sorry Mel, he really will. But you are being really stupid you know, staying in your room and letting him think he has ruined your bloody life. You need to show him that you can deal with it, I don't think for one minute he has taken time off work has he?" Melissa shook her head and Susan continued, "So you are bloody well ruining your chances of Art School if you keep skiving off and then you will have missed too much to catch up. Do you really want to have lost the man you say you love *and* have to go back to school to retake the Upper Sixth again next year?" "But you don't understand Susan. I love him so much I don't see any point in anything if I can't have him. I just know I will never love anyone ever again and I will never be happy, never. I saw us living together when I finished Sixth Form and even if I went to Art College in London we would be together most weekends, either there or here in Lancashire. How can I go to school and function when I will see him every bloody day until he leaves in February? How can I care about anything if I can't have him? I need him Susan, I need him so much." She couldn't continue, the pain of talking about him manifesting itself in every cell of her body, her tears the only outward sign of the wreckage inside.

"Right, that's it Melissa Johnson! OK if you did want him back how could you do it looking a bloody awful mess, lying in a dark room and listening to sodding Leonard Cohen who makes me want to slit my wrists when I am happy, so God knows what he makes a depressed person feel like doing! I think you are crazy even to give him the time of day after the way he has treated you. But if you want to show him that what he loved in you still exists then you bloody well make yourself beautiful, which isn't hard for you, and get back to school. You do the best you can and show everyone, especially him that you are not a quitter; you owe it to yourself and your awesome talent to at least do that Mel. Also you love bloody school work, you must be doing your nut, not having all that work on your hands!"

Susan did not believe, from what she had heard, that Jonathan would change his mind but if the thought of that possibility at least got Mel out of this room then it had to be worth a shot didn't it? What's more likely is that she will probably see him for what he really is once she gets back there, Susan thought sagely! She will see that he is a sad, ancient teacher who was just having fun with a gorgeous young girl and didn't know the meaning of love. He was clearly breaking all those rules that must exist about having sex with students; he should really have been preparing boring lessons, or chatting up someone of his own bloody age who could probably cope with all this rejection. Older women who were still single would obviously be used to being dumped wouldn't they! But her friend Mel who had been so happy didn't bloody well deserve to be made so miserable, God even the chip butties hadn't helped that much! She really did it have it bad didn't she?

Melissa mulled over everything Susan had said when she was at last alone and listening once again to wonderful Leonard Cohen, who seemed to have experienced all the tangled emotions she had been propelled through over the last couple of years. Maybe it would be a good idea to go back to school, even if he didn't change his mind she would be a visual reminder of what he was giving up and what she knew he would be missing already. She knew that Susan didn't understand the depth of her feelings for Jonathan or his for her, and more importantly she could never convince her that Jonathan had been sincere. So she didn't try. Melissa knew that Jonathan's heart was breaking and she knew he would be worried about her absence from school. So she resolved to return. There was a glimmer of hope that he would see her and realise he could not leave; there was a slight possibility that he would go to London to be closer to Jack but not return to his relationship with Lydia; there was even a remote chance that these suppositions were not illusory.

Chapter twenty two

Melissa returned to the Sixth Form and was supported with such assiduous love from Luke she wondered why she had been so lucky to retain his friendship after breaking his heart. Luke told her he would always be there for her and even though he did not know the name of the guy who had hurt her, he hoped to God he realised what a fantastic girl he had given up. The worst part for Melissa was seeing Jonathan and registering the mirror image of her own distress. Jonathan looked haggard; it was shocking for Melissa to see how devastated he was. He had clearly lost weight and although he was functioning efficiently and professionally he had lost the spark and humour that had so characterised his lessons.

They didn't speak privately until the last day of term and even then it barely amounted to a conversation. He saw her walking home when most of the other students had long gone with the usual gusto of release that came with the last day of term; Melissa was walking listlessly and he slowed down knowing she would get in the car. He stopped a couple of streets away from hers and said wistfully, "I'm so sorry for causing you this pain Mel, please believe me, please?"

"I believe you Jonathan and it's obvious that you are suffering too, but really we have said all there is to say and I just can't cope with being close to you right now. Please don't do this again. Promise me?" He nodded his head and slowly reached for her hand and caressed it whilst his eyes searched for hers in the dark. If their eyes met now Melissa knew she would kiss him, cling to him and thus instigate the endless cycle of regret, recrimination and unendurable melancholy that had only just mercifully subsided within her. She could not contemplate that course; she must protect her reinstated equilibrium. There must be denouement, and it must be effective from this moment, or she would not be able to function let alone survive the weeks until he went to London for good. So Melissa found the strength to avert his gaze and as she got out of the car, he whispered he loved her and she responded tremulously, "I love you too my dearest Jonathan and I always will." She ran home and when she reached her room she threw herself on her bed and gave way to her sorrow.

The weeks went by punctuated by a typically mediocre Christmas and a wonderful New Year party at Sally's house. Melissa managed to smile a little, laugh once when really pushed, and be fastidiously nurtured by Luke and Sally. Sally had invited her friend Steve in the hope that he could attempt at least to cheer Mel up. After their half term visit to his farm in the Lake District, Steve had confided to Sally that he thought Melissa Johnson was the most beautiful and unusual girl he had ever met. He had been filled in by Sally about her recent break up with a boyfriend and could patently see that Melissa was taking it hard and he empathised with her.

He did not want to show overt interest in a girl who was so clearly suffering so he chatted with her innocuously and asked her about herself. She seemed relatively comfortable on this safe ground and when he revealed his hopes to go to Drama School eventually when he had saved enough money from the poorly paid job on the farm, she seemed genuinely interested. Steve explained that mandatory grants were not usually awarded for study at Drama School so he would have to apply for a discretionary award. This would entail collating letters of support, probably undertaking an audition in front of a panel of experts at the local authority, and even then he was not guaranteed success. Melissa was interested in Steve's career plans and had she not been on auto pilot in order to function socially, she may have pursued the conversation further because what really intrigued her was his ultimate goal of becoming a theatre director. In happier times she would have shared her own aspirations with him and told him of her interest in theatre design, but as it stood she was barely holding on, clutching at her glass so tightly as if it could steady her. She knew that when she left the party and was alone in the dark with her thoughts, she would visualise Jonathan with Lydia in London and thus embark yet again on this compulsion to torture herself with jealousy and fruitless longing.

What Melissa didn't know was that when Jonathan was staying with Lydia and Jack in his old house which he would soon be living in permanently, he slept in the spare room. Jack had asked him about it once, because hadn't Mummy and Daddy slept closely together in Spain? Jonathan had told Jack that he was sleeping badly at the moment, which was true, and so he mustn't sleep with Mummy yet because she needed her sleep to get better and he would disturb her. Jack was satisfied and Christmas had been so great with Mummy, Daddy and his English granddad and granny all together. He had been cuddled almost as much as when he was in Spain - the only thing missing was ice-cream like his abuela made for special occasions; unfortunately neither Mummy nor granny seemed very good at cooking.

Daddy had made the Christmas dinner and it tasted really nice but he was so full of chocolate he couldn't eat much of his and he got told off! But he had only eaten so much chocolate because there was no ice-cream, so really it wasn't his fault and he didn't see why Daddy had said he must save some for the rest of the holiday. Nice things needed to be eaten when you really felt like them otherwise they weren't a treat were they? I mean if you had them every day they would become like cornflakes or something – just sort of normal really! Grown ups really were funny!

It was the beginning of February 1971 and Melissa knew that Jonathan would be gone in a few weeks. She had survived so far, immersing herself in her studies, but the New Year had brought with it a tenuous thread of hope that Jonathan may change his mind if she could spend some time alone with him like they used to. He had spoken to her about some pieces of art work he wanted to give her and Melissa had clung to those words like a drowning woman holding on to a disintegrating piece of driftwood. Hadn't he really meant that he had missed her and needed to be with her one last time? His physical appearance had slowly improved but Melissa who knew him so well, realised he was not even remotely recovered from their break up and continued to yearn for her as she continuously longed for him. So when he rang and asked if he could pick her up and take her to the cottage, she gained sustenance from that almost invisible thread of knowledge. She could think of nothing else all day; visions danced in her head – visions of holding Jonathan one last time and perhaps ....perhaps then he wouldn't be able to go through with it. Yes he would tell her it was all a mistake and he had to be with her for ever.

The hostility of winter's looming glower seemed to have pervaded the once welcoming ambience of the cottage. When they walked through the front door, Melissa knew in an instant that this was the last time she would be truly alone with this man she had wanted to be with forever. Where once the glow of welcoming Tiffany lamps created an atmosphere of shared possibility, there were now endless boxes and a stark ceiling light revealing transience. Where once the kitchen resounded with their laughter and the polished surfaces reflected their smiles of sheer happiness as they talked animatedly and cooked together with love, there was now a redundant space. Where once a studio witnessed the combined creativity of a gifted artist and his beautiful model, there were now only the echoes of a fragile happiness. It was to the bedroom which was almost unchanged except for the fact that Jonathan had placed Ophelia on the floor ready to be wrapped and packed that they sought refuge from the reality of Jonathan's imminent departure. They had walked upstairs - mere automatons; the room had beckoned as always with its insistence that they love each other, the only room in the house not overflowing with the unremitting signifiers of termination. They sat on the edge of the bed fully clothed and without any words being said, she turned his face to hers and through the pain they found each other's lips.

When they made love, as they both knew they would, it was as if they had travelled back in time to their first wonderful evening of lovemaking here in this room on this bed covered in white. Their joy in each other, their final and all consuming journey to an unparalleled ecstasy that neither of them would ever find with anyone else, was as perfect in its finality as the first had been in its possibility. Very few words were spoken but they had communicated their consummate love for each other in every stroke, kiss, sigh and tear and so now as he slowly stoked her face he was finally saying goodbye and she was finally accepting it. It must be endured.

They were collecting for Mr Pritchard's leaving present and did Melissa want to contribute anything? Melissa stood rigid unable to respond either with words or action, stultified, inert, but not through disbelief. After today she would never see him again. She could not possibly place any money in the envelope and instantly she determined to be absent from school tomorrow when the Sixth Form students would surprise their favourite teacher with a party and with what would probably be an exceptional present judging by the amount of money they had collected. She had endured enough and would not partake in this charade of revelry; fate held in store an event that would test Melissa's resilience to the utmost.

The day started like any other, with Carol leaving the house without a word to either Stuart or her daughter, the door slamming her permanent disapproval and the now dislodged letters on the telephone table scattering her bitterness visibly. Stuart was working a short day and would be back earlier than Carol and actually asked Melissa if he could help her cook a meal to surprise his wife; Melissa was constantly in awe of Stuart's ability to ride the storm of Carol's unremitting disapproval. She agreed to assist him knowing that it would be therapeutic – cooking seemed to soothe and calm her and the surroundings of the kitchen , even if it was not Jonathan's, imbued her with creativity. No doubt whatever they prepared would be scorned and only partially eaten by her mother but Melissa's generosity of spirit ensured that, despite Carol's behaviour, she would try to assist Stuart in his attempts to please her no matter how fruitless.

Melissa had made herself a little lunch – just some cheese and an apple accompanied by some fresh crusty bread and a glass of red wine she kept secreted in her room because her mother resolutely refused to buy any. She was reading a book on Brecht by John Willett whom she had recently discovered was an exceptional authority on this fascinating man. For a moment she did not register that the sound of the door bell was resounding through the house, she was lost in the pleasure of discovery. She knew Luke was not working today and had tentatively mentioned the possibility of coming round although nothing definite had been arranged. Melissa was so glad they could be together without any feelings of awkwardness and felt genuine and unreserved pleasure in his happiness with Sally. If he did call it would be a welcome distraction from the thoughts of Jonathan which would incessantly invade her senses when she was not occupied. She closed the book now because whoever was at the door was seemingly impatient and was keeping their finger permanently on the bell so it insisted on being answered.

When she tried to recall it later it was as if the rest of this day occurred in someone else's life; the sheer disbelief that anything so iniquitous could be perpetrated against her already fragile stability made it hideously surreal. She barely pulled the door ajar when it was forcibly wrenched from her hand and she was pinioned against the wall, the man incoherent and smelling so strongly of alcohol it made her instantly nauseous. What was it he was saying, she could barely understand him as he began to tear at her clothes and press his face to hers. A flash of intuition registered recognition, somehow she knew this man who was hurting her now. She managed to pull herself away and began to run upstairs hoping she would make it to the bathroom and manage to lock herself in, her survival instinct taking charge. As she reached the landing two things happened simultaneously as he caught her and pushed her into her mother's bedroom: she heard her mother's name being spoken and she looked up at the bloodshot eyes and knew this was her father, Jay.

She screamed repeatedly that she wasn't Carol, she pushed and she fought, but he seemed like a man possessed with intent and was so drunk he seemed to have the strength of two men. She heard him saying Carol's name over and over again intermingled with disgusting suggestions that made Melissa even more frightened that he would succeed in what he had so clearly come here to do to her mother. Now she was sobbing and found she could not summon up the strength to push him away but in her despair she managed to say who she was, "I'm your daughter, I'm your daughter..........please stop..........*please, ...I'm your daughter ...it's Melissa.*"

Stuart thought it was strange that Melissa had left the door open and what was even more disconcerting as he walked in was the fact that he could hear her sobs from the hall. He became worried that she had regressed to the state of depression that had taken hold of her last December and almost ran upstairs to make sure she was OK. Why wasn't she in her room? The sobbing intensified and what Stuart saw when he found his step-daughter in his and Carol's bedroom would haunt him forever. Stuart was a gentle and inexperienced man who stared in disbelief, but the evidence of some form of attack was clearly being presented to him. Melissa was rolled up in a ball, her clothes torn and her face stained with utter misery. His instinct now was to comfort her and protect her although he knew he was too late for the latter and so he took her frail body in his arms and sat rocking her whilst her pitiful crying permeated the house.

And that was what Carol saw when she came home; her husband and her half naked daughter sitting entwined on her bed. She saw what she wanted to see, failing to rationalise the situation she began to rant and scream at both of them, her perverted sense of logic implying joint complicity. The injustice of it made Stuart shout back at Carol and Melissa gathered some strength, pulled her clothes about her and staggered to her room. She could hear her mother screaming, "Get out of my house both of you. You can continue your sordid little affair somewhere else. I will not have either of you under my roof for a moment longer. I just knew something was going on. You both disgust me, especially you Melissa. I know you used to dress like a little tramp but deep down I didn't really believe you would act like one. But how wrong I was, how *very* wrong. *Now get out, JUST GET OUT!*" She sounded deranged and Melissa could now hear the noise of drawers being opened and things being thrown around her mother's room. For a moment she was terrified, where would she go and in this state? She was too traumatised to rationalise fully but one thought was paramount she must get to Susan's and then she could deal with everything else later.

Susan proved to be the best friend Melissa could hope to have and without any hesitation whatsoever, Susan spoke to Tom and they both agreed that Melissa should have their spare room for as long as she needed it. Melissa had assured them that she would only be there until the exams were over and she would give them some money from her Saturday job. Melissa asked Susan if she could just be alone for a couple of days, she really needed to isolate herself from everyone. The thought of having to speak let alone go to school or function even in limited company was inconceivable. She felt utterly violated and physically sick every time she thought about what occurred yet she could not bring herself to seek help, she determined to deal with it herself. How could her father have come back after all that time and been so very drunk he didn't even recognise his own daughter, surely she looked so different to Carol? How could any man behave in such an appalling way towards women? What had he been doing in Lancashire and why hadn't he been the father she remembered – why had he come back and spoiled her dream of him, her few fond memories from when she was little? There really weren't any answers at all and there was no comfort in supposition.

She went with her friend to collect her stuff from 'that bloody unhinged cow' Carol's when she was out at work and Susan ensured that Melissa was as comfortable as possible in the small second room. Melissa was so grateful she cried continuously and Susan devoid of her usual humorous retorts and solutions found herself just cuddling her friend because it was the only action which alleviated the misery. Tom who was rather taciturn but essentially a very sensitive young man left the 'girls' to it, he thought it was best if he was not party to Melissa's reasons for leaving home. He just wanted to please Susan who was just the greatest, sexiest girl he had ever met.

Melissa had told Susan the basics of what had happened but she could not speak the words that would describe the finer details of what occurred; it was as if their very utterance would bring the events back in all their shocking brutality. Susan was satisfied but what she was totally ignorant of for the time being was that Melissa Johnson was pregnant. Melissa was in denial for some weeks although her body asserted its condition relentlessly with morning sickness manifesting itself every day and lethargy replacing youthful energy. When at last she acknowledged it remembering with absolute clarity that she had stopped taking the contraceptive pill at the end of last November, she made a decision. Melissa accepted that although she would never keep this baby, she was also fundamentally against abortion, so she would give it up for adoption. Yes it was a hard decision borne of principals rather than practicality and she would not know until she gave birth whether or not she could cope but there it was – she did not want this baby.

She determined to confide in her closest friends. Her mother had not even bothered to find out where she was and Melissa now believed that all she had in the world were her friends and her future career. There would be no baby in this future, just her. She was beginning to think that she had to rely on herself and herself alone, because her only love had deserted her and her mother had disowned her, so apart from her very good friends, she must be self reliant. She was resolved, she would start

Art School a week or so late after having this baby who would be given up for adoption. What her friends would say she didn't know, but she was certain that whatever their views they would fully support her and her decision whatever it entailed.

There were times when she broke down and stayed in the little room listening to sad songs which served to amplify her distress but in so doing were therapeutic; there were times when she decided to give up Sixth Form this year and restart next year when this bloody mess was over with; and there were times when she longed with utter despair for Jonathan's arms, his eyes penetrating to her soul and the intoxicating sound of his voice. If she told him about what had happened he would comfort her and she knew it would assuage her pain. She had a compulsion to telephone him, she was about three months pregnant and some vague stirring of romanticised hope permeated her senses with a vision of the two of them walking towards a misty horizon vaguely imbued with promise. She phoned his school and although his voice conveyed reluctance, she arranged to meet him for lunch in London on a day when he had a free afternoon. Melissa could barely afford the train fare but Jonathan said he would reimburse her when they met. He could not possibly get up to Lancashire.

All the way to London, Euston station, Melissa wondered if she was really doing the right thing, what if she was just going to exacerbate her own sense of loss, protract the suffering for both of them. She consoled herself with the fact that he had not refused to see her; she attempted to convince herself that her intentions were innocuous; she selectively forgot her resolve to continue alone and to forget about this man who had rejected her. When she saw him at the café, her heart soared and all she could think of was her need to throw herself in his arms and take their relationship back to last summer when it was untainted by remorseless change. Of course this elation was mirrored identically in Jonathan's heart; she looked thin he thought but she was his Melissa, still as alluring, as effervescent and as sensual as ever.

"Darling Jonathan, darling," was all she could utter as she literally threw herself into his arms which willingly and firmly enveloped her thin frame.

After many minutes had slipped by unnoticed he said, "Melissa, what are we doing? What the hell are we doing? God you look beautiful my wonderful girl – I've missed you more than I ever thought possible. No don't move, don't leave my arms – stay just for a moment while I smell you. You still wear the Patchouli oil which always sent me crazy with lust for you and you feel so good. Hold me tighter my darling." So it was still there, not even remotely hidden or dispelled but shining its presence like a beacon for all to see.

They still loved each other but he was settled, would not change the situation even if she asked because his wife and child were so happy it was a joy to be with them. His life lacked what only Melissa could give him but he knew he had acted in the best interests of everyone. He knew he would always love Melissa Johnson, but they would never be together. Last week he had tentatively made love with Lydia when she initiated it and it was familiar and pleasant, but not passionate, intense and all consuming as his lovemaking with Melissa had been. He could live with it, it made Lydia happy and he had found a peace in her arms after months of agonising and self-reproach about the pain he had caused his Melissa. Sometimes when he thought of her he felt a torturous pain that would remain for hours and he would long to see her, hear her and touch her like he had just now. God he loved her, would it ever be easy? But what good would come of this meeting? He sensed something was wrong and as they talked about school and other general and innocuous topics, he knew she wanted to confide in him about something but she was becoming more reticent as the conversation veered randomly from subject to subject. He noticed with dismay that she had been attacking her fingers mercilessly and the skin was sore around two of her nails, one was bleeding – clear evidence that she was distressed.

Melissa couldn't tell him. How could she? Jonathan was in no position now to comfort her and help her dispel the sickening image of Jay's depraved face as it moved closer to hers. He loved her still and she him, but what good would it do to tell him she was pregnant when there was absolutely no possibility that he would change his mind and be with her. So she was having a baby, why did she think he would leave his seven year old son and wife to be with her for a child who was not yet born? So she resolved not to tell him and add that burden of knowledge to his life; it was clear his son and wife were happy and she knew she could cope being without him, even if at times it was almost unbearable. So the unspoken hung in the air between them like a wayward note from a once familiar song destined never to be heard.

Before she left he gave her the poem and asked her not to read it until the train had pulled out from the station. "Please don't be sad when you read it Mel, only think of how much I loved and *still* love you. Be happy Melissa and enjoy your time at Art School, I can't tell you how thrilled I am that you were accepted at such a brilliant College. I know that one day I will come across your name, perhaps in a theatre programme or in some quality magazine, because I believe without any doubt whatsoever that my Melissa will be a success. Goodbye my darling." She couldn't say the word, that final goodbye, so she asked him to leave now before she went to the platform; she stood motionless like a sentry, vigilantly guarding her own composure and watched her beloved Jonathan walk off to a different future.

Epilogue

Melissa had made all her friends promise not to come to the hospital when she went into labour; it was the only way she could cope and the only way she could ensure she would maintain a clear head after the birth. It would not be a joyous occasion and if her friends came to see her she may lose her resolve. They had all protested and Susan especially had not understood the perverse logic that seemed to cloak most of her friend's decisions. Sally and Luke had worried that she would become depressed if she did not have visitors and was left alone to observe all the other mothers caring for their new babies. How would Mel cope with visiting time, they had asked each other, because she would be in the same ward as all the other new mothers and would be the only one without visitors, surely this would compound her sense of isolation.

Melissa thanked them not only for all their well meant concern but also for their support, without which she doubted she would have achieved such excellent grades: A for Art, A for English and a creditable C for History. But she would do this alone and if it meant she suffered then so be it; she must relinquish her baby and despite her firm resolve she knew she would experience the dichotomous anguish that only a woman who gives birth and then does not become a mother can experience.

When Joyce had heard Melissa's story, she was uncertain even then who the father of this baby was; had the poor girl actually been raped by that dreadful father of hers or had she managed to fight him off. The story made her shudder; she had been right when she had thought this girl had suffered more than anyone so young should suffer. She thanked God yet again for her wonderful Jim and for her loving family even though her life might seem a bit too normal to some folk, at least she was surrounded by love and that counted for a lot. This Melissa Johnson was intelligent and very sensitive otherwise why would she have collapsed after going to see her little girl? Perhaps she would keep her and find a way to combine her studies at Art School with the responsibilities of being a mum. But I have never had to be a single parent, thought Joyce, and couldn't possibly appreciate the hardships of bringing up a child without help. On the other hand Joyce knew only too well from being with some of her other patients over the years, that when a girl had been forced to have sex and the result was a baby, she very rarely wanted to keep it. Yes she understood that very well. If Melissa was *her* daughter she would have respected her decision and given her lots of love and hearty food to build her up; she really was so thin it made you want to give her all the care and love she should have received from her own mother. She for one could not forgive that awful woman who had thrown this lovely girl out of her own home - she was not fit to be called a mother; Carol was a disgrace.

When Melissa left the hospital she was alone; her past lay in the nursery with the other babies but her sorrow remained in her heart as a reminder. Her very palpable feelings of anger and hatred had subsided when she had looked at the tiny baby she had given birth to, she hoped she would be loved and cherished and never have to endure unbearable pain or have to make intolerable choices. She had felt such an affinity with Joyce and wished, like she had once wished about Brenda Scott, that her own mother had been more like Joyce. She vowed to keep in touch with her even though they could not be in physical contact on a regular basis because she would be living in London, but they could write and telephone. Joyce had listened and supported her through the last week when at times she had felt she would not be able to cope with yet another form, or yet another 'discussion' with a well meaning professional. OK they had to ensure that she was fully aware of her rights and of the implications once the whole procedure was set in motion, but why were there so many of them? She couldn't wait to get out of the hospital and distance herself from this now completed process. One thing she had decided to do was to name the father on the birth certificate.

She went to Art School glad to have her dear friend Luke starting at the same time. Sally was at University in London so Melissa really was cushioned in this momentous move to such a cosmopolitan city. Occasionally her thoughts lingered on the fact that Jonathan was also living in London; perhaps unwittingly their paths had crossed or possibly they had even been at the same theatre, blissfully unaware of each other's presence. As time went on and she visited Lancashire less and less except to see Joyce and Susan who was now married to Tom, she thought of him less. Melissa could not bring herself to date anyone for many years, much to the consternation of many a persistent suitor. She was contented with the company of her friends, her studies and her memories of a love that would in all probability always be unparalleled. She did not want to embark on any course that had even the remotest potential for pain.

Initially she had struggled together with Luke to find work in their chosen fields whilst Sally on the other hand had been offered a position with the firm she had worked for without pay during her gap year. Luke had decided he must move back to Lancashire to be with her even though the possibility of an opening as an illustrator would be reduced considerably. So Melissa had found work in a small interior design company to pay the rent on her tiny studio, but worked as a volunteer at weekends and some evenings for a theatre company based in south London. Her dream of becoming a theatre designer was still a dot on a cluttered horizon, barely visible, but with Melissa's tenacious determination, it was certain to become a reality one day.

It is 2001 - a new century; Melissa is forty eight, a successful theatre designer and had been married to Steve for eighteen years. Steve had often thought about Melissa from the moment he had met her and somehow he had sensed that their futures would be entwined. He had no tangible reason for thinking this, just a strong belief in fate and his intuition. Steve had been involved in a few casual relationships with women but working as an actor/director in a touring repertory company for most of his twenties, tended to make serious relationships difficult to sustain. He had been really broke for most of that time and it was not until he got an amazing chance to direct a production of Bertolt Brecht's *The Mother*, for a prestigious innovative theatre in south London, that he began to earn reasonable money. It was during the first production meeting when he was introduced to a well respected young designer, that he met his kismet. Melissa Johnson instantly recognised the tall, blonde, affable director and to the amazement of the rest of the Company they hugged for what seemed like an eternity: *bloody hell you expected that sort of 'luvvie' behaviour from actors but not the director and the designer!*

They had an ease with each other that they both found refreshing and they worked together on the production with such a frisson of creativity it was remarked on by everyone who came into contact with them. Melissa translated Steve's vision into an amazing set, incorporating the symbolism and stylised minimalism he had envisaged. The production was an unqualified success and marked the beginning of what turned out to be a short courtship before Melissa and Steve got married back in Lancashire with all those who were dearest to them present, even Joyce managed to make it despite her Jim being a bit poorly. Sadly this diagnosis had been far from the truth, because her beloved Jim died later that year and Joyce was never quite the same again, losing some of her robust grittiness and displaying signs of fragility from time to time.

Susan and Tom remained happily married and had three children. Luke and Sally had lived together for four years but now she was working in Scotland and living with another architect from her firm. She kept in contact with Melissa mainly by email and the occasional letter. Luke, after spending some time struggling to establish himself as a children's book illustrator in Manchester, had trained to be a teacher and was now happily teaching Art at their old school! Melissa often remarked on the irony of that when she met up with him and his wife Trudy who was also a teacher at the school, although her subject was English. They saw each other infrequently but relished each other's company when they did get together.

Melissa and Steve had two children quite early in their marriage, both boys, and Melissa found to her surprise that she was fiercely maternal; she had worried that she might not be because after all she had given up a baby once. She was comfortable with Steve; they had so much in common and admired each other unreservedly. Steve thinking Melissa was one of the most innovative and creative theatre designers in London and Melissa similarly in awe of her husband's skill as a director.

Steve knew that Melissa had given a baby up for adoption; he had not pressed to find out the name of the father and was content for Melissa to tell him as much as she felt able to. Melissa visited Joyce about twice a year and they often talked on the phone; Joyce knew more than anyone else about what had happened to her thirty years ago. Today she had to call her friend who now lived in sheltered accommodation; Joyce who was there at the beginning would now be a part of its conclusion.

"Hello love, well this is a surprise!" Joyce said with affection, "So how come I am getting another call from you when we only spoke two days ago? Not that I mind at all, I could talk to you every day, you know that love."

"It finally happened Joyce, she found me." Melissa's tone and the very close bond that existed between these two women was all Joyce needed to realise that Melissa was talking about the daughter she had given up. Joyce was worried for Melissa, it wasn't always a good thing to be found, some mothers took it badly and Melissa sounded very quiet.

"Was that OK for you love, I mean it must have been such a shock which is why you are calling me I expect. She will be thirty now, a young woman - does she look like you or…." Melissa knew that this was the time to reveal all the details to her dearest friend.

"Joyce I need to tell you something I have never revealed to anyone, because talking about it made me relive the horror of that day and I couldn't face bringing those images back to life. When Jay attacked me, I really thought he would rape me, it seemed inevitable – it was what he had come for and he was so strong Joyce………..he….." she stopped talking to reach for a tissue, Melissa had given way to the inevitable tears. As she had so astutely pointed out, talking about it took her instantly back to her house on that appalling day when she was fighting off a drunk who thought she was his ex-wife. She managed to continue, "I was resigned to it Joyce because I just thought he would hurt me more if I struggled and if you had seen his eyes, you would have been as frightened as me, I know you would; they were filled with such loathing and hatred you couldn't imagine. The only thing I thought might register with him was if I said who I was – that I was his daughter; at first he continued and I don't know if he didn't hear me or just chose to ignore it. It was when I said my name that he seemed to collapse onto me, he was like lead and then he began to sob Joyce; he lay on top of me and sobbed. Then as quickly as he had arrived he was running down the stairs and barely coherently amidst the sobs I could hear him saying that he was sorry. *Sorry*! God what he put me through has tortured me all these years even though he didn't rape me. So my mother threw me out as you know and despite my attempts to re-establish some form of contact, she hasn't spoken to me for years."

"You poor, poor love, and you were so very young and just a fragile little thing. You still are! God so you were pregnant with *Jonathan's* baby! It was Jonathan who you had loved so much who was the father and yet you still gave her up. Did you ever let him know about your pregnancy love?"

"I did see him one last time Joyce. When Karen knocked on the door I knew who she was instantly, she looks so like him, it was like looking into his eyes and being transported back to that awful day thirty years ago when he rejected me finally and utterly. He had made a new life with his wife for the sake of his son Joyce. What good would it have done to tell him? He had chosen his path and I had to take mine."

"So you didn't tell him love? He never knew?" Joyce almost whispered.

"No I didn't Joyce." Melissa was tugging now at the broken skin around her right index finger, making it bleed.

Gaynor Hensman

I just watched him walk towards a different future, Melissa thought, whilst I remained rooted in the moment, unable to say goodbye yet again to someone I loved. She reached into the front compartment of her briefcase once she had put the telephone down. In the very bottom beneath some bills she found the envelope Jonathan had thrust in her hand just before he left her on the station that last time. She opened it and read the poem:

STOLEN DAYS

*I think of you
and those days
we almost had to steal.
You, walking, smiling,
dreaming, loving –
still the same,
except for a tiny corner
of your mind,
where my smile hides,
ready to reveal itself
and remind you.
Soft concealed whispers
and honey eyes
conveying a need.
Sun on our smiles
and darkness as we touched.
Love on a forbidden tide,
but tides must turn –
and we who sat on driftwood
as the tide came in
must remain on the shore,
wilting in the heat of reality.*

Jonathan

She went downstairs and placed it in the fire and as she watched the flames lick and ignite it, she began to feel a little diminution of the pain she had unwittingly evoked every time she had read

Jonathan's final words to her. Now at last she had found the strength to say goodbye and with it came the certain knowledge that she had not wilted or floundered. She had made a choice thirty years ago, an intolerable and irreversible choice, but slowly and progressively she had developed a life for herself which contained no broken promises – only sweet possibilities.